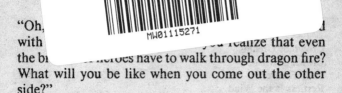

"Oh, ___ ___ ___
with ___ ___ you realize that even
the br___ ___ heroes have to walk through dragon fire?
What will you be like when you come out the other
side?"

Now the fire was inside her.

Devlin felt it, hot, brushing her skin. The heat licked
at the tender flesh of her throat, leaving a burning
trail. Her hands swept up to thrust the flames away,
but they were silken, melting over her fingers. Sweet
God, she'd never suspected that fire could be cool,
moist silk. A dragon lover, fashioned of flame.

She shifted, drawing it closer, wanting it to consume
her, and it slipped beneath the folds of her chemise,
pressing closer, until it opened, hot and wet, closing
upon the crest of her breast. She crushed her terror
and stared into its eyes—eyes blue as ice, eyes blue as
the torrent that raged inside her. They floated,
whirled. Together. And he led her to the brink of a
gold-spun cliff. She stared into the pool below. An
ocean of sapphires, emeralds, with lacings of pearls at
the tops of the cresting waves.

"Dev . . . ah, Dev . . ." The rasped words whispered
across her skin like the sweetest prayer, Myles's mouth
raining kisses down her throat. . . .

Books by Kimberly Cates

Crown of Dreams
Crown of Mist
Only Forever
Restless Is the Wind
To Catch a Flame

Published by POCKET BOOKS

CROWN
of DREAMS

KIMBERLY
CATES

POCKET BOOKS

New York   London   Toronto   Sydney   Tokyo   Singapore

This book is a work of fiction. Names, characters, places and
incidents are either products of the author's imagination or are used
fictitiously. Any resemblance to actual events or locales or persons,
living or dead, is entirely coincidental.

An *Original* Publication of POCKET BOOKS

POCKET BOOKS, a division of Simon & Schuster Inc.
1230 Avenue of the Americas, New York, NY 10020

Copyright © 1993 by Kim Ostrom Bush

All rights reserved, including the right to reproduce
this book or portions thereof in any form whatsoever.
For information address Pocket Books, 1230 Avenue
of the Americas, New York, NY 10020

ISBN: 0-671-79601-1

First Pocket Books printing January 1993

10 9 8 7 6 5 4 3 2 1

POCKET and colophon are registered trademarks of
Simon & Schuster Inc.

Cover art by John Ennis

Printed in the U.S.A.

To my brother, David, who was the inspiration for Myles's devilment. Maybe it's a good thing I couldn't talk Mom and Dad into selling you to the Gypsy King after all.

CROWN OF DREAMS

CHAPTER

1

England, 1745

*L*iancourt Castle rang with the sounds of wailing. The only feminine eyes in the entire estate not misted with sentiment and sorrow were the tip-tilted Gypsy-green ones of Devlin Chastain—hers were smoldering with anger.

Her white silk stockings a muddy ruin, she paced her chamber, heedless of the pins and needles and seamstress's shears abandoned on the floor, heedless of everything save the raw fury pulsing through every fiber of her being.

The silver gauze of her half-finished wedding gown was laced and pinned and basted around her, trapping her as certainly as a partridge trussed up for roasting. The hem of the glorious garment was smudged and dusty from her dash an hour earlier into the courtyard below.

She had feared some calamity had struck, such an uproar was being raised below. She had feared the fields were on fire, or that the sheep were ill, or that England itself was sinking into the sea.

But when she'd burst, stocking-footed, through the doors and dashed into the muddy courtyard, she'd found an even greater disaster grinning down at her from a prancing Barbary stallion.

He had come home.

The bane of her existence.

That thrice-cursed son of dogs.

Lord Myles Farringdon, Viscount Liancourt.

Devlin kicked a sewing basket in frustration, spilling its contents in a river of thread, fabric snippings, and glinting metal, to mix with the mess already on the floor.

She should have known he would return, just so he could manage to make a disaster out of the happiest weeks of her life. She should have known he would find a way to ruin the wedding she had been anticipating for five years—*five years* in which she and her betrothed, the most Honorable Braden Tracey, had waited for each other, perhaps not patiently, but sensibly. Five years in which the very fates themselves had seemed to conspire to keep them apart. Five years that were finally to end in fountains of roses and a lifetime together.

After such a long wait it was only fair that everything should be perfect. Everyone should be happy. That even she—capable, rational Devlin—should have the pleasure of playing the role of bride, with the grace of a princess for just one infernal day.

But now . . . now Myles had managed to botch everything, as certainly as he had botched everything that was important to her ever since they were children running about the castle grounds.

He had ridden in an hour ago, spurring his ghost-gray stallion through the front gates, a roguish grin on his devilishly handsome lips, his eyes alight with the quests of knights errant. His wind-blown chestnut hair had tugged free from its queue, to ripple in glistening waves around his granite-hewn jaw, and skim his broad muscled shoulders while his mantle was a splash of crimson against the mist.

And the news he had brought had driven all thought of wedding feasts and rose-arches and gowns of silver gauze from the minds of everyone who surrounded him.

"Scotland has fallen to Charles Stuart's hand," Myles had said, his face alive with eagerness. "And I go to fight at his side."

Devlin had felt the blood drain from her face, a sick

lurching inside her as she stared into the aristocratic features of the reckless boy she had always known, grown now into a man.

While the others had crowded around him, weeping with both joy and trepidation, babbling their hopes that the Young Pretender might regain the English throne as well, Devlin had stormed away, trying to blot out the image of Myles Farringdon's foolish, gloriously dashing face, his eyes sparkling with the thirst for adventure.

No, nothing like a tidy rebellion to muck up a mere wedding, she thought with a pang of hurt. Nothing like a fool spouting treason to ruin a lifetime of dreams.

Well, St. Stephen skin them all, let them march merrily along to the devil with him, then, if they'd no more sense. In two weeks' time she'd be mistress of her own home, with a husband who was all a woman could wish for in a man— intelligent as well as handsome, practical as well as charming, ambitious as well as possessed of enough fortune that they might live comfortably. Happily.

Even the most seasoned statesmen at Hanover Court judged that the Honorable Braden Tracey was a man to be reckoned with. A man with a diplomatic brilliance remarkable for his twenty-seven years.

In point of fact, the only flaw Devlin could find in the man to whom she'd pledged her troth was Tracey's unfortunate friendship with Myles. An affection that had developed during the years Myles had been fostered out to the Tracey family and had become their son's best friend.

Unbearably restless, Devlin stalked over to where her own sewing box stood. It had been a gift from Myles one Christmastide, given, Devlin was certain, because he knew how much she detested wielding a needle. Exquisite, elegant, the box had been enameled with a scene of rollicking unicorns and dreamy-eyed maidens, fantastical dragons and knights daring their wrath.

Myles's eyes had twinkled beneath his lashes in suppressed merriment when every other woman in the room cooed enthusiastic praises over the blasted box, urging

Devlin to open it. And when she had, the entire thing had been stuffed to bursting with Myles's small clothes, none too clean and all in sad need of mending.

Shaking herself free of the memories, Devlin plunked herself down on a stool. She gave a squeak of pain as a pin stuck through the dress and bit into her buttocks, and she raised up enough to yank the dangerously spiked fold of gauze from beneath her before plopping down again.

Trying to distract herself, she snatched up her favorite petticoat and began to stitch furiously to mend the tear she had gotten in the garment while gathering herbs to brew a soothing posset for Lady Caroline, the castle's gentle mistress. But even fixing her attention on mending—the task she despised above all others—even clutching her fury like a burning talisman could not fully mask the apprehension gnawing deep in the pit of her stomach as Myles's impassioned words echoed through her mind.

I go to fight at Charles Stuart's side. . . .

Charles Stuart's side, indeed, she thought, ferociously jabbing her needle into the fabric. How many times had the dispossessed Stuarts attempted to regain the English throne in the fifty-five years since James II lost his crown to William of Orange? A dozen? Maybe more.

The number scarcely mattered. The result had always been the same. Failure, heartbreak, and the public execution of the dreamers who had been foolish enough to follow the Stuart drum.

Yet even if she bludgeoned Myles with those irrefutable facts from dawn till dark, she knew it would be to no avail. He would just laugh at her, his eyes alight with idealism, as he whipped out some nonsense about victories touted in legends—of Agincourt, Crécy, battles spun into the hero tales on which he had gorged himself as a boy.

The trouble was, he'd never bothered to study the uglier battles like Bosworth Field, or Worcester, or the Battle of Boyne. He'd spent too many hours poring over glorious victories in his history books to be troubled by the much more plentiful grindings of defeat.

A thumping from the corridor beyond made Devlin

glance up, surprised and vaguely pleased that some astute seamstress might at last have realized that she had been abandoned. But that fleeting thought vanished as the chamber's door swung open, admitting a serving wench who obviously had not the slightest idea Devlin was even in the room.

Ever since the day Mary Maginny had been retained at a servants' fair, Devlin had maintained that the chit's head was empty as a cracked lark's egg. But the girl's body was so lush and her disposition so willing that the men in the household showed a marked lack of concern over her want of good sense.

Devlin had suffered watching the girl's flirtation with Myles since before he'd wielded his first razor, and the thought of dealing with the woman now was almost more than Devlin could bear.

But Mary barely glanced at Devlin and muttered a watery greeting as she straggled into the room, arms laden with garments so absurdly rich and elegant they could only belong to Myles. The woman clutched the lush velvets and brocades against her breasts, stroking the cloth with her chapped hands. The tears coursing down her irritatingly pretty cheeks could have filled every washtub in Liancourt's laundry chamber.

Devlin gritted her teeth against Mary's aggravating sniffles, hiccups, and sobs as well as the sound of a cloth brush's bristles whisking over fabric. She wanted to shake the wretched chit, tell her she was a fool to weep for a man who had been courting a headsman's axe since the day he was born. But she knew that to do so would be an exercise in futility. To the simple folk of the castle, Myles Farringdon was their own special hero—Hotspur riding into legend, the Evergreen Gallant, bold and laughing, his blazing courage bathing their drab lives in reflected glory.

It was not until the wench blew her nose with deafening force for the third time in as many minutes that Devlin's thinly leashed control snapped, sending her bolting from the chair.

"Stop it!" she blazed. The girl shrieked in surprise, paling as if the shadows themselves had berated her. "You will cease this caterwauling at once!" Devlin raged. "You're driving me wild with it!"

For an instant the maid just stared, but then she sprang to life, indignant. "If you had a woman's heart inside yer breast, instead of lumps of Latin and Greek, you'd be weeping, too! Master Myles is the finest figure of a man I ever knew, and he goes . . . he goes to die," the chit snuffled, fat tears running down her cheeks.

"Well, he might have at least had the decency to wait two weeks until I am wed," Devlin grated, stinging under the girl's censure—which echoed Myles's teasing of nearly four years ago.

"Is there a woman buried under all that Latin in there, Dev?" he had joked, snatching off her prim gray bonnet and making her hair tumble from its pins in a cascade of red-gold. "Just once it would be nice not to get frostbite from a touch. . . ."

Unexpected tears bit at Devlin's eyes, and she forced them back.

"How can ye even *think* of going forth with the wedding when Master Myles will be swallowed up in war?" Mary demanded, indignant.

"It will be easy enough, I assure you. I will merely walk up the aisle in the Liancourt chapel and take vows before the vicar, and Tracey will slip the ring upon my finger—"

"Shame upon you! Master Myles—"

"Don't you go off wailing about your precious Master Myles to me, Mary Maginny! Three years he has been away. Three years of gorging himself on pleasure at the Hanover Court in London, and in France with his rakehell friends. Did he bother to dash off more than a handful of letters in all that time to let us know he was alive? Oh, no. Yet as soon as he has tidings that will drive everyone mad with worry, he rides home straightaway to tell us."

"But 'tis grand news! Grand! For years we been praying that Bonnie Prince Charlie would come home. And Master Myles is like the knights of King Arthur, bold Lancelot and—"

"Lancelot? Now, *there* lies true measure of Myles Farringdon's character. Wasn't Lancelot's claim to legend running off with his most trusted friend's wife? Yes, I bet Myles could find some way to make even that seem noble as well."

"How can ye be so cold, miss?" Mary demanded, injured. "'Specially when ye owe yer living—aye, and that of yer mama—to his lordship's generosity? Were it not for the master, you'd not have dowry enough to attract a miller's 'prentice, let alone a fine man the like of Mr. Tracey."

Devlin felt as if the girl had rammed a mallet down upon a particularly tender tooth.

"Myles Farringdon was still terrorizing his tutors when my mother and I first came to Liancourt. It was Lady Caroline who invited us to stay. And as for my dowry, Myles's grandfather, the duke, is my guardian. He arranged the financial aspects of the wedding contract."

"Now ain't those pretty turns of phrase," Mary said saucily, smoothing out a crease in a pair of doeskin breeches. "From how I hear it, your mama was nearly a beggar when she come here, with you only five years old. A charity case, what with yer papa losing everything speculating and then doing away with hisself."

Devlin stiffened against a soul-deep jab of pain, her memory filling with images of the father she had loved. The father who had not loved her enough to go on living, fighting. Who had killed himself, robbing Devlin of the one thing she'd treasured above all others—his love. It was a crime for which she would never forgive him. "My father is no concern of yours," she said quietly.

"Well, *you* wasn't any concern of the Farringdons, either, if I may say so. If her ladyship hadn't been so sentimental over the affection yer mama and she shared when they was girls, ye would've been grubbing for yer living with the rest of us, spite of the fact ye're a knight's daughter."

"I've earned my place in this castle as much as you. I've cared for the sick, kept the household in order, and tended Lady Caroline—"

"And what shall we do without ye when ye're gone?

There'll be no one to pour yer foul tea brewings down her ladyship's throat and no one to poke about in that musty old library ye seem to love so much. I wonder how pleasant 'twill be in her ladyship's chambers if the young master never comes back."

Devlin tried to block from her mind the images the chit's words conjured in her imagination. The sunny, peaceful rooms of the invalid Lady Caroline would be draped in black crepe mourning. The lady's blue eyes, usually as serene as mountain lakes, would be filled with a grief too deep and too terrible for one so frail.

If Devlin had one niggling sorrow amid the joy of her upcoming wedding, it was parting from the mistress she loved so well. And to leave Lady Caroline to an agony of uncertainty and grief was almost more than Devlin could bear to contemplate.

"Believe me, her ladyship will be worrying herself into a fever over nothing," Devlin said, crushing the sharp stab of panic inside her. "Myles Farringdon would never do anything so obliging as to get himself blown up by some discerning cannonball. He'd move aside at the last instant and miraculously save half a regiment, just to torment me."

"But ye'll never know, will ye, cause ye'll be quit of Liancourt, and be trying to warm the sheets of yer Mr. Tracey by then. It won't be none of yer concern whether the master comes back or no."

"Me lord *is* comin' back," a belligerent child's voice echoed from behind them. "When the true king of England be crowned."

Devlin turned to see the cook's ten-year-old daughter glaring up at her. Little Nellie's eyes were glittering with fierce loyalty.

"Myles promised to bring me a bit of blue ribbon that Bonnie Prince Charlie has kissed," the child said. "An' I get to see the cori . . . cari . . . the crownin' when they send bumblin' George back t' Germany."

"Of all the ridiculous—" Devlin tried to hold on to her temper but couldn't.

Dumping the petticoat into a basket at her side, she

caught the child by the arms, their faces inches apart. "Nellie," she said with forced gentleness, "there isn't going to be any ribbon, there isn't going to be any crowning. There are just going to be a bunch of bloody dreamers running off on a fool's errand."

The child paled, and Devlin felt a twinge of regret. She looked away, remembering the child she had been, believing so fiercely in wonder, in magic, in a strong, tall man who laughed, and loved, and tossed her high in his arms.

The image made Devlin ache somewhere deep, hidden. "Well, even if disaster strikes, you needn't fear for Myles's safety," she said, releasing Nellie. "I'm certain that even if he is in the thick of the fighting, he'll manage to escape. Run along, now, and practice your letters. I've a treat for you if you can get all the way to Z."

"For shame, miss, upsetting the child!" Mary chided, as the little girl dashed from the room. "It will all end up glorious. You will see. His lordship will come blazing through the gates with the whole of England laying at his feet."

"The only grail Myles will find will be one filled with Blue Ruin. And as for England laying at his feet, from what I've heard, the female half of it has already been laying between his bedsheets." The words slipped out before Devlin could stop them, and she fought the urge to clamp her hand over her mouth in embarrassment.

"Perhaps you would like to join the distinguished throng of my admirers?" A low, masculine chuckle raked across Devlin's nerves. "Then you could give me your opinion of whether I'm worthy of so much adoration."

Devlin spun around to find her nemesis lounging against the door frame, a rosy apple in one hand, the mesmerizing sensuality simmering beneath his drooping eyelids belied by the slightest twinkle of amusement peeking out from thick black lashes.

Heat surged into Devlin's cheeks as the maid left off sniveling long enough to chortle her approval.

"I wouldn't so demean myself if you were the last man in England!" Devlin snarled, but already she could feel nigglings of hurt, the familiar sensation of all in the room banding with the insufferably charming Myles against her.

But then, hadn't it always been so? From the time she had skipped about Liancourt in short skirts even her mother had been one of the viscount's adoring throng. And nothing, from attempting to be the best little girl in Christendom to being a very devil, had been able to draw her mother's attention away from "the young master" to the daughter of her own blood.

And as for the rest of the household, Devlin could mop up the cuts on Nellie's knee, tutor the child in reading so she'd not be ignorant, rescue linens bubbling too long in starch kettles, and hide a hundred of Mary's mistakes from that curmudgeon of a housekeeper, Mrs. Smeaton. But in the end, it never mattered—not when up against the blazing white smile of the abominable Lord Myles Farringdon.

"In case you've forgotten," she snapped, "I'm to marry your best friend two weeks hence."

"Ah, yes, the grand wedding." Myles shrugged broad shoulders, the laugh lines about his mouth deepening. "Must've slipped my mind. Heartbroken I'm going to miss it, of course. Stopped by Tracey's townhouse before I left London to give my regrets."

"Before . . ." Panic congealed in Devlin's chest. "Oh, Myles, tell me you have not been filling his head with this madness—"

"You may rest easy, madam. I am certain all the gunpowder in the king's armory could not blast your bridegroom from your side this time. It seems the prospect of marriage has temporarily dulled his taste for adventure. One can only hope that there will be time for him to join us when we march into London."

"Don't you dare intimate that Tracey is a coward! Not once in all the years you've been friends have you managed to best him at anything—chess, fencing. Why, last time you visited he had you at the point of his rapier a dozen times!"

Myles's eyes flashed midnight, the tiniest twitch at the corner of his lips betraying the fact that her verbal riposte had found its mark. Then his lashes drooped with bored arrogance as he flicked an imaginary speck of lint from the lace spilling from his cuff.

"What can I say, milady?" he drawled, shrugging his broad shoulders. "Tracey flies into a temper unless I let him win."

Furious, Devlin started to sputter a rebuttal, but Myles held up one strong hand with a long-suffering groan.

"If you're intent on nominating the man for sainthood, I'd recommend you send the list of his virtues to the Holy Father in Rome and not bore me to tears with them. I fear I'm a bit tired after the welcome I received in the castle yard."

His gaze swept over her in an irritating appraisal. "I suppose that stuff you're bound up in must be wedding frippery. I know you loathe sewing, Dev, but you *are* going to stitch that up before you make Tracey the most miserable of men, are you not? Poor fellow would be skewered to death if he came within an arm's length of you. And I vow such an eager bridegroom will want to get a good deal closer."

Devlin flinched, his words stirring up memories of a dozen veiled taunts cast off by sly maids about the length of her engagement these past years.

She searched for something to say, some way to hurt Myles back, knowing all the while that he was patently unflappable when in one of his obnoxious moods. But her eyes narrowed at the sight of a slightly damp patch on the exquisite amber velvet of his frock coat, the fabric just a little crumpled, as if someone had buried her face against it and wept.

Devlin winced inwardly at the scene that rose in her mind—Lady Caroline Farringdon embracing her only child, that gentle, learned, most beloved of mistresses heartbroken, but doubtless attempting to be brave.

Anger bit deep, the senselessness of this madness tangling in Devlin's mind with the waste of her own father's death. She shot Myles a glare filled with loathing.

"Since we were discussing opinions a few moments ago,

my lord," she bit out, "I would like to know what your mother thinks of your plans. Not that it would matter a fig to you."

The light in Myles's eyes faltered, and a look of worry crossed his face. "My lady mother understands loyalty. Duty."

"That was never in question. Tell me, though, does her ladyship understand stupidity, my lord?"

Myles's face paled, his lips a hard white line. "Stupidity?"

"What else would one call turning traitor to the crown?"

"Traitor?" Outrage flashed in his eyes, the quick, hot fury that was as notorious as Myles Farringdon's dazzling smiles. "The English throne belongs to the Stuarts, not to a pack of Germans who can scarcely speak our language. I go to restore the crown to its rightful owner."

Devlin's gaze raked him with scorn designed to fuel the flames. "I doubt that King George will see it that way. Nor Parliament, which has been ruling in his stead. Tracey says that the odds are against—"

"Odds? Odds? This is my country, not a cursed game of whist! I have a duty to fight for what I believe in, Dev."

"Your *duty* is to take care of your mother. Protect her. Not break her heart and put her in danger along with everyone else at Liancourt."

"I would give my life to keep my mother safe. Keep"—his voice thickened, and he turned, pacing to the far corner of the chamber—"keep everyone here safe."

"Oh, but of course," Devlin said. "You'd fling your life away in some grand gesture, and gladly. But I doubt you have the courage to be sensible, to tend to your responsibilities instead of racing off on some crack-brained adventure. You have a duty here, Myles. Estates—"

"Devlin? Child, is that you bellowing in there?"

Devlin stiffened at the sound of the all-too-familiar voice. She turned toward the door.

Red-faced, a kerchief stuffed beneath the lace edging her ample bosom, Lady Agatha Chastain entered the sewing room for the first time since work had begun on Devlin's wedding gown. Her eyes were swollen beneath her lace cap, her face creased with a very real grief above the crumpled pile of elegant white stuffs clutched in her arms.

"Ah, yes, there you are, daughter," she sniffled, oblivious to Myles's presence. "I knew I would find you as soon as I heard the shouting." Agatha glanced at Devlin's silvery gauze clothing. "You've smudged yourself already, I see. And the gown not even finished!"

"I ran out into the courtyard when Myles rode in," Devlin said, defending herself. "From the sound of it, I thought the whole castle was tumbling down."

"I told Caroline we should garb you in black so stains would not show," Agatha said, clucking like a fractious hen. "Well, you may quit preening before mirrors this instant, miss, and set yourself to important matters. It seems Myles has nearly ruined his clothing of late, with no lady to mend for him. He said it would mean much to him if you would tend to it."

"I'll just wager that it would," Devlin said, sending the viscount a killing glare. Myles lounged, half hidden in the shadow of an armoire, an expression of such supreme innocence on his face that Devlin wanted to box his ears.

"Oh, Myles!" The short, plump Agatha's face was radiant when she noticed the tall young man. "So you have found Devlin yourself! How clever of you!"

Giving the garments to Devlin, Agatha went over to him. Her hands reached up to cup the viscount's cheeks in a caress rife with adoration and love.

To anyone else watching, the scene might have been heartwarming. But the sight only served to deepen the bitterness inside Devlin, lacing it with an old, sharp tang of hurt. For never had Devlin, the child of Agatha Chastain's body, experienced any of the love that the lady lavished upon the reckless boy who possessed all of her motherly heart.

"My dear, dear Myles," Agatha said, a flood of tears welling over thinly lashed eyes. "My dear, brave boy."

Devlin saw a flush steal up beneath Myles's high-slashed cheekbones, but he did nothing to escape the older woman's embrace, merely slipping his arms about Lady Agatha's stout waist and patting her with some gentleness upon her back.

"Now, now, Mother Aggie, you mustn't carry on so. When I ride off tomorrow I don't want to remember the prettiest girl in Liancourt with tears all down her face."

"Bah! You're a fine wicked rogue, Myles Farringdon, you are. Have been since I first tended you so many years ago." The tentative smile that had creased Lady Agatha's face wobbled, then shattered into a gulping sob. "I only wish you were still a lad of seven, so I could keep you tucked up safe in the nursery."

"If Myles were still in the nursery, he'd only find ways to set it on fire, Mama," Devlin said, her throat tight with a longing she tried to keep buried.

"Stop it, Devlin, just stop!" Lady Agatha blustered, turning reproachful eyes to her daughter. *"Can* you not be civil to our Myles until he leaves tomorrow morn? Or must you p-plague him until you ruin even this little time I have with him before h-he goes away?"

The lump in Devlin's throat tightened, and she swallowed hard. For once in her life she wanted to give way to weeping as furiously and gustily as everyone else in the castle seemed wont to do. But it was not for Myles—rather, it was for the little red-haired waif she had been, watching while her mother pressed sweetmeats into another child's hands, worshiped another child's smiles.

She caught her lip between her teeth to still its quivering and busied herself by scooping up her sewing box.

"I'm sorry, Mama," she said, her voice strained. "I'll try not to plague you until *after* the viscount leaves."

"Don't strain yourself upon my account." It was Myles's voice, laced with an incongruous mixture of teasing and empathy. "You might burst if you thus contain yourself. And besides, I'm already full of scarrings from the sharp side of your tongue."

"Perhaps once she is married she will leave off her sour ways," Agatha said with a shake of her head. "Though I must admit sometimes I almost feel sorry for Mr. Tracey, saddled as he will be with her blue devils. Perhaps you should warn him."

"Tracey could hardly help being aware of all my legion flaws, Mama," Devlin said, trying as hard as she could to keep her voice light. "Whenever he's visited Liancourt you've made every effort to point them out to him. It's a wonder he plans to marry me at all."

"Well, he's taken his sweet time about the matter. Most likely looking over other prospects with this fine rogue." She jabbed Myles teasingly with one finger. "Five years," Agatha chuckled up at Myles. "Can you imagine?"

Stifling a sob of frustration, pain, Devlin turned and fled.

She heard Myles call after her, his voice laced with enough regret to make Devlin wince.

With all the haste she could muster Devlin rushed down the corridor toward the library that had ever been her haven. But even when she reached it, slamming the door behind her, she would not allow the tears to come.

CHAPTER
2

White Stuart roses drifted a fragrant coverlet across Liancourt's garden, blossoms kissed by the apricot hues of sunset, casting an aura of enchantment within its ancient stone walls.

Paths, neatly clipped years ago, had been narrowed by encroaching weeds, even a few intrepid nettles daring to poke their heads up amid the blossoms.

Garbed in nothing but a pair of black breeches, a shirt of thin white lawn and riding boots, Myles Farringdon perched in the crook of an aged rose tree, thinking about the past.

It had all seemed so simple during his boyhood, the world full of goodness and heroes and courage. It had not been until the day he had ridden away from Liancourt to be fostered out to another noble family at twelve years old that he had discovered that the world was not like the hero tales he had read at his mother's knee, that matters were more complicated in real life than in books. And that sometimes, when the hero knelt before his lady fair, she summarily kicked him in the teeth.

Devlin.

Myles's lips curved into a rueful grin at the memory of her hours before, in her bedraggled finery, her eyes flashing

16

green fire, her cheeks rosy, her temper so hot that if he'd dared to touch her, he'd have been scorched.

How did she manage to look like a queen even in a half-finished gown, her arms full of soiled garments? Her hair had been pulled up at the top of her head in a tousled autumn-gold knot, tendrils of it clinging to her cheeks, while snippings of thread dusted her from head to toe like the first snowflakes of winter.

How was it that she could always make him feel like a bumbling clod in the presence of some kind of royalty?

What was it about her that set him on edge? She made him angry, made him laugh, made him aware of an emptiness inside him no one else had ever seen. But she never looked at that vulnerable space she had exposed. She only brushed past him, her full, red lips curled in disgust, her nose thrust into the air as if he didn't exist.

But soon she'd not have to go to such pains to ignore him. She would walk down the aisle of the Liancourt chapel to wed the virtuous Braden Tracey and be quit of the infamous villain Myles Farringdon forevermore—save for occasional visits during which she could doubtless melt away into her countless responsibilities as chatelaine of Tracey's holdings and political hostess extraordinaire.

No, she would most assuredly breeze past Myles whenever he was about, favoring him with a distracted smile and some social platitude like "Haven't got your head blown off in a duel yet, Myles? Will miracles never cease?" She would bestow upon Tracey one of those besotted smiles that made Myles want to retch and then would whisk off, quite capable, intrepidly busy, agonizingly responsible, while the years slipped away unnoticed like beads from a broken thread.

Myles fingered the memory of five years ago, when he had strode into the stable to examine the latest issue of his favorite mare and discovered a flushed, disheveled, infuriatingly eager Devlin reveling in Tracey's practiced caresses.

By the saints, he had hated Tracey that day. He had come within a sword's breadth of calling him out, dueling over the affront to Devlin's honor. But in the end Myles knew he had shared in too many amorous adventures of his own to condemn Tracey for long.

Back then, seduction had been the order of the day for both Myles and Tracey. It had consumed them in much the same way it did most young rakes when they first recognized their own sexual prowess.

Yet even then Myles had made certain that the ladies involved were fully aware of the rules of the game.

Devlin had never suspected that it was a game at all. Nor had the Duke of Pothsby when he heard of how the girl beneath his protection had been compromised. There had been a lengthy meeting in Liancourt's library, with Myles only able to pace on the other side of the door, wondering if Tracey would come out alive. But the duke and Tracey had exited two hours later, both looking astonishingly congenial, after which Tracey had gone off to beg Devlin to make him the happiest of men.

Myles had never understood why it had been so difficult for him to wish them happiness. There was no reason he should not have rejoiced at the news of the betrothal with the rest of the family. He had always thought Tracey the finest of men—admired him for his keen wit, for the fierce competitive edge that ran just beneath the surface of Tracey's calm exterior. Myles could think of no man he would rather have at his side for a night of revelry, or when crossing swords in a fight.

Yet when Tracey had emerged from the library with the news of his impending nuptials, Myles had not felt any of the emotions he should have.

Instead he had felt oddly hollow, betrayed, a confusing sensation that roiled in the pit of his stomach until he had gone to his rooms and downed enough Madeira to find sweet oblivion. And it took a great deal of Madeira to fell the Viscount Liancourt.

In the end, the only thing that made the whole affair bearable was the fact that Myles believed Tracey loved Devlin in his way. At least, as much as Tracey would ever be capable of loving any woman.

She was everything Tracey admired, everything he had

marked upon his list for an ideal wife. Too much beauty and brains by half, a tongue witty enough and sharp enough to slay unfriendly Tories, and that damnable caution that all but guaranteed that she'd not make any costly social mistakes while Tracey was weaving his webs of diplomatic intrigue.

And as for Devlin, it was a miracle she had not already commissioned a bust to be done in Tracey's honor—set up in a garden somewhere so she could drape laurels upon it night and day. He was everything Devlin dreamed of. Everything Myles was not.

He grimaced and fumbled at the open collar of his shirt in a gesture more instinctive than conscious, his long fingers closing about a gold disk suspended on a chain about his neck. He ran the pad of his thumb over it, a kind of ache closing about his heart.

Though he could not see the image, he knew it by heart—that of St. Jude, his robes pooled gracefully about him, his eyes turned to heaven.

The holy medal had been a gift from Devlin one year at Christmastide. Myles had been unaccountably touched, hoping that somehow they might reach a truce with each other. But when he had gone to thank her she had fixed him with eyes solemn as a baby owl's and told him that St. Jude was the patron saint of the hopeless. And if she'd ever known anyone in need of that saint's intercession, it was Myles.

The breeze wisped cool across his cheeks, and Myles closed his eyes, an unaccustomed sense of melancholy drifting over him.

From the time they were children Devlin had taken fierce pleasure in predicting the most gruesome of ends for him—everything from being shot by a jealous husband to falling into shark-infested waters in a drunken stupor.

Perhaps he would oblige her and prove her right at last.

Insanity, stupidity—a mission for fools—more than one older, wiser man had thus judged the Stuart cause. Even Tracey, usually his compatriot in such escapades, had pleaded with Myles, begging him to remain neutral until it was clear which way the sword would fall—especially when Myles revealed the mission he was racing off to embrace.

Myles was stung by a pang of guilt as he recalled his attempts to persuade Tracey to throw his lot with the rebellion and seek adventure at Myles's side. He had convinced himself that his obsession with entangling Tracey in the uprising had been because the man would be a powerful ally in Charles's cause. But Myles had not allowed himself to think of the peculiar desperation crystallizing inside him, or of what Devlin's reaction would be, what it would cost her to wait once again for the golden-haired Tracey at the chapel's barren altar.

She was right. He was a bastard. Maybe he was mad as well. For two years emotions had been seething inside him, restless, wild, almost frightening. He had cast himself into the role of rakehell with a vengeance, wagering staggering amounts on the turn of a card, lavishing stunningly expensive gifts on high-priced courtesans. But it had not been until he'd been afflicted with the "Stuart madness" that he had begun to feel somehow sane.

The Stuart crusade to regain the throne had spanned three generations, filling history books with one wild, futile quest after another and a list of arrests and executions daunting enough to make the bravest of men take pause.

The young Prince Charles had never set foot upon English shores, had never pressed deep into the bustle that was London or run his fingertips over the stones of the great Tower to feel the pulse of history within.

And yet, Myles thought bitterly, Charles Stuart was far more a monarch than the pop-eyed, stubby German masquerading upon the English throne. During his stay at court Myles had seen the man called George II, had felt the beringed hands of one of the king's mistresses pawing admiringly over his own broad shoulders. He had felt soiled somehow, sickened, as he listened to their guttural German in the same hall where Elizabeth I had heard of the victory over Spain's great armada, and to which Henry V had returned in glory after the triumph of Agincourt.

In the place where heroes had once dwelled King George

prattled like a whining schoolboy of his homesickness for his beloved Electorate of Hanover—and of how he was going to travel off to the tiny principality again as soon as he was able.

That in itself had raked at Myles's temper, but when he'd had to endure listening to the king revile everything British, from the weather to the countryside, and declare that he'd never stoop to bed an Englishwoman, as they were all ugly and dull and undesirable, Myles had felt a rush of fury deeper than anything he'd ever known. It had been all he could do not to mount a rebellion that instant.

His outrage had been so wild, it was inevitable someone else should take note of it. Before the night had even ended a courtier cornered Myles over a glass of Madeira, whispering grand tales of having had an audience with the "king across the waters" and the young "Prince of Wales" in their banished court in Rome.

Fascinated, Myles had begun to prepare that very night for a trip to the continent and had raced to Italy at a killing pace.

It had been the devil of a journey—but Charles Stuart had proved worth every aching muscle, every sleepless night. And as Myles had listened to the tall young prince with his regal bearing and lively dark eyes speak earnestly of his dreams for England, the resolve Myles had first felt in the Hanover Court had hardened into something as terrifying and as compelling as the resolve that had lodged in the hearts of Galahad, and Lancelot, and the bold Sir Gawain as he faced the Green Knight.

Wonder . . . Myles had felt it in abundance. Yet also, for perhaps the first time in his life, he had felt a sense of foreboding, unable to deny the harsh reality of what this course of action could cost him.

But when a night of revelry with the young prince had resulted in a dangerous mission more secret and mystical than any Myles could ever have imagined, it was as if his whole life had been preparing him for this one shining moment.

Myles's eyes focused once again on the sweet-scented

garden. The roses were still velvety soft, the twilight warm, as if nothing had changed since he'd run about the paths as a boy.

Yet everything had changed. Everything.

That was why he had come there—perhaps for the last time. He had wanted to see those he loved just once more, to try to explain.

His mother, possessed of an inner strength that more than compensated for the frailty of her body, had wept, yet understood—smoothing back his hair, kissing his cheeks as she bade him to be brave, to bring honor, if not victory, to the noble name he bore.

Mother Aggie had clutched at him and sobbed, giving him the pleasure of teasing a smile from her while he patted her wrinkled hands.

Only his meeting with Devlin had gone awry. He had wanted to take her aside and tell her the things in his heart. Tell her about the restlessness inside him, the strange, twisting ache that drove him to be reckless, wild. He had wanted to hear her promise to be happy with Tracey. To run barefoot in the meadow once in a while. To laugh. Oh, God, to laugh.

But even before he rode through Liancourt's gates he had known deep inside that where Devlin was concerned, his wishes would remain just wishes—as impossible to fulfill as a child's dream of putting reins upon the moon.

Somehow, despite his best intentions, it always ended badly between them—with Devlin fleeing from him, those haunting, Gypsy-green eyes filled with anger or pain or scorn.

Ever since five-year-old Devlin Chastain had arrived at Liancourt she had been attempting to shoo him away from her. His earliest memories were of that piping, incredibly stubborn little voice saying "Go 'way, Myles, you are bothering me."

It should have been infuriating, or at least aggravating enough to make him want to go seek out more amiable company—company all too easy for him to find. But there had been a fascination in that small, heart-shaped face that was so earnest, so serious. There had been a challenge in attempting to make her break into a smile. Christ knew, she had such a winning smile.

Not that she'd often favored *him* with its light.

Why was it that from the time he was a lad he had tripped over himself to gain her approval? Why was it that none of the other laurels he had earned mattered at all?

He had wanted her admiration, had nearly broken his neck a dozen times over to gain it. Yet the things that made other girls' hearts flutter did not put the tiniest ripple in Devlin's infernal calm.

Even this scheme to aid the Stuart cause Devlin had twisted into some kind of irresponsible game. A game whose forfeit would be a headsman's axe—punishment for seeking something so elusive as one bright, glittering dream.

He winced at the memory of how Devlin's peach-blushed skin had paled with distress when she feared Tracey might be espousing the Stuart cause—remembered that reaction in stark counterpoint to the scathing contempt on her face when Myles had revealed his own neck-deep involvement.

His long fingers sought again the holy medal at the base of his throat, his hand closing around it until its edges bit into his palm.

St. Jude, patron saint of the hopeless . . .

No, he should wear another saint, one symbolic of boundless hope, absurd hope, absurd measures of hope.

With a resigned sigh Myles let the medal fall from his fingers to be warmed by the hard wall of his chest.

He shook himself inwardly, driving away the brooding thoughts. There was no point in dwelling on Devlin's scorn. No point in dwelling on the darker possibilities that might serve as consequences for his actions. Such thoughts would do nothing to change whatever ultimate fate Dame Fortune held in her fickle hands.

He forced his body to relax into the contours of the aged tree, the physical exhaustion gained in three days of tearing across England on horseback finally asserting itself until the thick fans of his lashes drooped, closed.

He must have dozed for a little, because when he woke up with a start the sunset tints on the roses had deepened to orange, the tangle of vines and thorns beneath inky-dark with shadows. He shifted against the coarse bark bracing his back, one hand lifting up to knead a kink in the muscles of his neck.

It was then that he saw her—her hair tumbled down from its knot, the last rays of sun glinting upon the red-gold strands. She had shed her wedding finery and was garbed in a gown of the dismal blue she favored because she knew he detested it. There was something in her hands, something white and soft, and for a moment Myles hoped that it was roses. But he should have known Devlin Chastain would never do anything so frivolous as to pluck blossoms and twine them in her hair.

No, far more likely there was some rare herb grown amid the blooms, something foul-smelling, tasting like bile, which Devlin would consider magnificently good for one's constitution.

He considered calling out to her, but it was infernally pleasant to watch her without her being all stiffened up with her disapproval of him.

Myles's eyes narrowed as he peeked through the tangle of leaves and branches, attempting to discern what Devlin was about with . . . what was it? A garment of some sort?

Stealthy as a cat, he levered himself upright so he could get a better view.

She jumped a bit, then stuck one finger in her mouth like a child, as if to cool the sting of a thorn or bramble. But after a moment she went back to whatever business she was about.

Well schooled in deviltry himself, it took Myles but a moment more to solve the mystery going on beneath him.

The little hellcat! Myles thought to himself, grinning. By St. Stephen, if she wasn't elbow-deep in nettles, cheerfully rubbing them into what could only be *his* shirt! And she called *him* incorrigible!

Carefully, silently, Myles eased himself down from his perch, making certain he made no sound. He had practiced such stealth in a hundred childhood games, and it stood him in good stead now as he crossed the ribbon of pathway and made his way across the garden. He paused, just far enough behind her that his shadow wouldn't alert her to his presence.

She was applying herself to the task at hand with great energy. The curve of her cheek, just visible to Myles, was flushed with a more beguiling pink than any bloom he had ever seen, and that bewitching dimple, more rare than a falling star, was twinkling at the corner of her lips. Ah, she was enjoying herself, certain sure. He might have been tempted to creep away and leave her to her pleasure.

Might have been.

Except for the still-fresh sting of her taunts hours before. Except for that undeniable compulsion to aggravate her that he could never manage to contain.

At that moment she hunkered back on her heels, regarding the shirt with a sigh of such consummate satisfaction that even the vaguest thoughts of retreating unnoticed melted away.

He kept his voice deadly solemn as he said, "I fear you have missed a spot."

With a startled squeak she wheeled, attempting to lunge to a standing position at the same time. Her skirts, already tangled in the brambles, caught on one of the wooden pattens protecting her slippers. Myles tried to grab hold of her arm, to steady her, but she yanked away from him with such force she tumbled in an ignominious heap, bottom first, into the patch of nettles.

The squeal of surprise was lost in a squawk of pain. "You knave!" she cried, attempting to right herself. "You misbegotten, detestable—"

"For God's sake, Dev, stop it!" Myles grabbed her by the arms and hauled her to her feet, despite her struggles to escape him. "You're going to get your hands full of thorns!"

"They're *my* hands, and I'll get them full of thorns if I want to!" she bellowed, her face flaming scarlet.

"Fine, then! Fine!" Myles shouted at her, releasing her abruptly. "Take a bath in the damned things just to spite me!"

He half expected her to do as he'd suggested. Instead she glared at him, defiant, burying her palms against her skirts.

25

He knew the exact second she realized she was still holding his shirt. Her eyes flickered away from his, and she thrust the evidence behind her back, just as little Nellie, the cook's child, might have done.

"You've had your fun at my expense," she said, her chin jutting up. "Now go away, Myles, and find someone else to bedevil. I'm sure that twitter-brained Mary Maginny would be just overjoyed to worship at your shrine."

"Before I do anything, perhaps I should change into some fresh clothes. My *shirt*, for example, is wrinkled beyond redemption."

Devlin's teeth caught nervously at her lower lip, and he could see that she was attempting to stuff the garment she held behind her back into a snaggly rosebush.

"Why bother changing, when the stupid chit will just get the fresh one crumpled with wailing over you?"

"It's a matter of being gallant. I'm certain Tracey would tell you the same. After all, what fun would it be for a lovely maid to weep upon her master's breast if his shirt was reeking of . . . shall we say . . . *nettles?*"

Devlin's mouth gaped open, then snapped shut, and she glowered at him. Cursing under her breath, she ripped the shirt from its hiding place, unmindful of the way the thorns snagged at her fingers and the fine fabric.

"Tracey would not demean himself by trifling with serving maids," Devlin snapped. "And as for your shirt"—the breath whooshed from Myles's lungs as she slammed the garment, and her fist, into his stomach—"I hope you choke on it!"

Myles felt a twinge of irritation, with Devlin and with himself, as he remembered Tracey's most recent dalliance—a harmless enough flirtation with a buxom downstairs maid at his London townhouse. Myles himself had been strangely put out, discovering the two of them, all but disrobed, on the settee in the green drawing room, but the flustered Tracey had only slapped Myles on the back, attributing the lapse to a bit of pre-wedding jitters—and an excessive eagerness to be in the arms of his bride.

After all, Tracey had said, with an earnest light in his eyes, he would not want to frighten Devlin with an overabundance of passion.

It should have comforted Myles that Tracey was so resolved to be gentle with her, that he had a care for her innocence. But instead Myles had felt the blade-sharp edginess cut inside him, fraying at something he could not name.

Myles tore his gaze away from Devlin's defiant one, fearing that, perceptive as she was, she might sense the turbulent path of his thoughts and set her mind to prying free whatever secret he might hold.

With determined levity he forced himself to focus instead upon the bundle of lawn and lace clasped gingerly between his two fingers, examining it with one brow arched in what might pass for amusement.

"Choke upon it?" He echoed her words of moments before. "I must admit, I hadn't considered making a meal of it at all—that is, unless *you* are planning to be meddling in the kitchen before the evening meal. No doubt you could do Catherine de Médicis proud, serving up poisoned tarts, or some such to make me miserable. Although, I must admit, the nettles in the shirt were a much more original idea."

"It would have served you right if I had taken the blasted thing to Old Ned's cot in the stables," she fumed. "You would've had the worst case of lice in three counties. You know I detest mending, but you thrust a mountain of it on me when you know I have a million things to prepare for the wedding. Tracey arrives in two weeks and I have all my packing to do. Not to mention teaching Cook how to brew the possets I use to soothe your mother's headaches. Now if you'll kindly get out of my way—"

Myles gritted his teeth in irritation, uncertain why he didn't sketch her a mocking bow, and let her sweep past in the high dudgeon she seemed to adore. But at that instant, he glimpsed the pale outline of her hand against her skirts, a slight reddening showing across her knuckles.

The little fool! What had she done to herself?

He planted his feet apart, effectively blocking her way.

"You are welcome to go to the devil if you please," he

27

said, manacling her wrist with his fingers. "But first . . ." Brooking no resistance, he dragged her hand from where she had it hidden in folds of fabric. She cursed him, struggling like a sparrow in a snare, but he held firm.

"There are two ways we can do this," he said with forced patience. "You can either give me your hand freely and let me look at the mess you've made of your palms, or I can go into the castle and announce to everyone present at dinner what you were doing here in the garden. After which I will summon the footmen to hold you down while I examine the damage you've done to yourself. It is your choice. It makes no difference to me."

"You would humiliate me before the whole castle? Oh, of course you would, and take the greatest of pleasure in it."

"Almost as much as you would have taken, my dearest, were I to have gone off on my quest itching madly. Come now, at least I did you the good service of *warning* you. Giving you a chance to avoid being—how did you say it?—humiliated. It was a courtesy you were not about to extend to me."

"I should have Tracey call you out! I should have him thrash you to within an inch of your life for threatening me—"

"What bloodthirsty creatures you women are. Nasty business, duels. There are real bullets in those pistols, you know. Might land you into widow's weeds before your bride garb is even finished."

"I'd shoot you myself, and gladly!" she vowed, leveling him a killing glare. She tugged savagely against his grasp one more time, then, with an oath that seared his ears, surrendered.

Myles held her captive a moment more, savoring the fact that she wasn't attempting to yank away from him— enjoying it, despite the fact that he had shamelessly coerced her. The fragile skin of her wrists was warm against his sword-callused fingers, and he could feel her pulse racing in fury beneath his hand.

He was stunned to find that for a moment he wondered

what it would be like to make her fall prey to a more exquisite fire.

With a stab of guilt he forced himself to pay attention to the task of discerning what harm she'd done to herself. He turned her palms up into the light. What he saw made him wince, then swear.

"Of all the idiotic schemes! *Next* time you want to drown me in nettles, just tell me, and I will be happy to oblige you. *Without* your having to go to the trouble of tearing up your hands in the process." Releasing her, Myles withdrew a clean handkerchief from his pocket.

He stalked to the manmade pool that glittered silver a dozen strides away. Kneeling beside it, he dampened the cloth in the cool water.

"It is not so bad," Devlin said stubbornly. "In fact, I had only pricked myself once before you sneaked up behind me, scaring the life out of me. If I had not fallen . . ."

"Ah, I see." Myles straightened and paced back to where she stood. "This, too, is my fault. I suppose Tracey would have knelt down and helped you work the nettles into his clothes."

"Well, what were you doing in the garden anyway?" Devlin snapped, defensive. "No one comes here anymore."

"If you'll remember, this is the place I always came to be alone, when I needed time to think. Now, your hand, milady." He reached for her with his long, tapered fingers.

"No! It's not necessary to muck up the wounds with that filthy water. I . . ." she stammered and fell silent for a moment.

"You *what,* your horridness?"

"I brought along one of my salves," she said belligerently. "Just in case."

Myles couldn't resist. The tension that had been building inside him burst free, unexpected. He threw back his head, laughing until tears stung his eyes.

"You mean to tell me that all the while you were furiously plotting your revenge you stopped long enough to think of . . ." He grabbed her by the shoulders and kissed her heartily on the cheek. "Ah, Dev, Dev, the ever-practical. You never cease to astonish me."

She pulled free, scrubbing away his kiss with her knuckles like a fractious child. "Astonishing a dolt like you is no great feat, I warrant," she said, withdrawing a small tin from the embroidered pocket tied about her waist. She attempted to wrench off the lid, but Myles swiped the container neatly from her grasp, shaking his head.

"What else have you in your pockets, girl? A stiletto to fend off brigands, pen and ink to write out a ransom note?" He twisted off the tin's lid, setting it carefully on a decorative stone. "Damn, but I'd not be surprised if you had Prince Charlie himself tucked away there, trussed up like a Christmas goose."

"He wouldn't fit. But if I could get my hands on him, I would find a way to squeeze him in, just to keep you from flinging your life away on his behalf."

Myles's fingers paused in their task of dipping up some of the salve, and his eyes caught hers, holding them for but a heartbeat. His voice was unaccountably unsteady as he began to gently work the soothing concoction into her injured palms. "Would it trouble you, then? To see me lay my life down upon a field of glory?"

"Glory?" she fairly laughed into his face. "Is that what you call it? God knows, there must be a million ways a resourceful blackguard like you can get his head lopped off as traitor. I've not the slightest interest in which method you've chosen. No matter what mad scheme you're involved in, you wouldn't listen to any words of caution *I* might say anyway. So there is absolutely no point in getting myself all riled."

He worked the salve into her raw skin with gentle, circular motions of his fingertips. "Ah, but maybe I *would* listen this time, Dev. You might be my lady light. My savior."

She scooped the tin out of his hand and whisked on the lid. "No, I'll not exert myself over your fate. If you are addlepated enough to follow Charles Stuart's lead, you deserve whatever befalls you." Tucking the small tin in her pocket, she began walking resolutely toward the garden gate.

"I can only thank God that Tracey was not duped into such an outrageous course. But then he is far too honorable, far too prudent to—"

"Oh, aye, the man's an accursed saint!" Myles's hand flashed out, closing upon a handful of blue sleeve, spinning her to face him. He was sick, heartily sick, of her slavering over the man like a moon-sick calf. And he was mad as hell that even this once she could not bloody listen, not bloody hear what he, Myles, had to say.

His lips curled back in a sneer. "Tracey was so honorable, he all but ravished you in the middle of a stable five years ago, with all the finesse of a groom tumbling a milkmaid. And he was so prudent in choosing his trysting spot that half of the estate caught a glimpse of what you were about. I vow, gossip regarding the incident had made its way thrice around London before you'd even managed to pick the straw out of your hair!"

Devlin's cheeks flushed scarlet, her lower lip quivering in rebellious fury. "We didn't . . . didn't plan it. It just . . . happened. And we were betrothed before the night was out."

"Well, let me tell you, if I hadn't come upon you in time, you'd have been a damned sight more than *betrothed*. The way you were clinging about Tracey, you would've skipped the ceremony and gotten right to the wedding night."

She yanked against his grasp, attempting to free herself, indignation blazing in her eyes. "It isn't like that between us! Not anymore—"

"It should be," Myles barked with a belligerent thrust of his chin. "Five bloody years! If I loved a woman, wanted her, I'd not wait five bloody minutes!"

"That is because you are no better than that stallion of yours, rutting around after every mare he can sniff out! Don't you dare reduce the attachment between Tracey and me to such base impulses! You know nothing of the admirable qualities of a man like Braden Tracey."

Anger boiled within Myles, welling up, spilling free. "I believe you have the villains in this particular melodrama confused. *You* were the one in danger of being ruined, and

Tracey was in danger of doing the *ruining*. I'm just the stupid sod who kept it from happening."

For an instant her eyes glistened, overbright, glossed with what he feared were tears. But her voice was quiet, contemptuous as she spoke. "You just cannot bear it, can you, Myles? Just cannot bear the thought of my being happy."

"Don't be a fool, Dev! Of course I want you to be happy."

She laughed, a hollow, aching sound. *"You* are the fool, Myles Farringdon! An arrogant, insufferable fool."

"So you persist in telling me," he bit out with swift, sudden savagery. "Maybe it is time I give you some grounds for your estimation of my character."

What possessed Myles in that moment he was never quite certain. He knew only that one instant he was glaring into those eyes, wild and green as a forest, and the next second he was dragging Devlin into his arms.

She gasped in outrage, one small fist connecting solidly with his chest as his mouth crashed down onto hers, fierce, plundering. His anger, his frustration inflamed his roiling emotions until he felt on fire with something oddly terrifying, dark, a side of himself whose mask he'd never before torn away.

He'd wanted to pay her back for all the names she'd ever called him, all the scorn she'd heaped upon him. He'd wanted to show her that a man—*any* man schooled in the art of physical pleasure—could wring response from one as innocent as she.

But he was stunned to find that most of all—perhaps even the reason he had veered three days' ride out of his way to reach Liancourt—he'd wanted to do this.

Kiss her, just once, before he rode off to die.

The sudden certainty rocked him to the core of his soul, and he shoved her away as if she'd turned to poison in his arms.

Sputtering, spitting fury, Devlin wrenched free, her hand slamming into his cheek in a slap so hard his ears rang with it.

He raised his fingertips instinctively to the burning print her palm had left, and they stood scarcely an arm's length apart, glaring. Silent. The only sound was his breath, ragged in his ears, her breath, exhaling in sharp, indignant puffs. She was quivering as she rubbed at her lips as if to cleanse them of something vile.

And it was vile, what he had done. Kissing the hell out of his best friend's betrothed.

"What th-the blazes did you do *that* for?" Devlin's voice slashed blade-sharp across nerves alive with guilt and something fiercer, more terrifying.

"I don't have the damnedest idea."

"You're insane! Do you know that? Crazed!"

"For once I agree with you! I must be mad, kissing a hellcat like you! But you don't have to fear any more assaults to your sensibilities. By tomorrow noon I'll be gone, and in the meantime I'll not trouble you further."

"Not if you value your life!" Her eyes flashed fury. "You're a bastard, Myles Farringdon!"

"I suppose I am. But perhaps you'll be fortunate, and soon I'll be a *dead* bastard, out of your way for good."

"Don't you dare try to make me feel guilty! I refuse to—"

"You mistake me, madam," he said, voice harsh. "I wouldn't attempt to make *you* feel anything at all." Myles sketched her a bow, dripping with scorn.

"I hope you never come back!" she cried after him. "Never!"

"I shall do my best to accommodate you. And give my sympathy to your bridegroom. I wish him good luck. He'll sure the devil need it!" Myles pivoted on his heel, striding down the garden path.

Devlin watched him disappear into the lengthening shadows, her whole body aquiver with indignation, fury.

Crossing her arms, she turned her back to him, as if to blot him from her mind. But her gaze fell upon something pooled upon the ground. Myles's shirt, its lace still so crisp she could almost see it falling over his sun-darkened hand, the fine ripples of lawn sleeve stitched full enough to fit broad shoulders, tautly muscled arms.

She stomped over to where the garment lay, wanting to grind the muddy heel of her shoe into the rich fabric.

But at that instant the tiny slice of sun yet visible above the horizon cast shadows upon the snowy cloth.

Devlin's breath snagged in her throat as the pools of darkness spilled across the material, seeming almost like stains of blood.

"It's only the sunset . . . the sunset," she said, her voice quavering. "Damn you, Myles . . . you and your mad imaginings!"

Her jaw clenching, she bent down to grab up the flowing white garment, but the feel of it, smooth and rich and warm, as if Myles had just dragged it from his shoulders to go swimming in a stream, made her stomach lurch, her knees quake.

Her mind filled with images of that tall, hard-muscled body bound up in an unfeeling shroud, that ready laugh silenced, the light in those teasing blue eyes extinguished forever.

She sank down onto the moist turf, the dampness seeping through her petticoats, making her whole body feel cold, strangely empty.

"I hate you, Myles," she whispered, her throat aching. "Hate you . . ."

She was still murmuring those words a moment later as she buried her face in the soft white folds of his shirt and sobbed as if her heart would break.

CHAPTER

3

*M*orning sun streaked through the window, the bright rays ruthlessly exposing Devlin's folly of the evening before. She looked at her reflection in the gold-framed mirror, her eyes staring back at her, puffy and reddened from a night devoid of sleep. With a sigh of self-disgust she drew her red-gold hair away from the left side of her face to examine the disaster that lurked beneath the curling strands.

Reddened welts streaked the tender skin from her cheekbone to the fragile dip of her temple, and a raw, stinging rash blended back into the wispy curls along her hairline.

She had been stunned when she had noticed the first nigglings of heat upon her cheek, but had thought the slight stinging was only the burning of her foolish tears. It was not until later that she had realized the full extent of her idiocy—she had fallen into the very trap she had so cunningly devised for Myles, all but scrubbing her face in the nettles that had been destined to drive him mad.

But the most intolerable blow of all was that the instant Myles saw her he would know with excruciating certainty that she had been making an imbecile of herself over his upcoming departure.

Devlin gritted her teeth at the thought of what the

insufferable rogue would say to her, how his eyes would twinkle with suppressed merriment, gloating triumph. He would be so blasted solicitous she'd want to strangle him. And she would have to use every ounce of her willpower to keep from playing right into the blackguard's hands.

She had spent the whole night trying to avoid such humiliation—brewing possets and mixing poultices in a desperate attempt to ease the mayhem the nettles had wreaked upon her skin. But though the swelling had eased, and the itching was no longer maddening, there was nothing in her packets of herbs and powders that could do anything to relieve the even worse misery Myles's kiss had wreaked upon her peace of mind.

Why, by the saints, had he done such a thing? she asked herself for the hundredth time. Why had he dragged her into his arms with that unfathomable look upon his face? The act of his lips crashing down upon hers was something even she could not misconstrue as a jest. There had been no teasing in his eyes, no laughing at her discomfiture. There had only been his hands, hard, as they urged her body against his, his mouth, hot, open, almost . . . *desperate* . . . in a way Tracey's kisses had never been.

Devlin's stomach fluttered, and she swallowed hard at the image of Myles's storm-blue eyes, the fire that had burned beneath the thick veil of his lashes.

"I'll wager he was desperate," she muttered to herself, fiercely. "Desperate to make certain that Tracey would not find out about his villainy! Tracey would never be so barbaric! Since we've been betrothed he's treated me with nothing but respect—" She broke off in midsentence, and she could almost hear Myles's sneering laughter at her words.

"Respect, Dev? Respect is what you hold for vicars and war heroes and stodgy, pompous asses who are martyring themselves over political causes. . . . You give a damned sight more than that to a woman. . . ."

Devlin closed her eyes, trying to drive away the mocking sound. But her attempts at escape only made matters worse, for that lazy, insolent grin of his flashed upon the backdrop of her eyelids, his voice filling with a rough, weighty heat.

"If I loved a woman, wanted her, I wouldn't wait five years." His words echoed in her mind. "I wouldn't wait five minutes. . . ."

She pressed her hands to her breast, aggravated to feel that her heart was bounding crazily, her senses swimming with the memory of roses and that wild, wind-tossed scent that was Myles's own.

"The man is a philistine! A scoundrel! A cheating, lascivious brute! Grabbing me like that when he knows . . . he *knows* that . . . that Tracey and I love each other."

But even as she spoke she knew she would never forget the look in those thick-lashed blue eyes, the odd burning, the blazing of shock and something almost akin to grief.

Grief? Devlin thought. How ridiculous. As if he had anything to grieve over! He was riding off like all men had since the beginning of time—doing exactly what he pleased, while the womenfolk in his life were left to gather up the pieces when things went awry, as they inevitably did.

He had probably gone about the whole estate, kissing every girl whose lips he'd never sampled—like a greedy child, not wanting to miss out on any sweets before he was hustled off to the plainer fare of Eton.

Doubtless he had approached the kiss in the garden the same way—pleasing himself, then forgetting it as he dashed off to indulge in some new diversion.

Devlin's mouth set in an unyielding line. If he ever dared attempt to take a nibble of her again, he'd regret it. He'd find those straight white teeth of his rammed down his insufferable throat.

"It doesn't matter," she told herself. "In three more hours he will be gone, and then I can devote myself to getting ready for the wedding." Yet some part of her knew that even Myles's departure would not banish him from her thoughts. And the wedding would be long past before things around Liancourt settled back into the calm routine that had existed before Myles arrived.

No, Myles would ride away without a backward glance, but Devlin knew from a dozen previous partings that for days, weeks, maybe months afterward the echoes of his presence would surround Liancourt.

Countless times before, Devlin had endured the aftermath of Myles's departure. She had been the one who busied herself with soothing those who were distraught, sorrowful, wandering about like lost children. She had bullied her mother into perking up and had gently but firmly distracted Lady Caroline from dwelling on Myles's everlengthening absences.

But this time—this time would be unbearably worse, an agonizing eternity of waiting . . . waiting for news that could only be tidings of disaster.

Even Devlin's usual sanctuary—that citadel of common sense and unrelenting logic, the Lady Caroline's chambers—would offer no escape. For already Myles's mother was sad and listless, twisting about her frail finger a ring Myles had fashioned of sealing wax years ago.

And already Devlin was facing the hard, painful fact that if tragic news arrived about Myles, she herself would be a world away in London, unable to brew heartening teas for Lady Caroline or to read her diverting stories, unable to sit quietly at Lady Caroline's side, letting the silence say things their lips could not.

In a way, it was as if Devlin were gone already, as if she had crossed some invisible line, snipped some thread of parting, and was waiting like a child's sailboat for the rippling waves to drift her away.

Never before had Devlin been tempted to shirk her duty to the mistress she genuinely loved. And as the time of her wedding approached she had stolen every moment she could to spend with Lady Caroline, their time even more precious since it would soon come to an end.

But this morning it was difficult to wind her way up the stone staircase, knowing that hours once spent in companionable study and intriguing discussions about everything from Plato and Machiavelli to the latest works of Swift and Fielding would be lost now in silences heavy with unspoken fears. Knowing, too, that Myles would doubtless steal away at some point during his preparations for his upcoming journey to spend a few precious moments with the mother he adored.

Devlin swore and paced to where sunlight spilled rainbows through the mullioned windows. In a secluded rear courtyard, far from the bustling heart of the castle yard, she could see Myles's enormous stallion, bridled and saddled at the ready. The beast had been isolated because of its propensity for tearing at any other horse that came within reach with its hooves and teeth. A few bundles were already tucked in the shadow of the old gate, doubtless containing vital necessities—the first load of Myles's elegant wardrobe, his dice box, and a small fortune for the viscount to gamble away.

She was tempted—sweet Lord, *how* she was tempted to wait, watch, until that demonic horse was gone, busy herself somewhere else in the castle with other duties, avoiding Myles at any cost. She wanted to hide away until the wrenching anguish of his leaving was over, until that lazy blue gaze of his could no longer travel knowingly over her face.

No one in the whole castle would even suspect her cowardice, for everyone at Liancourt knew the weight of her responsibilities. No, no one would suspect she was hiding, Devlin thought. *Except* for Myles.

And to allow him such a victory was inconceivable.

Especially when such a capitulation would mean deserting Lady Caroline when she needed Devlin the most.

In the day since Myles's arrival her ladyship's fair skin had grown even paler, her face taking on a haunted look before Devlin's very eyes.

Devlin grimaced, glaring at herself in the mirror. "Enough," she told her reflection sharply. "He is not even gone yet, and the whole castle is drowning in misery! What will it be like in a month? A year? At this rate, everyone will waste away to ashes from worrying about the rogue. And why? Knowing Myles, the rebellion could be a grand success, Charles could sit upon the throne, the whole world could be rejoicing in the Stuart's restoration, and Myles would be so immersed in his revelry that he would not even remember to write us a letter and tell us."

But the one pleasure she was certain Myles would never give up was the opportunity to torment her this morning about the silly rash on her face.

Resigning herself to her inevitable ordeal, Devlin glanced one more time at her reflection. She abandoned the green satin ribbon with which she'd planned to catch back her unruly hair, instead allowing the cascade of red-gold curls to hide at least the brightest welts upon her cheek—God knew there was no sense giving him any more to gloat about than was absolutely inescapable.

Shaking out a quilted petticoat of the most dismal shade of gray she could find, she started resolutely from her room, stopping for a moment to retrieve a pillow stuffed with fragrant herbs she had stitched for Lady Caroline in the wee hours of morning when sleep had stubbornly continued to elude her.

Outside her ladyship's room Devlin paused, steeling herself, then rapped softly on the door.

"Come in," said Lady Caroline, her voice slightly thick with tears.

Tucking the pillow beneath one arm, Devlin opened the door and entered the room.

The only light came from the fire crackling merrily on the hearth, a tiny kettle of fragrant herbs and dried flowers upon the grate filling the room with the scent of long-lost springtime.

Deep, welcoming chairs and full inkwells with quills sharp and ready beckoned to Devlin, as they had ever since that long-ago day when she had first come to study within these bright rooms.

With reluctance Devlin turned her gaze to where Caroline Farringdon sat upon a settee, a thick coverlet drawn over her as if to ward off a chill Devlin knew had nothing to do with the nip in the breeze beyond the castle walls.

A dressing gown of white silk was tied with rose satin bows beneath her ladyship's chin, while the silver masses of her hair seemed to draw all the color from her face.

"Devlin, child." Her ladyship's gentle voice shook Devlin from her thoughts. "Have you come to bring me sunshine?"

"I should hope so, my lady. It is dark as a tomb in here," Devlin said, then she stopped in horror. "I mean it is no wonder you're not feeling yourself, stuck up here in the shadows."

Biting her lower lip, Devlin hurried across the room and opened the heavy damask window hangings. She shifted Lady Caroline nearer the window and tucked the pillow beneath a cheek that, despite its pallor, remained as smooth and soft as a girl's.

"Mm," her ladyship sighed, burying her nose in the pillow. "It smells of lilacs and lavender and sweet new roses."

The older woman caught Devlin's hand and squeezed it gratefully. "You are a good girl to bring me roses, since I cannot visit them myself any longer." Her lips curved into a gentle smile as she looked up at the portrait that graced one daintily papered wall. A man with flowing dark curls and Myles's devilish smile peered out at the world from beneath a cavalier's dashing plume.

"My grandfather planted those roses himself, you know," Lady Caroline said. "A gift to my grandmother before he followed King James into exile. Stuart roses. He charged her to see them blooming when he returned in glory to English soil."

"I remember the story, my lady."

"You were but a tiny wisp of a girl when first I told it to you. You got that look upon your face, so solemn, your brow furrowed, your lips frowning. When I asked you what was amiss you said that you thought it unfair—for my grandfather to have planted all those flowers, then leave them for someone else to tend."

"You laughed," Devlin said softly. "I could never understand what was amusing."

"You were, my moppet. So earnest, so quiet, always trying to make sense of such fancies, legends, even when it was impossible. And Myles, embracing the most fantastic of tales as if they were gospel-spun." Her fragile smile vanished. "I wanted all good things for you both. Saw so much in you that I loved. Your intellect—so quick, so decisive. Myles's imagination, richer than any other I had known. And now I reap the fruits of what I have sown in both of you. The absence of your smiles, Devlin, child. And Myles . . ." She fingered the lace at the cuff of her dressing gown.

"It is my fault, you know," Lady Caroline said. "My doing, that Myles is intending to fly off on this mad escapade. My fault that my son will be in danger."

"How can you say so, my lady? Myles was leaping from the stable rafters, trying to fly, from the time he was able to walk."

"That may be, poppet. But who do you think gave him the idea he could fly? Who filled his imagination with Minotaurs and Pegasus wings and wild-eyed griffins to be tamed?"

"As if a team of horses could have dragged such notions from Myles's head once he latched on to them! You take too much upon yourself, my lady."

"So my husband always said when Myles was small. Yet soon he will be gone—my boy." Her voice cracked, and in a heartbeat Devlin was at her side, catching Lady Caroline's thin hands up in her own young, strong ones. "You mustn't take on so," Devlin urged, her heart aching as tears welled over Lady Caroline's lashes and coursed down her cheeks. "Myles . . . Myles would not wish it. You do not want your eyes all reddened when he comes up to say good-bye. He'll bellow loud enough to bring the turrets tumbling down, insisting we're neglecting you."

"He would, wouldn't he?" Lady Caroline said with a slight chuckle that was so sad it broke Devlin's heart. The older woman dabbed at her cheeks with a handkerchief edged in Brussels lace. "I cannot tell you how much it helps me, knowing that you love Myles. Fear for him, too."

Devlin turned away, her cheeks burning. "Y-yes, milady."

Her fingers wove into the folds of her skirt, and she was stunned to realize that *she* was the one in need of the familiar people, places, in this time of upheaval. She could hardly imagine being cut off from what little news might trickle in about Myles. Far off in London it could be weeks before she would know he'd been wounded, captured . . . or, more unthinkable still, lay dead upon some battlefield.

She cleared her throat. "I was wondering just this morning if it might . . . might be best to draft a letter to Tracey and postpone the wedding a bit longer. In case you need me."

"I'll not hear of it! You already altered your plans once on account of my health. And then it was Tracey's diplomatic mission to India that foiled your plans, and mourning for his grandmama. There will always be something intruding, child. You must grab up your happiness when you can. You"—she paused, peering intently into Devlin's face—"you *are* happy, child, at the prospect of becoming Tracey's wife?"

Devlin stared at her. "Of course I am! It's what I've wanted forever—"

An urgent knocking upon the door silenced Devlin's words, the panel bursting open to reveal her mother, Lady Agatha, her hands fluttering in high agitation.

"Your pardon, C-Caroline. D-Devlin. You must pardon me, but it is too bad of him to come charging in at such a time."

"What deviltry is Myles about now?" Devlin nearly leapt to her feet.

"'Tis not Myles!" Agatha burst out, affronted. "'Tis that other. The—the odious beast who—" She pressed her hand to her heaving bosom. "He came charging in as if he were lord of the castle, demanding to see you, milady."

"Agatha, calm yourself and tell us what this is about."

"Why, 'tis as I told you already. He is here. Your papa-in-law, the duke. And worked right up into an unholy temper, even for him. Terrified the very wits out of the stable lad who took his horse, and near drove poor Beasley's teeth down his throat, flinging open the door in such a fury."

"The duke? Here?" Lady Caroline asked rather faintly.

Devlin felt a fierce rush of protectiveness sweep over her,

and instinctively she moved to stand guard between her gentle mistress and the doorway.

Roald Farringdon, Duke of Pothsby, was a hard-bitten boil of a man with a temperament so rancorous it rivaled a wounded boar's. Totally engrossed in his role in the House of Lords, he'd had little to do with his daughter-in-law, and Myles, his heir, since they had buried his son sixteen years before.

The scarcity of his visits had proved a fortunate circumstance for all concerned, since the crotchety old man and his grandson could scarcely be in the same room together without coming to verbal blows.

All during the years Devlin had lived at Liancourt the threat of the duke's interference had lain beneath the peace of the estate like a sleeping Vesuvius, ever poised to wreak havoc upon an extremely vulnerable Pompeii.

Even amid the wedding preparations there had been a certain amount of ambivalence regarding the fact that the duke had sent an imperious missive that he would deign to lend his august presence to the festivities.

But it was one thing to have the formidable nobleman charge into Liancourt when expected—a dozen servants mustered and at the ready to keep him from wreaking havoc with his gruff commands and fierce complaints. It was wholly another matter to have the Duke of Pothsby arrive when the whole castle was seething with the news of Myles's infernal Stuart rebellion.

"Devlin." Lady Caroline shook Devlin out of her thoughts, recovering with remarkable aplomb. "You must run and warn Myles at once. And send for Marguerite. I can hardly receive His Grace in a dressing gown."

Her voice was lost in a brusque bellow that seemed to rattle the very windowpanes. "You will not be troubled to receive me at all, madam, as long as you bring that blackguard son of yours to heel!"

Agatha Chastain leapt to the side, as if the devil had crept up behind her.

"Where is he?" the duke roared. "Where is that thrice-cursed son of Satan? You shall serve him up to me at once!"

"The only thing we are serving here is medicinal tea for her ladyship. She is not feeling at all herself."

"Sh, Devlin." Lady Caroline attempted to climb to her feet. Devlin hastened to steady her, shoring up legs too weak to bear even her ladyship's slight weight for long. Lady Caroline turned her melting violet eyes to the duke. "Your Grace. Such an—an unexpected—"

"You may leave off the pretty lies, ma'am, for I'm not such a fool that I can't imagine your reaction to my arrival. As for not expecting guests, that is obvious, since you are lounging about in your dressing gown even though the day is half gone."

"She is ill, blast it!" Devlin began, but the duke cut her off with the wave of one hand.

"You may save your breath, girl, for I give no credence to such limp excuses. This weakness is what comes of stuffing too much learning into a woman's brain, poor feeble organ that it be. And this . . . this inexcusable disaster is the result of a mother who allows her son to run wild when he should have had a strong hand at his reins."

"Disaster?" Lady Caroline echoed. "I do not understand."

"Then perhaps you should ask your son for an explanation! No doubt the whelp would be at the end of a chain somewhere were it not for that fine Tracey lad coming to warn of the danger."

"Tracey?" Devlin repeated, sick dread knotting in her stomach. "Myles said . . . said Tracey had nothing to do with—"

"Braden Tracey would not serve up such a fool's trick!" the duke barked. "The boy has far too much sense for it. I but wish the same could be said for that idiot who calls himself my heir! Now tell me this instant where he can be found."

"M-Myles?" Lady Caroline pressed one thin hand to her heart. "He is here. It just so happens he—he has come for a visit."

"Is that so? Perhaps you had best pass along word to your servants that they should prepare for further company."

45

"Further company?" her ladyship stammered.

"Yes, madam. Soldiers. Hordes of them, who are presently tearing apart the countryside in search of your son."

"S-Soldiers?" Panic crushed Devlin's throat.

A tiny cry breached Caroline Farringdon's lips, and Devlin grasped her arm to steady her as she swayed beneath the impact of the duke's words.

"Sweet God . . . no," Agatha wailed.

"The best you can pray for now, woman, is that he escapes with his life," the duke snarled. "If the king's men get a noose about his neck, they might not even trouble themselves to take him to Tower Hill before dealing him a traitor's death. They may just string him from the nearest tree and flay whatever information he possesses from that idiotic hide of his with a cat-o'-nine-tails—and the devil with the fact that he's successor to a dukedom."

Devlin whisked Lady Caroline down onto the settee. "It will be all right, milady. I'll find Myles," Devlin said, wheeling to dash for the door.

She cried out as she slammed headlong into a hard masculine chest that blocked the portal. Strong hands closed about her arms to steady her.

Myles.

He looked like a warrior king facing a headsman's axe.

Ivory breeches clung like a second skin to thighs powerful enough to keep even the wildest Barbary stallion at bay, and a deep red ribbon caught his dark hair back from a face whose hard planes and angles were not softened, for once, by the light of his smile. Lines of weariness fanned out from eyes that appeared strained from lack of sleep. But there was no other evidence of Myles's usual lazy ease.

Instead, his whole body seemed rigid, tense, his mood as dark as the cloak slung carelessly across his shoulders.

Devlin clutched at the front of his wine-dark frock coat, the gold-thread embroidery in the shape of the Liancourt crest scratching her palms as she arched her head back to look into his face.

A flush swept high on his cheekbones, his breath ragged,

as if he'd run from whatever corner of the castle he'd been in. Devlin's eyes caught his for a moment, just long enough to see a flicker of some unnameable emotion in them before he shuttered it away. And in that instant she was certain that he had been avoiding her with the same energy as she had him, and that only when he'd heard that the duke had come had Myles rushed to rescue his mother from the dragon who had tormented her for so many years.

"Oh, Myles!" Devlin choked out, attempting with her weight to keep him from charging into the chamber. "Your grandfather—"

"Ah, yes. My grandfather." That lazy gaze scanned the room, lighting upon the duke. "I should have guessed His Grace had arrived. The servants were in such a blather, it sounded as if the barbarian hordes were sweeping through England."

"You may save your tasteless jests for the soldiers who are even now thirsting for your blood!" Pothsby roared, advancing on Myles.

"Soldiers?" Myles's face whitened, and Devlin could see the effort it was costing him to maintain his aura of carelessness. "I thought all of His Majesty's guard dogs were standing watch over Hanover. God forbid the Electorate should be in danger. England—now, England is expendable."

"Blast it to hell!" the duke bellowed, the corded blue veins in his temple throbbing. "Are you too thickheaded to realize what you have done? The whole of England knows."

"Knows?" Devlin saw Myles's eyes darken. "What do they know? How do they know? I've done nothing."

"Nothing save hold court with Prince Charles in Italy. Nothing save vow fealty to him and swear to fight to the death in his behalf. Maybe no one knows what this *mission* Charles entrusted you with might be. But Braden Tracey assures me that they know it exists, boy."

"Tracey told you . . ."

"He all but killed himself in his efforts to reach me, warn me. Arranged passage on a ship to France. The devil is in it, you fool. There are countless men, even now, vying for the pleasure of being the first to wrench free whatever information you hold."

Myles thrust his shoulders back, every line of his iron-honed body screaming arrogance. "I'd like to see them try it."

"Do not fear. They will! And if you think your rank will spare you or that my power in the government can shield you, you are wrong. Fatally wrong!" The duke's face was purple with rage. "You are branded traitor."

"Much of the country is loyal to the Stuarts! When Charles rides into England a wave of supporters will rise up behind him."

"You cannot truly believe that! The people are far too prosperous, too complacent to risk such a venture. Those who remember the days of Stuart glory are old men like me! Men who have grown wise enough to long to die in their beds instead of at the point of some Hessian's sword! And God himself could not win England with only barbarian Scots and a handful of hotheaded lords like you!"

"Would you care to place a wager on it, Your Grace?" Myles's voice was cold, so lethal that even the duke of Pothsby seemed to take pause. The blue eyes that could be so warm and laughing were diamond hard. "I shall salute you when we ride in triumph through London's gates."

Never had Devlin seen the duke back down when faced with opposition. But in the light of Myles's savage resolve, the old man wheeled away, pacing wildly.

"No," Pothsby blustered, obviously shaken by this reversal. "You shall fling your life away on some futile gesture and bury the name of Farringdon forever! For ten years I have commanded you to wed, to get an heir. I was certain you would end thus, leaving no one to inherit!"

Twin devils danced in Myles's eyes. "I knew I forgot something besides packing my neckcloth. I will do my best to impregnate some unsuspecting female before I leave, sir." Myles turned toward Devlin, raising one dark brow. "What say you, Dev, would you care to attempt it?" But a sudden sulky bitterness clung about the curve of his mouth. "Ah, but I had forgotten. You are to marry the virtuous Tracey. Perhaps if I die, Grandfather, you might adopt him, and he and Devlin can fill up the nurseries—"

"I'll not be made the butt of your infernal jests!" Pothsby cried, "nor have you jeer at the name I have brought to honor."

"Honor?" Myles sneered, his eyes flashing. "Is that what you call it?"

With a bellow of frustration the duke grabbed Myles by the shoulders. Devlin dived between the two men, but Myles's hands had already closed upon his grandfather's, tearing them away.

"Please!" Devlin pleaded. "Both of you!"

"Bah!" The duke spun away in disgust and something Devlin sensed was very close to despair. "Why do I even exert myself? 'Tis too late already! The boy is lost to me! But I'll not have him dead! No, I'll not have it, do you hear me?"

He turned to jab one gnarled finger at Myles's chest. "You'll be on that ship sailing to France before this night is out if I have to nail you in a hogshead barrel and roll you aboard myself!"

"Stop it! Both of you, just stop!" Devlin felt tears of frustration knotting in her throat. She stalked to the window to hide the dampness spilling over her lashes. But as she stared out across the lands she loved her anguish melted, raging forth into raw, biting terror.

A group of soldiers rode toward Liancourt's front gates, their regimental coats staining the hillside crimson and their swords gleaming in the sunlight.

CHAPTER

4

*D*evlin wheeled toward Myles, but he was already at the window. He turned, ashen-faced. "Soldiers. At least a dozen of them, maybe more."

"Hide him!" the duke, pale but fearsome as ever, demanded. "There must be somewhere to—"

"No!" Devlin cut in. "The soldiers might question the servants, frighten one of them into talking. They know every cranny in this place. I'll take Myles down the back way. His horse is there, hidden from any who enter through the front gates. Your Grace, you must go down and try to distract them."

"Are you crazy, Dev? If I leave, they might harm all of you. Damn, I should just surrender—"

"The devil you will!" Pothsby roared. "I'll find a way to smooth things over for the others, boy. But you . . . I'm not certain even I could save you from death. Go! Go now!"

"You could lose everything helping me! Everything you've worked for."

"Do you think I care when 'tis held against your death?" Pothsby said, rummaging beneath his frock coat. "For once do as you are told!"

Myles swore, then wheeled to Lady Caroline. He caught her in his arms, fierce, kissing her cheek. "Mother, you mustn't worry. Everything will be all right."

Devlin could feel the pain in both Myles and Lady Caroline, could feel the desperation as they clung for one last, infinitely precious moment.

Myles's face was etched with anguish as he tore away and raced toward the door. But Lady Agatha flung herself before him, her eyes wide. "The Dower House—go to the Dower House! Remember . . ."

"I will," Myles promised, then he ran headlong into the corridor beyond.

Devlin started after him, but Pothsby's hand closed about her arm to stop her. She spun around, yanking free, furious, frightened, but before she could speak the old man extracted an ancient dueling pistol from beneath his frock coat, a powder flask bound to the weapon by a silk cord. The duke thrust them into her hand. "Give these to the boy. Aid him."

Devlin nodded, then, jamming the heavy weapon into the waistband of her petticoats, she ran.

Heart pounding, breath rasping, she attempted to catch up to the racing Myles as he plunged deeper and deeper into the winding maze of corridors at the rear of the castle.

With every footfall Devlin expected to turn a corner and find a soldier's leering face, death glinting upon the point of his sword.

Already the sound of distant cries of alarm from terrified servants was echoing down the hallways, making the chill that always clung there seem deeper, darker, like that of a fresh-dug grave. The soldiers were searching, doubtless already raking through Liancourt's halls.

Myles glanced back at her over his shoulder, his face grim, furious. "Dev, get the blazes out of here!" he hissed. "Get away before you're dragged into it neck deep!"

"You think I'd . . . trust you to . . . escape on your own?" Devlin gasped, breathless. "You'd . . . find some way to . . . botch it. Now *run!*"

For once it seemed that Myles had taken her at her word,

or that he hoped to outdistance her, his speed accomplishing what his words could not. But desperation drove her hard as he ran down the last flight of stairs.

She all but sobbed with relief as she saw the heavy paneled door at the foot of the stone risers. Iron rattled as Myles wrestled with the door's latch, then flattened his hand against the panel to push. The panel held against him.

Emitting a black curse, Myles slammed his shoulder against the door in an effort to convince the warped boards to give way. With a screech loud as cannon fire the aged oak surrendered to his strength, swinging open to reveal the courtyard beyond.

Startled by the noise, Myles's stallion whinnied, plunging against the lead that bound him. The stirrups swung wildly against his barrel, driving the beast to renewed frenzies. Bundles lay tumbled in disarray upon the turf, but the courtyard was barren of servants—and of the soldiers, who were most likely swarming over the front of the castle. Still, Devlin knew they would have only a brief reprieve, before the soldiers rode to the rear of the castle to cut off any escape.

Myles turned, grabbing her arm, his eyes afire with frustration, fear for her. "I'm all but free. Get the blazes out of here!"

"No! Now hasten, before you bring the whole castle down on us with your railing!"

Consigning her to every demon ever spawned, Myles spun away from her, bolting toward his stallion.

By the time Devlin had retrieved one of the bundles and wheeled toward Myles, the beast was untied, somewhat soothed by the presence of the master he trusted.

"What the devil is that?" Myles snapped, slinging the reins over the stallion's neck.

"Things you'll need," Devlin said as she affixed the bundle to the saddle. "Clothes. Coin."

The sounds of alarm were getting closer now. Catching up her voluminous petticoats, she ran to the iron gate and flung it open.

Myles's hand closed upon the pommel of the saddle, his glossy boot catching the stirrup as he swung up onto the ghost-gray stallion. His eyes locked with hers, the blue depths brimming with gratitude, regret. "Dev, tell the old man . . . tell him I—"

"Tell him yourself! In a letter when you're safe in France!" Devlin said, rummaging for the pistol at her waist. "Now get out of—"

"Halt!" The gruff command made Devlin wheel, scream, her gaze fixing upon a lone cavalryman, his speckled horse blocking the path from the gate. A pistol was clutched in one of the man's beefy hands, the barrel leveled at Myles's chest.

Desperate, Myles groped at his side for the sword or pistol that had always armed him, and Devlin could see in his face the sickening instant he realized he had nothing with which to defend himself.

He swore, but the sound was lost in a blare of powder and smoke as the soldier's weapon roared.

With instinct born of desperation Devlin ripped the duke's pistol free.

"Dev, no!" Myles's horrified shout raked her.

But it was too late. The recoil jolted through her, nearly sending her sprawling.

The speckled horse reared in pain, fright, plunging as the pistol ball grazed its rump. Devlin caught a glimpse of the soldier catapulting through the air, skidding across the turf as he was thrown from the saddle by the terrified horse. There was a hiss like steel scraping bone, a flash of silvery-blue death as the cavalryman drew his sword, his face bright red with fury. Devlin's blood froze in terror.

But it was as if in that instant the very heavens opened, dragging her up, weightless, as Myles grabbed her wrist and yanked her up behind him on the frenzied stallion's back. The pistol flew from her hand as she struggled to grasp Myles's waist and gain her balance while the horse bolted madly for the gate.

Fear streaked through Devlin as she saw the soldier's sword arc toward them, but Myles's stallion veered sharply, and the blade slashed harmlessly, through the air as the gray raced through the aged iron gate into the open countryside beyond.

"He missed us!" she cried out. "I can't believe it, Myles, he missed us!"

But her brief surge of relief was shattered by the report of yet another pistol, from another direction. Shaking her hair from her eyes, Devlin turned to glimpse a dozen red-coated figures running from various parts of Liancourt—the stables, the front gate, the orangery—dashing for their horses. All the soldiers who had been searching for Myles in the castle were alerted by the pistol fire moments before.

It seemed impossible that the horse could race any faster without falling, without plunging both her and Myles to their deaths, but it thundered toward the rim of the woodlands only a few leagues away as if it sensed that its riders' lives hung in the balance.

Shots rang out, orders for Myles to halt echoing on the wind. Devlin clung closer to him, knowing that if she lost her hold she would fall. Knowing that if she fell, it would seal Myles's fate forever. For he would never leave her behind now. She closed her eyes, praying, frantic, as she heard the hoofbeats of the soldiers grow clearer, more terrifying. They were gaining, and Devlin knew in that soul-sickening moment that even Myles's stallion could never outdistance the seasoned cavalry mounts while carrying both of them upon its back.

Cooler air struck Devlin's face as they plunged into the dim, leaf-sheltered maze of trees, the horse racing deeper and deeper into the tangled woodland. A woodland Devlin recognized only too well.

"Where are you going?" Devlin cried, despairing as Liancourt's hunting park closed about her. "The whole place is walled in! We'll never find a way out of here."

"We'll see about that," Myles said darkly.

Devlin felt a scream knot in her throat as he reined the gray off the faint track, straight into the tangle of vegetation beyond.

She heard the soldiers' shouts of frustration, the sounds of confusion as they attempted to crush a dozen horses into a single file, to give chase through the cramped aperture. Their difficulties gained Myles's stallion precious time.

Branches raked at their arms and legs, threatening to tear both Myles and Devlin from the saddle or fling the running horse to its knees. But even that terror was magnified a thousandfold as Devlin's eyes suddenly fixed upon the course Myles had set for them—one that seemed to slam directly into a high stone wall.

Surely even one as reckless as Myles could not really believe the stallion could clear it.

"Myles, for the love of God!" The words ended in a panicked shriek as the horse veered sharply at Myles's command. The wall towered above Devlin's head, and she stared in horror, expecting at any moment to be crushed against the huge stone barrier. But at that instant Myles reined the horse to one side.

Devlin cried out, stunned. The stone seemed to part before them as if by some magical spell, revealing a narrow opening.

Harsh stone scraped at her legs, tearing burning scratches in her skin despite the shielding of petticoats, but Devlin didn't care.

The wind whipped back her hair, the wild speed of the stallion beneath her filling her with a sharp surge of triumph.

"We did it, Myles!" she cried out, jubilant, her arms tightening around his tautly muscled waist. "Blast it all, we did it!"

"Did it?" His voice was scored with undertones of sick fury, tinged with a very real despair, the devil-take-the-world laughter she'd expected over their unlikely victory soberingly absent. "Damn right we *did it.*"

Devlin stiffened as if the edge of the cavalryman's sword had trailed down her spine, leaving a steely chill whisper of foreboding. "Myles . . . what . . . what ails you? What—"

"Why can't you listen?" he bit out, savage. "Why can't you ever bloody listen?"

Dread formed a cold lump in Devlin's throat, choking off

her response. She swallowed hard, struck with a sudden compelling need to be quit of the whole affair.

She shook herself inwardly, telling herself that she only wanted to leave Myles to his "grand adventuring" while she worked her way back to Liancourt and a sensible bath with steamy-hot water.

But the need grew deeper, more gripping with every unsteady beat of her heart, a thin film of alarm seeming to sift over her skin like dust from the faint road.

A dozen miles had flown past when her gaze snagged upon the squat structure that was the cottage of Robin Doolittle, one of Myles's more prosperous crofters.

"Myles, wait," Devlin commanded, tugging at the folds of his cloak. "We've gone far enough."

"Far enough?" Myles shot a glance back over his shoulder. "What the devil—"

"I want to get off. I'm certain Robin can see me back to Liancourt before nightfall, but if we go on much further—"

"Liancourt?" Myles echoed, his voice thrumming with disbelief.

"I live there, if you recall it. At least until the wedding. I need to hurry back before—"

With a curse Myles yanked back the stallion's reins, pulling the animal to a bone-jarring halt in the shelter of a copse of trees. When he levered his weight onto one hip and angled to face her, the knife blade of foreboding sawed deeper inside her.

"Go back? Damn your stubborn eyes to hell! Don't you know what you've done?" Fury and hopelessness were carved deep in his face. "You've helped a man judged as a traitor escape capture and, worse yet, left a score of witnesses to testify upon it!"

"I had no choice! Y-You would be dead if I hadn't helped you."

"I doubt the king would have counted it much of a loss! You'll be hunted now, as sure as I am. A fugitive—"

"Oh, no, Myles, I'm no fugitive," Devlin said with a wild little laugh. "This has been infinitely entertaining. Wonderfully diverting. But I'm going home now. Getting married."

She attempted to slide off the horse, but Myles's hand manacled her wrist, torment in his eyes.

"Don't you understand? There isn't going to be any wedding, Dev." His voice tore, jagged-edged. His eyes locked with hers.

"You can never go back to Liancourt now."

CHAPTER
5

She attempted to slip along under her to Myles's hand tightened her arms.

"Unless you—"—someone wouldn't going to be any reaction. Myles him trying to drag about him even naked with her.

"You are a very quick to about it."

*M*yles's words plunged into Devlin's consciousness with the force of a fist, driving the breath from her lungs in a rush of fury, denial. With a cry she shoved away from him and scrambled down from the stallion's back.

Myles swore, dismounting in one swift movement, his jaw clenched, his eyes full of both challenge and regret. "Damn it, Dev. I don't care if you're furious at me, hate me, curse me. Go ahead. Saints know, I deserve it. But you know full well what I say is true. The consequences—"

"No, I don't know it! I refuse . . . refuse to . . . Damn it, Myles, you're not ruining my life again!"

"Dev, you have to think. The authorities—"

"All right! All right!" she broke in, twisting her fingers together. "The . . . the authorities might . . . might be . . . unreasonable. I might not be able to go to Liancourt now. But Tracey . . . Tracey can remedy things. He's powerful, resourceful. *And*"—she tipped up her chin, belligerent—"he loves me."

"I believe that he does." There was nothing comforting in the hard tone of Myles's voice. "But that doesn't change a damned thing."

"It changes everything! What would you, a man who

spends every hour racing about, greedy for anything garbed in petticoats, know about commitment? Trust?" She thrust out her hand, the betrothal ring of the Traceys glinting on her finger. "Do you have any idea what this ring means, Myles? It means that Tracey and I have pledged our love, our faith. Loyalty. I'm not about to lose that."

She saw Myles wince as if she had pierced him with some unseen weapon. He raked his hand back through his flowing chestnut mane, and she could see him battling his formidable temper. But when he spoke his voice was quiet, even.

"Devlin, Tracey is a good man. A fine man. Christ, he's like a brother to me. There is no one I would rather have on my side in a battle, in some gaming hell, or in the House of Lords. But the hard truth is—Devlin, to wed you now, he would have to give up his home, his family fortunes. His ambitions."

Devlin flinched, hating the way Myles's words shook her confidence, hating the way they tore at her certainty that all would be well.

She closed her eyes, picturing Tracey as she had last seen him, clothed in steel-gray velvet, his eyes blazing with intellect, shrewdness, and triumph as he told her of his latest victory in the House of Lords.

"Your husband will be a power to be reckoned with in King George's realm, my sweet," Tracey had told her. "The whole of England will be at my feet, begging for the favor of the Honorable Braden Tracey. And you will stand, proud at my side. . . ."

Devlin turned away, unwilling to allow Myles to see the sudden terrible doubt rippling through her. Because it was far too painful to contemplate, she tried to crush the uncertainty.

True, Tracey had been alight with his victory. One of their favorite pastimes had always been reading political tracts, dissecting Machiavelli, the workings of the state. When they had been locked in such furious debates Tracey's eyes had glowed at her with a passion that was more powerful than the heat she felt when they kissed.

Even his monthly letters had been filled with news of the ebb and flow of political forces, of Parliament gaining power over the throne and gradually slipping the reins of control from the oblivious George of Hanover's hands.

Usually there was a line or two of sentiment at the end of the letters. Hoping to find her in good health. Some had even carried a postscript about wishing she were near, so he could see her sweet face, hear her most valued opinions.

Doubtless, if Myles were ever betrothed, he would dash off reams of letters scrawled full of his impatience, filled with endearments and wild, reckless promises he had no intention of keeping.

Just because Tracey did not do the same didn't mean that Tracey's love for her ran any less deep, was any less abiding.

Devlin turned and glared at Myles. "Tracey will come for me. You'll see."

"Wonderful. Would you mind telling me *how* the devil he'll know *where* to come rescue you?"

Devlin sucked in a breath to rebut him, but the words choked off in her throat. Her cheeks burned. "I . . . I shall send him word where to find me."

"Fine. Send word for him to fetch you in Scotland, because that is where you're going."

"I'm not going anywhere with you! I'm staying right here."

"What are you going to do, Dev? Camp out beneath a hawthorn for . . . how long? Three weeks? Four? While your letter winds its way to London—if Tracey is even still *in* London."

"Don't you dare mock me!"

"I wouldn't *dream* of it! I'm just trying to understand your plan. Have you thought about inconsequential things? Like food?"

Devlin blinked, and his mouth curved into that insolent smile she hated.

"No?" He shrugged. "Well, what the hell? You can eat

berries and roots, and pray like blazes that the soldiers who are searching for us don't discover you in the meantime. Of course, it might be best if they *did* discover you. At least before some unsavory cutthroat stumbles across you—a rack of bones from starvation and exposure."

"Robin Doolittle could take me in. Hide me."

"I'm sure you want to convince poor Robin to get mixed up in this mess. Especially after what has happened to you."

"You're a bastard, Myles Farringdon!"

"I know." Myles knotted his hands on his hips. "Where you are concerned, I believe I've managed to make it into an art form. Now get on the damned horse! You might not mind sleeping with scores of night creatures crawling across you, but personally, I'd prefer a roof over my head. It's been the very devil of a day for me, too. I—*son of a bitch!*"

His gaze suddenly locked upon her face as he shoved her tumbled hair away from her cheek. Concern showed in his eyes. *"What the hell happened to your face?"* he all but bellowed. "Did a branch strike you? Hurt you? Why the blazes didn't you tell me—"

The rash from the nettles seemed aflame, on fire because of the heat in her face from embarrassment. She thrust her chin up and said nothing. Myles stroked her hair, still holding it back from her face.

"The nettles," he said softly while one finger traced the tenderest of the spots near her temple. "It's from the nettles, isn't it?"

Devlin was terrified that he would somehow guess that she had gotten the painful rash while weeping over him. And in that moment she loathed him for all that he had said, done, since the moment he had accosted her in the garden. Hated him most of all for the unforgivable sin of being rational when it seemed the whole world had gone mad.

"I hate you!" she cried, tears of frustration and despair burning her cheeks. "I hate you!"

Myles grabbed her about the waist, slinging her up onto

the horse. His eyes were dark with fury and something more as he snapped, "You only hate me when I'm right."

The heavy gray sky was misting, and thunder rumbled, a distant, oddly mournful sound.

Myles shifted weary muscles against the damp leather of the saddle, painfully aware of Devlin sitting behind him, agonizingly silent since their angry words three hours before.

The rage he had felt had long since dissipated, tightening into an ache that clenched about his chest. But Devlin's own fury was still hot as a new-minted coin, burning him, though she had not said a word.

She was holding her body as far away from his as possible, barely touching his waist with her fingertips, as if he were something reprehensible, which he supposed he was.

Far better to plunge to the rocky ground below, he thought, far better to break one's neck than to depend upon someone as unstable and irresponsible as the notorious Viscount Liancourt. Myles swore inwardly, swiping at gritty eyes with the back of his hand. He turned his gaze to the horizon. A smear of stone upon the crest of a hill assured him that they would soon reach their destination—what remained of the Chastain Dower House, Devlin's birthright.

Yet even the thought of getting warm and dry in the half-ruined structure was little comfort. For the weight of the coming storm seemed to press down upon Myles's chest, the burden of his guilt seeming almost too great to carry.

Sweet Christ, what had he done?

Tearing Devlin away from the home she so loved, from the multitude of people she fretted over, cared for, ordered about in that voice that brooked no argument. Shattering her hopes of wedding a man she had waited for for over five years. A man she loved. All but worshiped.

A man who would never have her now.

Myles closed his eyes, despairing, as he pictured Braden Tracey's face when he received the news that his betrothed had fired upon one of the king's soldiers. There would be fear for her safety, even a lover's despair, but those fierce emotions would not be able to withstand the underlying force of Tracey's ambition, his sense of honor and duty to his family name.

Tracey would grieve, rage, curse Myles's recklessness, Devlin's impetuosity, and the fates' injustice, and then he would square his shoulders and perform what he deemed a painful necessity. He would excise Devlin from his life with one slash, as cutting and final as a blow from any sword.

And it would be all Myles's fault.

He gritted his teeth against the acid-hot lashes of self-recrimination that raked him. He should have beaten the girl away with a cudgel to get her to abandon him—should have ridden into the very jaws of the soldiers at Liancourt rather than allow her infernal meddling.

There was no name vicious enough to call himself for dragging her into the midst of this mess.

Christ, he thought, it wasn't fair that she should be robbed, not only of Tracey, but of Liancourt as well.

Myles's jaw knotted, his throat constricting.

Though he held his ancestral home in great affection, he had spent his childhood imagining adventures far away from the safety of its walls. From the time he could toddle about he'd been attempting to slip through the gates to explore the tantalizing delights that lay beyond. But Devlin . . .

Even when they were children he had known that the sprawling castle meant far more to her. And in one rare weak moment she had even admitted that her one reservation about becoming Tracey's bride was the fact that she would be leaving the place she so loved. The castle that had insinuated itself into her very soul.

He sighed, his mantle doing nothing to warm away the chill that closed about his heart.

Damn it, Dev, he wanted to rail at her, I would do anything to restore Tracey to you. Liancourt as well. Anything. By God, he thought, hadn't he done so once already?

He'd been twelve then, and full of mischief. He and

Devlin had been even more quarrelsome than usual that summer, turning the whole of the estate into their own private battleground. Wild pranks and full-scale wars had everyone in Liancourt stuffing bits of wool in their ears to shut out their bellowing. And no one in the castle so much as dared take a spoonful of sugar without checking the bowl for spiders.

He had been in his mother's chambers, filling the ink-pot Devlin always used with some foul-smelling concoction he'd stirred up in the stable yard, when a burly footman had brought Lady Caroline back from an airing, Mother Aggie trailing behind her with an armload of comforters and pillows.

Knowing that his mother would be furious if she caught him tampering with the tools of Devlin's studies, Myles had ducked behind Lady Caroline's huge writing desk to wait for an opportunity to escape. But when he heard the ensuing conversation of the two women he so adored, he almost wished he had sprung out into the room to suffer their scolding.

Even now Myles could remember how his stomach had knotted at the solution Lady Agatha had devised to put an end to the mayhem: sending Devlin off to the home of some distant cousin the girl had never met.

Peeking from behind the desk's mahogany corner, he had seen the shock in his own mother's face, and the sorrow. And it was as if he could see a foreshadowing of Devlin's devastation reflected in Lady Caroline's dark eyes.

"I—I cannot think such drastic measures are necessary," Lady Caroline had said. "This mischief between the two children can be annoying at times, I know. But it seems unfair to banish the girl when Myles is equally responsible."

"Never say so, my lady! Devlin is dependent upon your charity. It is her duty to defer to the young master in all things, while Master Myles is only just high-spirited, adventurous."

"Adventurous is a boy climbing to the top of a tree or riding a horse beyond his skill to control. It is not creeping into another child's bedchamber and shutting a wild fox-cub in her drawer."

Myles had squirmed, wanting nothing more than to bolt for the study door, but it was as if Lady Agatha's words had rooted his feet to the spot.

"Pah!" the bustling woman said with a dismissive wave. "It was nothing to warrant the tantrum the girl threw. She had no clothing in there, or ribbons, thank the heavens. Only that batch of papers she's been scribbling on these past months—"

"They were essays on which the child had worked very hard." There had been regret in his mother's voice. "I had promised her I would send them to my brother, the bishop."

"Well, now you will be saved the bother." Lady Agatha smoothed the coverlets back onto his mother's bed. "And as for Devlin, I am certain Cousin Alexander must have some books stuffed away somewhere. As long as the child can go poking about them, I'm sure she'll not be aggrieved at all to leave . . . not even her own mama." Lady Agatha had given an injured sniff. "It is unnatural how little the girl cares for me. You are so fortunate, dearest Caroline, in your son."

His mother seemed about to protest, then stopped with a weary sigh, almost as if she were surrendering somehow. "Agatha, please stop to consider before you send the child away. It is so difficult for her to meet new people, and I know of few who could stay ahead of her in her studies. It would be a tragedy if a mind such as hers were to be wasted."

"She would do better to spend her time learning proper humility. No, I promise you Devlin will be fine, once she is settled. I fear it is the only way. Now let me help you into your dressing gown, my dear, and—" Agatha Chastain had closed the French doors leading to the chamber, blotting out Myles's view of the room, reducing to faint murmurs the voices beyond the carved oaken panels.

He had stared at them, his stomach pitching. Then he had turned and fled the room, feeling more despicable than he'd ever felt in his life.

Even now, at twenty-seven, Myles remembered how he'd dreamt up countless wild plans to save Devlin from such a plight. He considered running away and joining a troupe of players. He thought about joining the army.

But it was later the same day, while practicing with his elderly sword master, that he'd seized upon the perfect solution. Master Auvergne had been bemoaning the fact that Myles had no brothers or neighboring sons of noblemen worthy to test his skill against—an old complaint, one Myles hardly listened to anymore.

But the words had scarcely left du Pree's mouth that afternoon before Myles was casting aside his sword and dashing to his mother's rooms.

For three days Myles hounded, cajoled, and pleaded with his mother, begging her to send him to a family where there was not "just a worthless girl" hanging about. He would never be a warrior without someone worthy to serve as his opponent, without a father to teach him the ways of swordplay.

In the end Lady Caroline had wearily agreed, and he had been packed off to the Traceys of York.

He could still remember staring out the window of the coach, watching everything he knew fade away into the distance. His mother had been attempting not to weep, but Mama Aggie had had no such compunctions. Devlin had curtsied a stiff good-bye, still angry over the ruined essays. And Myles had not been able to forgo a parting riposte, catching her in an enthusiastic hug just long enough to slip a harmless garden snake into the pocket at her waist.

Yet even then he knew he'd done the right thing in leaving Liancourt. It was far better for him to strike out on such an adventure than for Devlin to suffer the agonies she would have endured being torn away.

And before they'd traveled a dozen miles he had been craning his head out the window and begging John Coachman to let him drive the horses.

Now Myles's memory relentlessly catalogued every ill turn he'd ever done Devlin. He'd never meant to hurt her, damn it. But that hadn't made the pain cut her any less deeply, hadn't made her despise him any less.

And this time there would be no easy answers, no way to rush in like a knight astride a white charger to mend things, sending her back to her prince and her gray stone tower.

This time he had destroyed her dreams.

A tiny sound like that of an animal caught in a snare startled Myles from his thoughts. He peered over his shoulder to see Devlin's face, and his chest gave a painful squeeze.

She no longer wore that hard, angry expression that had seared him upon the endless miles of their journey. Rather, her face was ice-white, her eyes huge and filled with emotion —fear, anticipation, grief, loss, and dread.

Myles drew rein and shifted to one side.

Her fingers tightened in the taut muscles at his waist, and he sensed a tremor working through her.

"Dev?" He switched both reins to one hand, reaching his other up to cup her cheek in his hard palm. She didn't so much as blink at the contact. That above anything made the dread coil deep inside Myles.

"Wh-where are you going?" she asked in a faint, lost tone.

"What do you mean, where are we going?" he said, as softly as though speaking to a skittish wild bird. "I'm taking you to the Dower House. We'll shelter there for the night, then go to join with the Stuart forces."

"But after Papa . . . died, and we left, everything was destroyed. I used to dream about it. See flames against the sky, hear the house screaming."

Her fingers were shaking, her legs, cupped beneath the backs of his thighs, quivering in a way that alarmed him.

"Silly, wasn't it?" she said, with an attempt at her usual bravado. "Ridiculous thought that stones could"—she swallowed hard—"could scream."

Myles's fingers clenched and he was uncertain what to say, hating the sudden, strange helplessness he felt. Memories flitted through him of when Devlin had first arrived at Liancourt. For a time she had been ensconced in the

Farringdon nursery with him, Mama Aggie installed as nurse.

He could remember waking up to the sound of Devlin's sobs, Mama Aggie's voice low, yet granite-hard, railing at the girl to cease her wailing, that she was being a stupid gudgeon, weeping about things that had never happened.

Three nights Myles had heard the crack of flesh striking flesh, and Devlin's sobs had shifted into heartbroken snifflings that had made Myles squirm in his own small bed.

The last time he had heard the slaps Myles had not been able to bear it. He had crawled from beneath his coverlets and crossed the room in the darkness, pleading with Mama Aggie not to strike her anymore. The very next day five-year-old Devlin had been moved to the attic chamber she had kept for years.

And Myles had been left to wonder if she still cried up there, alone.

He shook away the memories, peering into those wide sea-green eyes. He wanted to break whatever spell held her. Wanted to make her smile just a little. Even if it was to sneer at him.

"When I was a boy I used to dream that I had shrunk down to the size of a thimble and was being chased by a petticoat that slunk across the floor," he said.

Something flickered in Devlin's eyes, something desperate, something grateful. "Portent of things to come," Devlin said. "The cuckolded husband's breeches were probably giving chase a moment behind."

Myles skimmed the edge of his thumb along the velvet-soft curve of her cheek, as if his touch could bring back the bloom of color that had faded there. He smiled. "I don't know about the breeches, but the petticoats never caught me. It was right terrifying, I can tell you."

Devlin's lips formed a fragile smile. "I always knew you were a coward."

He tugged at a tendril of red-gold hair, but his own smile was stiff with regret. "Dev, I was thinking . . . well, maybe it would be better if I just dashed into the Dower House for a moment, and then we could ride a ways, sleep under the night sky."

Despite the haunted look in her eyes, Devlin's brow creased in puzzlement. "It's going to rain. The thunder—"

Myles shrugged. "I've slept in the rain before. Sometimes, when you stay out in a storm, it's as if you can hear the very gods warring—Zeus and Mercury, Thor and Loki—all gathered from a dozen different legends."

Devlin looked away. "I've already been shot at, abducted, bellowed at, and had my wedding spoiled. I don't intend to add catching my death from lying out in the rain all night."

Exasperated, Myles let his hand fall away from her cheek, stinging at the fact that even now, when he was attempting to do her a kindness, she managed to make him seem an inconsiderate oaf.

"I just knew you weren't eager to return to your father's house. Thought I might spare you the trial."

Devlin shrugged. "I can't imagine why you would want to go to the Dower House in the first place. But since we're nearly there already, and are about to be trapped in a downpour, I cannot see why we shouldn't seek shelter beneath its roof."

Suddenly Devlin's eyes narrowed in suspicion, her head tilting in question. "Why *are* we going there?"

"Your mother told me long ago of some trinkets that were hidden away within the walls."

"That is impossible. There was nothing left—"

"Apparently they were secreted away in the old stone part of the house. She's not even certain what is there, save for a sword whose scabbard is studded with gems. She wanted me to retrieve the things years ago, but I was always too busy. A failing in character for which you and I can only be grateful, because now whatever coin we can get for that sword will see us to Scotland."

Myles winced as Devlin's nails bit into the flesh at his waist, her gaze suddenly hard and affronted.

"You are telling me that *my mother* sent you scrounging after my father's belongings and did not even bother to mention their existence to me? That she let me believe we were stranded at Liancourt, dependent on your charity for our very survival, when there was a jeweled sword lying in some hole in a wall somewhere?"

Myles looked into her eyes, saw the devastating hurt, the fierce betrayal. "Dev, I'm certain there was a reason she failed to tell you. For a long time you were having nightmares—"

Devlin's eyes widened in an ice-pale face, and she flinched slightly. "You knew about the nightmares?"

"I would have had to be deaf not to, considering that we were sleeping in the same room! Blast it, Dev, I was only saying that your mother might have been trying to protect you when she chose not to tell you about the sword. She might not have wanted to remind you of your father."

"Don't you dare tell me she was attempting to shield me somehow. She never bothered to shield me from the fact that my father was judged a failure and a coward, gambling away his fortune on mad financial schemes and then killing himself to avoid the consequences of his actions. She never bothered to *protect* me from the fact that he chose to die and leave us alone, helpless—*penniless*—to face the disaster he had made. No, she made that quite bloody clear to me, even before we came crawling to your doorstep like beggars with their bowls!"

"Devlin, for God's sake, I didn't say it was right for her to keep it from you, I only said—"

"That she was doing me a *kindness?* Showing how much she *loved* me? Well, perhaps you haven't noticed, my lord, but the only person my mother seems incapable of lavishing love upon is *me!*"

Myles hated the anguish he heard in her voice, hated that at least some of what she said was true. "Dev, I know things have not always gone well between you and your mother, but I don't think she set out to hurt you."

Tears broke over her lashes. "Do you know what it would have meant to me? To have something of my father's? Anything? The riding crop he carried when he made the rounds of his tenants? The old gray cloak he favored, the one that smelled of brandy and spice? Anything . . . just so I would know that he—he was real. That he loved . . ."

Myles swung one booted leg over the stallion's neck, sliding to the ground. Then he turned to pull Devlin down into his arms. He had comforted more than his share of weeping women, but this time . . . this time was different.

Devlin's pain seemed too great to be contained, even by one of her formidable inner strength. And there was something doubly awful about the way the grief tore at her, because never, in all the time Myles had known her, had he seen her thus shaken.

He pressed her close against his chest, as if the warmth of his body could thaw the chill of hurt, grief, betrayal. She seemed delicate somehow. So damned small. God knew it was hard to remember she came scarcely to his shoulder when she was scratching his eyes out like a fury! But here, now, he could sense how fragile she really was beneath it all, how lost.

His hand stroked her hair with a fierce protectiveness the depth of which stunned him, the silky strands of her hip-length curls snagging on his sword-toughened palm.

He cursed Agatha Chastain for her idiocy regarding Devlin, and he cursed himself even more heartily for not shunning the Dower House, for not taking Devlin and making a dash for the border, relying on his wits to see them to safety. The whole of the king's treasury would not be worth the misery now etched on Devlin's face.

He cradled her, feeling something break inside him. He pressed his cheek against her wet one, rocking her as if she were no bigger than little Nellie. But he knew full well that this pain was not so easily healed as skinned elbows and broken dolls.

Instinctively his lips brushed against her temple and lingered there. The first chill drops of rain struck his skin, as if even the sky mourned.

"Go ahead, Dev," he breathed against her tear-moistened skin. "Cry it out, sweeting."

71

He sensed the change in her, as swift, yet subtle, as the scent of a storm upon the wind. She had almost let herself melt against him, be comforted, warmed. But now it was as if he could feel crystals of icy aloofness forming inside her, compelling her to push him away with hands that had curled in the fabric of his shirt a moment before.

"It's raining harder" was all she said. "If we don't get to shelter, we'll be soaked to the bone."

He looked at her flushed face, her eyes not grieving, but empty. Horribly empty.

"Damn it, Dev, it's all right to cry after all you've been through today! There is no sin in breaking down for a little while. It's only me. Myles. There's no one else to see you—"

"Leave it alone, Myles," she said, resolutely mounting the stallion.

"Damn it, Dev! You don't have to be some bloody bastion of strength! You're not a marble statue with no feelings! You're a woman! You should be railing at me in a fury—crying, cursing—anything would be better than sitting there, pretending this never happened!"

"Better for whom?" Her voice was whisper-soft, her eyes quiet as they peered at him from beneath thick lashes.

Myles stared up into the face that he had known when it was still speckled with childhood freckles. That stoic, heart-shaped face that seemed suddenly like that of a lost angel—not one who lounged about looking elegant on some cathedral window, but rather the most practical of angels, so busy polishing up the stars she had no time to consider how much beauty she was missing.

He wanted to help her, wanted somehow to wash away her pain. But he let his hand fall away from the warm rose-softness of her skin, knowing that the greatest kindness he could show her was to turn the other way.

Silent, he mounted the stallion and spurred the animal into a graceful canter until the smoke-blackened walls of what had been the Chastain Dower House loomed above them. And when Devlin slid from the horse's back and stood poised at the gaping hole that was the doorway to her nightmares, Myles gave her the most difficult gift he could give her.

He rummaged a candle from the bundle slung over the saddle and struck flint against his iron striker to set the wick aflame.

Then he pressed the taper into Devlin's hand and let her walk into the house alone.

CHAPTER

6

*T*he candle flickered, dancing in a ring of light with the shadows that lurked in the entryway. Spiderwebs, delicate as lace, draped the blackened corpses of gilt cupids that had once frolicked across the ceiling. Dust motes drifted like restless spirits, the dusky gold of twilight filtering through the shattered window to form puddles of gray upon the floor.

Devlin turned her gaze to the marble staircase that rose in a stately majesty that even time and ruin could not disguise and remembered sliding down the wide railing into her father's waiting arms.

She remembered how large it had all seemed when she was five years old, peering through the carved posts at the top of the stair to catch a glimpse of her mother's glittering guests. They had arrived in wave after breathtakingly beautiful wave on the nights of the Chastains' frequent entertainments—musicales, soirees, balls from which the music drifted up to Devlin.

But her favorite pastime had been creeping from her bed long after her nurse was snoring in the next room. She would steal down the stairs and stand just outside her father's study, listening to the important men within talk of politics and diplomacy, until it seemed as if her wonderful father held the fate of the whole wide world in his hands.

There had been times when she had been discovered at her forbidden pleasures and scooped up into Josiah Chastain's strong, warm arms. But there had been no scoldings, only an indulgent hug as he would ask her to tell her own opinions on whatever the topic. His guests might have laughed, but her father had always listened solemnly, so she had never minded.

Often he had even excused himself from his guests long enough to settle her back in her own small bed, kissing the tip of her nose in their nightly ritual to chase away any mischievous pixies that might be hiding bad dream dust amongst Devlin's sprinkling of freckles.

How often they had giggled together at the absurdity of the game, for never once had Devlin been troubled by night terrors.

Until the night that she had fallen prey to the most horrible nightmare of all. Losing her father forever.

It seemed unfair, unjust. One night she had been curled up on her father's knee, listening to stories and playing with the trinkets she loved to rummage from the enameled chest upon his dressing table. She could remember drifting to sleep as she often did, her face nuzzled against Josiah Chastain's simple waistcoat, the frill of his neck cloth tickling her cheek.

She had dreamed of thunder, but she had loved storms then. Had dreamed of the cool wind nipping at her nose, whispering through her hair. It had been wonderful, exhilarating, and she had stretched out her arms to fly into the glorious purple clouds. But instead of the marvelous soaring sensation as she was swept up into the sky, there was a disquieting lurching as the currents of air buffeted her, sweeping her higher.

Odd, so odd, that even now, many years later, she could remember it so clearly—the unfamiliar bite of fear that rippled through her, the bruising thump on her shoulder that jarred her awake. The world had seemed a blur, a patch of moonlit countryside flashing past her at an alarming rate, framed by what looked like a window.

Devlin could still recall scrambling upright, confused, startled to find herself in a coach, careening into the night. She should have been comforted by the familiar sight of the Chastain equipage that had carried her a hundred times before, the deep red interior set aglow by the lanterns swinging at each side of the driver's seat.

But this time it was as if she were riding within a gaping wound, the shadows in the coach seeming to drip down the walls like blood.

An acrid stench singed the insides of her nostrils and clung about her stained nightgown, filling her with sick, cloying horror while the wind whistled through the coach's open windows, penetrating the thin cloth of Devlin's nightgown, cutting to her very bones.

She had cowered in the corner of the coach, her heart feeling as if it were trying to beat its way out of her breast.

But when her eyes had locked upon her mother her terror had lanced deeper still.

Agatha Chastain sat in the seat opposite her, suddenly seeming like a stranger in her limp apricot gown, wringing her white hands in her lap. Lady Agatha's face had been robbed of its accustomed layer of lead paint and rouge, and her features looked haggard.

And Devlin had been terrified, paralyzed, wanting nothing more than to run back to the Dower House and into the safe haven of her papa's arms.

She'd sobbed and pleaded with her mother, begging her to take her home, to find Papa. It had been the first time her mother had struck her. Full in the face, hard. It had seemed in that moment that the world Devlin knew had shattered. And somewhere amid the broken shards she had lost her father forever.

The nightmares he had always kept away with his kiss had found her then, filling her nights ever after with tortured images of a writhing, scaled monster, its devil-flames devouring the Dower House, swirling out in deadly tongues that beat against the stone.

The windows, aglow with the backwash of the flames inside, peered after Devlin with demon eyes and hungry, fanged mouths, greedy for her soul.

And in the dreams her mother . . . her mother had sat, oblivious, upon the highest stone tower, scolding the servants and sewing her fancywork while the dragon savaged everyone around her.

Devlin walked to where silk paper curled back from the wall like the petal of some macabre flower. She touched it, the charred edges crumbling to dust beneath her fingers.

How many nights had she been tormented by the dream? How many times had she awakened, her whole body shaking? How many times had she seen the most horrifying dream image of all—the one so devastating it catapulted her from sleep?

The image—that of Josiah Chastain framed in the monster's eye—his hands pressed desperately against it, as if it were a window, his face contorted in agony as the monster's minions fed him to the flames.

Remembered horror ate inside Devlin like poison, her palms slick with sweat, her throat constricting as the familiar mists of the nightmare enveloped her.

She had wanted to find that it had all been a dream—that the Dower House still stood, white upon the hillside, the library full of books, the drawing room stuffed with elegant lords and ladies.

She had wanted to root about in the kitchen, have Cook carve her off a slice of sour apple or a shaving from the sugar loaf tucked in the pantry.

She had wanted the horror to go away.

But every day she woke in the unfamiliar bed across the chamber from the strange boy who stared at her with eyes so blue it hurt her to look at him. Every night she lay in bed trying desperately to stay awake, consciousness her only weapon to keep the dragon at bay.

Devlin winced at the memory of how small, how frightened she had been. In the first week at Liancourt she had tried to tell her mother of the dreams, had whimpered for her father, for the home she had loved. But instead of the soothing, the comfort Devlin had craved, Agatha Chastain had berated her, slapped her, and had at last dealt her the final, most devastating blow of all.

"Stop this! Stop this raging!" Lady Agatha had said, shaking Devlin until her teeth rattled. "Your father will never come fetch us! Will never take us back home!" Devlin had wanted to scream a denial, wanted to stop up her ears, block out the appalling things her mother was saying, but Lady Agatha went on, relentless.

"He is dead, child! Dead! And not through the villainy of any dragon, or even through the evil of another man! He killed himself because he was a coward—too weak to go on living once he'd squandered everything we own on some mad speculating scheme!"

Sobs had racked Devlin, seeming to tear her apart, but still her mother had raged. "He left us, girl, penniless, alone. He didn't love either of us enough to go on living, keep fighting. . . ."

Devlin's eyes stung as she remembered her fierce disbelief, her rage and confusion that her mother could tell her such horrible lies.

But in the weeks that followed she had heard the whispers of the servants, felt their sly glances whenever she passed. The saucier of the scullery maids had made no effort to conceal her scorn, telling Devlin that she needn't stick her nose up in the air so proud-like—that she was nothing but a charity child thrust upon Liancourt's master.

A charity child . . . Devlin had been witness to enough of her father's good works to know what that meant. She had been too hurt, too proud to ask her mother if it were so. But as the weeks went by and Sir Josiah Chastain's wife eschewed her accustomed silks and satins and set about serving as nursemaid to the blue-eyed boy, Devlin had felt a sinking sensation in her stomach, certain that what the mean-spirited maid had said was true.

And if the fact that Agatha Chastain had no money was

true, then the story about Devlin's father must be true as well.

He had abandoned her in the most final way possible. He had left her for all eternity without even telling her good-bye.

Within the space of one night she had gone from being the cherished only child of a powerful, wealthy man to being a burden, dependent on the charity of a family she had never known before.

Even her mother, who had always treated Devlin with a sort of careless kindness, had changed utterly from the smiling, gay butterfly of a woman she had been into one who seemed to blame Devlin for stealing away her wings.

Strange, it had all seemed so strange. And the dream-dragon with its fangs and claws had reveled in it, feeding upon Devlin's confusion and terror, her anger and her grief, until she'd feared it would devour her, just as it did her father night after endless night.

When Lady Agatha had told Devlin that the Dower House had burned, Devlin had accepted it silently, stoically. For it had been consumed a hundred times in her dreams.

But she was awake now. Awake. And the sight of the lovely mansion left tortured by the flames made the nightmares seem suddenly, horribly real.

The sound of a footstep startled her, and she turned to find Myles standing there, his hair clinging damply to his brow, his mantle wilted around broad shoulders.

"It was so quiet in here I was . . . was afraid you'd fallen through the flooring," he said softly.

"It's marble. Imported from Italy. Papa used to say it was cut to last a thousand years."

Myles's gaze swept over what had once been her home, and Devlin was certain he could picture all its former splendor in his imagination far more vividly than she.

"I remember my own father talking about how lovely it all was," Myles said, reaching out to run a fingertip over the scorched arm of a sculpture of Aphrodite. "My parents came to a ball here one night. Father said that all the greatest minds of England were gathered here, all the thinkers, the most powerful diplomats, the most dazzling of ladies. I remember him saying that the hope of all England had been housed beneath your father's roof that evening."

Myles paced to a tattered canvas hanging in ragged strips from a half-seared frame as he continued.

"I was barely eight when your father died, Dev. But even I knew that Sir Josiah was much loved and respected before . . ."

"Tell me, Myles," Devlin asked, bitter. "Where were all these great thinkers, these saviors of England, on the night my father was so hopeless he knotted a bell-pull around his neck?"

"Damn it, Dev, don't!" Myles snapped.

"Where was your father, who thought everything was so lovely here? Where was my mother? Off planning a menu for next week's musicale?"

Myles took a step toward her, and she shook her head, holding up one hand. Silver droplets on her lashes caught sparkles from the candlelight.

"Go away, Myles. I want to be alone."

Holding the candle before her, she started up the wide stone stairs.

Myles watched her, her hair gleaming like polished copper in the wreath of light from the candle, her shoulders trembling just a little beneath the dreary gray of her gown.

His jaw knotted as he remembered the time he had found a fox cub caught in a snare, its flesh torn and bleeding from its own teeth as it had attempted to sever the leg that was holding it prisoner.

He had worked to free it, despite the slash of its fangs upon his own hand. He had wanted to carry it to Devlin, to have her poultice it and bandage it. Heal it. But in the end the animal had escaped him, dragging itself away to hide its pain, alone.

Hide like Devlin was hiding. Just last evening he had been teasing her in the rose garden, the ribbon of her life stretching out before her, serene, everything clear and safe.

And now there she was, wandering like some lost little waif in the burned-out shell of the house she had left eighteen years before, her life as shattered as the great entryway with its ruined paintings and flame-blackened statues.

Damn it, how had everything gone awry? He had shrouded his mission in the utmost secrecy. The only man he had told of his quest had been Tracey—Tracey, whom he trusted with his life. Tracey, the man the duke had said warned of the disaster at hand.

Could someone have overheard the discussion Myles and Tracey had had a week ago in Tracey's study? Or had word of the Stuart threat spread insidiously through England, driving those subjects who were loyal to King George to be on their guard, waiting, watching . . .

What had his involvement in Charles Stuart's cause already cost him . . . his family . . . Devlin? What would the final grim total be when the dust of battle had settled?

Myles thrust his hand deep in the pocket of his frock coat and paced the entryway, trying to recapture the glittering excitement, the wild enthusiasm he had felt when he had ridden his stallion through Liancourt's gates the day before. But all he could see was Devlin, curled in some chamber she half remembered, crying her heart out with no one to hold her, rock her, brush soothing kisses against her hair.

Not that she would want any such attentions, he thought with wry grimness. No, she'd most likely fling herself kicking and clawing at anyone who disturbed her mourning.

She didn't want him. Had never wanted the comfort he'd so often yearned to offer her. No, it had always made things worse instead of better.

But how long could he stand waiting down here, helpless, useless? How long would Devlin burrow herself away from him, tending to wounds of the spirit that he could feel as if they scored his own skin?

Restless, frustrated, he walked to the doorway and stared out into the deepening twilight. It would be dark soon. Maybe the best thing he could do for Devlin was to ready a place for her to sleep, and then . . . then seek out what had driven him there.

The sword that Agatha Chastain had always told him about.

The sword that was wreathed in legend.

An hour had passed before Myles tethered the stallion in what remained of the stables behind the great house, filling the feed box with hanks of sweet grass he had cut with a scythe he found tucked in what had once been the feed room.

He had lingered as long as he could over his tasks, wanting to fill the time, to keep from thinking of the consequences of what he had done. But far too soon there was nothing left to do. The stallion was nibbling at the green blades in contented oblivion.

The campsite Myles and Devlin would share was as comfortable as Myles could make it.

He had fashioned a makeshift bed in what had been the Dower House's music room. The belongings from the bundle Devlin had tied to the saddle had been unpacked and examined.

Myles grimaced as he perused the small, precious store of supplies. A dice box, a parcel of sweets, a pair of diamond shoe buckles, and three clean neck cloths were the most useful of the articles, save for the flint and steel and candle stubs he had found earlier.

He supposed he could sell the buckles for a tidy sum, and as for the dice . . . Myles's mouth curved in a hint of his old bedeviling smile. He was so skilled at gaming that the pair of dice alone would carry the two of them to Scotland in fine style, if he so desired. Yet at the moment he would have been happy to stay damp and hungry and tired as hell if Devlin would just come back down those wide marble stairs and start ordering him about in her usual way.

Myles stretched stiff shoulders against the fabric of his frock coat and slipped off the heavy folds of his mantle. Was she upstairs, weeping her very heart out even now? Was she sobbing herself sick, up there all alone?

Myles flinched at the image.

He walked to the window, watching the rain trace patterns of silver on the glass. How long he stood there he didn't know. But suddenly it occurred to him that in his efforts to make a comfortable place for Devlin he had all but forgotten the reason they had come there in the first place.

The sword.

Always before when he had considered the weapon he had felt a kind of tingling excitement. But now, with Devlin so miserable, and with things so tangled, his anticipation had subsided.

He turned away from the window and retrieved the candle, then he stepped back into the corridor and made his way through the unfamiliar chambers.

The wooden end of the Dower House was a shambles, a rubble of fallen timbers, blackened, burned; but the older section of the house was stone, and though its furnishings were scorched and ruined, the chambers themselves had withstood even the savage onslaught of fire and abandonment and that most lethal enemy of all—time.

He closed his eyes for a moment, trying to picture Devlin as she must have been when she lived here, an earnest, busy child, always bustling about with that solemn expression of hers. Or was it possible she had laughed here, in these rooms? Had she dashed about, a wild little hoyden, laughing and dreaming until tragedy had crashed down around her?

Was it possible that he didn't know the real Devlin Chastain at all? He closed his eyes, imagining her wandering around this ruined house, searching for all the joy she'd somehow banished from her heart.

It was a thought so painful that he quickened his pace as if to escape it, and continued his wanderings through the rooms, following the fragments of instructions he remembered from those Lady Agatha had given him so long ago.

The sword was supposedly hidden in a priest hole—a secret room tucked deep in the recesses of the building to hide fugitives in the years Catholicism had been dubbed a crime.

Myles turned yet another corner in the winding passageway, and a chill passed through him as deeper shadows embraced him.

It was almost as if he were walking backward in time. The flames had not touched the chambers he passed now, yet it appeared as if thieves had made this section of the Dower House their own.

Settees were overturned, their cushions slashed. The contents of featherbeds had rained down like drifts of snow across Aubusson carpets that had been torn up from the floor. A clothes press had been overturned, the wood of its back shattered by the butt of a musket or a frustrated brigand's boot. Had the intruders been seeking the sword? Myles wondered. More importantly, had they found it? His gaze sharpened as he scanned an upended set of shelves, and he was surprised to notice that every book that had stood upon it had been torn open and flung aside, as if someone had been searching through them.

For what?

Surely no thief could hope to find a sword pressed between the yellowed pages.

Myles knelt to leaf through one of the volumes, the illuminations so exquisite they took his breath away. Cavaliers dashing across a field of battle, a knight charging into a sea of infidels during the Crusades, sea nymphs carrying Sir Francis Drake through an arch of white-capped waves.

Unable to consign the beautiful volume back to the refuse littering the floor, Myles slipped it into one of the spacious pockets of his frock coat and frowned.

He could understand slashing mattresses and cushions in which treasure might be secreted. He could understand why thieves might have smashed in the backs of furniture that might hold a secret stowing place for a jeweled sword, or a stash of coin.

Yet what could they have been searching for in the volumes scattered across the floor?

And if the intruders had been common thieves, why would they have left so much of value? Things like the pure silver candlestick clasped in his hand, or a dozen other precious objects he had seen in his wanderings through the halls.

Strange. It seemed so damned strange. . . .

And yet, when one stopped to think, was it any stranger than the fact that in all the years Agatha and Devlin Chastain had lived at Liancourt no mention had ever been made of returning to the Dower House for even the briefest of visits? To see if anything—some treasured heirloom, some beloved portrait—remained. Even if all was lost through the speculating disaster to which Sir Josiah had fallen prey, didn't it stand to reason that even the most ruthless of creditors would not begrudge a grieving widow and her daughter some personal keepsake?

Why had Agatha closed the door so completely upon this chapter of her life? Why hadn't she attempted to resurrect at least something from the ashes—to retrieve at least a portion of the valuables to be found there?

She had always made such an issue regarding the dependency of both herself and Devlin upon the Farringdons, when maybe, if she had merely parceled off this holding, they could have lived comfortably, if not in luxury.

A splash of wax from the candle burned Myles's hand, and he swore, switched the sconce into his other hand, and sucked on the stinging patch of skin.

Christ, he was acting like a fool, he thought, wandering about, half dazed with the questions whirling in his mind. At the moment none of this mattered—none of the mysteries, the questions, the inconsistencies unsettling him. All that mattered was retrieving the sword and getting Devlin to safety.

Resolved, he paced to the side of the room where Lady Agatha had said he would find the hidden panel. He shoved a gilt chair and a ruined torchière out of his path, baring the section of wall she had told him about so long ago.

The wall was paneled with wood that fit into its moldings in intricate patterns and swirls doubtless designed to make the cracks of the secret doorway invisible to prying eyes.

Long minutes passed as he searched for the pattern that identified the location of the entry to the room. But then he saw it. A quatrefoil, the shade of its wood but a whisper darker than the rest.

He braced his palm against the side of the carving,

attempting to slide the panel over, but it seemed fused, as if it had put forth roots that had twisted deep into the wall.

Myles set aside his candle, then turned back to the secret door. Gritting his teeth in determination, he wedged his shoulder against the thick slab of oak, shoving at it with all his strength. He strained against it, beads of sweat gathering at his brow, but the panel wouldn't budge. He swore, giving it one last mighty shove in frustration. A grating sound shattered the silence, and the hidden portal slid back with an abruptness that almost sent Myles sprawling.

Light from the candle beside him revealed a chamber that seemed nearly tomblike.

Musty, dank, the dust of nearly two decades filled his nostrils, sending him into a choking fit as the grit he had stirred up with his boots bit at his nostrils and made his chest burn.

His eyes teared, and he had to swipe at them with his shirtsleeve, fighting to focus his vision and peer into the cramped room.

A bed that seemed too small to accommodate even a child like little Nellie was crammed into the alcove, a warm coverlet smoothed over the bed in colorful precision, as if prepared for a guest expected to arrive at any moment. A candle in a plain pewter stand stood at the ready upon a table the size of a serving maid's kerchief, along with a bundle of quills, a penknife for sharpening them, and a small bottle of some substance that must once have been ink.

Where the rest of the house had been ravaged by fire and ransacked by thieves, this room was undisturbed, everything just the way it had been left years before.

Retrieving his own lit taper, Myles ducked his head to avoid the low ceiling and stepped into the tiny alcove. Even Devlin would not have been able to stand up straight. He sucked in a deep breath, unsettled by the way the priest hole seemed to close its stony fist around him, squeezing the air from his lungs. His imagination leapt to how it must have been while in use—a priest hiding, listening, praying, while the priest hunters' dogs stalked him, hungry for his blood.

Christ, it would have driven Myles mad to be locked within this chamber for more than five minutes without the sunshine and the wind and the sweet sense of reckless freedom. How must this room have seemed to a man barred inside it for weeks on end? Months? Imprisoned . . .

Myles swallowed hard at the image and shuddered. In all the preparations for his mission for Charles Stuart his greatest fears had not been of torture or death. He knew he had the courage to face these old foes in the name of a cause he believed in. But he broke out in an icy sweat at the thought of being imprisoned, of being one of the living dead that paced the cells at Newgate or in London's dreaded Tower.

He tried to brush away the dark thoughts, but they clung to him, unyielding. His own darkest fears warred with his most precious of dreams.

Heart pounding, Myles lit the candle on the tiny table, filling the alcove with light. He scanned the interior of the priest hole, searching the walls for the tiny etching Lady Agatha had told him about. When candlelight skated over a stone midway up the wall Myles's hand froze, his eyes locked upon a crude cross that had been cut into the ashlar.

Slowly, carefully, he knelt upon the aged mattress, the feathers giving beneath his weight. With the tips of his fingers he traced along the lines of the stone upon which the cross appeared, shaping the block until his finger slipped into a crevice at the bottom of the stone. To the casual observer it seemed no more than a nick from an awkward stonecutter's chisel, but as Myles worked his fingers deeper into the bottom of the stone he could tell it had been carved with all the precision of a latch upon an exquisite pocket watch.

The stone abraded his skin as he began to pull against it, but after a moment there was the sound of stone grating against stone and the feel of the blocks moving ever so slightly against each other. Finally it came loose, raining a fine mist of dust over the thighs of Myles's breeches, revealing behind it a hole dark as midnight.

Myles reached for a candle and held the taper near the recess. For an instant he knew a crushing disappointment, since the hidden cranny seemed to be empty as a beggar child's eyes. He stretched his other hand into it to feel the floor of the nook in disbelief, but his palm didn't brush harsh stone. Instead it plunged down, a burning pain driving into the skin beneath his thumb.

He cursed at the sting, yanking his hand back to see a drop of blood welling upon his skin. Blotting the blood upon his sleeve, Myles pushed the candle deep into the recess.

A tangle of gold and silver glittered against the stone like a gnome king's treasure, ropes of pearls and emeralds shooting prisms of fractured light over Myles's trembling hand. A ruby brooch thrust its needle-sharp fastening upward, the glinting point ready to lance the hand of any who trespassed.

Sweet Jesus—there was a bloody fortune there! Myles dipped his fingers into the drift of jewels.

Where the devil had they come from? Lady Agatha had always maintained that there was nothing but the sword and maybe a few negligible trinkets hidden away there. Never had she hinted that there was a king's ransom.

No wonder thieves had been tearing the place apart!

Myles scooped out handfuls of the jewels, spilling them across the coverlet, then suddenly stopped, his fingers tightening upon a diamond stickpin, its intricately wrought setting extremely unusual—a griffin's head, its eye a blazing jewel.

Myles's fingers tightened around the object, the image of himself as a small child echoing through him. He could see the pin embedded in a waterfall of lace. Could see himself attempting to feed the mythical creature bits of a broken tart with his tiny child hands.

God's blood—the ornament had been his father's! What the devil was it doing there? Buried in this wall? Had it been a gift to Sir Josiah from Averill Farringdon? Some token of regard? If so, why hadn't the financially beleaguered Chastain sold it off to meet his debts?

God knew the coin from the griffin pin alone could have

supported Devlin and Lady Agatha in the height of luxury for five years!

Myles's brow creased at the thought of Devlin's fierce pride and what the value of this pin could have saved her—the grinding, ever-present humiliation of being dependent, of having little save the clothes upon her back to call her own.

It didn't make a damned bit of sense! But then, did anything make sense anymore?

With numb fingers Myles slipped the pin into the pocket of his frock coat and turned again to the opening in the wall.

The space was empty but for several sheaves of vellum paper, which he pulled through the opening into the light.

The yellowed pages glowed in the candlelight, every inch crammed with scrawled handwriting. Myles squinted at the pages, making a cursory attempt to read them, but dampness and time had made the lines illegible.

He searched the cranny one final time, running his fingers along the stone joints until suddenly he brushed something hard, metallic—the basket hilt of what must be the sword, he thought. Slowly he eased it from its hiding place.

In the moments when he'd discovered the riches buried in the wall he had all but forgotten the sword. But now it struck into his soul like a bolt of lightning as he took in the workmanship of a quality not seen since a hundred years before.

An enameled dragon gripped the jeweled scabbard in fearsome claws, its teeth locked with those of a rampant tiger, while a legend in Latin was carved beneath them in beautiful scrolled letters.

I battle my own demons.

Gripping the hilt in one hand, the scabbard in the other, he withdrew the blade, the lethal length of steel gleaming, beautiful, deadly. Dragons writhed upon the blade as well, etched with the greatest detail upon the glittering metal. Myles tightened his grip on the hilt, attempting to settle the weapon into his hand, to make it but an extension of his sword arm, as blades had always been before. But for some reason the rapier felt slightly awkward in his grasp.

Undaunted, Myles settled the hilt deeper against his callused palm. And as he watched the candlelight gild the rapier's blade, as he touched the intricate etchings, felt the superb resilience in the tempered steel, he cursed himself a hundred times for not riding to the Dower House years before. To whom had the rapier belonged?

He reached out his thumb to test the blade, and it was as if he could feel the thundering terror in the breasts of countless foes that had lost their lives at the point of this sword.

"Myles?"

The sound of a voice made him wheel around.

But no wraith from a century past danced in ghostly robes in the chamber behind him. Rather, it was Devlin, her lips set in a stubborn yet infuriatingly serene line, her eyes wiped free of any traces of tears.

"You little idiot!" Myles barked. "Never sneak up on a man with a sword! I could've skewered you before you had time to blink."

"It's not my fault you're standing there in a fog. I've been calling you for nearly half an hour. The only way I could have announced my presence more clearly was to light a keg of gunpowder under you."

Myles's jaw knotted, aggravated that Devlin seemed so calm when he'd been tearing himself apart with guilt the better part of two hours, imagining her crying her eyes out in a corner somewhere.

"Did you find your musty old sword?"

"Yes," Myles said, extending it toward her.

Devlin reached out a tentative finger as if to touch the scales of the dragon, and her lips parted just a whisper. For an instant Myles suspected that she, too, had been drawn in by the web of mysticism, the beauty that seemed to surround it. But before her finger brushed it she jerked back her hand, her lips compressing again.

"It's dusty," she observed, brushing back the riot of sunset curls cascading over her left shoulder. "If we make a paste of ashes we can polish it up before you pawn it."

"Pawn it?" Myles exclaimed, outraged. "Are you mad?"

Devlin stared at him. "I thought that was why you dragged us here in the first place."

"It is. I mean it was. But not anymore." Myles unfastened the scabbard's old-fashioned buckler, fixing the weapon around his own taut waist. "Besides"—a slow, mocking smile crossed his lips—"we won't be needing any such paltry sum as this sword might bring anyway. Not when we have all this."

He stepped aside with a flourish, and he reveled in the fact that Devlin's mouth gaped open. The jewels scattered across the mattress cast out sparkles that were trapped in her eyes, eyes that flashed with quicksilver emotions—shock, awe, then pure, hot fury.

She brushed past him, scooping up a handful of the stones, her fingers tightening around them as though she would crush them to dust if she could. "My mother—these are what she sent you for?" Devlin whirled to face him.

Myles took her stiff fist into his own, his eyes meeting hers. "No, Dev. I am certain she didn't know they existed. But thank God they do. Don't you see, there is enough here to get us to Scotland, and from there . . ." Myles's hands swept up, curving about her cheeks. "Dev, I can book you passage to France now and set you up in a foreign court in the luxury of a reigning princess."

"Tracey is coming for me."

Myles rolled his eyes heavenward, gritting his teeth against an oath. "Of course. How stupid of me to have forgotten. Let us just say that the two of you can run to the Continent and set up housekeeping together. I am certain Tracey will adore Italy—"

"Don't mock me, Myles. Do you know how much this is worth? Do you know what a difference it might have made? Mama and I could have had our *own* house. She wouldn't have had to worry so much, tend to matters in another woman's home . . . mother another woman's son. She might have had time for . . ."

Devlin turned away, but not before Myles caught a glimpse of pain, and his memory filled with a vision of her watching through a break in the rosebushes while Agatha Chastain had cosseted him.

He felt something twist in his belly.

A sigh went through Devlin. She cast the jewels back onto the mattress and paced out of the priest hole into the room beyond. "It doesn't matter now, does it?" she said softly. "What might have been?"

"I suppose not," Myles said. He followed her, his gaze tracing the curves of her face, those firm lips so temptingly rosy, so innocent.

What might have been . . .

He rubbed his eyes with the fingers of one hand, suddenly struck by the memory of himself pacing outside his grandfather's study the day the duke had arranged for Tracey to become Devlin's bridegroom.

There had been one poignant moment Myles had felt a desperate regret slash through him, the sense of having lost something precious with a careless wave of his hand. Then he had crushed the strange emotion and had attempted to wish Tracey happy . . .

Devlin's voice intruded, drawing him back to the present.

"What is important," she went on, "is what to do now."

"I thought we had that settled."

"No. I've been thinking—"

"God preserve us!"

"You were right for once, at least in some of what you said. About . . . about Tracey's love of politics. About what . . . what a sacrifice it would be for him to surrender those ambitions, even for me."

Myles regarded her, wary of this Devlin, who actually seemed to be considering his views. And yet, just a moment before, she had flung out the fact that Tracey was coming for her, as if she'd not veered a whisper from her resolve in the hours since they left Robin Doolittle's cottage behind.

"While I was wandering about I believe I came up with the perfect solution. For everyone."

"I'm pure perishing to hear it."

"This rebellion you are so set upon . . . it seems to me

that the only way to straighten out this coil is to make full certain that Charles Stuart does indeed gain England's throne."

"Pardon me?" Myles choked out.

"Don't you see? If Charles were crowned, you could go back to Liancourt and marry and provide your grandfather with a nursery full of grandsons. There would be plenty of high positions in the government in need of enterprising politicians. Charles would be extremely fortunate to find a man like Tracey. In truth, there is no limit to the heights he might reach."

"Oh, I see. I'm good enough to spill my blood in Charles's cause, but once the fighting's over, my only function will be impregnating some whey-faced heiress to satisfy my grandfather. While Tracey—"

"You needn't be quarrelsome," Devlin interrupted. "I'm sure you will be quite good at it. From what I hear, you are every bit as accomplished in the art of wooing as Tracey is in the workings of diplomacy. Many women would place a higher value on your . . . er, gift—"

"But not you. Never you." Myles felt a sudden urge to shake her.

"What I think doesn't matter a damn, as you are so fond of saying. What is important is the fact that if Charles gains his throne, I will no longer be considered a traitoress. Tracey could remain in England, doing what he loves, and we could marry."

"Dev, I hope like hell everything comes aright in the end," Myles began, but Devlin cut him off with a wave of her hand.

"At least three other times you Jacobite men have mucked things up, plotting rebellions that fizzled into ragtag defeats. You'll just do so again if allowed to go your own way. So it seems to me that the only way to get through this is for you to tell me everything about this vital quest you are in charge of, so that I can figure out what to do."

Myles all but strangled on a laugh. "So that *you* can figure out what to do? *About the whole bloody Jacobite rebellion?*"

"Not the whole rebellion. Just your portion of it. Tell me,

what is this mission you are risking your life for? It must be something of vast importance."

Suddenly Myles found he couldn't meet her eyes. His cheeks stung, and he turned to busy himself, scooping some of the jewels into his pockets. "There is not much point in discussing my mission at the moment, since I shall have to alter all my plans for the time being anyhow. Charles must be warned that there is someone in London privy to the darkest secrets surrounding him. If the quest for the crown was unearthed, then there is no telling what other information has been revealed."

"But your mission. Myles, after what transpired today, I have a right to know."

"I am to gain Charles a crown."

"I know, I know. Off of King George's head—"

"No. I don't know where I am to find it. Sometimes I'm not certain it even exists. But it must, Dev. It must."

Myles stole a glance at her face and saw there exactly what he had feared—scorn, disbelief, and a hard edge of temper.

"You're talking in riddles, Myles."

"This whole mission is *about* riddles. About magic. About a fortune teller who spun out the future . . ." Myles paced to a settee and flipped it upright, then sank down onto the lumpy, torn cushions. "It's so hard to explain."

"I'm tolerably intelligent. Attempt it."

"When I was in Italy, in the exiled court of James, Charles Stuart and I became quite friendly. Most of the Englishmen he'd met were older men, men beaten down by the defeats of fifty years. Cautious men, Devlin, always bending in the winds of diplomacy, waiting for their house of cards to tumble down about their ears. It had gotten so that the slightest rumor could spook them like an untutored filly. Even when the signs were propitious, they would be discouraged by the slightest adversity. James himself was embittered, aged, weary. I was young, Devlin, strong. Full of hope."

"You mean you were a hotheaded rakehell, charging neck or nothing into situations where only a madman would tread."

"Exactly." Myles shot her an arrogant grin and patted the seat beside him.

For an instant Devlin looked as if she were going to remain standing just to spite him, but after a moment of consideration she plunked herself down as far away from him as possible.

"So," she prompted him. "Being of the same warped mind, I suppose Charles took a liking to you?"

"I believe so. There were half a dozen of us who spent time hunting, riding, talking. One night we disguised ourselves as traveling players and went about the countryside. We came upon a band of Gypsies, a caravan hidden away in the hills. The women were dancing about a fire, their black hair swirling, their bodies graceful, spinning madly against the night. We couldn't resist stopping for a while. A dainty little morsel of a girl teased us into allowing her grandmother to tell our fortunes—"

"I have absolutely no interest in your amorous encounters. Just tell me about the mission."

"I'm trying to, if you'll have some patience!" Myles snapped. "Anyway, the prince and I went along with the girl to the cart. We didn't believe in mystic nonsense, didn't believe in foretelling what was to come. But damn it, Dev, it still makes my skin crawl—the things the crone knew about us, the things she foretold."

"She probably just guessed from the looks of you that you were wealthy, which would be obvious from the rings on your fingers and the quality of your horses. Then she doubtless told you all your dreams were going to come true and you were going to be rich as Croesus, handsome and beloved as Adonis, and—"

"And that the ragged-garbed musician with cracked shoes and a dirt-smudged face was King of England?"

"K-King . . ." Devlin stammered, her eyes reflecting the wariness Myles himself had felt upon hearing the hag's words. Then Devlin shook herself, her nose crinkling. "The woman must have seen through your disguises somehow. She must have known—"

"On more than one occasion Prince Charles's very life has

depended upon his ability to fool others in such masquerades. There are spies everywhere, men whose life's work has been attempting to abduct the prince, to neutralize that threat to the Hanover throne. No, Dev. It was uncanny. The woman was blind, her eyes filmed over—but she could see . . . see so clearly."

Devlin's tongue stole out to moisten lips suddenly dry. Her eyes were wide, fixed on his. "What . . . what else did this woman say?"

"She said that the cards foretold a betrayer and one betrayed, while I . . ." Myles looked away. "She said that one of our party would be the keeper of miracles."

"You said she was blind. How could she see the cards? Blast it, Myles, she was a charlatan. She didn't know that Charles was really a prince, she merely thought it amusing to fill some poor, dull-witted peasant with grandiose dreams, thoughts that he might have been stolen from some monarch's cradle. It was merely coincidence that he really was of royal blood. How much coin did you give to this hag? Doubtless she thought if she told you such wild lies, you'd all spill your purses."

"She wouldn't take any coin at all—not even what was due her. She knelt on the ground before Charles and kissed the hem of his mantle. And then she turned to me, and she told me that I was the only one among them who had the power to break a curse."

"A curse? What next—some charm against the evil eye? Some demon spirit possessing—"

Myles grasped her by the arm, his whole body tense, on edge at the raking up of the disturbing memories.

"The woman was real. What she said was real. I could feel the magic around her like a veil. It touched me, and I— Damn it, Dev, don't look at me that way! If you could have seen her, heard what she said to me, even you would have been shaken."

Devlin reached out and touched his arm lightly, but Myles tore away from her and lunged to his feet. He began pacing as if the chamber had suddenly become too small.

"Tell me, Myles. I'm listening." The words were quiet,

soothing, as if an angel had reached out to smooth a tempest-tossed sea.

"The woman said that there was a curse upon all of the Stuarts. That Charles could only become king when that which was lost was returned to those of his blood."

"I don't understand."

"Neither did I, until the Gypsy told us the tale. When Charles's grandfather first attempted to regain his crown he, too, landed in Scotland. He was named king, and a coronation was planned. All was in order, save for the fact that no one had thought to secure a crown for the ceremony."

"My father used to tell me the story sometimes. I always thought that was a fairly important oversight."

Myles wondered what it must have been like for her father to hold her on his knee and look into those solemn green eyes. To watch her questioning every nuance of the story, to see her chew at her bottom lip in contemplation.

"No one knew what to do about the lack of a crown," Myles continued, "until one of the rebels' wives came forward with the suggestion that they fill a basket with treasures given up by those following the Stuart cause. She proposed that the jewels be pried from the settings, the gold melted down, and the lot of it melted together into a crown that was not only royal, but a symbol of the devotion of all who fought for the king's return, a symbol of all that was good, all that was noble in the Stuart cause.

"There was a woman among the company who was recently betrothed to a wild Irish warrior—a man she loved with the fierceness that beats in all Irish hearts. She was poor but proud, and when the basket came, all she had to give was the betrothal ring her beloved had slipped upon her finger. She gave it gladly and shed not a tear over its loss. Until . . ." Myles felt as if a shadow were whisking over him, a sense of foreboding, as unsettling as the Gypsy hag's hands.

"The king was defeated," he went on, "and fled to the Continent. Those who followed him"—Myles paused, swallowing hard—"they were sought out, cut down, the Irishwoman's beloved among them. When she found her betrothed lying on the field of battle the crown was there, too, abandoned in the heather nearby. She cursed the Stuarts. Cursed the crown. And set out to destroy the symbol of all she'd dreamed of, all she'd lost. But before she could fling the crown into a bog a woman by the name of Wakefield spirited it away, and it lies hidden, like the Holy Grail, waiting for someone to retrieve it from the mists of legend."

"You tell the story even better than my father did," Devlin said quietly, and Myles was struck by the fact that he had never heard her speak in quite that tone of voice before, had never heard her willingly mention her father except to defend him from someone else's insults.

"He was always fascinated by the story because his grandmother was a Wakefield. Julianna Devlin Wakefield. That is how I was saddled with this abominable name."

"I always thought it was a wonderful name. Strong, unique, like you are. I cannot see you saddled with some milksop plain one."

He reached out a finger to smooth back a tendril of hair that clung to her cheek like the kiss of a lover. Her eyes met his, and there was a softness in the green depths that stole his breath away.

"I believe there *is* a crown, Dev," he said. "That it is out there waiting. Maybe waiting for us. I've been studying the legend since I was a boy. And since the night at the Gypsy camp I've been delving into it even further."

"How would you find it, this crown? When men have been searching for it a hundred years without success? Where would you even begin the search?"

"The Gypsy hag told me one clue to the puzzle. She said that *the dragon will lead to where water sprites dance.*"

Devlin curled up her legs and wrapped her arms about them. "I'm afraid there aren't many dragons about anymore," she said, resting her chin on her knees. "Heroes like you slew them all. I often thought it was unfair. After all, the dragons couldn't help being what they were. If the knights had left them alone, they might have been perfectly amiable creatures."

Myles chuckled. "Tell that to the maidens they served at their dinner parties. Though God help the dragon who attempted to have roast Devlin for a meal."

She didn't even blink at his attempt at a jest; she only stared thoughtfully at the patterns painted upon the walls. "Even if the crown *had* existed, some enterprising Irish barbarian would have melted it down and sold the jewels off long ago. They made a bad bargain, following the Stuart king. They lost everything. As I fear you will."

"Some things are *worth* risking everything for, Dev."

Myles was stunned to find his throat suddenly tight as he looked at her—the freckles of childhood vanished from her face, the corners of her eyes tipped up with their fans of thick lashes, her full lips a deeper rose than he had ever remembered them.

"Come down from your ivory tower, Dev, and have an adventure just once in your life," he urged her.

"That's what you said the time you cajoled me into jumping off of the stable rafters. I twisted my ankle so badly I couldn't walk for a week."

"Ah, but I felt so guilty, I spent the whole week entertaining you. And the next time I caught you when you tried."

"Is that what you called it?" She smiled, and he knew she was remembering, too, how he had bullied her into jumping again, and how they had rolled together across the fresh straw, laughing. She had done it a dozen more times, she had loved it so much, her hair flying, her eyes sparkling. It had been the one time she had trusted him, truly trusted him.

God, he had forgotten how sweet that had been. He closed his eyes for an instant, thinking of gardens and roses and her lips parted beneath his.

"Dev," he said at last, "did you know that on the night Charles was born the astronomers claimed that a new star appeared in the heavens?"

"How did they know it was for him? I'm not trying to be difficult, Myles," she added hastily, shifting to face him. "But there were thousands of other babies born that day besides Charles Stuart. That star might have been for any one of them."

"And what about the storm that swept through Hanover that very same night, devastating everything in its path? Can you deny that it was an omen? A warning for German George to beware of the newborn Stuart prince?"

"There are dozens of storms like that all across the world. They can't all be signs from God. It would be too exhausting, even for Him. And yet . . ."

She pleated a fold in her dove-gray petticoat, a wistfulness clinging about her lips. "It would be wonderful to believe what you say, Myles. To hope."

Her voice was soft, touched with the tiniest quaver. "It is just that so many people have already lost so much in the name of the Stuarts. So many lives ruined. So many dead."

He took her hands in his, wanting to soothe her. "This time things will be different," he said. "We have the support of the French king, an army raised by him. Ships stuffed with soldiers and arms and the gold to supply them. Combine those with the Highlanders and the Englishmen loyal to the Stuarts and we will be invincible. We will sweep into London, Dev. Splendid. Triumphant. Years later you will be able to read the tale in your history books, but you won't be able to taste the bite of adventure in the air, Devlin. Hear the drums. Feel the glory pulsing."

He saw her shiver, but she said nothing.

"Jump, Dev. Just this once. I won't let you fall."

CHAPTER

8

*M*yles was snoring.

With a groan Devlin pulled the cloak they were sharing as a blanket over her ear in an effort to block out the soft, grating sound that made it impossible to ignore the fact that the Viscount Liancourt was stretched out in slumber a few inches away, his long, lean body clad in nothing save a pair of breeches and an unlaced white shirt.

It should have been comforting after everything that had happened to Devlin in the last few hours, should have been soothing to feel the heat emanating from those iron-honed muscles, feel his breath ruffling the curls against her cheek.

And it should have been amusing to have him snoring away like the aged butler at Liancourt, often caught napping in the sun. But Burrow's mouth had always hung open, unattractive, limp, while Myles . . .

She turned again to look at him, the light from the small fire built in the music room's fireplace dancing in seductive patterns across the bronzed planes and angles of his face, magically transforming it into an even more breath-stealingly beautiful picture than when he was awake.

A light stubble darkened the line of his jaw, his lashes absurdly long against the arrogant slashes of his cheekbones.

His hair was tumbled in waves like warm molasses over the wadded-up frock coat he was using as a pillow, while his long fingers were curled into the fabric gently, almost tenderly, as though it were a lover's tresses.

His lips were parted, the sleepy curves making one think of the rumors of bone-meltingly erotic encounters that had made the Viscount Liancourt nearly a legend.

Devlin caught her bottom lip between her teeth and resolutely turned her back to him, pulling the cloak with her, but Myles groaned in protest at the loss of his coverlet. Obviously well-practiced in battling for the bedclothes with quilt-greedy partners, he rolled after Devlin, flinging one arm heavily over her waist.

Devlin shoved it away, thinking of how sweetly he had cared for her in the time since they'd exited the bedchamber above. How he had insisted that she eat the half-crushed sweetmeats rummaged from his frock coat's pockets—the only food they'd had between them. He had given her his fresh neck cloth to sponge the grime from her face and had set her damp slippers before the fire to dry. Then he had offered to make the noblest sacrifice of all—giving her the cloak that would serve as their only covering while he went off to shiver in a corner a modest distance away.

Already unnerved by his kindness, Devlin had told him not to be ridiculous, that he'd catch his death of cold. It wasn't as if there was any chance that they would fall on each other with untameable passion. There was no reason whatsoever why they couldn't be perfectly civilized and share the single covering they had between them.

But all those hours ago she hadn't suspected how small the cloak would seem when it was spread over Myles's broad shoulders. Or how disturbing it would be to hear the soft, rhythmic pattern of his breathing, almost feel the beating of his heart.

She hadn't suspected that he would touch her, unconscious as he was, his hands reaching toward her by instinct, as though he always expected to find the soft warmth of a woman's body beside him while he slept.

He nuzzled closer, his breath now whispering against the

nape of her neck. Dev gritted her teeth, thinking she should have let him freeze.

If she'd possessed the sense God gave a goat, she would have scooted out from beneath the warm woolen folds and found another place to sleep. Or better still, she would have ripped the cloth from Myles's grasp and bundled herself up in another corner, indulging in the pleasure of watching his lips turn blue. Surely if they were pinched up with cold, they wouldn't seem so . . . appealing. Her eyes wouldn't be drawn to them time and again.

And yet, despite her inward grumblings, the fact was that it seemed cold enough to store chipped ice in the ruins of the house.

Slapping a wave of hair away from her chin, Devlin rolled over yet again, glaring at Myles. She pushed at one broad shoulder to roll him onto his back, but her palm connected with the hot satin skin of his chest, where his shirt lay open.

She jerked her hand back, knotting her fist against the strange sensation that fled through her. But Myles was oblivious. He lay flat, one long-fingered hand splayed over the bared, hair-roughened plane of his chest. The V between his thumb and first finger framed the darker shadow of his nipple, his middle finger accenting a ripple of muscle that disappeared beneath a white fold in his shirt.

The chain of the holy medal she had given him so long ago trailed in a thin stream of gold over his knuckles. The contrast of the fragile chain against the tensile strength of Myles's hand was unbearably alluring.

There was something about him, seductive, dangerous, and very different from the Myles she had known since a child.

Myles smelled of leather and wind and idealism. It was worlds away from the polished, cultured, and cologned scent of Tracey.

Tracey.

A dull throb of pain clenched inside Devlin at the thought of her fiancé, and she wondered if he knew yet of the disaster that had befallen her—if he suspected that the woman he was to wed, the woman who was to have been one of the premier political hostesses in all of England, was bedded down upon the marble floor of a half-ruined house, hungry, hunted. Heartsick.

She blinked back the hot sting of tears. Sweet God, what would he think if he could see her now? Practically lying in Myles's arms, her dress a torn mess, her hair uncombed, her fingernails dirty.

It had always been uncanny how even after a day's hunt Tracey was as pristine as if he had just left the capable hands of his valet. Not a strand of his sun-gold hair was ever out of place, his neck cloth always in crisp, precise folds, not so much as a bead of sweat trickling from his brow no matter how hot the weather or how wild the chase.

No, Devlin couldn't imagine the Honorable Braden Tracey as Myles was now, with his hair tousled, his clothing wrinkled, his shirt falling open in disarray. She couldn't imagine Tracey feeding her sweets and warming her slippers near the fire.

Of course, Tracey would never be so foolish as to put himself into a situation where such things were necessary. He would always have enough wit about him to make certain that there was a serviceable roof over his head and an acceptable meal, properly cooked, laid out upon clean plates.

If Tracey had been the one stalked by King George's soldiers, he would never have wasted precious moments needed for escape in kissing his mother, begging her not to worry. He wouldn't have paused in the courtyard to thank Devlin for her aid but would have swung astride his horse and ridden out before the soldier had found them.

No, Tracey would have been far too sensible to make the mistakes that Myles had during the wild, reckless moments of his escape. And yet Devlin couldn't banish the image of the desperation in Lady Caroline's face when the soldiers had ridden in, couldn't dismiss the strength Myles's embrace had seemed to infuse into his gentle mother.

And despite everything it had cost Devlin, she couldn't help but be just the tiniest bit glad that Myles had offered his mother that gift of strength—a strength Lady Caroline would doubtless need to draw upon during the agonizing months in which she waited for word of her son's fate.

Myles moved, running his hand upward from his chest, to nudge a lock of hair away from his forehead. He let his arm fall bonelessly back in a curve over his head and buried his face in the crook that it made.

Damn him, Devlin thought with some violence. Damn him for being so patient with her, for being kind, when she would have far preferred his tauntings and arrogant quips. Damn him for shrugging in that careless way of his, telling her he wasn't hungry, when his stomach was growling moments after she had eaten the last sweet. Damn him for spinning out the story of the crown, his eyes misted with dreams that had made her want to plunge deep into his obsession, heedless of the pain she would feel when those dreams shattered, as they inevitably would.

"Jump, Dev," he had whispered. "I won't let you fall."

But what could Myles Farringdon know about the cost when one's world crumbled around her? What could he know of the disillusionment, the bitterness that ate away the rosy ribbons of fantasy, leaving nothing but dismal gray?

Everything had always come so easily to Myles—even the worst scrapes he had gotten himself into always miraculously unraveled and solved themselves.

"Oh, Myles," she whispered sadly. "Don't you realize that even the bravest of heroes have to walk through dragon fire? What will you be like when you come out on the other side?" she asked silently before turning over, determined to fall asleep.

The fire was inside her.

Even asleep Devlin felt it, hot, brushing her skin. She writhed against it, but it only grew more insistent. White flames that wound about her, tighter, tighter.

She whimpered softly as the heat licked at the tender flesh of her throat, leaving a burning trail. Her hands swept up to thrust the flames away, but they were silken, melting over her fingers. Sweet God, she'd never suspected that fire could feel like cool, moist silk. A dragon lover, fashioned of flame.

She shifted, drawing it closer, wanting it to consume her, and it slipped beneath the folds of her chemise, pressing closer, closer, until it opened, hot, wet, closing upon the crest of her breast. She crushed her terror and stared into its eyes—eyes blue as ice, eyes blue as the torrent that raged inside her.

They floated, whirled. Together. And he led her to the brink of a gold-spun cliff. She stared into the pool below. An ocean of sapphires, emeralds, with lacings of pearls at the tops of the cresting waves.

She wanted to dive deep into the wonder that glittered there, wanted to drown there.

Jump, the dragon urged her, his voice a low growl.

She opened her eyes, the hues seeming too bright to bear. And suddenly there was only blue, sapphire blue, glowing at her from Myles's eyes.

But this Myles was different, so different from the Myles she knew. His arms were banded about her, strong, gentle, his fingers smoothing the last ribbons of darkness from her hair.

"I told you, Dev," he murmured in a voice like warm honey. "I wouldn't let you fall."

She clung to him as the waves of terror gave way to exhilaration, the fire of moments before now filling her very veins with a wild, sweet sensation.

She arched her neck, raising her face to his, and suddenly the fire *was* Myles. His hands laced through her hair, his mouth hot and open upon her lips.

Devlin moaned low in her throat, and she clutched him closer. She jumped when his large, sword-toughened hands skimmed over her hungrily, tracing every curve, every line of her body from waist to hip to the fragile skin of her thigh.

Heat, white heat.

"Dev . . . ah, Dev . . ." The rasped words whispered across her skin, his mouth raining kisses down her throat. Her clothing seemed to have melted away magically, but she didn't care, didn't feel anything save Myles's lips and tongue as he trailed his mouth down the curve of her collarbone to the swell of her breast.

Her breast . . . every nerve in her being seemed centered there, waiting for something she didn't understand. And then she knew, for Myles's mouth fastened, sweet and hungry, upon the aching point of her nipple.

Her back arched, and she felt herself floating, at one with this Myles who was driving her mad with his caresses. She was flooded, not with despair, but with desperation, wanting, needing—

Something hard, heavy curved over her hips, Myles's thigh, sinewy from years of riding. He dragged her deeper into his body until it seemed as if they were melded, melting.

"God . . ." Myles gave a guttural moan. "You feel so . . . sweet. Heaven . . ." His palm, hard and callused, swept up her thigh to cup her buttocks, his fingers kneading the firm flesh as he arched against her, something rigid nudging with mind-numbing sensuality against her stomach as he rotated his hips.

Devlin gasped, stunned that such a thing could happen, even in a dream. But suddenly there was a sharp pinching sensation in the soft flesh beneath her hip, a scraping that seemed spawned not of fantasy, but a reality that jolted her awake in one heart-stopping instant.

She tried to sit up, to shake free of the dream, but something heavy was pinning her down. She tried to cry out, but it was as if her struggles stirred Myles, making him more aware. Firm and hot and open, his mouth crushed her lips, his tongue invading the cavern of her mouth.

Oh, sweet Jesus! she thought, wild with panic. It was Myles—*Myles*—the real Myles with his devil grin and his taunting—

She wrenched her lips away from his and shoved against his chest, wild with the need to escape, but he was as immovable as a granite block. Desperate, she opened her mouth and sank her teeth into the first flesh she found—the muscled curve of his shoulder.

"Son of a bitch!" Myles roared, jolted awake. One palm slammed into her ribs as he levered himself upright. His eyes were wide open, angry, disoriented. The hand that had been doing those scandalous things to her seconds before was pressed to the place she had bitten him.

Devlin swallowed hard, and she could taste the saltiness of his blood.

"You little vampire! What the devil did you do that for?" he demanded, outraged.

If it were possible to die of embarrassment, Devlin would have done so that very moment. "You—you accosted me!"

"*Accosted* you?" Myles yanked back his half-opened shirt, straining to see the wound she had made. "I don't see *you* bleeding like a skewered pig! Hellfire and damnation, I was only—"

"You were all but smashing me beneath you, you great hulking oaf!"

"That cloak is damned small. You'll have to pardon me if I was trying to stay under it to keep warm!"

"Keeping *warm* had nothing to do with it. You were sticking your hands all over me, and your mouth, and—"

Myles froze. She saw his Adam's apple bob in his throat. "I was asleep!" he protested. "I must have rolled over and . . ." His gaze flicked to where her chemise was in patent disarray.

She clutched the garment shut, her chin tipping up as if daring him to challenge her. But his eyes traveled from her fists, knotted in the fabric, to where her lips were reddened, her cheeks slightly pink, abraded by the stubble of his beard.

"Oh, Christ," he managed to choke out, hastily grasping the edges of her chemise and awkwardly rearranging it to cover her bared skin. "Dev, I'm sorry! I didn't even know—"

"You didn't even know *who* you were accosting? How comforting! You merely slogged over to one side and grabbed hold of the first thing that breathed? I should have made you bed down with your horse!"

"Dev, I didn't mean to. Didn't set out to . . . to . . ."

"Paw at me?"

"I was asleep, too! I must have—have thought I was . . . someplace else."

"Don't you mean that you must have thought you were with some*one* else? God knows, if you're no more discriminating in your affairs than this, it is a miracle you've not been stricken with the French pox. I should mix you up a posset in case—"

"I don't need a damned posset! I don't—don't have any diseases, and—" She was pleased to see that he was looking as unnerved as she had been moments before, a dark red stain at his cheekbones visible even in the crackling light of the fire. His eyes were glinting with that familiar flash of temper, and she was gratified to know that she'd struck him a telling verbal blow.

"Damn it to hell, I've already said I'm sorry, and I am!" he said between gritted teeth. "Sorry as the devil! But I was dreaming—"

"Well, you can keep your apologies *and* your hands to yourself and bloody well go and dream somewhere else!" Devlin bellowed, grasping the folds of the cloak and yanking it away from him.

She saw him shiver as the chill air touched his skin, but then he stiffened, as if he would rather die than betray his discomfort.

"Maybe I'll go find a wolf den to sleep in!" Myles snapped, clambering to his feet. "God knows, they'd probably be more congenial company! Not to mention the fact that I'd have a hell of a lot less chance of getting bitten!"

Grabbing his coat from the floor, he stalked over to where a pedestal and urn had been toppled in the far corner. He plunked himself down on a slab of marble floor and propped his head upon the pillar with such irritation that Devlin heard a dull thump and a low, stifled curse.

"I hope you cracked your head wide open!" she told him as she pointedly wrapped herself in the woolen cloak and scooted nearer the hearth. "I hope you freeze. Your blood could use some cooling. It's not good to keep it in a fever all the time."

"The only fever I'm afflicted with is the need to strangle you. Now leave me the hell alone! Being a lecherous bastard, I want to get back to that dream I was having. Of course, first I'll have to puzzle out who I was with in the fantasy. Was it Mademoiselle Alcase? The Marchioness de la Merridaine? Or was it that plump, pretty actress that took the stage when last I was in London?" He laughed, the sound designed to grate upon Devlin's nerves.

"You're despicable! I can't imagine why I even thought for a moment that you could be anything but a self-centered, self-indulgent—"

"I may be all those things and worse, madam, but considering my crime, I think you'd best add a few other characteristics as well. Like being able to kiss a woman until her bones melt."

A squawk of outrage rose in Devlin's throat, and she attempted to dredge up some name, any name spurious enough to call him. "H-How dare you, you contempt-ible—"

"Save your breath, Dev! I've always been best at dreaming —and if my memories of this particular one are any indication, *you*—Miss Primrose Proper—were enjoying the blazes out of it until you woke up!"

"I—I was not! I detested—" She cut off the protest, prompted by the very devil to say the one thing she knew would wound Myles's overinflated ego the most. "If you must know, I was dreaming of my wedding night with Tracey."

In the glimmer of firelight she saw Myles pale, some unreadable emotion streaking across his face. Wounded pride? Arrogance brought low? Or could it have been, for a heartbeat, just a heartbeat, that there had been hurt in the Viscount Liancourt's eyes? "The devil you say," Myles growled, low.

But Devlin merely tossed back her fall of curls, still stinging from his tauntings of moments before.

"Of course," she said with a strained laugh, "I should have known it wasn't Tracey. He is much more tender."

"I can be so tender I could singe your hair ribbons right off!" Myles roared, injured. "Your precious Tracey could never make you feel the things I made you feel."

"You'd best just take your losses and run, sir, for Tracey is far more accomplished in kissing than you."

"More accomplished? I have it on the highest authority that I—" Myles stopped, muttering a most satisfactory expletive.

"You were saying?"

"Never mind." He scowled thunderously.

"Then I shall bid you good night," she said with frigid politeness. She rolled over, pointedly turning her back to him.

But the enveloping silence did not accept the millions of excuses she offered for her response to Myles's kisses. She was rocked with the knowledge that never, in the five years she had been pledged to become Braden Tracey's wife, had she experienced the soul-savaging wonder she had known in Myles's arms.

She closed her eyes, trying to imagine the last time she and Tracey had rendezvoused in the library to share a kiss—a kiss that *had* been tender, gentle, all those things Devlin had always believed she wanted in a lover.

Since that first encounter in the Liancourt stables that had precipitated their betrothal, Tracey had been the consummate gentleman, never indulging in the fierce demands Devlin had tasted so briefly in the hay-scented darkness of the stables.

She had sensed how much effort it had taken to leash himself, had admired him for his thoughtfulness when he had insisted that he would do nothing to further jeopardize her reputation—or, he had added with a chuckle, to risk again bestirring the duke's formidable wrath.

She had never understood the faint restlessness his kisses had stirred in her, the vague dissatisfaction she'd not recognized until this instant.

Tender? Gentle? They had been wonderful, sweet, the brush of Tracey's lips filling her with a contented warmth.

But Myles's kisses had flung her far past that lukewarm

feeling into a mad rush of sensation she had never even suspected existed, let alone known that she craved.

Damn Myles to hell, with his mocking words, his infernally skillful lips, his masterful hands that seemed to take fiendish delight in their knowledge of how to hurl a woman off of the razor's edge of sanity. Damn him for making her aware of an emptiness inside her that Tracey had never filled.

Devlin's fists knotted in the folds of the cloak, the fabric still holding the scent of Myles, the rough velvet abrading her palm reminding her of the feel of his beard-stubbled jaw grazing her cheek, her throat, her breasts. She wanted to scream, she wanted to hit something, she wanted to cry until she was drained of all feeling.

She blinked back tears, feeling lost. The emotion cut deeper still when Myles's soft voice came to her through the darkness.

"Dev . . . sweet dreams."

CHAPTER

9

*M*yles forcibly restrained himself from spurring the stallion hell for leather up the rutted road that led to Edinburgh. Raw exhilaration, fierce anticipation thrummed through his veins, wild and intoxicating.

For days now, as Myles and Devlin made their way north, they had heard news that a string of stunning victories had culminated in Charles's triumphant march into Scotland's capital. The Stuart forces had wrested the city from King George's commanders.

Swift, daring, Charles Stuart had dispelled the dismal clouds of gloom that were the legacy of his father's previous rebellions, the young prince seeming to burst through those failures like bright sunshine.

Myles had been insatiable when it came to gaining word of what had transpired, grilling every peasant, every nobleman, every dairymaid met upon their travels in hopes of unearthing some tantalizing new bit of information. Devlin, peering down from the sorrel mare he had bought her at a farmers' fair the day after they had left the Dower House, had accused him of alerting half the countryside that he was a Stuart sympathizer with his insistent questions.

He'd ignored her grumblings. Every fragment of news he learned increased his loyalty and the resolve he felt inside.

Charles was conquering.

Not only towns and land, but men's hearts as well. Myles could feel it.

A shiver of pure delight rippled through him, and he braced himself high in the stirrups for a moment in an effort to see the city where Charles was now holding court. But a thick mist obscured anything farther away than two horse-lengths. Only the fact that Myles was able to make out the rutted ribbon of road before them made it possible to continue this final leg of the journey, and even then Devlin was quarrelsome as a bee trapped in a whiskey keg.

She had argued that there was no sense in going ahead and risking riding off a crag somewhere, since the last word Myles had heard was that the prince had settled at Holyrood House for the time being. Charles was reportedly busy attempting to fashion the administration of the country that was now his to rule—an enterprise that had earned even Devlin's grudging approval.

And Devlin's approval was something in very short supply of late. Myles grimaced and sank back against the saddle. In an effort to steal a surreptitious glance at her he lifted his tricorn from the wind-tangled waves of his hair, then resettled the headgear at a more comfortable angle.

She was riding with her back ramrod-straight, her eyes fixed upon the road as if she truly did expect to plunge off some precipice. Beneath the emerald-green hood and plain linen cap he had bought to disguise her as a wandering musician's wife, her red-gold hair was knotted into a braid so tight she could likely use it to knock a man into the next century. And Myles almost felt as if he'd like her to try it.

He shifted the mandolin that hung on display from his saddle, his part of the guise that had seen them safely through endless miles of English countryside. His eyes narrowed in a scowl. The restless, resentful feelings that had beset him ever since they rode out from the Dower House were deepening, simmering—threatening, as they had far too often, to boil over into scalding-hot temper.

Devlin had been by turns sulky and withdrawn, outraged and angry, disdainful and disgusted. Worst of all were the times she was quiet, when he would catch glimpses of a lost, haunted light lurking beneath her thick lashes. The confusion of an innocent lamb caught in some huntsman's snare.

His snare, Myles thought, his threatening temper fading into self-disgust and a relentless sense of guilt. She had fallen into a snare he had perfected through countless romantic entanglements. A snare in which more than one woman had lost herself during past years.

Yet the beauties in those affairs had all been purposely seeking the flame that was to be found in the Viscount Liancourt's arms, while Devlin had merely set out to share a cloak with him.

He should have known better, he thought grimly, remorse scourging him afresh. But then, he had been dreaming, too. What he had not yet said aloud was that he had been dreaming of Devlin, who had melted against him, her lips pliant, eager beneath his, her body molding to his with a perfection that had bewildered him.

He shook himself. No. That was no excuse for his despicable behavior.

Blood and thunder, he cursed inwardly, couldn't he have been satisfied with the havoc he had already wreaked in Devlin's life?

Without question, that night in the Dower House had been the rakehell Viscount Liancourt's finest hour, he thought angrily—all but seducing an innocent under his protection—in his *sleep,* no less! And if his own memories of the dream he'd been reveling in that night were any indication of the passions that had been firing deep inside him, Devlin had doubtless received far more of an education regarding the dealings between a man and a woman than she had bargained for.

You might hope so, you arrogant oaf, a voice whispered inside him. But she is betrothed to Tracey. Most likely you taught her no pleasures into which her fiancé has not already initiated her.

Myles felt claws of jealousy rip deep.

Had that been the reason Devlin had turned to molten flame in his arms? Because she'd done so before with Tracey?

Anger, hot and bright, rushed through Myles, and his jaw knotted. Had that tryst he'd broken up in the stable been but a prelude to far more lusty pleasures?

God knew, in the eyes of most of the world a betrothal was nearly as binding as marriage, and therefore as open to carnal delights.

Had the two of them been stealing away to the meadow, to love each other beneath the spreading branches of an oak? Had Tracey taken her to the hidden garden where Myles himself had first tasted her lips? Or more painful still, had Tracey used the ploy he and Myles had resorted to so often when they had been enamored of some alluring damsel at a house party somewhere? Had he waited until the rest of the house slept, and then stolen into Devlin's very bedchamber?

Blind, killing fury ripped through Myles, and he ached to have his hands about his foster brother's throat as he pictured Devlin in that simple, virginal bed with its plain white bed curtains, the dressing table beside it scattered, not with bottles of color and scent, but with vials of her possets and elixirs, the window ledge holding thriving pots of herbs to the thin rays of sun.

He could picture her in the unadorned nightgowns she favored, her hair rich, tousled sunset upon the pillow, her lips parted, betraying a sensuality that even the most childlike of surroundings could not disguise, if only a man had the patience, the power to set it free.

The thought of his best friend's hands smoothing over that petal-soft skin, wringing from Devlin the sighs and whimpers Myles remembered from the haze of his own dream, filled him with such savage fury it frightened him.

Damn it to hell, he thought, even if Tracey *had* been overeager to stake his marital claims upon Devlin, who was Myles to say him nay? They had the duke's approval. Devlin loved Tracey. And Tracey—Tracey was as fine a man as England had ever seen.

No, *he* was the one who had had no right to touch her. *He* was the one who was the scoundrel. Attempting to blame Tracey for sins that were Myles's own was dishonorable. Disgusting.

He had all but made love to his best friend's betrothed. Had wanted to—sweet God, had wanted to with a mind-shattering need that had left him numb, stunned. And God knew he might well have carried the entire affair to its culmination if Dev had not had enough wits about her to stop him. He had been groggy, drunken on the taste of her, and yet awake enough to remember how cataclysmic the effect of kissing her had been.

And all the excuses he could spin didn't matter a damn, because the truth was he had lied. He had not been spinning fantasies about his former mistresses when he had caressed her. He'd been thinking only of Devlin. Dreaming of Devlin. Loosing a fire that had given him no peace since the moment he had ridden through Liancourt's gates and seen her running through the courtyard barefoot, her half-finished wedding gown a glorious tangle around her.

Sweet God, he should have known it had been a mistake to come there. A mistake to see her, readied to become the Honorable Braden Tracey's bride. But he hadn't suspected then the reason he had returned, hadn't suspected until that emotionally charged moment when he had dragged her into his arms in the rose garden and had kissed her until it felt as if his very soul were shattering inside him.

But after that kiss it had been the most grievous, inexcusable of mistakes to allow her to follow him into the courtyard and into disaster, and from there to the more mind-numbing disaster of easing his long body beneath the folds of the cloak she had drawn about her.

Once, when they had been children, Devlin had accused him of always wanting whatever plaything someone else had. He'd denied it heartily, and yet, as a man grown, he couldn't deny the fact that at least between him and his foster brother there had always been an underlying sense of competition to give an edge to their friendship.

From the time they were boys the two had been all but inseparable. It had only been in the past year that Myles had begun to feel a distance between them, as if they were seeking far different lives, far different futures.

Myles supposed that it was natural enough. He and Tracey *were* different—fire and ice.

Was that what this tangle with Devlin was about? Was it that Tracey had taken one of Myles's toy soldiers—a plaything that Myles had cast in a corner and forgotten until someone else had shown the slightest interest in it?

True, he and Tracey had frequently vied for the favors of the same women.

But this . . . what had happened—*and almost happened* —in the Dower House was a far different matter indeed. Seducing his best friend's prospective bride was a crime worthy of only the lowest villain.

"Who goes there?" The harsh voice snapped Myles from his musings, and he reined in his horse while peering into a circle of light spilling from torches that illuminated the gate that led into the city.

A giant of a man glared out from beneath a wild bush of dark hair, his sword glimmering in the light.

Myles swept the tricorn from his head. "I am Lord Myles Farringdon, Viscount Liancourt, here with Mistress Devlin Chastain."

The guard eyed him with suspicion.

"Farringdon?" A voice rose from a din of what sounded like merrymakers passing beyond the gate. "Did you say Farringdon? If that's Lord Myles, there's not a man in all Scotland more loyal to the Stuart cause than he!"

"Cameron!" Myles cried, swinging down from his horse. "Harry Cameron! Damn your eyes, it's good to see you, man!"

Masculine shouts and feminine shrills of greeting from the others in the party echoed around Myles as the bluff, redheaded Scotsman emerged in the circle of light from a lantern suspended near the gate.

His bull-like body was swathed in the Cameron plaid, but a pair of doeskin breeches encased legs thick as tree trunks, soft leather boots enclosing powerful calves that seemed incongruous when set against the man's short stature.

"Open the gate, MacDonald, you fool!" Cameron cried, thumping one hand against the offending portal. "This is a man who would shed his blood for Charles in the wink of an eye!"

With much muttering the guard opened the gate, allowing the blustering Harry to rush through, engulfing Myles in a gruff embrace.

"I would've judged you halfway to Ireland by now, my friend—off chasing your dreams," Cameron said, sweeping Myles into the protective walls of Charles's capital city.

"And I would have imagined you ensconced at the fireside with that little wife of yours perched upon your knee." Myles glanced over long enough to see that Devlin, in a surprising show of good sense, had gigged her own mount into following. The gate swung into place behind them, effectively trapping Devlin inside the walls, and with a surge of something akin to triumph Myles turned back to Cameron. "Tell me, is Arabella still pining after me?"

"If you're asking whether my bride is still worried over your chances of getting hanged, drawn, and quartered, I'd have to admit she is."

"If she was *my* lady, I vow I'd call you out over the place you held in her affections!" a stripling of about sixteen summers with shaggy gold hair and eyes that still held a boyish innocence pronounced. "'Twould be pistols at dawn—"

"Well, if you be challenging my lord, Sandy, my boy, you'd best send your mammy a letter regarding your last wishes. He could shave that fuzz you call a beard right off with a single shot."

The boy blustered a protest, but Harry only laughed, cuffing him none too gently on the shoulder.

"Besides, you've doubtless not had enough experience with the fairer sex to recognize the signs that the girl is head over ears in love with me. Why she'd want anything to do with a rack of bones like the viscount here, I'd have no way of knowing. Not when she has a fine figure of a man the like of Harry Magnus Cameron to keep her warm at night!"

Harry declared, thumping his fists upon his barrellike chest.

Myles chuckled as Harry turned to slap him on the back. "Ah, well, I suppose I have no choice but to endure your company tonight, Farringdon. Bella would dump me down a well certain sure if I didn't bring you home straightaway."

"Don't be so selfish, Harry," a camp follower's voice, husky with teasing sensuality, broke in. "I'd like a chance with this fine 'rack o' bones,' as ye call it. I could think of about a hundred things I'd like to do with yer Lord Farringdon, if he would be pleased to follow me to my tent. No charge, ye understand," the woman cooed, pressing her lush body against Myles's chest, one slender hand running in an appreciative path down the side of his face. "Just a welcoming party to show you just how . . . *excited* we all are that ye've come."

A portly, red-faced gunner chortled. "He's not even through the gates three minutes and Christina is trying to get him out of his breeches! Some fellows have all the luck!"

Christina gave a low growl in her throat and rubbed her thigh against Myles's long one. "Has nothin' t' do with luck." She strained on tiptoe, her mouth skating a path down the cords of Myles's throat.

Myles's thoughts were suddenly filled with images of Devlin beneath him, her breasts crushed against his chest, her lips moving under his. Restless—she had been restless, eager when his fingers had plied the erect peaks of her nipples, and he could still taste the feverish need he'd had to close his lips with delicate hunger upon them.

God. Myles groaned the curse low in his throat as he pushed the camp follower away.

A harsh guffaw shattered the agonizingly painful, gratingly pleasant vision of Devlin Myles had fallen prey to, and he glanced over to see one of Harry's men downing a draught of ale from a leather pouch.

"Christina, ye blind cat, can't ye see he's already got a lady?" the man bellowed, delivering a slap to the harlot's backside. "She'll scratch yer eyes out if ye don't take care."

"She can have the blackguard and welcome!" Devlin snapped, her face all shadows beneath the shielding of hood.

Whistles and roars of laughter pierced the mist, pricking at Myles's pride. In the light of the lantern he could just make out the supreme satisfaction upon Devlin's pursed lips, and he wished for the days when he could have dumped a bucket of water over her head or filled her bed with spiders in retaliation.

"Now don't be getting all flustered up over poor Lord Myles's regarding Christina, here." Harry moved to soothe her, the Scotsman's keen eyes surveying Devlin with open curiosity. "She's a bold baggage, Christina is, and my lord can't be helping that he's such a handsome devil."

"Aye," an Irishman called out, loping over to where Devlin sat astride her mare. "The son o' Satan always has the bonniest lass in the whole camp when he's about. So let's have a look at ye, now, sweeting, an' compare—"

The Irishman reached up to pull Devlin down, and Myles all but choked on a laugh as she kicked the dolt full in the chest. Unfazed at meeting with such adversity, the man gave a hoot of good-natured laughter and hauled her down despite her protests.

"Take your hands off me!" Devlin sputtered. "I'm not a horse to be judged at market!"

"Methinks ye'd make a right fine filly, all fire," the Irishman said. "It's no wonder Lord Myles wants to tame ye." Holding Devlin fast with one arm, he tugged back the hood she had drawn over her face. A gasp tore from the man's chest as the lantern light turned her hair fiery red and glistening gold.

"By the cross o' St. Simeon," the man said faintly, "I'll give ye a month's pay for an hour in yer arms."

In the space of a heartbeat Myles's amusement turned to fury. "Take your hands off her!" Myles snarled, scooping Devlin into the protective curve of his arm.

The man who had pulled back her hood raised his hands in surrender, his face still holding a lust-filled expression that made Myles's pulse rage.

"Now, then, Farringdon!" Harry said, trying to calm Myles. "O'Keefe here didn't mean a speck of harm to the wee lass. Did you, man?" Cameron gave the Irishman a none-too-gentle poke in the ribs.

The Irishman glared at Myles as if he'd have liked nothing more than to draw swords and settle the dispute over Devlin in the most primitive and permanent way possible.

The dark-haired camp follower slipped between the two men and smoothed the bodice of her gown over lush breasts. "Come now, the both of ye. O'Keefe here isn't tryin' to steal yer doxy, my lord, pretty though she be. Let me take her to where the rest o' us 'ladies' are stationed, an'—"

"Mistress Chastain is no doxy." Myles's voice cut through with a savage edge, his gaze flicking to Devlin's outraged face. "She—"

"Go on back to the fleas in yer bed, Christina," Harry said sharply. "Why, any one of us can see that she's not like you."

Myles's hand relaxed a bit against Devlin's waist at the knowledge that at least Harry had the wit to gauge Devlin's circumstances. But the bold Scot's next words drove any such hopes from Myles's head.

"Why, with a face the like of hers, all aristocratic and proud, she could only be Lord Myles's *lady* mistress."

"She's my lady, period, Harry!" Myles roared. "Mistress Chastain—"

"I know she be your lady. And she'll be treated as such," Harry said, his broad face creased. "There be a wee sweet house down from the barracks with a bed soft as down where you can visit her whenever you've a mind to. Very discreet-like, and—"

"I'll not be visiting her at all!" Myles bit out. "Not that way!"

The confusion in Harry's face deepened, and O'Keefe glanced at Devlin, then back to Myles, disbelieving. Disbelief was mirrored in the faces of the other men.

"Well, if the bleedin' fool is goin' t' waste her, I *will* take the house, an' be damned to 'im," the Irishman snapped, a murmur of agreement washing through the crowd.

Myles felt the rage in his belly seethe, burn. And in that instant he knew full well there was only one way to drive that infuriating light from their eyes.

"You'll not even speak to her—O'Keefe, no, nor any of you others—without the respect you'd deal out to a bloody queen. Mistress Chastain is a lady. *My* lady."

His mouth set grimly with warning, and his voice was level, laced with a bitter irony.

"Before a fortnight is past she is to become my wife."

CHAPTER

10

*M*e? Marry *you?"* Devlin choked. She staggered back, appalled at what she thought must be some kind of twisted jest. But before she could react further, congratulations erupted all around her and Myles, the crowd pressing close to kiss cheeks and slap backs.

"Lord have mercy upon you, my sweet," Harry exclaimed, dealing her a fiercely joyous kiss. "You must be a saint to chain yourself to this scoundrel!"

"A saint!" Devlin sputtered. "I'd have to be *insane!"*

"And so you are, my darling," Myles called out, snatching her out of his friend's grasp. "Insane with love for me." Whoops of laughter drowned out her reply as Myles's long, lean body all but swallowed her in a hard embrace. She wanted to pound her fists against his infernally handsome face until he admitted it was all a horrible prank. But with the craft of a cunning spider imprisoning its prey, he had pinned her arms against her sides, his body crushed so unyieldingly against her that she couldn't breathe, let alone move.

Furious, defenseless, she flung back her head to demand to know why he was doing this, but she had scarcely opened her mouth when his crashed down upon it, stifling all but a choking groan of protest as he pillaged her lips with a force that left her head spinning, her eyes filling with hateful tears.

Tears that stunned her, as did the odd sense of hurt and betrayal that sliced through her fury.

She struggled to draw a breath, mortified beyond imagining at being thus mauled with a crowd of onlookers cheering Myles on.

When she couldn't have cried out to save her own soul Myles pulled his lips away from hers, sliding them to where his fingers now knotted in the red-gold waves at her temple, his voice low, harsh, his breath hot and ragged as he muttered for her alone to hear. "Not a word, damn it, to call me liar."

"Y-You are one!" she croaked. "A—A vile, d-despicable—"

"And if you'd listened to me in the courtyard, you'd be standing at the altar a week from now making calf's eyes at Tracey!"

The words were like a slap in the face. Devlin reeled with them, her tirade of fury and denial dying in her throat. "Why? Why are you doing this to me?"

"For the blasted entertainment of it!" There was fire in Myles's eyes, and in that moment she sensed he was somehow trying to protect her. But instead of gratitude, resentment flashed through her, along with pure outrage that she should be beholden to him.

"I hate you!" she choked out. "Hate you for this!"

"I don't give a tinker's damn," he hissed in a deadly whisper. "Just do what you're bloody well told!"

He stepped back, keeping one hand clamped around her waist so tightly it made her ribs ache.

"Since my secret is out, you will all understand why I am so eager to get to my quarters and see my betrothed settled comfortably after such a long ride. Harry"—Myles turned to the stocky Scotsman—"I fear we left in a great hurry, with half of George's army on our heels, so if you could direct me to a place where we might find lodgings and then help me root out a mantua maker and a proper lady's maid, I would be eternally grateful."

"With this grand news of a wedding in the offing, I'll not hear of anything save that you stay with Bella and me! We've a grand place right near Holyrood, way too big for just the two of us."

"No," Myles said. "We couldn't possibly impose—"

"Impose? You wound me, man! After all you did for Bella and me? Sweet God, I—"

"It was nothing, Cameron." Myles's voice was edged with what was almost embarrassment.

Harry cleared his throat noisily, looking abashed. But after a moment the devil danced again in the Scotsman's bright eyes. "Look at it with a dose of Scottish practicality, then, if you must. You need a chaperon for your betrothed, and who better than a respectable married lady like my Bella? As for clothing, I vow your Mistress Chastain seems near of a size with my wife. We could have her outfitted in a lambkin's wink."

Harry turned to Devlin with a winning smile made all the more appealing by Myles's reticence. "Bella would be overjoyed at having a bit of feminine company. I know she's been pining for her sisters ever since I scooped her away from the vicarage in Norfolk, though she'd never admit it for fear of hurting me. Say you'll come along home with me, sweeting. It wouldn't be the least bother. In truth, you'd be doing us Camerons a kindness."

The thought of trundling off to a strange household to meet some paragon of womanhood who was still wrapped up in the first throes of matrimonial bliss was almost more than Devlin could bear.

From the time she could remember she had been notoriously wretched when plopped in the middle of a gaggle of girls, their heads filled with nothing save coiffures and flirtations and the latest fashions from Paris. She had heard their veiled whispers behind their fans, had seen them smirk over everything from her awkward needlework to her unbecomingly keen intellect.

Often it seemed she didn't even have to say a word before they knew that she was different—a sin for which even the most charitable miss seemed unable to forgive her. The only thing that held even less allure than subjecting herself to such a scene was continuing to stand in the middle of Edinburgh's streets, ringed by a pack of men who were still gawking and chortling over the kiss Myles had dealt her.

"I'd be grateful to sleep in a barn tonight," Devlin finally said, her shoulders sagging.

Harry gave a hoot of laughter and slipped his arm about her, maneuvering her from Myles's grasp.

"I fear my stables are full, dearie," Harry said as he guided her down the cobbled street. "You shall have to content yourself with the featherbed in the chamber upstairs. I know it will be a hardship after what you are accustomed to, but we must all make sacrifices for the cause."

Devlin mustered enough energy to shoot Myles a killing glare. "Do you think that a *human* sacrifice might help your cause? We could find a druid altar somewhere and sprinkle goats' blood around and sing magical chants. And then we could burn someone's entrails in a bronze cup."

Harry followed her gaze to where it was pointedly fixed upon Myles's glowering face.

Cameron roared with laughter. "By God, Farringdon, I vow you've finally met your match! I can see why you're mad in love with the girl!"

Something twisted deep inside Devlin, leaving in its wake a bitter, aching grief.

Mad in love with the girl . . .

The words echoed through her as she trudged along beside the Scotsman, filling her with remembrances of when Myles had kissed her in the Dower House. Sparks had raced through her veins, radiating outward in whirlwinds of ecstasy from where his mouth had caressed her, tasted her.

That had been the madness of which Harry jested—that dark, swirling current that had almost dragged her under in the moments before she and Myles had fully awakened. But Myles had not been lost in that maelstrom with *her,* hadn't begun that mad, careening plunge into passion with her face burned into his heart, her body branding itself into his soul. It had only been a dream, a fantasy, doubtless peopled by some dazzling Aphrodite or peerless courtesan.

Maybe women like this Arabella Cameron drove men insane with love for them, but simple, practical Devlin Chastain was not the type of female who could be faulted with launching a thousand ships, shattering a kingdom because of the passion she inspired.

Even Tracey was not "mad" in love with her. He loved her, true. Respected her. Shared her interests, her ambitions, her beliefs. There had even been passion—in that brief, fire-hot encounter in the stables so long ago.

But never had she seen in Braden Tracey's face the light that had shone in Harry's face when he had talked about his Bella. Never had she felt in Tracey's fingers the eagerness, the hunger that had filled Myles's hands with fire the night they had spent beneath his cloak.

She swallowed hard, her fingertips stealing up to touch the bruised swells of her lips, still hurting from the callous, punishing kiss Myles had pressed upon her moments before. The kiss that had taken something away from her, instead of filling her the way the other one had.

Her memory smarted beneath the image that had raked at her upon the endless journey—Myles's face when he had awakened with her pressed so intimately in his arms, that stunned, almost sickened expression that had darted into his eyes, the way he pulled back from her, his hands knotting as if to crush the feel of her from his skin.

She stared down at the road before her feet, grateful for the mist that obscured her downcast face from the view of Harry and Myles, who flanked her on either side.

And she hated Myles—not for the kiss or the humiliation to which he had subjected her beside the Scottish capital's gates. But rather for pointing out a gaping void inside her, for dangling before her a taunting image of a kind of love she could never hope to have.

Not that she wanted it, she told herself hastily. Were she ever afflicted with such passions, she would only make a fool of herself. But could she ever feel more the fool than when she had awakened to the humiliating awareness of Myles's caresses?

She squirmed inwardly, hazarding a glance at Myles's face. In the dim light she could see the square line of his jaw jutting out, determined in a way that unsettled her.

A sick feeling knotted inside her. What if Tracey should hear of Myles's claim that she was to become his viscountess? Tracey and Myles had shared the same set of friends since they had trundled off together to Eton, and though men continually accused women of being gossips, Devlin knew full well that there was nothing on earth more dangerous than a group of blustery, heedless men with a delicate, sensitive secret.

In the snap of one's fingers they would manage to make the most horrid disaster possible out of whatever news they had gained. And she would wager half of the silver plate at Liancourt that the bumbling idiots Myles had lied to moments before would be tripping over each other to break the news to Tracey that his betrothed and his best friend were about to be chained together in the bonds of matrimony—the news announced by the viscount merely eight days before Mistress Chastain was to have become the Honorable Mrs. Braden Tracey.

Fear hardened like an icy stone in Devlin's stomach as she pictured Tracey's golden head bent, those intelligent eyes filled with anguish at the thought that she had betrayed him with his closest friend.

Tears seared the backs of Devlin's eyes, and she clenched her fists so hard the nails cut into her palms. Oh, God, what had she done? Tearing after Myles, letting him bully her into fleeing to Scotland instead of riding to find Tracey at once and enlisting his help out of this dreadful tangle.

Cease this nonsense at once, she berated herself sharply. There would be time to tell him about this ridiculous charade Myles was insisting upon, claiming she was to become his wife. Tracey would be as outraged as she was that Myles had done such a thing, had trapped her into going along with this madness. But Tracey would understand that she'd had little choice in the matter, wouldn't he? Please, God, he would have to understand. . . .

A sudden tug on her arm made her slam to a stop just before she would have smacked headlong into the iron gate of a fence that ringed a quaint old house.

She shook herself, stunned at how far they had traveled while she had been lost in her thoughts. Glancing up, she caught only a vague impression of windows glowing with candlelight and a face pressed close to the panes before the door was flung open, revealing the most beautiful girl Devlin had ever seen.

Delicate and sweet as a cameo the girl's features were set against a perfect foil of rich marigold curls. Silk ribbons trailed through them in crystal-blue streams, exactly matching eyes that were trusting and full of merriment.

Without an instant's hesitation the girl flung herself into Harry's outstretched arms, seemingly oblivious to the company he had in tow, and her laughter rippled out like harp strings brushed by an angel.

"Harry Cameron, I should never speak to you again for keeping me waiting so long!" the girl said, burying her face against the man's thick chest. "I've been waiting for hours to thank you . . . ever since Ranald delivered it! The most beautiful thing I've ever seen."

"Not a whit as beautiful as you, Bella-love," Harry said, glowing at her praise as he dropped a tender kiss upon those dainty curls. "But look at the other surprise I've brought you! This is Mistress Devlin Chastain, come to be company for you."

Bella turned her smile upon Devlin, scooping up her hands with soft fingers. "Welcome. I'm so pleased."

"No more pleased than Mistress Chastain will be, I vow, once you get her settled. She has just arrived after dashing across England with only the garb upon her back and is in need of a hot bath, a warm supper, and a set of fresh-laundered clothes, if my judgment is correct. Just the sort of coddling that you so love to do."

"I shall have her toasting her feet before a hearth fire in a trice, then," Arabella said with a resolute nod. "And you, Harry Cameron, will fetch your pistols at once and call out whatever beastly scoundrel has delivered her here in this shameful condition!"

Her diatribe was cut off by Harry's hearty laugh. He gave her a mocking bow. "As ever, dearest, your wish is my heart's command. But I fear that if I face off against this particular villain, you will find yourself a widow. You see, I found Mistress Chastain with her nose pressed against the city gates in the company of some half-crazed viscount—"

"Viscount?" Bella squeaked, wheeling toward the figure still shrouded in the shadows. "Not . . . *Myles!*" With a shriek of joy she hurtled toward Farringdon, and Devlin felt a stab of something akin to jealousy as Myles enfolded her in an affectionate embrace.

"Hello, Bella." Was there a wistfulness, a sadness in the subdued tones of Myles's voice? "I thought I'd come back one last time to see if I could convince you to run away with me. But I can see that you are as addlepated as ever about this stubborn bull of a Scot, so my hopes are dashed."

"Poor Myles! I can see just how dejected you truly are!" Arabella teased, hustling the lot of them into a cheery entryway with a friendly smile at Devlin. "He really is the most shameful rogue."

"His days as a rogue are numbered, I fear," Harry announced, tugging off his plaid and throwing it over the stool in the corner. "It seems that our Myles is to console his broken heart by following my excellent example and marrying."

"I fear it is true," Myles said. "I am about to make Mistress Chastain the most fortunate of women."

Arabella pressed her hands to the pink and blue satin covering her breasts. "I can scarce believe—"

"That anyone would have him?" Harry interjected. "I confess I had a bit of trouble imagining it myself. But after speaking with Mistress Chastain here, I trust she will be up to the task of bringing this scoundrel to heel."

"Stop it, Harry!" Bella scolded, eyes blue as violets filling with concern as they took in Devlin's expression. "This is wonderful news! I'm so happy for both of you. I hope . . . hope you find even half as much happiness as I've found with my Harry."

A lump of misery hardened in Devlin's throat, and she looked away, but not before she glimpsed the worried look that was in Arabella Cameron's eyes.

"She was talking about relieving Myles of his entrails earlier," Harry offered, seemingly unaware of Devlin's distress. "I take such threats as a good sign."

"Yes. O-Of course," Arabella stammered, her voice threaded through with unease as she looked from Devlin to Myles, then back again. "Harry, escort Myles to the study and have Bristol warm him a brandy while I take Miss Chastain abovestairs and get her settled in the n—I mean the extra bedchamber."

The uncharacteristic somberness that had fallen over Myles's face lightened, and Devlin saw his gaze lock with Arabella's. A flush stained the girl's cheeks, and her lashes drooped low at his open regard.

Myles reached out to hook a finger under Arabella's round chin and tipped the girl's face up to his. "So Harry has turned you into a mama, has he?" Myles said in a tender voice that Devlin had rarely heard. "I should have known the moment I saw how your eyes were shining. I hope this baby knows how lucky it is to have you."

"It will know." Harry's voice was gruff with love. "I'll spend all my life telling my son or my daughter the miracle of how plain Harry Cameron was blessed with an angel to rock the cradle."

"Not an angel," Arabella said, stepping over to press herself against her husband's side. "Just the happiest woman in all the world."

Devlin watched crystal tears spill over Arabella's lashes. "I was watching at the window when you came, wanting to thank Harry for the gift he sent me this afternoon. It was a cradle, all carved with thistles and roses entwined."

Myles cleared his throat, and even to Devlin's ears his voice sounded a little unsteady. "And when is this cradle to be filled with the newest Cameron?"

"Near Christmas, I think," Arabella said, her palm cradling the child growing within her. "I only . . . only hope . . ." She hesitated, her smile trembling. "There is so much to be done yet in Scotland before Prince Charles can feel secure in this kingdom. I am certain he will not set out for England before winter is over."

Devlin saw Harry Cameron's lashes lower over troubled eyes, saw his arm tighten about the wife he so obviously adored. And in that instant Devlin had a sick premonition that when Harry Cameron's child came into the world its father would be far away, lost in the maze of blood and glory that men called war.

She looked at Myles, wanting some sort of reassurance, but he, too, was silent, his gaze hooded beneath the tousled dark fall of hair that tumbled across his brow.

The silence grated at Devlin until she felt compelled to break it. "Have you been feeling ill in the morning since you have been with child?" she asked Arabella.

The girl seemed taken aback by her abrupt words. Arabella flushed scarlet. "Wh-why, I . . . I fear I've been a little distressed."

"She told me she feels as if she's swallowed a raw egg in the morning," Harry put in. "Shell and all."

"Harry!" Bella cried, aghast.

"Those are your words exactly!" the Scot insisted. "Just this morning you said—"

"I'm sure Myles's betrothed is far more interested in getting warm and being fed than in hearing some list of maladies springing from childbearing!"

"Actually, Devlin likes nothing more than hearing an accounting of somebody's ills," Myles said in a sour voice. "It gives her an excuse for pouring her possets down an unsuspecting victim's throat."

Devlin felt her own cheeks flame, and she shot Myles a glare. "My mother and I live at the Farringdon estate. I was always fascinated with writings about ancient cures."

"And when she found a particularly vile one she couldn't wait to test it out on one of my unsuspecting crofters. No wonder some of them have been so eager to emigrate to the Colonies!"

Devlin bristled as Harry all but strangled on his laughter. "I'm good at what I do," she defended herself. "I've cured everything from gout to colic. When it came to midwifery, my mother squawked when I wanted to follow old Dame Griselda about while she made the rounds of the expectant mothers on the estate. She claimed it wasn't proper for a girl of my station to be exposed to such things. But I told her that there couldn't be anything *more* natural than bearing a baby and went along in spite of her objections."

"Devlin is not given to taking advice," Myles said, a bite in his voice. "And the more sound the advice is, the less likely she is to heed it."

"If I had heeded my mother's wishes, I would probably be a weak-spined girl who couldn't open her mouth without saying something foolish about hat plumes or stays."

Devlin's jaw was set firmly as she crossed her arms over her chest. "I learned a great deal following Dame Griselda about. I taught her a thing or two as well about how to make women more comfortable when they are breeding."

Arabella's eyes widened at the use of such a frank word, but Devlin continued. "I can't understand why women try so hard to hide the fact that they are with child, nor can I fathom why men feel obligated to ignore the fact that the women around them look as if they have swallowed a pumpkin."

"I—I don't know," Bella said in a confused voice. "It is just that . . . well, when one is in a delicate condition—"

"I don't think you delicate at all. From the first time I witnessed a birth I've said that if men were the ones charged with having babies, the human race would have died out with Adam."

Myles's growl of aggravation and Harry's protests were lost as Arabella hustled Devlin up the stairs.

Devlin was not certain what she expected from Arabella after airing such unconventional views, but it was not the trill of bright laughter that tripped from the young woman's lips.

"Oh!" Arabella cried, leaning against the top stair rail, breathless with mirth. *"How* Nan would love you! She is always running around in Papa's breeches, lecturing on the injustices of being born a woman! And Lizzie would have you in the library in a moment, making a list of the books where you learned about healing. If you are able to play the pianoforte, too, you would snatch up the affections of Till as well, for she's enchanted by anything musical."

Devlin stared at her. "I—I couldn't carry a tune if it was in a molasses keg. I fear Till, whoever she is, is destined to be disappointed."

"Whoever? Oh! Forgive me!" Bella Cameron said, linking her arm through Devlin's and guiding her through the passage toward the end of the sparsely furnished corridor. "Nan and Till and Lizzie are my sisters back in Norfolk."

"But I thought your husband said . . . he said you lived in a vicarage. That your father was a minister."

"Not the kind of household in which you'd picture such an upbringing, is it?" Bella asked, ushering Devlin through an open door, then disappearing into the darkness at the far end of the room.

Devlin heard her fumbling with something, and after a moment a taper flamed to life, bathing the room in a soft golden glow. Copper-printed curtains draped the bed; a crewel-worked chair was stationed in readiness beside an intricately wrought cradle. A bit of sewing was tucked upon the cradle's feather ticking, a needle gleaming in what was to be a tiny cap for the coming baby. Devlin couldn't resist going over to where it lay, trailing her fingers over the silk-spun lace.

Bella's voice followed her, laughing and sweet.

"I fear many of the women of the parish didn't consider it a proper way to bring up four daughters either," she said, bustling over to a washstand. "But Papa . . . he was never one to be swayed by other people's opinions—except God's, of course."

She smiled as she dashed water from a pitcher into the bowl nested beneath it. "He called us his garden of wildflowers, and in the years after Mama was swept away by fever he let us all grow up any way the Lord saw fit."

Devlin felt a swift sting of envy that had nothing to do with Bella's pretty features, her sweet friendliness, or her good fortune in her marriage to Harry Cameron. "That must have been wonderful," she said slowly. "Having someone encourage you to use your gifts, nurture them, instead of struggling against them. I have always felt like— well, something like an overlarge foot being shoved into a tiny dancing slipper."

"A dancing slipper?" Bella's laugh tinkled out as she turned from withdrawing linen towels from the clothes press. "Whatever do you mean?"

Devlin turned her face away from the girl's searching, friendly eyes, feeling exposed. Yet for once she did not mind it as much as she knew that she should. She took the towel from Arabella's hand and began scrubbing her face.

"It's just that my mother made it her mission in life to shape me into her idea of what I should be, as her only daughter. But"—she let out a sigh—"I fear that I was something of a disappointment to her."

"That is impossible! I've known you only a little time, but already I can tell that you are supremely clever. Witty. And Myles . . . he has often spoken of how well-read you are."

Devlin let the cloth droop to the washbowl, surprised that Myles would have talked of her at all to this laughing angel-sprite of a woman, let alone have painted an image in the least complimentary. "Doubtless Myles was amusing you all at my expense. He seems to find it endlessly funny that a woman should have a thimbleful of brains."

"No! No! It was not like that at all. The truth is that Myles is fair bursting with pride over your accomplishments. He swears that you are a master in subjects that would make most Oxford scholars' brains ache."

"Myles? Said that about *me?*"

"Myles spoke of you a great deal before he left for court.

Of course, now I can understand why, what with your secret engagement and the marriage to come."

Devlin looked into eyes as wide and innocent as meadow-kissed violets and couldn't bear to deceive this girl a moment longer.

"There is not going to be any wedding. I would not marry Myles Farringdon even if the king himself decreed it."

Arabella's mouth opened in astonishment, and Devlin could see the girl searching for words. "I . . . see."

Devlin sank down upon the crewel-worked chair and let her eyes close.

After a moment Arabella's voice intruded in soft, apologetic accents. "Forgive me if I seem to be prying, but did you and Myles have some sort of tiff upon your journey?"

"Myles and I have been merrily attempting to kill each other since I was a child," Devlin said, suddenly very weary.

"So Myles has told us." A dimple danced at the corner of Arabella's lips. "I don't mean to—well, to interfere in things that are none of my affair. And you must tell me straightaway if you want me to leave you in peace. I just feel the need to tell you that emotions always run high before a wedding. So it's not surprising if you and Myles are arguing."

Devlin looked away from Bella's earnest face, feeling a kind of hopelessness clench about her as she acknowledged that the girl's words were true. Her emotions *had* been raw, her nerves frayed to the breaking point in the weeks before her wedding to Tracey was to have taken place. A wedding Myles now insisted would never be.

Devlin felt Arabella's fingers drift down upon her shoulder, the touch warm, comforting as the girl evidently mistook the reason for Devlin's sudden pensiveness. "When Harry was pleading his suit with my papa it was awful. I spent the entire week in tears. Of course, Lizzie would say that it was no wonder, for Papa almost denied Harry and me permission to wed. Harry was already committed to following the Stuart cause, and though Papa, too, believed in their divine right to rule, I think he was fearful that I would be . . . hurt somehow. The Stuarts . . . they have tried so many times to regain what is theirs. And after each failure the consequences . . ."

Her voice trailed off, and Devlin found that she could empathize with this father who had wanted to protect his daughter from calamity. But Arabella went on, her eyes shining beneath thick lashes.

"If it had not been for Myles's help, I am certain Papa would have stood firm, and I would even now be breaking my heart with grief at the vicarage."

Arabella's eyes sought Devlin's hopefully, doubtless expecting her to be charmed that Myles had done such a kindness. And it did disarm her for a heartbeat before common sense reasserted itself, insisting that Bella's father should have locked his daughter in a stone tower rather than allow her to career off on such a mad course, even for her beloved Harry Cameron.

Devlin looked into the young woman's fragile yet radiant face. What would Arabella Cameron look like a month from now? A year from now, when all these Stuart dreams lay in ashes at her feet? Would her eyes still glow with that innocent, joyous light when she was fleeing across the countryside with her fugitive husband? Exiled forever from the bevy of sisters she so obviously loved, and from the father who had been persuaded to go against his better judgment?

Or worse, yet, would those angelically sweet features be covered with grief as she stood over Harry Cameron's fresh-dug grave with his newborn baby in her arms?

Devlin laced her fingers together, squeezing them until they hurt.

"Devlin." Bella's voice was soft, tentative. "May I call you that? I know it is early in our acquaintance, but already I feel as if I . . . as if we were friends. I know it must seem silly, but—"

Devlin looked at the young woman, knowing she should hurl up the protective walls that had always shielded her. But somehow, during the handful of minutes that had passed since she had entered Arabella Cameron's front door, she seemed to have lost the ability to do so. Still there was a hint of reluctance in her voice when she said, "Of course you may call me Devlin. I'd be glad if you did so."

"Very well, then. Devlin," Arabella said, pleasure lighting her eyes. "I hope that you and Myles will be able to solve whatever trouble lies between you at the moment. Harry teases me unmercifully because I worry about Myles so much. It's a habit, I fear, ever since Myles and I met."

Bella's smile was soft with remembering. "It was during my first Assembly in Doughton Hall. I had sipped a bit too much punch, I am ashamed to say, and was a little too tipsy to handle the attentions the gentlemen were paying to me."

Devlin could imagine quite clearly how appealing the girl must have been that night, even to the most cynical and jaded young buck.

"I would wager the gentlemen were the ones who were half drunk, when they looked at you," Devlin said with just a tinge of envy as she recalled her own first ball. She, too, had committed a social faux pas. But hers had been of a far less thrilling nature. Instead of stirring up a sensation amid the beaux she had avoided them altogether by stealing away to her host's library and spending the night with her nose buried in some rare first editions. It had been surpassingly pleasant until Myles had come to drag her by the ear back to the dance floor. She had spent the dance he had forced upon her plotting her revenge upon him.

But her memories slipped away as she glimpsed Arabella's face, which held an expression of regret mingled with a kind of resigned amusement.

"I was more than a little pleased with myself that night. Abominably vain over my little triumph. You see, the fashionable set had been predicting for weeks that I would be absolutely ignored, since I had neither wealth nor a high-placed family."

"Then they must've been blind, or else utter fools," Devlin scoffed, and Arabella shook her head in self-disgust.

"I know I was an idiot to be so pleased, but when the local squire's son invited me to walk with him in the gardens I was quite soaring with delight. Though I knew I oughtn't, I went, and . . ." Her cheeks flushed. "I fear his mama had filled his head full of tales regarding the scandalous freedom of the Reverend Macy's girls. He became quite insistent I should favor him with a kiss." Bella bustled over to a clothes press, rummaging behind its doors to draw out an armful of clothing.

"Luckily for me, Myles—evidently dragged to the country for a fortnight of hunting—charged out of the shadows and threw my suitor headfirst into the holly bushes."

Devlin grimaced, aware of how much Myles must have enjoyed rescuing a damsel in distress. "Of course, while he was swabbing your tears he was probably hoping to steal a kiss of his own," Devlin said, shaking her head.

Arabella dumped the clothing she was carrying upon the bed and turned. "No, it wasn't like that at all. No brother could have been kinder or more tender. In the scuffle I had stained my gown, and my hair had fallen askew. He mopped up the damage himself and arranged my coiffure as expertly as though he had served as a lady's maid a hundred times."

Devlin chewed at her lower lip, a disturbing uncertainty gnawing at her. She had known Myles forever. Why was it that sometimes she felt as if she looked into his face and saw someone entirely different from the person everyone else saw?

"So you and Myles became fast friends?" she couldn't resist asking.

Bella nodded. "He came often to the vicarage—brought books for Lizzie, music for Till. And he raced across the countryside on horseback at a pace mad enough to satisfy even Nan."

Devlin attempted to reconcile her image of Myles—drowning in gaming hells and worldly women—with this picture of him sitting in a humble vicarage amid a cluster of innocent girls.

"I cannot even imagine Myles doing such a thing," she couldn't stop from saying.

"I think he found peace around the fire with us. A peace he needed. Badly. He was so restless. It made me afraid for him." Bella fussed with the garments, smoothing out imaginary wrinkles with her fingers. "The two of us spent so much time together that I think Papa even hoped that one day Myles and I . . . that we would . . ."

"Marry?" Devlin asked, somewhat stunned that a father who was reportedly as loving as the Reverend Macy would encourage his daughter to form an alliance with such a notorious rakehell as Myles, despite the fact that he was heir to a dukedom. "I know Myles's position would mean security, and his wealth is considerable. But—"

"Oh, it was not because of Myles's station in life or his fortune that Papa favored him. It was because Papa knew Myles would always be good to me. But we were only friends. Good friends. Trusted friends. And when Harry came along and I fell in love with him, it was Myles who intervened on our behalf and convinced Papa that a love such as Harry and I shared was a rare and wonderful thing—worth any risk."

"Myles would say something like that," Devlin said, unable to keep an edge of censure from creeping into her voice.

Bella watched her for a moment, quiet. "You are very lucky, you know," she said at last. "Very lucky to have a man like Myles love you."

"Myles *doesn't* love me! Myles doesn't even *like* me most of the time!" Devlin blurted out, feeling as though Arabella Cameron had not heard a word she had said regarding her relationship with Myles. "I told you we're not going to marry. We'd strangle each other before we even got to the bridal bed!"

She stopped, chagrined to see Arabella staring at her with round, solemn eyes. Forcing her voice to gentler tones, Devlin said, "I am betrothed to another man, Arabella. I was to wed him at Liancourt eight days from now. But I got mixed up in Myles's escape when a group of soldiers tried to arrest him as a traitor. I ended up having to flee England myself. This nonsense about a marriage between Myles and me is spawned by some misguided notion that—I don't know—that he is protecting me somehow. It is all a charade."

"Is it?" The low, masculine voice startled both Devlin and Bella. They turned to see Myles framed in the doorway, those blue eyes hooded, his mouth a hard, unyielding line.

"I assure you, madam," he said in a voice like velvet-sheathed steel, "I have never been more serious in my life."

CHAPTER
11

Arabella gaped at Myles and Devlin lunged to her feet, both looking as horrified as if he had just informed them Devlin was to be chained in a labyrinth and sacrificed to some dreaded Minotaur.

"Stop this playacting at once, Myles," Devlin snapped. "I've already told Arabella everything! She can be trusted with the truth!"

"The truth?" Myles leaned against the door frame, attempting to feign some semblance of his usual careless grace, but his gut was churning at the look of betrayal in those sea-green eyes. "The *truth*, my love, is that I have already sent two missives off in the charge of the Camerons' footman. The first letter is to be given to the nearest clergyman, requesting that he make the necessary arrangements for us to be wed. The second message was sent off to Holyrood House to ask that Prince Charles himself lend his august presence to the affair."

"You told the prince? The *prince?* That we are to wed?"

"And so we are. Two weeks from tonight." Myles made a great show of flicking a speck of dust from the lace at his wrist. "I presume that should give you and Bella enough time to arrange whatever feminine absurdities you require."

"The only thing I *require* is for you to sit in that chair, take up a quill and ink, and tell both the prince and the clergyman that there will be no wedding."

"Myles, truly," Arabella pleaded, catching at his coat sleeve. "I cannot think that it was wise of you to—to act so precipitately without discussing this with Devlin."

The chastising words raked him with the guilt he had felt before he had even breached the chamber's door, but he only gave a lazy shrug. "Devlin and I do not *discuss* anything, Bella," he said. "We only bellow at each other until it is a wonder neither of us is deaf. However, as you can see, my betrothed and I *do* have a great deal to address at the moment. If you would excuse us?"

Arabella's agitated gaze flicked between the two, and Myles was certain they must seem like duelists faced off upon some dawn-swept hill. "I . . . I'll only be in the next chamber," she said in a nervous voice. "If you need me . . ."

She let the words trail off, and Myles winced at the tremor in her voice, knowing that the gentle Bella had always been loath to deal with confrontation. But if the Camerons were to remain insistent that he and Devlin lodge with them, he supposed the household had best grow accustomed to dealing with drawn daggers.

"Don't worry, Bella. Despite Devlin's dire predictions, I won't strangle her, and I much doubt she has the strength to strangle me, no matter how much she might like to."

He looked back at Devlin. The sight of her standing silhouetted against the silk-papered walls ate inside him. Her head was flung back in defiance, her eyes clouded not only with fury, but with confusion and hurt.

Myles ached to go to her, take her in his arms. To explain. To comfort. To soothe. He wanted to stroke back the tumbled mass of her hair and tell her that he was sorry for everything that had happened—that he had mixed her up in this catastrophe. He would do his best by her. Keep her safe. He would do everything in his power to see her happy.

Not because he was duty-bound to do so or because he had ruined her in the eyes of society. Not even because she was ward to his family, a responsibility to be lived up to. But because . . . because he cared about her—so much that it hurt him inside.

And yet even before Bella slipped from the room, shutting the door behind her, Myles knew that he could not say any of the things he so longed to. He felt he deserved the fury and betrayal that glinted in those sea-green eyes. Deserved every bit of her hatred for the way he had destroyed her life—destroyed it all unknowing.

"Dev," he began, his fingers chafing at the signet ring encircling one long finger, "you have every reason to be vexed with me, but if you could just attempt to be reasonable—"

"Reasonable?" His words were lost in Devlin's roar of fury. "You swine! I could cheerfully boil you in oil! Roast you on a spit! I could—"

"I'm afraid that would be exceedingly bad judgment considering the circumstances." Myles gritted his teeth beneath the curve of his smile and battled to maintain a frigid calm. "The fact is that you will need to cultivate a civil tongue when speaking to the man who is to share the nuptial bed with you. Being a reasonable sort, I shall not require that you leash your temper entirely. I will be generous and insist only that you address me with a modicum of respect when there are other people around. I know it is a weakness in me, but I have this aversion to being made an ass in front of my friends."

"You won't need the least amount of help from me to look like a fool before them! Especially when you are stranded at the altar, with the prince and his whole court in attendance, and no one to serve as bride!"

"Oh, you'll be there, Devlin. Because neither one of us has a choice."

"I have choices aplenty, Farringdon!"

"Ah, yes, we've discussed them already. You have the choice of being a fugitive from English justice for the rest of your life—unless, that is, Charles regains the throne. Exile is such an attractive prospect, isn't it? Then there is the even more appealing one of being captured and tried for treason, with execution to follow. And lastly there is the little matter of you being socially ruined.

"If we were to marry, we could lessen all of these to consequences much more bearable. As my wife, you would not be judged so harshly for aiding in my escape. The authorities have, on occasion, shown great sympathy for a love-besotted woman led astray by her dastardly husband."

"I do not need their pity! When Tracey comes he will find a way to make things right."

Her words poured acid on an old wound. Myles flinched inwardly, but his eyes locked with hers, dark with resolve.

"Tracey isn't coming, Devlin. But even if by some miracle he should magically appear, there would be nothing he could do to save you from being charged with the crime of aiding me. Or to stop the scandal."

"I don't care if there is a scandal!"

"Tracey *will,*" Myles grated out, ruthless. "So will the rest of polite society. But let me warn you that once something like this is stirred up, they are not quite so polite. I have watched them pick at people's reputations until there is nothing left."

Devlin's chin tipped up. "I'd like to see them try carving me up with their gossip! I—"

"They'll do far more than *try*. Even *after* we are legally husband and wife. And if by chance we should conceive the heir my grandfather so desperately desires, they will sit about sipping their punch, ticking off the months until your confinement as carefully as though they were counting up the royal treasury."

Devlin blanched, and Myles winced at the thought that it was not fear of social reprisals that had made her face so pale, but rather the idea of marrying *him,* of bearing his child.

Myles closed his eyes for a heartbeat, his voice harsh even to his own ears. "Of course, even if we do pass the appropriate amount of time before producing a child, it won't matter. They'll merely squabble over everything from your broken engagement to my paramours to the fact that you were to wed my best friend."

He walked to where a decanter of Madeira stood upon a small gilt stand. Taking the goblet beside it, he poured a draught and drank it down in one searing gulp. He laughed, the sound rough, hollow.

"I am to be the villain in this little drama, you see," he said, saluting her with his empty glass. "While you will have the dubious honor of being commiserated with, seeing as you had the misfortune to be sucked down into the morass of my corruption. But never fear," Myles told her, returning the glass to its place on the table. "In time everyone will see that I mean to do my duty by you, and that you, of course, are devoted to me. Then they will trundle merrily on their way to find some other poor wretch to torment."

"And so for the rest of our lives you and I will be married? Absolutely miserable? For how many years, Myles? Twenty? Forty? Sixty years? Long after this scandal you so fear has faded into dust?"

Myles cursed and raked his hand through his hair. "Oh, yes," he snapped, battling an urge to shake her. "You'd see to it that we were miserable, wouldn't you, Dev? You'd make certain of it, because you never could bear being wrong."

"There must be another answer, another way."

"There is no other way. But even if you work your hardest to make sure you loathe being my wife, you'll fail. I'll make you a decent husband, Dev. Better than most."

"Not better than Tracey. Never better than Tracey!" Her words lashed him like a whip. But he kept his voice even as he peered into her eyes.

"How do you know, Dev?" he asked, "unless you let me try?"

Her lower lip trembled, but her eyes flashed bravely. "I know because I love him, Myles!"

Myles dared to reach out and clasp her hands in his. "I know that you love him. But maybe . . . maybe you could become fond of me. In time. I wouldn't press you, Dev. I swear it."

"Press me? You'd do as you always do—bludgeon me until you got your own way." She tugged her hands away

from his and sank into the crewel-worked chair, her fingers knotting in her lap.

He spun away, unable to bear seeing in her face the absolute certainty that Tracey would somehow save her. A certainty Myles knew would soon give way to despair.

"Devlin, I'd do anything to make it right. I swear I would march straight up to King George's sentries and surrender if it would do any good. But it is too late. We must do the best we can to mend this."

"I'm not marrying you, Myles." There was a tremor in her voice, and he couldn't keep himself from turning toward her.

Tears glistened in the thick fans of her lashes. "I'm going to wait. Wait for Tracey. I have to, don't you see?"

Myles looked away. "I suppose I do. I'll send a letter to him now, in the hands of a trusted messenger, telling Tracey what has happened, telling him where we are. That way, if he chooses to come, he will know where to find us."

"That is just the thing to do!" Devlin cried, eyes that had been dark with tears suddenly aglisten with hope. "Of course he will come. The instant he knows."

Myles gritted his teeth, taken with the sudden, fierce need to drive his fist into the wall. Instead he locked his hands behind his back.

"I will send the letter at once," he promised, "as long as we agree upon certain . . . conditions."

"Conditions?" Her old spirit flickered in her eyes. "What conditions?"

"First of all, you must continue to play at this game we have begun. You must at least pretend to be my betrothed."

"If you think for an instant that I will humiliate myself by slavering over you before your friends, you are sadly mistaken. I'll not do it, Myles. I won't."

"It is your decision, after all, but before you start poking your nose up in the air daring me to knock it down, I'd just like to tell you that the men you met at the gate are rather more well-mannered than most of those enlisted in the army here. These are men who have already put one foot willingly in the grave for Prince Charles. Many of them would not be loath to dive headlong into their caskets for a tumble with a woman like you."

The blood surged into Devlin's cheeks, and Myles sensed that she was remembering the scene outside the city gates—remembering her fury, her helplessness as O'Keefe hauled her from the saddle. Her eyes clouded with a kind of dread Myles had never seen there before.

"They are soldiers under their officer's command," she said. "They would not—"

"Not what? Steal a kiss? Or more, if they were in their cups? No one here knows that you are *Mistress* Devlin Chastain—Sir Josiah Chastain's daughter."

Devlin glared at him, her mouth opening as if to reply. He could see that she wanted nothing more than to tell him to go to the devil. But even she must realize that this was no jest on his part. Rather, it was a caution against a very real danger. Her lips set in an angry line.

"All right, damn you. I'll do nothing to expose the fact that this betrothal is a lie. But neither will I simper about in your wake, looking glaze-eyed and besotted! With a baby coming, I'm certain Arabella has much to do—sewing and such like. I'll stay here, help her."

"Oh, yes, I remember just how much you enjoy sewing." A bittersweet memory tugged at him, one spun of moonlight and velvet-white roses, of Devlin rubbing nettles into his shirt. A memory that still made him ache with the remembrance of how her lips had felt under his—innocent and sweet and right—so blasted right. He cleared his throat, forcing the images away.

"You'll not last two days bent over your sewing," he said in a voice just a whisper unsteady. "But if you insist on being stubborn, I'll not argue with you about it."

"That shows remarkable good sense. What other demands do you intend to set forth?"

"Preparations for the wedding celebration go forward—that includes readying a gown for you, arranging a wedding feast. Everything."

"It would be an abominable waste of money! Whatever tradesmen you employ will still expect to be paid, whether or not the ceremony takes place. And besides, the prince may have you off chasing after that infernal crown again by tomorrow night."

"From what Harry says, Prince Charles is in need of trusted allies at the moment. I would guess Prince Charles will find my presence here more beneficial than chasing off upon the crown quest. And as for the expense of the wedding preparations"—Myles gave a careless shrug—"I've been known to wager away more coin on the turn of a card. I can afford this gamble as well."

"Gamble? There is no gamble. I've told you—"

"Yes, there is, Dev." He caught her face in his hands, forcing her gaze to meet his. "That is the last condition I must set forth. If Tracey does not arrive, you must promise to go through with the ceremony. Marry me."

Myles saw Devlin's lips curve in disbelief, her eyes holding a certainty that she would be rescued by her precious Tracey, that she would be saved from the awesome calamity of being Myles Farringdon's bride.

"I would wager my soul to the devil himself that Tracey will come," she said.

"Fine, then. Consider it wagered. Two weeks, Dev. That is all the time we can give him."

"Two weeks? Why? Is there some rule that this betrothal cannot exceed two weeks? There is all the time in the world."

Myles turned away from her, his mind whirling with the information Harry Cameron had imparted to him minutes before. Information regarding Prince Charles's rebel court —the leaders even now locked in battle with one another.

Factions battling for supremacy were the lifeblood of any royal court, but such division among the Jacobites now could only weaken the Stuart cause, a cause that had miraculously survived the loss of men, arms, and the French king's gold to shipwreck, ill weather, and the interference of the English fleet.

Already Charles Stuart had surmounted incredible odds, landing at Eriskay with little besides the cloak upon his back and going forth to raise up a victorious army almost from the heather itself. But triumph was fleeting, and the fates often proved fickle, smiling upon such bold ventures for only a little while.

Myles felt the restlessness roil deep within him. He grasped Devlin by the shoulders, feeling the light, nervous trip of her pulse beneath his thumbs.

"I cannot say what will happen in the future," he told her. "I cannot judge how much time there may be before— before Charles pushes into England."

Devlin's face paled, a worried frown puckering her lips. "He cannot mean to do anything so foolhardy!"

"It would be the most daring sword-stroke any Stuart has ever taken. But that is the way legends are spun."

"Don't you mean *massacres? Slaughters?* Dear God, Myles, it would be insane!"

"Put whatever name you like to what comes, Dev. But before it *does* come, all this between us must be settled. I'll not go into battle carrying the knowledge that you are stranded here in Scotland, the king's noose about your neck, your virtue at the mercy of any rogue who cares to steal it. You'll have my name before I ride away. And all the protection the house of Farringdon can offer you."

Devlin stared at him, her eyes huge, haunted by fears with which he had burdened her. Frightening images from an uncertain future. And yet she had to face the images if she was to survive.

She seemed smaller somehow, more fragile, but the curve of her chin was as resolute as ever. "Surely Tracey can reach Edinburgh in two weeks. Especially if he is aware of how desperate my situation is."

Myles knew she was trying to convince herself, not him.

"All right, then, Myles, you have your wager," Devlin said with a nod. "Two weeks. But Tracey will come in time. You will see."

Myles stared into those eyes that were so certain and felt as if something fragile, precious inside him was falling to pieces.

"You will see. . . ."

God, he was afraid that he would.

That he would see her crushed, disillusioned.

That he would see her desolate when Tracey failed her.

And that he would see her dealt the most horrible blow of all.

He would see her become his wife while the world around them spun away into madness.

CHAPTER
12

*T*he master bedchamber at Tracey House was ablaze with candle fire. The light from three dozen tapers flowed down scarlet damask bed curtains to pool in the folds of the lilac satin gown and black velvet breeches that lay abandoned upon the carpet below.

Bedclothes folded back from silken sheets with almost military precision still stretched across the foot of the bed undisturbed, a single depression in the pillow at the head of the bed cradling the blond head of the Honorable Braden Tracey.

He lay there unmoving, his eyes hooded as he stared up into the excruciatingly beautiful features of Aloise Delacourt, la Comtesse Danay, as she writhed in thwarted ecstasy astride his lean hips.

Her eyes were black and fathomless, her lips bee-stung and ripe as cherries. Breasts, small and firm, were crowned with nipples the color of wine. The tempting globes bobbed enticingly as she braced herself upon her knees, undulating her hips in a desperate, primal motion, her long-nailed fingers swirling maddening patterns upon Tracey's hairless chest. But his face remained impassive, distant and cool as snow on a windswept mountain.

"D-Damn you!" Aloise choked out in a ragged breath, and she bent down to pluck at Tracey's own flat nipple with her fingers. "Damn you to hell, T-Tracey! I know you feel this! Know it!"

"Do you, my dear?" he asked, only the tightening at the corners of his mouth betraying his mounting pleasure. "How gratifying for you."

But the effort it took him to hold that careless tone made a tiny bead of sweat gather at his temple, drip down into the burnished gold wisps of his hair. Her body was all liquid heat around his throbbing shaft, her mouth wet and mind-shatteringly skilled as she opened it and took his nipple in a fierce kiss. Tracey felt her suck it deep into the cavern of her mouth, her tongue swirling, demanding as she ground herself down upon him time and again.

Skill she had in plenty, matched with a face and body that had half of the London court slavering to bed her. But Tracey only linked his hands beneath his head in an attitude of boredom, his lips a mocking, predatory curve as he tasted his own triumph.

"You have lost your wager, Aloise," he told her with a feigned yawn. "You would be wise to strike your colors and surrender the field."

"D-Damn you! I'll not!" she almost sobbed. *"C-Canaille! Filthy canaille!"* Her hips moved even more frantically, her fingers groping between them to aid her own release.

Lightning fast, Tracey's hand shot out, capturing her wrist, yanking her hand away from that part of her obviously now screaming for ease.

"You would not wish to be known as a cheat, my love, would you?" he asked in silky accents. "After all, you *are* the one who insisted upon striking this ridiculous wager."

"You were . . . were telling the comte that . . . not a woman alive could bewitch you unless you willed it so," the comtesse gasped out, yanking against his iron grasp. "That no woman . . . would ever move you to lose . . . your head."

"It is the truth, no matter how repugnant you might find

it," Tracey said, enjoying the sensation of her impaled upon his rigid flesh.

"But they know!" Aloise cried, tears of frustration and fury pouring down her cheeks. "They all know that I am your mistress! Everyone at the rout! E-Even the servants were s-sniggering behind my back! As if I . . . I could not drive you to madness. Me. La Comtesse Danay. I, who have driven men to hurl themselves from bridges for love of me. I, who have broken the hearts of kings—"

"I am well aware of your illustrious career between the bedsheets, my sweet. And have been quite impressed with the list of my predecessors. But if you are waiting to add me to the droves of lovesick fools who tear themselves to shreds upon the rocky shores of your passions, I fear you will be disappointed. I find you quite appealing. Delectable, in fact. But ultimately resistible."

With a curse as foul as a Fleet Street whore she shoved away from him and rolled to the other side of the bed. "If you had been Adam in the Garden of Eden, you'd not have been tempted by the apple! You would have flung it in Eve's face!"

"And saved the entire human race a good deal of trouble," Tracey said, levering himself onto one elbow. "I have always maintained that if Adam had only exercised a bit of restraint—"

"Dog! Unnatural dog!" Aloise shrieked. "I spit upon you! Never again shall I waste my charms upon your bed! Never again! No matter how you beg. I shall seek out that friend of yours—that viscount with eyes hot as the devil's coals."

"Farringdon?" Tracey's lip curled, his rigid control slipping but a whisper. "I fear you will have a difficult time in finding the rogue, let alone luring him to your bed. He is embroiled in some difficulty at present."

"Even so, he would be well worth the effort! I have heard from the other women at court—heard of the skill he possesses, enough to drive a woman mad! 'Tis rumored he can bring a woman to ecstasy with the barest touch of his hand, and that the weapon of love he wields is the mightiest lance in all England."

Tracey's fingers unconsciously tightened in a bruising grip about her wrist as he felt the gnawing sense of jealousy that had always tainted his relationship with Myles.

Aloise's eyes widened, and Tracey disliked the sudden gleam in her shrewd eyes. Her lips parted over sharp white teeth. "Liancourt was the one I wanted anyway when first I approached you at Lady Worthing's musicale. I had come specifically because I knew he would be there. I was without a lover at the time, and I was eager to sample the skill of the legendary Myles Farringdon. But he spent the whole night hovering over that stupid Revand boy who had lost so badly at the gaming tables."

"Ah, yes. I remember the occasion well." With fierce control Tracey forced himself to release her hand, schooling his expression into lines that would not betray his vulnerability to a she-wolf upon a blood scent. "Myles feared Revand would put a bullet in his brain rather than confront his father with his losses. The youth was quite desperate, as I recall. How inconvenient for you."

"I had to settle for you. Not that you have proved an *intolerable* lover," Aloise taunted. "However, I must say I pity this wife you are to take a few days hence. I have heard that she was raised in Liancourt's household. I fear it will be quite distressing to your betrothed to be switched from a steady diet of delectable pastry to one of dry bread."

Tracey felt his own blood heat, but not with passion. Anger pulsed deep as he felt his shaft begin to soften, wither.

Regardless of her spitefulness, Aloise gave a squeak of protest as he climbed out of bed and drew on a robe of gold-shot brocade. He fastened the loose dressing gown about his waist.

"What are you doing? I've not finished with you yet."

Tracey gave her a thin smile as he realized that she had been attempting to break his control in the only way left to her—fury. He looked into her eyes and saw that she wanted him to take her with violence. Disgust filled him.

"I would not dream of burdening your discerning palate with mere bread, my lady," he said. "Of course, I shall be

happy to write a letter of recommendation to my friend
Liancourt if you wish."

Aloise gave a disgruntled huff. "Perhaps I should interview your betrothed before I bestir myself on Liancourt's
behalf. She should know him quite intimately. Intimately
enough to enlighten me as to his . . . er . . . particular tal-
ents."

"My betrothed would know nothing of Liancourt's talent
in that regard. She is a lady of intelligence, with far too
much sense to be swayed by either Farringdon's appearance
or his reputed skill in the bedchamber."

"You mean that she is a bluestocking with the same pale
passion in her veins as you. Doubtless she will prove as
responsive in bed as a milksop, and—"

With lightning swiftness Tracey grasped her chin, his eyes
piercing hers, his voice thrumming with warning.

"You are not even worthy to wipe the dust from her shoes.
And should you ever dare to so much as speak her name
again, I promise you will regret it."

Aloise stared at him, her eyes wide, excited. Revolted,
Tracey released her. Snatching up the garments the woman
had strewn across the floor in the first heat of desire, he
threw them at her.

"Get dressed," he snapped. "I'll have your carriage
summoned."

He was turning toward the door when a sudden sharp rap
shattered the tension between them, a worried voice
penetrating the bedchamber's door.

"Mr. Tracey? Mr. Tracey, sir?" the voice of his butler
intruded.

"What the devil is it, Rouget?"

"A messenger, sir, just arrived. I'd not **have** disturbed
you, but he bears a missive sealed with the Liancourt crest. I
know you've been waiting for word from Master Myles."

Relief shot through Tracey, making him suddenly aware
that he had been tense ever since the day he had left
Pothsby's study, having warned the duke that Myles was in
danger.

He had known from the first that if Myles received word in time, he would make good his escape, had hoped that by now Myles would be gorging himself on wine and wenches in Paris. Safe. Far away from the unrest rippling through the whole of Britannia.

Still, it had been a dangerous gamble—one that could have cost not only his best friend's life, but his own career as well.

Not bothering to see if Aloise had managed to cover herself yet, he strode to the door and flung it open. He all but tore the missive from Rouget's hands. Breaking the seal with an eagerness belied by the slightest trembling in his hand, he unfolded the note and held it toward the light, scanning Myles's familiar bold scrawl.

Escaped under noses of King's soldiers, thanks to your warning . . . Tracey gave a laugh of triumph, but his brow furrowed, tension knifing between his shoulder blades as he read on. *You will be relieved to know I have repaired to Scotland and placed myself at the side of the prince for the battle to come.*

"Relieved?" Tracey echoed the scribblings in disbelief. "The fool was supposed to go to France, damn it. France."

He skimmed on, anxiety shifting to anger, disbelief.

Despite success in eluding authorities, regret to inform you I have encountered one difficulty. Devlin ran afoul of my escape attempt, and I fear things went awry.

Tracey felt his throat constrict, his hands clenching upon the paper until it crackled, tore.

Wish to God there had been any other way, but had to bring her with me. She is distraught over ruined wedding plans. Would see you.

Tracey stared at the words, reading them over and over as if they had suddenly been transcribed into some language he did not understand.

No, it was impossible. Devlin was at Liancourt, preparing to become his wife. He had received a letter from her mere weeks ago, rambling on about her gown and the preparations for the wedding supper. There had been lists of wedding guests to be gone over—all the most powerful, most influential men in government. She had been so determined not to forget anyone vital to his career.

This was unthinkable! he thought wildly. Some practical joke upon Myles's part to set him into a panic on the eve of his wedding. But even as he formed the thought he knew it wasn't so. It was true, Myles's letter—every horrifying, shocking, mind-numbing word. Tracey closed his eyes, images dancing in his head.

Devlin stranded somewhere within Scotland's barbaric borders, in the middle of an army about to go to war. Devlin afraid, hunted, alone.

No, not alone. Myles had been there. Myles. He would protect her, keep her safe. He would—

Damn the bastard to hell, *he* was the one who had allowed her to stumble into this calamity!

"What is amiss, Tracey?" Aloise's voice jarred his nerves, and he was suddenly aware of her sly eyes peering with pointed interest over his shoulder. "Did Liancourt indeed run off with your intended?"

With volcanic suddenness Tracey's control snapped, and he wheeled, his hand flashing out. He heard his butler's stunned cry, Aloise's shriek splitting the air as his palm connected, hard, wiping the sneer from the comtesse's smug face.

Her heavily jeweled fingers clutched at her rapidly reddening cheek, her sultry lips gaping open in shock.

"Get out," Tracey thundered.

Any sign of arousal vanished from the woman's face. Her eyes went wide with fright. Clutching her half-laced gown against her breasts, she wheeled and fled the room.

Fury raged through Tracey's veins as he recalled the last interview he had held with Myles in the study at Tracey House. Hadn't he warned Myles that he was courting Armageddon? Hadn't he pleaded with the fool not to be so reckless?

"Sir?" Rouget's voice interrupted his thoughts, the tones trembling. "Sir, wh-what is it? My lord Myles . . . is he hale?"

"Hale?" Tracey snarled. "Oh, aye, he's hale. In fact, it seems he has invited me for a visit."

"A—A visit, sir?"

"In Scotland. Have Sikes saddle my horse at once."

"B-But your wedding, sir. Forgive me, but—"

"Damn it, man," Tracey shouted, "do as you're told!"

The butler blanched, stumbling back as if he feared he would be the next to suffer this unprecedented use of his master's hand. Then he wheeled, racing to do Tracey's bidding.

Tracey sucked in deep, burning breaths, battling to get control of emotions rushing through him—helplessness, fury at the stupidity, the needless waste that had brought them all to this pass. Emotions more savage than any he'd ever known.

He crushed the letter in his hand, the wax seal crumbling to bits beneath his fingers. Then, with an oath, he flung it into the fire.

CHAPTER

13

A smug cupid cavorted at the base of the timepiece upon the mantel, his bow and quiver at his side, one plump arm looped about the naked shoulders of a sleeping maiden. Behind the filigreed hands sweeping about the clock's face a man uncannily like Myles poked his head through a tangle of delicately carved vines to see her, his chest pierced by a tiny gilt dart.

Devlin glared at the clock, tempted to wind it until its spring exploded, stopping time in its flight.

A fortnight Myles had promised her. A fortnight to wait and pray and drive herself mad with wondering whether or not Tracey was on the road somewhere, riding. She stiffened, wondering if Myles had truly sent Tracey the message at all.

He had seemed so certain that Tracey would not come, that only by becoming the Viscountess Liancourt would she be safe, protected. Yet even Myles could not be so despicable as to promise to send word and then fail to do so. Even Myles could not be so cruel as to let her wait these agonizing, endless days to suit his own purposes, could he?

And yet hadn't he made her vow to hold her tongue, telling no one that the preparations for the upcoming nuptials of the Viscount Liancourt and Mistress Devlin Chastain were nothing but a ruse? Or that she was waiting for another man to rescue her from the unthinkable fate of becoming Myles's wife?

Devlin spun away and stalked over to a small sewing box tucked upon a bench by the window, a half-finished gown for Arabella's baby there beside it. But she could not lose herself in the intricate embroidery or the working of delicate lace.

All she could think of was the relentless sweep of the hands upon the clock.

Since the morning Myles had been summoned to an audience with the prince the viscount had again been within Charles Stuart's exclusive inner circle, his responsibilities keeping him away much of the day.

And yet despite the distraction of molding a government, every time Myles returned to the Camerons' household he had been the most attentive of suitors, excruciatingly charming, intent upon seeing to her every comfort. He had fetched her books from the bookseller, seen her supplied with enough paper, ink, and quills to "scribble away" for the next five years. He had hired a small army of seamstresses to make her a wardrobe.

And as if that were not enough, he had brought her countless small gifts—an engraved box for writing implements, a carved brush for her hair, a cunningly wrought bottle of scent portraying the fable of the tiger and the fox—whatever ridiculous, wasteful bit of feminine frippery Myles had taken a fancy to.

She had first ordered, then cajoled, and finally begged for him to stop, cautioning him that he might later have need of whatever funds he had managed to raise from the jewels they had found at the Dower House. But he had only flashed her that infuriating grin and told her that it pleased him to surprise her with the presents. And, he had added, with the slightest edge of bitterness touching his voice, Devlin should know better than anyone that he always did exactly what he pleased.

In desperation she had lapsed into a stubborn, resigned

silence on the subject in the hope that Myles was getting some kind of mischievous enjoyment out of disconcerting her, and that, deprived of her protests, he would tire of the game.

But as the days of her self-imposed imprisonment in the Cameron household slipped past, Myles showed no sign of stopping.

He went on bringing her gifts astonishingly suited to her tastes. Even more frustrating, he plunged headlong into preparations for the wedding celebration that would never come, ordering up feasts and flowers, wedding clothes and wine so extravagant it gave Devlin apoplexies.

Even despite Myles's antics, the days sequestered away in Arabella's home had passed in an amazingly painless fashion. Devlin had expected to suffer, exactly as Myles had predicted, while being locked away in such close quarters. But she, who had always been solitary, had surprised herself by seeking out Arabella's company with almost alarming regularity. And Arabella had been every bit as hungry for companionship as Harry had claimed. Not that Devlin could wonder at the fact, as the days had slipped by and she had seen how often the young woman had been alone.

Both Myles and Harry were gone long before dawn each morning, buried in whatever political idiocy was transpiring at the prince's governmental seat of Holyrood House. Often they did not return until long after the tapers had been lit to stave off the darkness.

Harry would trudge in, his eyes lined with exhaustion as he stumbled into the room Bella jokingly labeled the grand salon. There the Scotsman would kick off his boots and stretch out upon the settee with his head pillowed upon his wife's steadily shrinking lap until dinner.

But Myles seemed to thrive on the very precariousness of the Stuart position. His step would always be as jaunty when returning as it was when he had left. He would fling his cloak and hat into the arms of a footman, jesting with the servants as if wagering the Liancourt fortunes upon Charles's success were of no greater import than wagering upon a carriage race. And the greater the odds against the horse he had backed, the more delicious the contest would be.

Devlin went to the window, rubbing her arms as she stared out into the twilight-shrouded streets. Couldn't Myles see that the whole city was teetering upon the blade of an axe, she wondered, waiting for the prince to turn its blade one way or the other?

She sighed as she watched people scuttle about on their various errands, their faces drawn deep into hoods, their heads bent as they pushed on in a harried, nervous stride. Even the lowliest stable boy seemed bent on hastening back to his own cozy fire. Why was it that they all sensed the tempest whirling nearer while Myles was seemingly oblivious?

Devlin chewed at the ragged edge of her thumbnail, the nervous habit surfacing whenever she was anxious. In the days since her arrival she had gleaned enough knowledge to gauge that this mad rebellion actually had a chance of success. A chance that could slip through the Jacobite fingers like slivers of moonlight if they fell into the trap that had snared so many armies before. The trap of feeling as if the gods were aligned on their side, the sense that they were invincible.

If only someone would make a decision—end this torturous waiting, not only for her own future, but also the fates of these people she had come to care about.

Arabella, gentle, laughing, almost painfully kind. Harry with his broad, honest face, his blustery affection. And Myles—always Myles. The fool. The dreamer. The man who stooped to wipe tears from a child's grubby cheek. The man who risked his neck to rescue frightened kittens.

The man who—despite her dreadful temper, despite the fact that she was in love with another man—was willing to marry her. To sacrifice his own future out of a sense of loyalty.

"Curse him, the man is a plague!" Devlin muttered aloud. "He's mad as a March hare." But even as she said the words, that odd sensation tugged at her heart, that feeling that made her want to throttle him and want to shield him at the same time—coupled with the sobering knowledge that she could do neither.

Her eyes returned to the window as if by will alone she could conjure Myles up, force him to appear somewhere in the street below. She pressed one hand against the glass pane, searching the mass of people who were wending their way home after their day's labor.

But nowhere along the street was there a tall, dashing figure astride a ghost-gray stallion, his cloak rippling back from broad shoulders.

Where was he? Sprawled in a chair in the prince's salon? Those long fingers of his curled about a crystal goblet? Was he flashing Charles that insufferable grin, that arrogant curve of his lips that boasted a careless courage and subtly scorned any man reluctant to follow his lead?

Others in either court faction might be resorting to angry pleas, might be railing and bellowing and roaring out their demands. But Myles would only lounge there in a way that made his opponents squirm as he sliced the floor away beneath them with his own style of irrepressible logic.

Devlin closed her eyes and twisted the betrothal ring Tracey had given her about her finger until the skin felt raw. It had been her one defiance, refusing Myles's request that she remove the Tracey diamond and replace it with a ring of Myles's own. For doing so would have made this madness of intrigue, rebellion seem far too real, would give it a finality that terrified her more deeply than anything she'd ever known.

Devlin started at the muffled sound of someone arriving below. For a heartbeat she held her breath, gripped with the ever-present hope that it might be Tracey's voice she heard, Tracey's step.

She dashed out of the room to the head of the stairs and peered down, her pulse hammering with desperate hope, but at that moment Myles stepped into view, surrounded by eager servants as he swirled his cape from about broad shoulders and swept his tricorn from tumbled dark hair.

A pair of bronze satin breeches clung to his powerful

thighs, a cream waistcoat embroidered with gilt griffins glinting beneath the sweeping edges of his amber velvet frock coat. His hair was caught back with a gold ribbon at his nape.

He looked every inch the hero about to be sacrificed upon the altar of some holy cause.

And Devlin wanted nothing more than to lock him in an ironbound trunk and keep him there, safe, until all this insanity had passed.

"Good evening, milord," the young footman, Jacob, said as he reached for Myles's cape and hat. "And how are things with the prince tonight?"

"Tolerable. Tolerable," Myles said with a shrug. "At least for a man whose cause is about to be lost."

Devlin felt her own pulse lurch in dread, saw the footman blanch.

"L-Lost, milord?" the boy choked out. "Tell me 'tis not so!"

The devil danced across Myles's eyes. "I'm afraid that I have it on the highest authority. Unless the prince remains barricaded here in Scotland until spring, my Lord Avenstea claims—"

"That old vulture!" the boy scoffed. "I thought he'd died o' the gout a dozen years ago. Don't tell me he's been telling the prince to sit on his sword in Scotland the winter through!"

Myles laughed, clapping the footman on the shoulder. "I fear it is true, Jacob. I thought the old scoundrel was going to shatter his quizzing glass, he was glaring at me with so much ire today while we were discussing the matter. And when I offered *my* opinion of the course he proposed, Avenstea turned so red in the face I thought he might explode."

"If only he would have," Jacob said with a heartfelt sigh. "I much fear Avenstea and his sort are going to rob the Bonnie Prince of his throne with their dallying."

The tension inside Devlin was near to the breaking point. "More likely they are the only ones with brains enough to preserve it for him," she said aloud.

At the sound of her words the two men in the passage looked up. Jacob looked as if his neck cloth had suddenly been jerked too tight. But Myles swept her an elegant bow.

"Ah, my beloved! My dearest heart—"

"It seems to me that this Lord Avenstea is the voice of reason. I think that your chances *would* be better if you strike in the spring. The French have promised reinforcements, and even the troops you have now will be better rested."

"Brilliant, m'lady! Brilliant!" Myles made a show of applauding her. "However, apparently it's not occurred to either you or Avenstea that King George's troops will *also* be more rested after an entire winter of guzzling ale by some hearth fire."

"Well, I—"

"I can tell you exactly how much that circumstance will help the Stuart cause. Just think, Dev, a pure ocean of Hanoverian soldiers spending an entire winter chafing under the defeats we have dealt them, burning with shame that a ragtag army has chased the King of England's troops straight out of Scotland."

"I don't see what that has to do with anything regarding the decision to remain in Edinburgh."

"Don't you, now? Do you know what defeat does to a man, Dev? Being made a fool of before all the world. Doubtless the court of France, Spain, even George's pitiful electorate of Hanover is pure buzzing with news of Charles's triumphs. George and his generals look like cowardly incompetents. No man—not even a stodgy farmer like George of Hanover—likes to appear the buffoon. Give the king and his generals months to reflect upon their failures, and they'll burst out in the spring fighting like cornered dogs, more savage than anything you've ever seen."

Devlin fingered a frayed bit of ribbon upon her sleeve as she considered his words. "That may be so, but you have beaten them before. Wouldn't you be able to do so again, more swiftly still, with the men and arms France has vowed to—"

"Jacobites have been waiting nearly three generations for

the French to give more than token aid to our cause. Who can say what that wily old Louis will choose to do when the seasons turn? No. We have the momentum now. Our men are still drunk on their victories—victories miraculously won. They do not believe they can lose in battle, Dev. And there is no weapon that is stronger than that kind of confidence."

"I think you are all fools. On both sides."

"That may be so. But thank God Charles seems to be as much a fool as I am. I predict that before autumn is out we will be thumbing our noses at German George in the heart of London Town."

"More likely you'll be having your noses *lopped off* at London Tower."

"Well, take heart. It seems you will have an opportunity to dissuade the prince from this mad course yourself. As ever your humble servant, m'lady, I have arranged for you to get your wish."

"My wish?"

"The wish you voiced at the Dower House. You were fair chafing to run the whole rebellion, if memory serves me correctly. It seems you may have a chance to do just that."

"You're being obtuse, Myles, and you're doing it on purpose. Tell me at once what the blazes this is about."

"I have been expounding your myriad virtues to the prince for days now, and His Highness is most eager to learn how to conquer England à la Chastain."

"Me? Speak with the prince?" Devlin's brow arched in thought. "Perhaps I could reason with him—"

"I'm certain Charles would find that infinitely amusing, as long as you did so while you were whirling about in a dance. You see, Cadman MacCreedy is giving an impromptu ball in honor of our upcoming marriage—at the prince's request."

"Oh, no, Myles." Devlin felt the familiar knot tightening in her chest at the mere thought of her promise to him. "You vowed I could stay here at Arabella's until Tracey—"

"Give it up, Dev. By now even you must know he's not coming. I've played along with your game as long as I can, but neither of us is going to offend His Highness by refusing this kindness."

"I'll be taken ill, then. A—A bout of the biliousness."

"You'll arrive at the ball upon my arm, your face glowing with joy, the picture of a happy bride. It will give you practice in smiling over gritted teeth, so that you may make it through the actual ceremony three days hence."

"But I have nothing to wear! Nothing suitable."

"I trust the seamstresses I have engaged can dredge up something. Something bright, something beautiful. Something worthy of the woman who is to be my wife."

Devlin stared at his implacable face, realizing that he was right, that if the prince himself was attending this fete in her honor, she could scarcely absent herself from it, no matter what excuse she could unearth.

And if she could not even manage to disentangle herself from a simple ball, what alternative would she have three days from now, when all of Edinburgh would be poised and ready to watch her become Myles Farringdon's bride?

CHAPTER
14

*T*he little French modiste fluttered about Devlin like a butterfly, her hands making adjustments on the gown now laced over Devlin's stiff corset.

For two days the woman had worked on the dress Devlin was to wear to the grand ball.

Only on the morning that Myles had hired the seamstress had the woman even tolerated Devlin and Arabella within her shop—and then just so that measurements could be taken and "mademoiselle's charms" could be properly gauged.

When both Devlin and Arabella had dared give the seamstress some direction as to what the gown should look like when finished, the woman had all but exploded in a puff of indignation, castigating them in French until the crystal in the candlesticks nearly rattled off of the table.

Madame DuPres was "only following my lord's instructions," the Frenchwoman had claimed. Such a romantic man the viscount was, such a handsome lover, not wanting his beloved to see the gown until she was to be dressed for the ball. Devlin should be ashamed of herself, *vraiment,* for prying about, spoiling the lovely treat he had in store for her.

Devlin had wanted to tell the woman that "prying about" to discover previous "surprises" Myles had arranged for her had saved her from eating a worm slipped into her soup, kept her from having her hair dyed with ink, and saved her the humiliation, not to mention the discomfort, of plucking a sharp-clawed crab from the toe of her riding boot.

But in the end she had shrugged off the whole affair of the dress, assuring Arabella that she didn't care if the thing was stitched in black with gray splotches. She didn't have the energy to worry about something so insignificant as a gown when her entire life seemed to be crumbling into ruin about her head.

But now, as Madame Juliette DuPres gave a final tug to the bodice's gilt lacings, Devlin knew with a sick certainty that she should have stood over the woman with a whip and a cudgel the whole time she was sewing. Knew that she should have mistrusted any needlewoman in Myles's employ.

In two hours she was supposed to be meeting Charles Stuart, Prince of the Blood, Regent—however temporarily —of Scotland. And there was not enough cloth in the front of her bodice to cover a child of ten.

She stared at her reflection in the mirror, flushed scarlet with embarrassment. Framed in gold, the square neckline plunged alarmingly low, while the magnificent sequined and silver gilt stomacher thrust her breasts upward in plump, pale mounds that threatened to spill from their fragile shielding of cloth.

The silk dress, brocaded with ribbons of gold, cascaded in a glittering waterfall over sea-green petticoats. Gilt shoes peeked out from beneath the snowy lace at the hem; even the garters were of matching green silk shot with gold.

It was beautiful—the most beautiful gown Devlin had ever seen. A gown wrought for a queen or a princess, a gown fashioned for some daring paragon of beauty, the court's most dazzling belle. Yet as she stared at herself she wanted nothing more than to tear it from her shoulders.

"So, so, so? Is it not the most heavenly of gowns? Is it not a dress for an angel?"

"I hardly think St. Peter would allow an angel to be garbed in something like this," Devlin said faintly. She turned to where Arabella stood frozen at the door of the dressing room, her eyes gone so wide with shock that Devlin feared the girl would collapse into labor on the spot.

"Oh . . . my," Bella gasped, wringing her hands. "Do you truly think . . . I mean, the gown . . . it is beautiful, but . . ."

"It is the latest fashion," the modiste said, much offended by the less-than-enthusiastic reception of her masterpiece. "I did much work to make certain 'tis exactly the kind of gown to give the viscount pleasure. This gown . . . it holds everything to bring the fire to a man's eyes. The bosom . . . it is a swell of snowy white above the edge of satin, your charms displayed so temptingly, as if only the bit of ruffle *here* is keeping them veiled from his eyes. The waist, it is tiny, and the petticoats, they have been contrived to flip up at the edges, giving your love glimpses of your ankles, glimpses that will set his body burning for mademoiselle."

"Myles does not need the least encouragement on that account, I can assure you," Devlin said, staring at her reflection. "He could glimpse anything remotely female wrapped up in a flour sack and dissolve straightaway into a puddle of passions."

"Ah, you are the most fortunate of women to have entranced a man so hot of blood. He will give you many nights of ecstasy in the marriage bed—breed in you fine sons."

Devlin felt an odd shiver work through her, a kind of excitement edged with raw terror. Her cheeks flamed at the images the seamstress's words conjured, images fired in her imagination by the all-too-vivid memories of Myles's kiss, Myles's hands, hot and hungry in the shadows of the Dower House music room.

She closed her eyes, her thoughts filled with scenes of her and Myles . . . together . . . *that* way. Her waistline swelling like Bella's, with everyone in the household aware of what must have transpired to start the child growing. Everyone knowing the things Myles had done to her . . . with her.

Myles would doubtless be bursting with pride at his achievement. Yet she suspected that no man alive would be more solicitous of a wife thick with his child, cosseting her until she was half crazed by his constant hovering. Devlin closed her eyes, a sudden picture painted upon her imagination: Myles bending over the cradle that had held seven generations of Farringdon heirs, his eyes shining.

Her eyes fluttered open, and she stared for a moment at the woman reflected back at her in the mirror—the woman whose eyes were troubled, whose teeth were nibbling at her lower lip. Nervous. Unsettled. An unexpected longing misting her features.

It was absurd, ridiculous, the reaction she was having to the seamstress's offhand words.

It was not as if Devlin had never thought of having children before. But such thoughts had only seemed to be one more facet of the business of marriage, something to be decided and then arranged.

Never had she suspected the *feelings* that would be streaking through her—the sense of intimacy, the fears, the strange, frightening hope.

Unsettled she turned to Madame DuPres, her chin set with a stubbornness Myles would have disliked.

"I am sorry, madame, but lovely as the gown is, I fear I cannot wear it."

"Y-You cannot *what?*" the woman shrieked, clasping her own bosom as though Devlin had just plunged in a knife.

"I cannot wear it. I would spend the whole night hiding behind the draperies, or tugging at the edge of the bodice until the whole of it tore away in my hands. And that would give Lord Myles a shock I can assure you he would *not* appreciate."

Arabella hastened over, looking vastly relieved. "I agree with Mistress Chastain. The gown is beautiful. And I am certain that—that Myles might like such fashions very much upon other women. But men are always such unreasonable creatures that I am certain he would be most . . . most aggrieved to see his betrothed so . . . so boldly displayed."

"You think he would not like it? Madame DuPres's most beautiful work?"

"I am certain of it," Bella said, rushing to unfasten the gown at Devlin's back. "Devlin, I have the sweetest apple-green satin tucked away. I am certain it would fit—"

"Wait." Devlin tugged away from Bella's hands, her eyes fixing upon her reflection in the mirror with a new, keen light as the young woman's words echoed in her mind. "Do you truly think Myles would dislike it? The gown, I mean?"

Arabella peered earnestly into her eyes. "Myles is infinitely more quick-tempered than my Harry when it comes to things such as this, and I can promise you that were I ever to go into company dressed thus, Harry would have me wrapped up in a swath of carpet and carried out the door over his shoulder before I could say farewell."

Devlin took a step nearer the looking glass, examining the way the gilt lace accented the flawless white of her skin, the gown's bright colors setting her hair ablaze with highlights of flame.

"Madame DuPres, I saw in a print once—a satire—a court beauty with a patch affixed . . . here." She pointed to the vulnerable flesh at the edge of the plunging neckline. "The men in the print were stumbling over each other, with their eyes goggling out."

"But of course they were," Madame said, eyeing Devlin with wary approval. "The mark of love upon the breast is most enticing. It makes men ache to place their lips upon it and—"

Arabella's gasp cut off the woman's words.

"Mistress Chastain does not desire men to put their lips anywhere of the kind!" Arabella said, bustling to place herself between Devlin and what Bella obviously saw as the corrupting influence of the French modiste. "And if Lord Myles even suspected that—that some other man was—was ogling his lady's . . . well, her *mark,* he'd most likely fling the culprit nose-first into the punch!"

"Perhaps that is the reaction mademoiselle wants, *n'est-ce pas?*" Black eyes sparkled.

"Of course she doesn't want any such thing!" Arabella burst in, distressed. "Devlin—"

"What else, Madame DuPres, would make Lord Myles wish to throw other men into the punch bowl?"

"A bit of rouge, so, and so," the Frenchwoman suggested, sweeping the tip of her finger across Devlin's cheekbone. "A touch of carnelian worked into the lips to make them glisten, red, as if they have just been kissed. And perhaps another tiny kiss of black velvet, affixed just beneath the swell of your lips, to draw eyes down, to make them wonder what you and the viscount have been doing in the garden . . . to make them wonder what it is about you that has made such a notorious rogue willing to bind himself to you for life."

Devlin's resolve faltered at the woman's words, and she fingered a ruched edge of silk. "I . . . I'm not certain I want others to be thinking of such things. I only wanted to bait Lord Myles—"

Madame DuPres's laugh tinkled out like crystal bells stirred by the wind. "Trust me, *ma petite,* there is nothing you could do that would stir up more anger in a man than to goad him with the knowledge that all the other men in the room are wondering what it would be like to take his lady into their arms, to take her into their beds."

"Devlin, I think this an exceedingly bad idea," Arabella pleaded. "There is no way of knowing what might happen when Myles's temper is roused."

"Well, it has not seemed to concern Myles overmuch what the consequences might be when my temper is aroused."

"But he'll not even let you leave the house if he catches so much as a glimpse of you."

"Ah, but men are so simple to fool, mademoiselle! A cloak fastened here"—the seamstress touched Devlin's chin—"and your lover will not suspect until it is too late."

"That is just what I am afraid of!" Arabella plucked at her skirts, distressed. "Devlin, I know you and Myles are not on the best of terms at the moment, but I cannot think—"

Devlin turned to the young woman, impulsively catching Bella's hands. "I'm not asking you to think, Bella. I'm asking you to be my friend. From the instant Myles and I left Liancourt he has been charging about, doing exactly as he pleased. He's been arranging my life, my future. And I"—her voice broke—"I need to feel as if *I* am in control of things again, don't you see? It's as if I . . . I'm losing pieces of myself and can never gather them up again."

She looked away, aware that a tear was trickling down her cheek, uncertain why she had suddenly been struck by this desperate melancholy, this strange ache that could only be banished by action.

Bella's fingertips trailed softly across Devlin's face, wiping away the salty wetness. "We'll gather the pieces up together," she said softly. "At the ball, tonight."

*M*yles lifted his chin and grimaced at his reflection in the drawing room mirror as he examined the stinging red slice where he had nicked himself at shaving an hour before. Five years it had been since he had sliced himself—and that had only been because one of his mistresses had flung herself at his back when he'd been about his task. But tonight he felt as skittish as a lad going off to his first assembly. He felt as raw and nervous as though he were going to approach his first lady-fair and ask her to dance.

It was absurd for him to feel so unsettled. God knew he and Devlin had danced together a thousand times before. They had shared the same dancing master—and both had taken the greatest glee in driving the poor man crazy with their battles. But this night . . . this would be far different.

Myles tugged at his neck cloth, the elegant fall of lace suddenly seeming too tight. He hastened back to the looking glass, straightening the ruffles back into their flowing perfection beneath the hard square of his jaw.

His hair was swept back from his deeply tanned brow, the dark masses left unpowdered because he knew how Devlin detested the fashion. It was gathered at his nape and tied with a black satin ribbon. His broad shoulders were encased in dark blue silk velvet. He felt a rushing excitement, an anticipation, as well as a gnawing dread that he would somehow fail.

But then, he was faced with the knowledge that the lady he hoped would peer up at him with longing in her eyes despised him, loathed him, and frequently held him in contempt.

Myles swore, digging his fingers into his pocket to feel the velvet-wrapped parcel within.

He had stopped at the silversmith on his way home from Holyrood House that very afternoon to retrieve the piece of jewelry he had left there two days before—an exquisite creation he had found in the treasures taken from the Dower House. He had stumbled upon it one night upon their journey, when he'd been unable to sleep—their supplies already alarmingly low, the road to Scotland seeming yet dauntingly long. Yet even though in the beginning he had imagined using a part of the treasure to finance their passage through England, he had later found himself troubled at the thought of selling off even the tiniest segment of the legacy for Devlin he'd discovered hidden in the priest hole.

He had been sifting his fingers through the tangle of riches, resigned to pawning off his favorite emerald stickpin and the set of diamond shoe-buckles his mother had given him last Christmas, when he glimpsed the glowing, softly luminous oval of ivory, all but lost amid the glitter of the other flashy gems.

There had been a woman painted upon the smooth surface, her dress from the days of the cavaliers, her pearl headdress adorning golden curls. Dust and age had dulled the finish, veiling it in a gray film that blurred much of the miniature. But as Myles had held it cradled in his palm a rippling sensation of familiarity, of *rightness,* had made him close his fingers around it and tuck it back into the pocket of his waistcoat.

The moment the prince had announced the plans for the ball Myles had known what he wanted to do. He wanted the ornament to be repaired, polished, made as beautiful as possible so that he could give it to Devlin on this night—a night of beginnings when he hoped to reach through her anger, her hurt, her sense of betrayal, to build something good between them. His gift of hope, of promise, to the woman who was to become his wife.

Yet never in his wildest dreams had he suspected the stunning beauty that would be revealed beneath the silversmith's skilled hands.

Myles smoothed back the velvet to see if the setting had been repaired and the tiny sapphires set as petals in the flowers surrounding the ivory miniature had been replaced. And his breath caught in his throat as he stared at the image worked upon the ivory, almost the only difference between the painted woman and the vital, living one seeming to be the color of hair and eyes.

Spirited, strong, the woman in the portrait gazed out at the world with much the same calm sense of confidence Devlin had always had. Courage shone vivid within the painted lady's face, her chin tipped up at a defiant angle so like Devlin's it astonished Myles.

And yet for all the boldness, the strength shimmering out of the image, there was about it a softness, a sweetness that clung about her mouth like some wondrous secret, a misting of something that had only rarely touched Devlin's features.

Tenderness. Love. Myles could feel them within the cavalier's lady as certainly as if she were spilling the emotions themselves into his hand.

And in an odd way it gave him hope. Hope that Devlin's heart was not so firmly fixed upon Braden Tracey as everyone had thought these many years. Hope that there was some part of herself that she'd never allowed any man to touch, not allowed any love to fill.

The sound of footsteps behind him snapped Myles back to the present, and he hastily returned the parcel of velvet to the dark recesses of his pocket. He cleared his throat and turned toward the doorway to find Arabella hovering there as though poised to flee at the slightest startling move.

She looked an angel in sky-blue satin, camellias fastened in her hair.

Myles crossed the room, taking Bella's chill hands in his

own. "And where, pray tell, is Devlin? I had begun to think that you and my betrothed were chained together at the wrist, you are so seldom apart."

"D-Devlin?" Arabella fidgeted with the wedding ring encircling her finger. "Why, I—I believe she slipped outside for a bit to . . . to watch the stars."

"Watch the stars? Devlin?" Myles queried, as astonished as though Arabella had claimed Devlin to be counting the sinners in hell. "This meeting with the prince must have unsettled her more than I had thought. I believe I shall steal out to observe this miracle. Tell your husband that we shall be waiting outside."

With a courtly bow in Arabella's direction Myles exited the house. The cool night breeze caressed his cheeks as he paused at the head of the stairs, watching for just a moment the lone figure leaning upon a crumbling pillar. Swathed in a cloak and hood from the top of her head to the tips of her shoes stood Devlin, a pensive Persephone peering out across the lost heavens.

His heart lurched as he glimpsed the curve of her cheek, just visible beneath the edge of her hood, silhouetted in pale ivory against the night. And he wanted to go to her, to slip his fingers beneath the rippling scarlet satin framing her face, to ease it back until he could thread his hands through her hair, skim his palms against her cheeks, lower his own mouth down to those lips that were at once so full of challenge and of the promise to be infinitely sweet.

Steadying himself, Myles walked to where Devlin stood, still seemingly oblivious to the fact that anyone had come to intrude upon her vigil.

He stopped an arm's length away, feeling strangely awkward. But he cleared his throat to alert her to his presence. She turned, and to his frustration he found that her face was still all but hidden in the shadows beneath her hood.

"Good evening, my lady," he said softly. "I was awaiting you in the drawing room."

"Were you?" Was there the slightest hesitation in her voice? "I . . . I was only just looking at the stars. They are quite pleasant tonight."

"Doubtless they count themselves flattered that you noticed them at all," Myles said, his hand slipping into his pocket to close about the waiting parcel. "I had been hoping that you would come down to the drawing room early so that I might give you something . . . a gift that I . . . well, that I hoped might add a certain beauty, a certain richness to the gown Madame DuPres created for you."

"You needn't have gone to any such trouble. The gown—it is quite complete as it is, and—and beautiful. I vow, I needn't so much as a bit of gilt lace to make it perfect."

"No, I am certain that the modiste made sure you were laced and stitched from here to eternity, but even so, a woman needs other ornaments besides her gown. She needs jewelry. Just a touch of some gem glittering upon the ballroom floor, catching up rainbows of light and sending them scattering to the ends of the room."

"No, Myles, I am quite sure that I don't need any such trinkets to—"

"I need to give them to you. Here." He extended the velvet-wrapped parcel toward her, his pulse speeding up with anticipation. "Take it," he urged. "I promise you it won't bite."

He could feel her smile. "Then you have not strung me a necklet of honeybees with stingers poised?"

Myles chuckled. "First the nettles in my shirt, and then honeybees about one's neck? I am afraid you are quickly overtaking me in the realm of mischief, my lady."

"You were a good tutor."

Myles was stirred by the husky note in her voice, and his own voice was a bit unsteady as he said, "You were always the better student of the two of us. I shall endeavor to be most cautious when in your company."

He was rewarded by the soft sound of Devlin's laugh, a laugh that was touched with a hint of nervousness.

"So," he prodded, "I give you my word as a gentleman that this parcel does not contain poisonous snakes, stinging insects, or even nettlesome plants."

Devlin took a step near him, her cloak brushing against his thighs. The contact of the rich fabric abrading those tensed muscles was mind-numbingly seductive. When she took the package the touch of her fingertips upon his palm sent jolts of awareness to heat his more private parts.

He swallowed the surge of desire lodged in his throat and watched her fingers carefully slipping the knot, wondering what it would be like to feel those same fingers, bare of their kid gloves, unfastening the fall of lace about his throat, opening the shirt that lay beneath it. His breath came fast, shallow beneath the weight of the imagined caress as he watched her unfolding the rich fabric from his gift.

The wrapping fell away, the glow from the lantern light cascading down across the ivory miniature.

Devlin gasped as she cradled the object in her palms and walked over closer to the coach's bobbing lamp. Myles could see even in the dim light how wide, how bright her eyes were, how unsteady the fingers that held the bit of jewelry, its ribbon rippling down from her fingertips.

"Oh. Oh, Myles." Soft, stunned, her voice warmed him. "It is beautiful."

"The woman must be your ancestor," Myles said gruffly, "for I found her image amid the other treasures we found in your father's cache of jewels. Look and you'll see that the similarity is truly amazing. She even tips her chin up at the same angle you do, as if she were daring someone to take a whack at it."

"We're not alike at all. This woman is beautiful."

"And so are you."

"Myles, you needn't stoop to stuffing my ears with your ridiculous compliments. We both know I am not beautiful in the least, and—"

"You are. Beautiful in the same way as this cavalier's lady. Strong. Capable. And yet possessed of a wonderfully keen wit."

"You were able to gauge all of this from the picture? You must be most astute."

"Only where this is concerned. Her name is etched upon the back, here." He turned the piece over in her palm and traced the line with his fingertip. "Lady Brianna of Arransea."

Devlin skimmed her thumb softly across the writing, as if attempting to assure herself it was real. "I remember Papa speaking of a Lady Brianna when I was small. There was a story . . . one romantic enough to satisfy even you."

"I could feel a tale within it from the first time I saw her face. Tell me."

"She was Irish . . . of simple blood in the time when Cromwell was laying Ireland to waste. She fell in love with an English noble pledged to the Royalist cause."

"Her love . . . did it end in heartbreak?" Myles asked, stunned at how deeply he cared about the fate of this woman captured forever in the bit of jewelry Devlin held.

"I'm not certain. I remember Papa saying that the lady married her love. But whether they were happy I cannot say."

Myles stared down at the painted image Devlin had turned in her hand, the cavalier's lady peering up at him as though she knew some kind of secret, something infinitely precious. Doubtless her love for her bold English lord.

Suddenly a thought struck him, and he grasped Devlin by the arm. "The sword, Dev. The one we found at the priest hole! It must have been Arransea's sword—Lady Brianna's husband's." Myles took up the necklet. "We'd best be getting to the ball. If you would just open your cloak, I could fix this about your neck."

Devlin's fingers went to the fastening beneath her chin, then jerked to a stop. "Oh . . . I forgot. I—I am garbed already, and . . ." Her eyes locked with his. "Myles, the necklace is beautiful. A wondrous gift. But I—I don't think . . ."

"It's magical, Dev. I can feel it."

"Enchanted crowns, and now magical necklaces?"

"Maybe the miniature is not magic, Dev," he breathed, "but I want it to be. Want it to be magic for us." The words left him vulnerable, and he wished to hell he could see her eyes.

The silence stretched out, long heartbeats filled with things he couldn't say, things she was not ready to hear.

"I suppose that I could use a touch of magic right now,"

she said after a moment. "Do you think Lady Brianna would listen if I petitioned her to shorten the road from London to Scotland, or to turn time backward to that last day at Liancourt when the soldiers came?"

Myles looked at her, glad that his own emotions were not visible to her eyes. "Sometimes we wish for things that we think we want without realizing that they are not the things we need to be happy at all. Maybe it is better just to trust the fates, rather than demanding . . ."

Demanding that Tracey come back into your life, he thought, when I want you now, need you. Demanding that I never had the chance to kiss you in the rose garden, or hold you in the Dower House. Demanding that we not be given this chance, this precious chance at beginnings. Because . . .

Because I love you, Dev.

The certainty jolted through him like a sword thrust, cleaving away years of denial, years of flinging himself into affair after meaningless affair in an effort to hold the truth at bay.

He loved her—Devlin the Terrible—the woman who had boiled his smallclothes in dye made of raspberries, the woman who had snipped the stitches in the seat of his breeches so that they would burst when he bowed to pretty Amanda Crawley. The woman who had sat up with him those endless nights when his mother had been teetering upon the brink of death, her small hands, already comfortingly capable, slipping some herbal brew between Lady Caroline's lips while Devlin managed at the same time to scold him for his lack of faith that his mother would get well.

Sweet God, when had it happened—this falling in love? Or had it been there forever, like the stars and the moon, hidden by the blinding light of day, but present, ever present nonetheless?

Had it been there during the days he had teased Devlin with his boyish pranks, attempting any crazed scheme to get her attention? Had it been there the day he had climbed into the carriage to become foster son to the Tracey family?

Had it been there—that tearing, restless, desperate sensation—when he had waited outside his grandfather's study, knowing that the duke was arranging her betrothal to another man?

Thunder in heaven, Myles thought, disgusted, he should have known long ago that he loved her—should have recognized a thousand signs.

Myles Farringdon, the notorious rake, the man who could gather a hive of beauties about him with a flick of one hand, was always finding them lacking when held up against Devlin's wit, Devlin's intelligence.

Myles Farringdon had come within days of watching the woman he loved walk up the aisle of the Liancourt chapel to become another man's wife, share another man's bed, bear another man's sons.

The very thought of another man, any man, even his friend Tracey, touching Devlin made Myles's blood boil. And he clung to the sense of unutterable relief that the fates, in the shape of one of King George's soldiers, had stepped in to give him one chance . . . one precious chance to win the only thing he'd ever really wanted. Not Devlin's approval, as he had thought all these years, but rather something deeper, something stronger. Something that even now might be forever beyond his grasp.

His breath seemed to freeze in his throat as he stared at her face.

I love you, Dev.

He formed the words with his lips, wondering if he would ever be able to speak them aloud, wondering whether he would ever see her eyes light up in answer.

His throat constricted as he realized that there would be only one torture more agonizing than watching Devlin Chastain become the bride of another man.

That would be to have her be his wife and fill the Farringdon cradle with his babes, all the while knowing that she did not love him at all.

Devlin sat quietly in the rocking coach, oblivious to Bella's nervous chatter and Harry's answering laughs. Oblivious to everything except the man sitting so close beside her, his shoulder brushing hers, his scent—leather, horses, and rare spices—teasing her nose, his kindness back at the Camerons' home filling her thoughts.

Her hands clenched on her lap, her mind whirling. Why in the name of God did Myles have to do such a thing? What uncanny instinct had made him dredge out from the whole sackful of jewels taken from the Dower House the one thing, the single object she would have wanted most of all?

Lady Brianna of Arransea.

The name rippled through Devlin's mind like the strains of a familiar lullaby—and in truth, that was what the story had been. The tale she had pleaded for when she had clambered upon her father's knee, the game that she had played while in the garden indulging in bouts of make-believe.

That had been when she still pretended things, when she, too, had treasured legends and myths and tales of heroism. When she had believed in enchanted crowns and happily ever afters, and in the fact that her father was invincible.

Before Josiah Chastain had ended his life. Before Agatha Chastain had chosen to exile herself in Caroline Farringdon's house, putting Devlin in the role of charity child. Before Devlin's whole world had crumbled beneath her feet, leaving her wandering, lost.

But during all that time the treasure had been waiting, enough jewels hidden in the nook in the wall to set both Devlin and Lady Agatha up in comfort for more years than Devlin could count.

It was unthinkable that her mother would allow her to suffer so deeply from pride stung with dependency on Myles's family. It was unthinkable that Lady Agatha had not retrieved Devlin's birthright, but in the end had tossed the lot of it off to Myles, as though independence was of no consequence. As though Devlin were not a daughter at all, but rather some sidesprit born on the wrong end of a barely tolerated husband's blanket.

The coach lurched, and Devlin hazarded a glance at the man sitting beside her, his long legs stretched across until they all but buried themselves in the folds of Bella's petticoats, his eyelids half-closed, as if meditating on something that at once troubled and delighted him. He caught Devlin's eye, then looked away, as if he feared she would read his thoughts; but tonight Devlin had enough thoughts of her own to duel with, enough inner battles to fight before the coachman drew rein amid the crush of carriages and coaches converging upon MacCreedy House.

Devlin nibbled at the full curve of her lower lip, agonizingly aware of the lining of her cloak brushing against the exposed skin of her décolletage—even more aware of what Myles's reaction would be when she at last shed the cloak to reveal that his gift was pillowed upon a veritable sea of exposed skin, rose-blushed bosom serving as a foil to display the image of the Lady Brianna.

For an instant, just as Bella and Harry exited into the night, Devlin had entertained the notion of slipping upstairs and enlisting Bella's aid in donning the green silk her friend had offered. But before Devlin could think of a plausible excuse Myles and Harry were hustling both women into the waiting equipage, neither man wanting to be late when their host was soon to be their king.

Devlin huddled closer in her corner of the coach, attempting to keep as far away from Myles as possible, but it was as if the man filled the equipage to bursting with his broad shoulders and long legs, the dark waves at the top of his head skimming the ceiling of the vehicle.

There was something daunting about him tonight, something in the way his voice had gentled when he had offered her the velvet-wrapped miniature. Something about his eagerness that she be pleased with his offering. He could be so infernally puzzling—first teasing her to the brink of tears, baiting her into a fury, then showing such tenderness, such kindness, all unexpected, like the sun bursting out during the midst of a summer storm. It put her off balance, it made her furious, it confused her.

And usually it goaded her into doing something abominably foolish, like spraining her wrist attempting to rig a pail of water over Myles's door, or staining her hands scarlet dyeing his smallclothes pink—or, she thought wryly, dressing herself to meet Bonnie Prince Charles with half her bosom falling out of her bodice.

Beneath the veiling of her cloak she tugged at the edging of silver gilt that cut across her breasts in an effort to draw it up higher, but the cloth fit skin-tight, the stomacher stiff as if it had been wrought out of iron. Not so much as the smallest bit of fabric could be coaxed to cover bared skin that was already burning with anticipated embarrassment.

A lull in the conversation between Harry and Bella made Devlin look up to catch her friend's troubled blue gaze, and Devlin was aware of how much the brave smile Bella shot her cost the gentle young woman.

"Myles, Devlin was so excited when . . . when she saw Madame DuPres's creation."

Devlin flinched at Arabella's attempt to aid in her prank.

"Bella," she said a little desperately, "please."

But Arabella merely plunged on. "It was all Devlin could talk about . . . how kind it had been of you to order it up. And to . . . to have it suit her so perfectly."

Devlin blanched as Myles's face angled toward her, the lantern light kissing his lips as they curved into a heart-melting smile. "I wanted it to be right for you, Dev. Everything you had dreamed. Madame DuPres had chosen a velvet the hue of apricots, but I thought this . . . the sea-green . . . was the same shade as your eyes."

"I thought you hated the color of my eyes, since you spent so much time trying to black them," Devlin said, battling to keep a light aura.

"Your eyes hold every color of green touched into a meadow."

Devlin all but choked, mistrusting the heavy, guarded expression in his eyes. "I—I can see full well how you have managed to accrue such a reputation with the ladies, Myles, but you are wasting your time attempting to flatter me."

"Am I? I wonder." His voice was liquid velvet touched with some dark secret she had never heard in it before. Her pulse hammered in her throat.

"Myles has always been the most gallant of rogues," Bella put in helpfully. "Why, the last time I was at a soiree with him I overheard him quoting whole rafts of poetry to Lady Cristofiori. She was garbed in the most stunning dress. All pink, it was, with the sweetest lace upon the bodice."

Harry's bluff laugh boomed out. "As I recall, there was scarcely enough material upon the woman's chest to give it such an illustrious title. 'Twas nothing but a quilt-patch here and here, Devlin, I swear to you. With a little scrap o' lace between 'em."

Devlin felt her stomach churn in time to the rocking of the coach, a coach now filled with Myles's darkening scowl.

"Blast it, Cameron, Devlin has no interest whatsoever in my past affairs. We've all of us hurled ourselves into reckless adventures when we were first men."

"Aye," Harry said with a teasing sigh. "Only *some* of us"—he leaned across to jab Myles in the knee—"*some* of us got the pleasure of indulging in a good many more such escapades than the rest of us poor sods."

Devlin felt Myles's arm tense where it brushed against her, his voice laced with anger. "Be that as it may, what matters is whether or not one continues to indulge in such games after he falls in . . . I mean after he pledges himself as husband. And I can assure you I've had my fill of women who cast their favors as freely as they cast their smiles, and liaisons with naught save a quick, hot passion that burns itself out before the next day. I want more now. So much more."

A strangled sound came from Devlin's throat, and he looked down at her, an odd hurt tingling the blue of his eyes.

"Is that so surprising, Dev?" he asked. But she didn't know what to answer. Didn't know what to say. She, who had always prided herself upon the witty repartee, the quick verbal riposte that disarmed one's foe.

It was as if Myles had wrenched away some weapon she had not known she possessed.

"Is that so surprising?" he had asked her, the arrogant lines of his face so sober, the smile gone from his eyes, from his lips.

She shook herself inwardly, turning to peer out the coach window in confusion as she battled with a dozen warring emotions, perceptions of both herself and him.

She had always assumed that Tracey wanted things such as she did—security, stability, a strong marriage to build a future upon. But when Myles spoke in that somber tone there was no questing for stability, but rather shared dreams; no wish for security, but instead a quest for joy. Some idealistic, fantasy-hazed union that he could weave into a lifetime of perfect dreams.

Some bastion of hope, of miracles, of faith that plodding, practical people like Devlin could never hope to capture.

The coach lurched to a halt, and Devlin was suddenly aware that it had drawn to a stop before the gray stone mansion of Cadman MacCreedy, tucked comfortably near to Holyrood House. The magnificent structures blurred before eyes suddenly misted with melancholy, a melancholy that did not fade even as Myles took her arm to assist her down from the coach, making her one more splash of color within a veritable rainbow of elegance and laughter.

Her feet felt leaden as he escorted her into the entryway,

liveried footmen hastening over to relieve the guests of their cloaks. Bella's was swept away first, and Harry's as well, and Devlin watched as the Camerons joined the throngs waiting to be announced by the footman, standing resplendent in front of the ballroom door.

Devlin felt a moment of panic as she watched her friend disappear, and her fingers clutched at the edges of her own flowing cloak. But she could hardly spend the entire evening huddled within the rich folds of velvet, no matter what the consequences of her foolish defiance might be.

Ever one to pay her forfeit for disasters of her own making, she straightened as a chipper cricket of a servant hopped over to her side.

She turned her back to Myles, who had been set upon by two exquisitely garbed men already chattering about wild schemes and reckless sorties.

With numb fingers she slipped the hood from tresses that had been swept high in an arrangement so intricate it had made Devlin's brain ache to look at it.

Trembling, her fingers moved to work the fastening of her cloak, the simple clasp seeming a mystery beyond solving. But after a moment the folds of velvet slipped away, the slight chill drifting over her shoulders, trickling down into the valley between her breasts to pool along the edge of the bodice until it seemed as though every nerve within her whole body was centered there, waiting for the brush of Myles's gaze, the fury, the horror, the hurt that would streak across his face.

For she would shame him, Devlin knew with sudden, sick certainty. She had never meant to, but she would shame the proud Viscount Liancourt here, among his peers, his friends, his prince.

She fretted her lip with her teeth, her gaze darting about, anxiously seeking some nook or some cranny where she might draw Myles off, some secluded place where they could be alone when she turned to display to him the full effect of the gown she wore.

Somewhere he could be shielded from the rest of these ogling peacocks, where his first reaction might be dulled before he fell beneath their keen, gossip-hungry gaze. But there was not so much as a piece of statuary she could dodge behind without wading through a score of other guests.

She flattened her palm against the bared skin, as if she could somehow hide it, the setting of the miniature impressed against her hand as the footman hustled away with her cloak.

Myles's hand rested lightly against her back, his breath stirring the tendrils of hair at the nape of her neck as he leaned close to whisper. "Surely this cannot be the same little termagant who dumped a whole box of the finest Poudre à la Marechale out her bedchamber window the last time her maid attempted to arrange her hair?"

"I—I thought I would try . . ." Devlin's tongue felt too thick in her mouth. "Madame DuPres insisted—"

Oh, God, she thought wildly, if only she could spend the whole night with her back toward Myles. If only she could feign illness. She fought a mad urge to race after the quickly disappearing footman in an effort to retrieve her cloak.

"The back of your coiffure looks lovely," Myles said. "And you perceive me positively agog to see what it looks like from the front." The familiar teasing note was in his voice again, gentled but a whisper with that disturbing new tenderness. "Turn around, sweeting."

"Turn around," Devlin echoed numbly, but she couldn't seem to force her slippered feet to move.

Myles chuckled, that rich, warm sound that seemed contrived to force everyone else in the room to join in his pleasure. His hands cupped her shoulders, his palms warm, hard, even through the layer of his gloves.

He spun her around in the same circular motion he had taken such pleasure in when they had been children playing at hoodman blind. Then he had whirled her and whirled her until she had been dizzy beneath the shielding of her blindfold, staggering so drunkenly she all but crumpled to a heap upon the grass of the courtyard.

But this time, when she came to a stop facing Myles, it was he who looked as though the very earth were writhing madly beneath him, setting his knees to buckling, and

Devlin wished desperately for the blindfold they had used as children so that she could wrap it about the dark waves of his hair, swathing his eyes in fine linen to hide the emotions warring within them.

The mass of guests about them appeared to blur, to fade, until they seemed alone in the crowded room, sick shock draining Myles's bronzed visage of all color.

The hands that had still rested upon her shoulders slipped limply to his sides as his disbelieving gaze raked a path from the plumes tucked in the curls at her temple to the reddened, glistening lips, and finally to her most reckless folly of all, the tiny patch of velvet affixed at the soft crest of her bosom.

And in that instant Devlin felt an inexplicable urge to burst into tears. "Myles, I—"

"I'm going to kill that infernal Frenchwoman!" His eyes were savage. "The very instant I get you the devil out of here!"

He grabbed Devlin's wrist, dragging her toward the footman who had just reappeared. "Retrieve Mistress Chastain's cloak at once. I—"

"No! No, Myles," Devlin hissed, glancing about at the clusters of curious onlookers filling the entryway. "You can hardly drag me from beneath the prince's very nose because I am not dressed to suit you!"

"Damn it, Dev, I'll not have you subjected to appearing garbed like a Fleet Street doxy!"

"I'm not being subjected to anything. I chose to look the way I do tonight."

"Chose to?"

"I was angry, Myles, at the way you . . . you were ordering me about, arranging my life," she began, her hands trembling.

Hurt blazed in his eyes, and Devlin felt as though she had shattered something precious, returned the kindness he had shown with a cruelty that disgusted her.

"I told you in the rose garden that next time you wanted to cause me pain you should just tell me what agony you wish me to inflict upon myself, rather than scratching yourself with nettles or undertaking some other crazed scheme," he said bitterly. "If you wanted to humiliate me before the assembled company, you should have told me. I would have been happy to appear wearing no breeches."

"It's true that I colored my lips and applied the patches to aggravate you. But you were the one who hired that dreadful Frenchwoman in the first place and insisted I not see the gown until I was dressing for the ball."

"I suppose that—shy, retiring flower that you are—it would never have occurred to you to come to me and tell me what that incompetent fool of a seamstress had done. Damn it, I told the woman how important it was for this dress to be perfect. I told her—"

"It seems that she was somewhat dazzled by the patronage of the notorious Myles Farringdon."

"What the devil?"

"She assured me that this was just the kind of gown that—that you preferred."

"On women I flirt with, dance with. But not on you, Dev. Damn it, not on you!" His voice cracked, and she saw a muscle in his jaw knot with the effort it was taking to hold his temper.

But for some unfathomable reason his words wounded her, needling her pride, stirring up her own formidable temper.

"I suppose you'd prefer *me* to be swathed up to my chin in cotton wool, my hair done up in two braids! After all, I'm not a woman. I'm just Devlin, a burden of duty to be borne about your neck!"

"Damn it to hell, don't you even begin to say that, think that!" Myles grasped her arms, his fingers pressing deep into the soft flesh. "You're different, Dev, different from all of them. You always have been."

"Maybe I don't want to be." Devlin's chin jutted up in defiance. "Maybe tonight I want to be one of these pleasure-drunk butterflies that flit about a ballroom, batting their eyelashes and waving their fans. Maybe I want . . . want men to notice me for once, instead of spending the whole evening as I have so many times before, listening to the other women making jest of me behind their fans."

"If another man so much as looks at you . . ." His eyes flashed murderously.

"You keep insisting that you want us to be wed. Want me to be your betrothed. Tell me, Myles, what would all of these illustrious friends of yours think if I were to appear in some modest, maidenly garb? Something a girl fresh from the schoolroom might wear? Can you imagine what speculation would entertain your friends, yes, and your enemies as well, as they attempted to figure out why the most noted rakehell in Christendom was enchanted with such an unsophisticated woman? A woman with no dowry to speak of, and no great beauty?"

"God forbid that they be fools enough to believe that I love you," Myles bit out.

The words twisted deep inside Devlin, and she gave a pain-filled laugh. "I am afraid that even with your grand skill at playacting you could never convince them of such a tale as that. No. They will be certain that you have been trapped into wedding me. That I have somehow snared you in a web of my own devising, and that you are far too honorable, too bound by duty to your family to cut me adrift as I deserve. You are not the only one between us who is possessed of pride, Myles Farringdon."

Blue eyes turned black as a storm-tossed sky. "You want to be treated as just another one of my women? You want them to believe that I lust after you, that I wish to display your charms as one would display a pretty trinket? So be it then." He sketched her a mocking bow, the heat of his lips just grazing the patch at her breast. Devlin leapt back, the wisp of moistness left by his mouth seeming hot as acid, making her skin burn.

"Blast it, Myles! Stop—"

Devlin was alarmed to see the recklessness, the hard, defiant light in Myles's eyes that she had learned to fear since childhood. His lips curved into a mirthless smile.

"You are the one who has insisted we play this game, my little dove," he purred. "And far be it from me to deny your heart's desire."

Myles captured her hand in his, forcing her to link her

arm through the crook of his elbow. "Now, shall we provide the prince's guests with enough of a spectacle to keep them gossiping for weeks?"

"I think I'd rather not," Devlin said, attempting to hang back.

"You'd best resolve to brazen this out, my sweet," Myles said, low, dangerous. "You've made bloody certain neither one of us has any other choice."

Myles cast an arrogant glance at the servant eyeing them with inquiry from the doorway. "You may announce us."

Devlin felt a shudder of something akin to dread ripple through her as the servant's voice rang out.

"Lord Myles Farringdon, Viscount Liancourt, and Mistress Devlin Chastain."

Devlin cringed inwardly as she felt dozens of heads turn toward her, people straining upon tiptoe, craning their necks to see the woman who was to be Farringdon's bride. A hush blanketed the ballroom, then swelled into a sea of whispering before the level of noise again grew to its previous pitch. If it had been possible to sink through the floor, Devlin would have done so gladly. But Myles was already piloting her relentlessly across the room.

Devlin caught a glimpse of Bella and Harry sipping refreshments with a bevy of bright-faced girls. But Myles did not go to join the Camerons. Rather, he guided Devlin toward a tall figure who stood at the far end of the room.

From the time she had been a child Devlin had heard tales of the exiled prince. In truth, during the past weeks she had cursed Charles Edward Stuart as soundly as she had cursed the fools who followed him. But as she looked upon the Young Pretender for the first time she was stunned to find herself moved in a way she had never suspected possible. For if ever there had been a prince fashioned in face and form and manner to win the hearts of even his most reluctant subjects, it was this man.

Dark wine-colored velvet encased shoulders only a little narrower than Myles's, Charles Stuart's tall, athletic build making him stand out amid the crowd of people thronging about him. A powdered wig was perched upon a noble brow, exceedingly handsome features made even more appealing by a pair of fine brown eyes.

Eyes that lit with pleasure when they fixed upon Myles.

"Farringdon! Welcome!" Charles called in bluff greeting.

"Good evening, Your Highness." Myles swept the prince his most gallant bow. "May I present Mistress Devlin Chastain? The woman who is to make me the happiest of men."

"The happiest of men?" Charles chuckled. "I wonder how many of our sex have said those selfsame words only to find themselves quite miserable by the same time next year."

Devlin felt those sparkling brown eyes upon her.

"Tell me, madam, what is it to be for our friend Farringdon? Do you intend to drown him in torrents of marital bliss or torrents of reproachful tears?"

Devlin dropped low into a curtsy. "I intend to drown him in any way I can contrive, Your Highness," she said with acid sweetness.

The prince laughed aloud, clapping Myles on the shoulder. "She is delightful, Myles, delightful."

"All I can say is that should I ever turn up missing, you would do well to search the lochs."

Charles flicked open a jewel-encrusted snuffbox and raised a pinch delicately to his nose. "I was beginning to fear that both you and your betrothed were missing. Travers and MacPhee were laying wagers upon whether or not you had decided to hie off and elope, leaving the lot of us mad with curiosity."

"No, no, Your Highness, we were but detained a while longer than planned. You know how women are, flitting about burying themselves in powders and perfumes, and fussing over everything from their garters to their petticoats before such a function as this. I fear I could not have blasted Devlin from before the mirror were I to rummage out every keg of powder in the powder magazine."

Devlin dug her nails into the muscled flesh of Myles's forearm, wishing for some sharp object to gouge him through the rich layer of fabric.

"Well, Mistress Chastain," the prince said, raising her

fingertips to his lips, "I can only affirm that the usual feminine delays would be worthwhile if the results achieved were always so lovely." The royal eyes swept in an appreciative path down, pausing long seconds at the place where the teasing, taunting little patch shone soft, dark, and inviting against the rosy swell of her breast.

Devlin's cheeks burned so hot she was stunned that they did not break out into flames.

"Thank you, Your Highness. I—I fear in the country, at Liancourt, we seldom have such illustrious entertainments as this, so I am not much of an expert when it comes to such affairs. But Lord Myles most generously offered me his guidance as to what I should wear."

She heard a sound low in Myles's chest and for an instant feared that he would contradict her, humiliate her before the prince, but Myles only skimmed a most seductive, patronizing caress over her cheek and favored the prince with a conspiratorial wink.

"I have always had a special gift for favorably displaying rare treasures, have I not, Your Highness? And my betrothed is the hardest-won treasure I have ever had in my possession. Unfortunately, unlike rare statuary or paintings or jewels, I cannot stand her in the corner of the gallery when something about her displeases me."

"And what, pray tell, could ever displease you about so beautiful a lady?"

"I fear that Devlin is most opinionated. In fact, all through our journey to join you here in Scotland she was devising strategies we should use to conquer England."

Charles laughed, and Devlin felt as if she would perish at any moment from shame. "So you are marrying a petticoat general, my friend?"

"A most accomplished general who can outflank me whenever she chooses."

"A dangerous predilection in a wife—especially one with a face as lovely as Mistress Chastain's."

"Devlin would never stoop to mere coquetry to get her way. No, it would be more like breaking out the heavy artillery and setting the cavalry to a charge. She has read more works on military strategy than you could ever imagine. And I can assure you that she has a set opinion on every military engagement in recorded history."

"Is that so?" Charles turned to Devlin, his eyes watchful, just a whisper cool. "And what think you of our chances, Mistress Chastain, were we to press on to London Town?"

Devlin hazarded a glance at Myles, then turned back to meet the prince's gaze with a level one of her own. "When I came to Scotland I did not believe your forces had any chance at all, matched against Hanover's might. But now . . . now I believe . . ."

She drew a deep breath, knowing full well what Myles's reaction would be to her next words. "Your Highness, you have managed to gain so much with so little. Scotland is in your hands. If you tend to this kingdom first, justly, wisely, you will win far more of your English subjects to your ranks than you will by charging across the border with your muskets blazing."

Charles gave her a look so patronizing her teeth clenched. "A most interesting opinion. And one with which many of my advisors would concur. However, I am afraid that your betrothed would most heartily disagree."

Myles looped his arm about her shoulders, his fingers toying with the long curl that lay pillowed upon the top of her breast. Devlin wanted to jam her elbow into his ribs. "Mistress Chastain and I agree upon only one thing," he laughed, his finger dipping near the tiny black patch, "and that is that the two of us *disagree* about nearly everything."

"Is that so? I predict that will make for a most . . . eventful marriage," Charles observed. "Are you certain that you want to court so much controversy within the confines of your own bedchamber?"

"Ah, but the bedchamber is where I intend to win my victories over her, Your Highness," Myles said with a laugh. "I have earned my title as rakehell most justly, and I intend to apply all my hard-won knowledge to, shall we say, *convince* my new bride to see things from my own vantage point."

Bawdy laughter erupted all around them, and Devlin felt

her whole body burn with humiliation. But she only smiled over gritted teeth. "Is that your battle strategy, my lord? Then I would recommend you call in reinforcements, for thus far I have not been overly impressed with the sorties you have made in that regard."

Myles's lips went white, his fingers crushing the curl he still held, and Devlin was glad she had returned in kind the verbal lashes he had been dealing her. She could sense the effort it took for him to release the lock of her hair, his fingers tense as he smoothed it back into place. His feigned a smile. "Strange, my love. I have never received any complaints before upon my prowess. Perhaps I shall have to be more vigorous in my efforts where you are concerned. Shall we lock in this latest battle upon the dance floor? I believe they are striking up a minuet."

Devlin glared at him. "I do not care to dance with you at all, my lord. Most especially—"

It was the prince himself who intervened, speaking to them as if they were quarrelsome children. "Off with the both of you! All of Edinburgh is waiting for this wedding you have promised them two days hence, and we order you not to disappoint them. Now dance, dance. Perhaps it will remind both of you of the far more passionate dance you shall be sharing once you pull the curtains about your nuptial bed."

Myles swept the prince a bow, then grasped Devlin's fingers so hard they ached as he propelled her out among the other dancers who had gathered upon the ballroom's vast floor.

Music drifted from the strings of violins, the keys of the harpsichord, the strains as sweet as Devlin's mood was poison. Myles swept her a bow reeking of masculine arrogance, and she dropped into an equally mocking curtsy, the gestures as filled with challenge as the movements of two duelists about to take the field.

"So," Devlin said as Myles began to guide her through the steps of the dance, "we are now commanded to marry by the prince, are we? Do you think that if I refused he would do me the favor of lopping off your head?"

"As taken as he was with you, he'd most likely allow you to wield the axe." Myles released her hand, circling with animal grace. "But I fear no such merciful a fate awaits either one of us. Rather, we are both destined to lay ourselves upon a block of another kind—that of the marriage bed."

"I have told you that it will not be so. Tracey will come. And even if he does not, I shall be damned before I take any such vows with you! You who made jest of me, humiliated me a-purpose—"

"I am not the one who intentionally wore a dress open to my very navel!"

"You would look ridiculous in a dress at all," Devlin said, laughing in spite of herself, "though I vow I'd give ten years of my life to see you rigged out in this one."

"I might consider it a fair exchange—making a fool of myself for a brief span in order to be free of your viperish tongue for an entire decade. Except that I fear I have far too much modesty to thus display myself. And when you are in truth my wife, I promise you that *you* will learn to feel the same."

"Ah, yes, I would be marrying Myles Farringdon, Viscount Liancourt—that paragon of virtue, advocate of seemly behavior."

Myles had the grace to turn scarlet. "You needn't attempt to change the subject. We were not discussing *my* myriad transgressions."

"And it is a good thing, too. If we began that gargantuan task, you'd be sporting a head of white hair by the time we had finished."

"And you, my poor dearling, would be pining away upon your spinster's bed, your virtue withered and bitter like fruit gone unplucked from its vine."

"Are you so certain my virtue would be unplucked, even if the chandelier were to topple down and crush me in the midst of this minuet?"

For an instant Myles looked as if he had indeed been struck by the huge confection of crystal and glowing candles that dangled above their heads.

His feet, customarily so graceful, faltered in the patterns of the dance. His fingers crushed hers. But in that instant she knew she would remember the expression that slashed into his eyes forever . . . the black-fringed depths rounded in shock and a swift, raw vulnerability, as if she had slipped a dagger between his ribs.

Devlin's own heart stumbled at Myles's pain, pain so sudden and unexpected it squeezed the breath from her lungs. Her feet felt leaden, the steps of the minuet suddenly as foreign to her as ritualistic dances brought back from Cathay.

She felt the other dancers' eyes upon her, felt Myles still battling to guide her through the patterns. His voice was raw but unyielding.

"Damn it, girl, dance! We have to finish the set or die in the attempt, for I would not have you shamed."

But as he turned her yet again toward the wide-flung doors at the end of the ballroom, what little remained of her equilibrium was yanked from beneath her, making her clutch at Myles's hard arm for balance. Her slippered feet seemed rooted to the floor, immovable, the other dancers blurring into smears of crimson and azure, lilac and amber.

"Dev? Blast it, Dev, are you all right?" Myles caught her in his arms as if he feared she would topple to the floor, his voice seeming to spiral down toward her from some distant cave, echoing and reechoing in her head as she stared at the strangely familiar figure half hidden by the footman stationed at the portal.

Candle shine glinted upon waves of blond hair, one broad shoulder encased in ice-white velvet visible beyond the servant's livery. There must have been half a dozen golden-tressed men within the room who had scorned the affectation of powdering their hair, and yet there was something in the way the newly arrived guest carried himself that was alarmingly familiar.

Devlin's hand shook as she strained to catch more than a glimpse of the man, joy, hope, and an unexpected dread wreaking havoc in her chest.

Then the blond gentleman stepped into full view.

Breeches as pale blue as a winter-struck sky were fastened about his knees with small diamond buckles. A silver waistcoat glistened beneath the impeccable neck cloth knotted under his chin, accenting features as classically perfect as a Greek Adonis. A remarkably high brow bespoke keen intelligence, while steady eyes beneath pale gold brows scanned the ballroom, seeming to take in everything, everyone, in but a heartbeat.

Devlin's breath froze in her throat as the servant's voice pierced through the hum of music, announcing this late-arrived guest.

"The Honorable Braden Tracey."

CHAPTER
17

*M*yles's whole body went rigid where it brushed hers, some throb of emotion racing from his hard chest into her, frightening her as he whipped about toward the entryway.

At that instant Tracey's eyes caught Devlin's, but she was already tearing away from Myles, scooping up her petticoats and racing headlong through the astonished dancers. She wanted nothing more than to fling herself into Tracey's arms, yet before she could act in so rash a fashion Tracey bowed to her, making it impossible for her to do so.

An odd, niggling hurt streaked through her as he raised her hand to lips strangely cold, stiff. "And so, milady," he said, his voice cutting as a sliver of ice, "I hear that congratulations are in order. Allow me to extend my heartiest felicitations upon your marriage to my *most trusted* friend."

Devlin's cheeks burned as Tracey gestured to where Myles stood in the center of the circling dancers, abandoned before the entire assembly when she had dashed off.

She felt a shard of regret gouge deep, but it was eclipsed by the flash of hurt she saw for an instant in Tracey's eyes. She caught at his hand in supplication. "Braden, you can . . . cannot believe that I would marry Myles!"

Tracey's eyes skimmed the nearby footmen, their faces impassive but their eyes showing bold interest in the exchange between the new arrival and Lord Farringdon's lady. Tracey's jaw clenched, and he guided her into an alcove behind a badly executed statue of Venus.

"How could I *not* believe that you intend to wed him?" Tracey demanded, his lip curling in scorn, his voice so low that the servants could not hear. "Since I arrived in the city three hours ago I've heard nothing save news of the viscount's upcoming nuptials with Mistress Devlin Chastain."

"The rumor that we are to wed . . . it was just a mad ruse Myles insisted upon to protect my reputation until we could reach you, make things right."

Tracey's gaze trailed a scathing path from her carefully arranged curls to the tiny black patch at her breast. "I can see just how deeply *my friend* is concerned about protecting your *reputation*. And as for this being a *ruse*, it would seem the both of you have gone to a great deal of trouble to play out this little jest. Basketfuls of roses to be brought in from all over Scotland, a feast planned fit to entertain a potentate. And wine—the finest to be had, imported from God knows where."

"Tracey," Devlin began, but he waved one graceful hand.

"Myles always did have the most uncanny knack for making water into wine. Yes, it seems that your marriage to Myles is to be quite the grand affair. Almost as grand as your marriage to me was supposed to have been."

"You don't understand. I never meant to marry Myles—"

"Then you've given a damned good imitation of it to the rest of the world. You ran off mere weeks before our wedding with a man so notorious for his womanizing that he rivals Bacchus. You set the city on its ear with your preparations for the ceremony. And then you attend a ball given in honor of these coming nuptials at the request of the prince and spend the night draping yourself about your *prospective bridegroom*, garbed in a fashion that would suit the most wanton mistress Myles has ever entertained."

Devlin's cheeks flamed, tears of hurt and confusion biting at her eyelids. "The prince commanded my presence here tonight. I've spent every moment since arriving in Scotland attempting to find some way to reach you."

"It would have been simple enough. You would merely have had to present yourself as planned at the altar at the Liancourt chapel two days ago."

Devlin faltered, battling back the tears as her mind filled with images of that beautiful wedding gown the seamstresses had been fitting upon her the day Myles had arrived. She had planned for the chapel to be banked with gillyflowers, and Cook had been set to working culinary magic for the feast Devlin and Tracey were to have shared.

If all had gone as planned, she would even now be the Honorable Mrs. Braden Tracey off upon her wedding trip to Italy and Greece, reveling in the Parthenon and the Colosseum, the works of Michelangelo and the statues of the ancient Greeks. Everything would be as she and Tracey had planned it for so long.

"I was half crazed when we had to flee for Scotland." Her voice quavered as Tracey's brow arched in cool disbelief. "There was nothing . . . nothing I wanted more than to become your wife. But I—"

Her words ended in a gasp as she felt a hand flatten against the small of her back. Myles's voice, edgy and tensile as a rapier's blade, cut through her stammerings.

"Dev, Tracey is well enough acquainted with my penchant for roguery to know that I am the sole perpetrator of this particular crime."

She looked up into Myles's eyes, expecting them to be filled with relief that he was to be shed of responsibility for her, expecting them to be filled with pleasure at the appearance of his best friend. Instead the azure depths were brimming with guilt, challenge, blended with a fierce regret as they fixed upon Tracey's face.

"This is my fault, all of it. And I'd not blame you if you called me out for what I've done."

"What you've done?" Tracey echoed, mocking.

"I fear I made a most ill-advised visit to Liancourt to bid my mother farewell before riding off upon my mission to secure Charles Stuart's crown. When things went awry

Devlin had the grave misfortune of being the only one available to save my unworthy neck."

"Your *neck*—along with the rest of you—should have been upon the ship the duke and I had hired to take you to France. Not hanging about, tempting the king's headsmen to measure it for an axe blade. Did you not even bother to think what could have transpired if you were caught within Liancourt's gates?"

"You of all people should know that I seldom think of such consequences."

"Perhaps someone should convince you to begin considering the consequences of what you do before you charge about, ruining people's lives."

Devlin felt Myles flinch, expected him to lash out in reply. But he only stood there silently as accusation vibrated deep in Tracey's tones. "God knows I've never been fool enough to attempt to deter you from your crazed schemes. I have even joined in on more occasions than I'd care to count, when I was younger and far more foolish. But I never thought you would be so craven as to drag Devlin into your madness."

She could feel the shudder of guilt that racked Myles, felt his pain as if it had been carried along some invisible connection to her.

"Five hundred guests were set to arrive at Liancourt for the ceremony!" Tracey grated. "The most powerful families in England were to have gathered in her honor! And you haul her off on some crazed race to Scotland, destroying everything."

There was something about the words that seemed to steel Myles, his eyes growing harder as he leveled them upon his friend. "It would seem that this unfortunate incident will prove to your illustrious political allies that I am a far blacker villain than either one of us suspected."

"Damn it, Myles, this is not some jest! I went to a great deal of trouble to assemble a list of guests worthy of this ceremony. Everything was mapped out to perfection! And you—you made the woman who was to serve as my bride into a fugitive from the crown!"

"That crown is none too steady upon German George's head. It could topple at any moment, carrying any charges against Devlin into oblivion along with it."

"And it could remain firmly planted upon the house of Hanover for the next hundred years, making both you and Devlin exiles for life! Even so, my first concern here is not the fate of the throne, but rather the fate of my marriage plans."

Myles jammed his hands in the pockets of his frock coat, guilt and belligerence carving lines deep into his brow. "I'm sorry as hell that I disrupted your *plans,* Tracey. And as for Devlin, I would do anything within my power to remedy things for her."

"Including sacrificing yourself upon the marital altar?" There was venom in Tracey's voice, and it drove deep through Myles's veins. Devlin could see it in the way his shoulders squared, his eyes glittered.

"Short of turning back time, I could think of no other way to make things right." Myles's voice was low, wearied in a way that made Devlin ache for him. "It is a less-than-desirable fate for her, I know, but it is the only protection within my power to give her. Yet if you can think of some other course we can take, I will travel it gladly. Tell me whatever forfeit you would have me pay, and I will meet it."

"Short of turning yourself over to the executioner, I can think of nothing that will change things. And after my betrothed has gone to such lengths to save you from his clutches, it would be most ill-mannered of me to insist you do so, though God knows you deserve no better. Since the day we last spoke in London you have done everything in your power to court this disaster."

How many times had Devlin cursed Myles the same way? Chastised him for embroiling himself in mad schemes? Yet despite her own anger with Myles and her desire to avoid Tracey's scorn, she could not escape the loyalty she and Myles had always felt toward each other when matters were at their worst.

"Braden, I know this is all quite . . . quite upsetting. But sometimes things happen that are . . . well, are truly

209

nobody's fault. Myles might act rashly sometimes, but he hardly planned for the soldiers to come thundering down upon Liancourt. And I was the one who insisted upon aiding his escape. I cannot be sorry I did, for if I hadn't, he would even now be languishing in the Tower, a prisoner of the crown."

"No, Myles can hardly be held responsible for any of this, can he?" Tracey sneered. "The fact that most men would say he was plotting treason is immaterial."

Myles's eyes narrowed, and Devlin glimpsed in them that fiery light that always filled them when he spoke of the Stuart cause. "Some men would call it treason. Some would call it holding loyal to the true king."

Devlin stepped between the two men, men worlds different from when she had last seen them together, hunting at Liancourt, Myles's ringing laughter punctuated by Tracey's more controlled mirth.

Then they had seemed perfect foils for each other— Myles's dark good looks and reckless disposition in counterpoint to Tracey's careful elegance and keen wit.

Yet now it was as if the two men were strangers, hostility raging between them.

"Stop it, both of you," Devlin demanded, laying one hand upon Tracey's waistcoat. "Instead of arguing about rebellion or about who is at fault, let's turn our energies to devising a solution to this difficulty."

"Solution?" A tick at the corner of Tracey's mouth betrayed his frustration. "I already attempted to come up with some rational excuse to cancel our wedding. Before I left London I charged my secretary to send word to everyone invited that you were taken ill, that Myles had kindly taken you off to recover your health at my request."

Devlin brightened a little. "That sounds wonderful. Perfect."

Tracey's expression soured. "It was so perfect that even in the brief time it took me to make ready for my journey I was treated to troughs full of commiseration, served to me by people who had somehow heard the news. The only problem was that while they were expressing their concern for your well-being, their eyes were filled with speculation as to whether, indeed, the rumors they had heard were true—that Myles was a fugitive, and that you had run off with him, not because of ill-health, but rather in a fit of passion."

Devlin felt as if he had struck her.

"Just think," Tracey proceeded in frigid accents, "of how amused they will all be when word filters back to London that Mistress Devlin Chastain was seen dancing with the Viscount Liancourt at a ball given by the Stuart Pretender in honor of their coming marriage."

Myles shrugged again. "Gossip can be quelled easily enough if one possesses the courage to brazen it through." Myles allowed the words to dangle there in the lull, and Devlin sensed that there was a challenge hidden somewhere within them, a taunt that both Myles and Tracey understood. "You might want to consider that while deciding your future with your betrothed."

Tracey sketched Myles a stiff bow. "Thank you *so* much for your sage advice, *friend.* But unfortunately Devlin and I shall have to muddle our way through the disaster you have created *without* your erudite judgment. If you will excuse us, I believe we will retire to the privacy of the gardens."

Devlin felt Tracey's arm link through hers, the gesture somehow disturbingly impersonal as he guided her through the maze of fluttering fans and eyes that were greedy with curiosity. She glanced back to where Myles now stood alone, the burnished waves of his hair framing features dark with worry, his mouth white, his jaw set.

She didn't know what crazed impulse within her made her want to tug free of Tracey's grasp and go back to Myles. Just long enough to smooth back the lock of hair that had straggled across his forehead. Just long enough to ease away the deep creases bracketing his lips.

The night air struck her cheeks, chill with the kiss of autumn, and Devlin promised herself that the moment she reached Bella's after the ball she would assure Myles that she truly meant what she had said to Tracey—that the happenings at Liancourt and upon the dash to Scotland were no one's fault. That they had only been one of fate's cruel little jests set in motion to entertain the gods.

The need to comfort him tore at her, as if she were being rent in two, uncertain where to go, what to say.

She matched her steps to Tracey's measured stride as he threaded his way through hedges washed by the glow of myriad lanterns. At the far end of the pebbled walk a lush arbor curved in a graceful arc, the branches of the trees interwoven over the years through the careful nurturing of some dedicated gardener.

Tracey led her into the entryway just far enough for the glow of one of the lanterns to thread fingers of light across his face.

Then he turned her in his arms and without a word pressed his lips firmly upon hers. Devlin arched her head back, astonished, as he moved his mouth across hers in the way that had once sent shivers of delight racing through her. Her palm flattened against his chest, the beat of his heart steady, the breath from his classically shaped nostrils wisping in shallow, even gusts across her cheek.

She wanted to submerge herself in these familiar pleasant feelings that were far less dangerous than the swirling currents Myles's caresses had evoked from her.

The thought of those hot kisses made her stiffen with guilt, filling her with an urgent need to prove to herself that what had happened in the Dower House had been nothing but a freak mischance—mere illusion spun of fire and smoke in comparison to the rich, warm reality of the regard she and Tracey shared.

But all she could think of was how unsteady Myles's hands had been as he had touched her, as if he were some mortal hero who had dared to worship a goddess with his hands. All she could remember was how his heart had raced and his lips had devoured hers.

A hard knot formed in her chest, and her eyes burned with frustration, self-loathing, and a very real desperation.

She pressed herself against Tracey, threading her fingers

through the perfectly combed strands of his hair. Her cheeks blazed with embarrassment as her tongue stole out in a daring caress against the tight crease of his lips. But even when Tracey's mouth opened, allowing her entry, she felt none of the burning sensations that Myles had awakened within her.

Desperate, Devlin kissed Tracey more fiercely, knowing that she would do anything, anything, to rid herself of the blue-eyed specter that drifted between her and Tracey like some sorcerer's veil.

Yet instead of deepening the kiss, welcoming it, Tracey went still. A tiny, anxious moan formed in Devlin's throat, her fingers tightening where she held him, but he pulled away from her, something flickering beneath his hooded eyelids.

"I—I've missed you," Devlin said, aware that it wasn't exactly true.

"Have you?" There was an edge to Tracey's voice, and Devlin felt as if he could see through the window of her soul, picture every shameful caress, every whimper, every sensation Myles had wrung from her. She swallowed hard, fighting to keep her voice even.

"Myles was certain you wouldn't respond to the letter, but I knew . . . knew that you would come for me the instant you got word that I was in trouble."

"How very wise of you to know that." Tracey's fingertips trailed down her cheek in a soft caress, but there was something in the set of his mouth that made dread curl in the pit of Devlin's stomach. "I would never have allowed anything to befall the woman I intended to take as wife."

"That is what I told Myles. I told him that we loved each other. That this difficulty would mean nothing to you."

"Despite my anger at this . . . inconvenience, I can only be relieved that the two people I care for most in the world are safe."

"Then we can marry. As soon as possible. You can carry me back with you to London." Devlin rushed on, a prickle of unease stirring the hair at her nape as she regarded

Tracey's averted eyes. "Powerful as you have become, I am certain that you can intercede on my behalf with the authorities, and everything can go on just as we planned it for so long."

Tracey pleated the ruffles of lace upon his chest, his face closed, hidden in the shadows. "Of course I shall do my best to help both you and Myles. I've made great strides over the past months with those who wield King George's governmental sword. Swords far more powerful than the mere steel ones Myles is so fond of. If I were to call in . . . shall we say a few vouchers for favors I have extended these past years, I should be able to reduce your peril considerably. Despite my frustration at how unnecessary all of this difficulty has been, Myles is like a brother to me. And you . . . you know exactly how vital you are to my happiness."

Devlin waited for the sensation she had anticipated during the weary wait for Tracey to come—the feeling that the weight of a thousand worlds was toppling from her shoulders as she transferred the burden of worry to Tracey's capable hands. But she only felt even more set adrift.

"We should marry right away," she insisted again, hope fluttering feebly in her breast. "We can spread around the tale that you came to Scotland to visit me, rushed to my side in agonies of worry. And that we could not bear to wait another moment to wed since my illness almost kept us apart forever."

Devlin paused to draw breath, and the silence within the rustling arbor seemed to grow heavy. She sank down upon the stone bench, her gaze fixed upon Tracey's face.

The shadows from the lantern illuminated the strong curve of his jaw, the prominent cheekbones, the lines fanning out from the corners of his eyes, the result of too many hours spent poring over his books. There was an obdurate set to his jaw, an impatience in the drumming of his fingers against his other palm. The explanations she and Myles had attempted to give to him seemed to have done little to soften the etchings of betrayal that clung about his face.

214

Devlin's fingers knitted together in her lap, her palms sticky with perspiration beneath the layer of her gloves, and it was as if she could hear Myles's countless gentle warnings that Tracey would never stand firm in his vow to wed her when to do so might endanger his ambitions.

"Tracey," she said, willing him to look at her with that reassuring, calming aura he had always possessed. But when he turned her breath grew raw in her lungs.

He cleared his throat. "Devlin, one of the things I admired about you from the first moment I met you was your intelligence. That ability to see things clearly, practically, in a way no other woman of my acquaintance ever had. But I fear that you are not being in the least practical now."

"Practical? I don't understand."

"I think that you do, although you may not want to." Those hands that had first taught her about passion in the sweet-smelling hay of Liancourt's stables closed over the curves of her shoulders, those keen eyes piercing hers. "Devlin, think. You say that we should marry now, concoct some monstrous tale about your illness and my eagerness to become your bridegroom. We can embroider the tale as we will, but the truth will eventually drift back to London."

"Why should it matter once we are wed? Let the old biddies wear out their tongues with gossiping! It will be too late then. They'll get over it, as Myles said. They'll find someone else to torment."

"Ah, but they will remember the scandal forever. Dredge it out whenever it can prove a useful tool to be turned against me. Powerful imbeciles take greedy pleasure in bringing a man more capable, more intelligent than themselves to his knees with just these sorts of whisperings."

The bench was rough beneath Devlin's fingertips as she curled them against the carved stone. "You are afraid of the mere whispers of gossip mongers?" she said, feeling the first dank stirrings of disillusionment. "Is your position in government so precarious that it cannot withstand so paltry a storm?"

Tracey's lips thinned. "The storm surrounding these happenings would be anything but paltry. It could destroy everything I have worked for, planned for. Everything. Gone."

"I see." It was as if Devlin's voice belonged to a stranger, as if she were watching the scene in the arbor from somewhere above the tangle of branches and leaves, as if it were happening to some other woman—perhaps the lady of high fashion who had stared back at her from the mirror hours ago. "So I am to be dismissed then, as a regrettable but necessary loss to your ambition?"

"No! Never." Tracey turned to her, catching up her hands, and the intent, possessive light in his eyes drove back a little of the chill that had closed about her heart. "I cannot give you up."

"But you just said that you dared not marry me."

"Marriage has little enough to do with love among the Quality. You know that, Devlin. We—we were most blessed that we had affection for each other and were to wed. But many people—respectable, honorable people—are required by circumstances to contrive other ways to find their happiness."

His thumb chafed at her wrist, the abrasion irritating rather than soothing.

"What are you saying?"

"I am saying that Myles is right. That the most expedient way of dissolving this mess is for you to become his bride. It will set you above the wagging tongues of the harpies that would rend you, and you would have the wealth of the Farringdons to buy you anything you care to possess. Not to mention the fact that the Duke of Pothsby would tear out the throat of any who dared to malign you."

"But what good would that do if I am already Myles's wife? To push away the gossip in such a fashion would do nothing to help you and me, nothing to make it possible for us to be together. I would belong to Myles then. Be pledged to Myles."

Tracey pressed the tips of his fingers together, contemplating the steeple they formed. "I know that we could never be legally wed," he said slowly, "but that does not mean that we could not love each other, Devlin."

"In what? Some platonic marriage of the minds, while we go off to the beds of other spouses?"

"I would not be so selfless as that." His eyes met hers, the steadiness now in evidence unsettling her to her very core as he went on. "I would have you come to my bed."

"Your—are you mad?" Devlin choked out, her head reeling. "Maybe it is all the fashion to disregard trivial matters like marriage vows among your set, but I would never . . . Myles would never . . ."

Tracey shrugged. "You heard him inside the ballroom, offering to pay any forfeit I might name. And this . . . this boon I would ask of him would be a relatively painless one. We've shared women before, Myles and I. And without such compelling reason as faces us now."

Devlin's stomach churned, and she pressed her palm against the silver-gilt stomacher, praying she would not be sick. "I cannot believe you are even suggesting . . ."

"Suggesting what? A solution to the difficulty we all find ourselves in? You claim to love me. You have belonged to me since you were newly a woman. And Myles . . . he knows full well that he is the sole reason we are to be kept apart. He is the one guilty of causing us this painful separation. Facilitating this . . . arrangement . . . is the least he can do."

"Arrangement." She squeezed the word between parched lips.

Devlin felt some part of her shatter within. But when she closed her eyes it was not even Tracey's callousness that haunted her; rather, it was the image of Myles waving his hand in breezy dismissal, granting her permission to pleasure herself in Tracey's bed whenever the urge should strike her.

"Listen to me, love." Tracey's voice was laced with the persuasiveness she had heard him use a dozen times, the irrefutable logic that he used to drug those he was arguing with into compliance. "As long as you get an heir by Myles—a son to carry forth the Farringdon name—he will not begrudge you a taste of pleasure in my embrace. Surely you can't be naïve enough to think that a man of Myles's reputation could be satisfied occupying only one woman's bed. And if he is to be dabbling in such entertainments, there is no reason you should not as well. Myles would be the first to tell you so."

Devlin clutched her fingers together in her lap until her nails dug deep into the flesh. She focused upon the physical pain, attempting to shield herself from a far greater anguish.

"I see," she said in a hollow voice. "You will have it all arranged between you, you and Myles. Everything worked out to your mutual satisfaction."

"Our satisfaction, darling." Tracey lowered himself to the bench beside her. "You will be satisfied as well. I shall see to it. I'll drive him from your mind, Devlin, from your heart, until whenever he makes love to you it is me you will be thinking of. Me you will be wishing for."

He groaned low in his throat and trapped her in his arms with more insistence than she had ever felt before in his embrace. His lips ground down on hers, a sensual kiss that already whispered that he thought her more mistress than mate. His hand swept between them to fasten upon her breast.

That contact shot awareness through the numb haze of grief that had gripped her, and she wrenched away from him, lunging to her feet with a broken sob.

"You and Myles neglected to consider one small impediment to all of your perfectly spun plans," Devlin choked out.

Ice blanketed Tracey's voice. "And what might that be?"

"The fact that *I* would never stoop to such . . . such a despicable arrangement. I would not lower myself to . . . to making vows to one man while breaking them with another."

In the lantern light Devlin saw Tracey's eyes narrow,

glinting with the same feral expression that drove fear into the hearts of seasoned political opponents three times his age.

"Is that so, my virtuous Mistress Chastain? Then why is it that when I kissed you I could taste another man upon your lips?"

Devlin's head whirled. She braced herself against the curving web of tree trunks and twisted limbs.

"Doubtless it was our most accomplished Myles who did such a fine job in tutoring you in the sensual arts in my absence," Tracey sneered. "And without my agreeing to any such arrangement, no less—a matter Myles and I will need to discuss at length, I fear."

"Tracey, it was not—not like that at all."

"It wasn't? Are you going to tell me that these practice sessions were all to further this *ruse* regarding your marriage? Tell me, Devlin, when was the charade to end? Were you going to leap from a bed stained with your maiden-blood and cry that it was still nothing but a jest?"

Tears seared acid-hot down Devlin's cheeks. Slowly she withdrew Tracey's betrothal ring from her finger, remembering how many times in the past she had held the glittering diamond to the sunlight, wondering what Tracey was thinking, doing, so far away.

"I wish that you would take this and go," she said, placing the ring in his palm. "I'll not play these—these sickening games with either you or Myles. I'll never—"

"Don't say never, my dear. I've learned from experience that whenever people do so, their vows come back to taunt them."

He bowed, the gesture as graceful and icy as though they had done no more than dance a minuet, as though they had not sat there in the arbor grinding any dreams they had once shared into bitter dust. "I bid you good night."

Devlin listened to Tracey's footsteps fading down the garden path, the sound seeming to crush something fragile hidden deep inside her. Hidden where she kept her deepest hurts, her darkest fears locked away from the rest of the world.

Laughter tinkled out from somewhere distant in the garden, the sound discordant as crystal breaking. Devlin's legs turned wobbly, and she lowered herself onto the bench, then buried her face in her hands and cried as if her heart was breaking.

CHAPTER
18

*M*yles stripped off his gloves, crushing them in his fist as he paced the shadowy corner of the garden like a prisoner awaiting his executioner, the night air burning his lungs in acid gulps. Damn it, what was happening out there in the arbor, where he had seen Devlin and Tracey disappear an eternity ago? What was Tracey saying to her? Doing to her?

Myles jammed the gloves into the pocket of his frock coat, his eyes closing against the jagged pain that tore through him at the images that raced in agonizing clarity across his imagination. Tracey at Liancourt soothing her in that practiced way of his while he unfastened her gown, smoothed it back from that rose-blushed skin. Tracey shedding his own immaculate garb and lying on a blanket of meadow grass beside her to teach her secrets as old as the Garden of Eden.

Secrets Tracey had every right to teach her as her betrothed. Secrets Devlin would doubtless be as eager to master as she was to learn anything new. Secrets Myles would have given his life to school her in.

But it was too late now, that magical first loving obviously plucked away by Tracey years before, without Myles ever once suspecting.

Myles stalked to where a statue of a shepherdess trailed its hand in a pool of flowers, cursing himself for a fool. It would have been none of his affair anyway—Tracey's trysts with Devlin. The man had proved honorable, vowing to wed her. And God knew Devlin had wanted Tracey for her husband. All had been perfect between them—a future filled with an endless string of political dinners and entertainments with the powerful of court. Endless debating on Copernicus and Sophocles and the theories of John Locke.

Yes, everything had been idyllic until Myles had returned to Liancourt—not to visit his mother, as he had deceived himself so many times before, but rather to crush his lips against Devlin's, to drown himself in the taste of her.

What had Tracey thought when he had received the letter Myles had written? What had Tracey felt when he had realized that the man he most trusted in the world had ruined his betrothal? In the moments within the alcove Myles had seen hints of the emotions Tracey must be feeling, all hidden beneath his icy facade. Betrayal, anger. Confusion, hurt. And most paralyzing of all, helplessness.

Myles drove his fingers through tousled hair, his gut twisting with guilt. Because despite what he had put Tracey through, he could not bring himself to regret those wild, sweet moments when he had taken Devlin's lips with his, could not have been made to relinquish the memory of her breasts imprinting themselves on his chest, her gasp of surprise, her soft moan of pleasure.

Myles arched his head back, his eyes burning as he stared up at the moon, adrift in tides of silver mist.

Were the two people he loved most in all the world paying the tithe for his sins even now? Was Tracey sitting there within the arbor, desperately trying to ease her pain as he severed the tie between them? Was Devlin shattering into little pieces that Myles would never be able to mend?

Frustration and fury at himself pulled Myles down beneath the waters of his own warring emotions. He was eaten alive with guilt—guilt at the anguish he'd put Devlin through, guilt at the ruin he had wreaked upon Tracey's plans of marriage. But most of all, guilt that he had betrayed them both. For as much as he loved them, he could not stifle the unforgivable hope that Tracey would indeed walk away from Devlin tonight, opening the gates to Myles's most cherished dreams.

Myles ground his fingertips against gritty eyes as self-loathing washed through him. In the weeks since he and Devlin had bolted from the gates of his ancestral home he had comforted himself with the assurance that the entire mishap had been beyond his control—one of those crazed, inexplicable happenings that no one could have stopped.

And yet now, knowing that he loved Devlin, knowing that he always had, uncertainty gnawed at him, taunted him with a dozen ways he might have averted the catastrophe that had snared her in its web.

"Bastard. You selfish bastard," Myles muttered. Dear God, what had he done? There had been such mocking challenge in Tracey's face when he had mentioned the wedding plans Myles had been laying out so carefully; there had been such accusation upon his friend's face.

Had Tracey somehow known? Suspected . . . what? That Myles loved Devlin? Had always loved her?

And now all he could do was to pace there, helpless, as he waited for the fates to cast their cards upon the table.

Myles gritted his teeth, jamming balled fists in the pockets of his frock coat, half mad with the need to charge across the shadowy beds of flowers and plunge into the leafy shelter where Devlin was hidden, to help her somehow, to hold her.

He started to swear, but at that instant a rustling made his gaze flash back to the entryway of the arbor, his eyes fixing upon a shadowy figure striding away.

Tracey.

Myles held his breath, straining to see if Devlin was near him, her smaller frame obscured by Tracey's taller one. But Tracey was alone.

And it was as if, in that instant, Myles knew what had happened within the arbor. He could feel Devlin's loneliness, her pain, reaching out to him across the garden. He rushed down the pebbled path, his throat tight, his jaw clenched, but as he neared the shelter woven of leaves and branches his steps faltered, stopped.

Soft sounds, wounded sounds were muffled by the branches. Devlin huddled upon the stone bench, the gown that had filled him with such fury an hour past a shimmering tangle about her.

"Dev," he breathed, her name an aching rasp in his throat as he stepped into the arch woven of trees.

With a choked sound she whipped around.

"G-Go away, Myles!" she sobbed out. "You were right all along. So there, I've admitted it. G-Go and gloat someplace else."

Myles swallowed, but the knot of regret still closed off his throat. "I'm not gloating, Dev. I wish . . ." He eased down onto the bench beside her, his hands feeling awkward, impotent as sorrow wrenched through her. "I wish you'd not waste your tears upon that infernal bench when I have a perfectly good shoulder for you to cry on."

He opened his arms to her, and she buried her face against his chest. There had been so few times as a child that Myles could remember Devlin giving way to tears. So few times she'd allowed anyone, most especially him, to comfort her, no matter how much he had wanted to.

But now, as he cradled her against him, rocked her, whispered soothing words against her temple, it was as if he were infusing every movement of his hands, his lips, with the succor he had wanted to give to her a thousand times before.

She was shaking, her breath ragged gasps of misery, her hands clutching at the front of his waistcoat as if he were the only safe haven in a roiling sea. And it made Myles ache to think that he had been the one who had caused this.

How many times had Devlin bellowed at him, warning him that someday his recklessness would cost him dear? He had laughed at her, teased her unmercifully. But never had he suspected that the greatest agony would come, not from driving his own curricle over a cliff or breaking his neck jumping his horse over towering fences, as Devlin had predicted, but rather from hurting someone else.

Oh God, Dev, oh God, he mourned silently, what have I done to you?

He stroked her hair, savage protectiveness welling up inside him. "I'm sorry," he breathed against her hair. His mind filled with the image of Devlin earlier that night, defiant, belligerent, so dazzlingly beautiful when he had first seen her uncloaked in the entryway.

He pictured her earlier still, outside the Camerons' house, her face glowing as she peered down at his gift.

But now she seemed devastated, so vulnerable.

"I—I hate it when I cry."

"Sh," he hushed her, rummaging in his pocket for a handkerchief and setting himself to dabbing at her wet cheeks. "It is only me. Myles. It doesn't matter."

"But it does. It does matter. Just as you said it would." She gulped down a sob. "You told me f-from the first that Tracey wouldn't marry me. I didn't believe you."

"I wish to hell I'd been wrong," Myles bit out savagely.

"You always did p-pick the most annoying times to—to be right," she said, taking the square of linen and scrubbing at her eyes.

Myles's lips pulled into a sad smile as he rocked her. "Ah, Dev, Dev," he crooned, "I'm sorry as hell."

"S-So was Tracey. Sorry, I mean. But he c-couldn't wed me because . . . because scandalmongers might use it against him. They might . . . might whisper about me behind their fans, or over their brandies! It might p-prove an embarrassment, and it seems that I am not worth risking such a terrible fate."

"I'd cast my soul into hell for you, and welcome," Myles said fiercely. He felt her tremble, but this time it was in a weak laugh.

"S-Some noble sacrifice that would be. Doubtless your soul is already thus condemned."

And for a heartbeat he wondered if it might not be so—that he was indeed to be condemned to a lifetime of being bound to her, but never being able to touch that soft, sweet corner of her soul she had allowed only Tracey to enter.

Gently grasping her shoulders, he eased her away from him, then cupped her chin with his palm. He stared into eyes reddened and swollen with grief, the sight worlds more wrenching than the pretty tears Myles had been treated to by countless court beauties.

"Devlin, listen to me. I know that you are hurting now. That this time with Tracey has proved a shock. But you have to know that he is the one who is the fool. He is at fault here, not you. Damn it, the man doesn't deserve you if he can hold your love so cheaply as to cast it aside for such a paltry reason. And in truth . . ." Myles looked away, his voice clotting in his throat.

"In truth, I don't deserve you either. But I . . ." He took her hands in his and stared down at her slender fingers, engulfed in his large bronzed ones. "I'd spend my whole life trying to make you happy if you would do me the honor of becoming my wife. In reality, not just . . . in ruse."

A tiny whimper escaped her, but Myles plunged on, desperate.

"Blast it, Dev, I'd be whatever it is you need me to be. I'd not even come near you unless you willed it. The only missives I'll even send you will be bank notes, to be spent however you wish. I've fortune enough to keep you in books for the rest of your life. And if we are indeed able to return to England, I could stay in London all season so you could be free of me. I would give you free rein at Liancourt, and you could fuss over tenants and tapestries and shoring up the east wing until my illustrious ancestors sing you hosannas from the family crypt."

"Myles, don't. I'll not make you an exile from your own home."

"Liancourt is your home, too, Dev. As for my being an exile from there—we can't be at all certain I won't be one anyway, after this rebellion is done. Even if Charles does regain his power, he'll need his allies at his side in court, to consolidate his position in England." He let his lashes drift low, his voice soft. "Being away from Liancourt would not concern me at all. If you were content."

"Content." There was something raw in her sad little laugh.

"Damn it, Dev, I'm not saying that I wouldn't . . . wouldn't want more."

"Yes, and doubtless you'd take it." Bitterness welled up in Devlin's voice as she shoved him away and bolted unsteadily to her feet.

"What the hell?"

"That is the way of things among men of the ton, I've been told. They take whatever they might wish. They arrange things quite amicably, as I understand it, with their wives overlooking their little indulgences."

Myles jammed himself to his feet. "What the devil are you talking about?"

"Mistresses. Courtesans. A staple of the masculine diet to rival beefsteak, from what I have heard. The gentleman of fashion, it seems, is a most generous fellow—willing to share not only his best hounds or horses, but his wife as well. Unfortunately, *this* wife would take exception to being passed about like a flask of wine to be sampled and shared, and—"

"Shared?" Myles bellowed, reeling from the accusation the flicker of lantern light revealed in her eyes.

"Yes. Shared. Between you and Tracey," she snapped, her arms hugged tight across her stomach, as if she were going to be sick. "It seems the two of you have done so before, and so he could see no difficulty in continuing the practice."

"That bastard!" Myles grabbed Devlin by the arms in a bruising grip. "Tell me that bastard didn't dare to hint that I . . . that you . . ."

"He didn't *hint* anything at all," Devlin flung back at him, her eyes huge pools of pain. "He stated it quite bluntly. I am to be a good wife and produce you a son to assure the Farringdon line. But after I do my *wifely duty*, Tracey was certain you would have no objection to my seeking pleasure in your best friend's bed."

Myles was shaking now. Shaking with wrath at the mere

thought of Tracey suggesting such a thing. Shaking with rage at the final, crushing humiliation Tracey had made Devlin suffer before he had cast her aside.

"Was that what he was out here saying to you?" Myles demanded in a flat, deadly voice.

"He was laying out the arrangements for the rest of my life quite neatly. He—"

"Plague take him! Listen to me, girl. I'd kill any man who dared lay his hands upon you. And if I take you to my bed, I'll pleasure you so deep you'll never have the will to take another lover."

Her eyes were huge in her face, and Myles could see the hollow bruises of humiliation still etched in that petal-soft skin. He was half crazed with the need to drive her pain away with his mouth, his hands, his very soul. But she was too fragile yet, the most delicate spindle of spun crystal, still seared by the glassblower's flame, and Myles feared that even to hint at what he felt for her would be to shatter her forevermore.

He held her a heartbeat longer, warring with his own self-control and with the far more threatening specter of the love for Tracey that still haunted her eyes. Then he stalked out into the garden.

He heard Devlin's call for him to wait, but the devil's own minions could not have stopped him from confronting Tracey now. He strode into the ballroom, murder bubbling in his veins as he scanned the brightly lit chamber. The cluster of men that had surrounded the prince had disappeared with their monarch, most likely into the gaming room set up for the gentlemen's entertainment. Couples were reveling in a set of country dances, feet flying in time to the frolicking melody spun by the violins.

But nowhere among the crowd was Tracey.

Myles glimpsed a flutter of blue silk as Arabella hurried toward him from across the room, her eyes wide with alarm. "Myles, where is Devlin?"

"In the garden," Myles snarled. "Go to her, Bella, and quickly. While I go to kill the bastard who left her there."

"That—that man who was announced a while ago? Your friend Tracey—"

"He's not my friend!" Myles growled, savage. "Not anymore. Now where the hell is he?"

"I saw him a little while ago," Bella said faintly. "He stalked about as if he were—were looking for someone, and then he went out into the entryway. I heard him summoning his cloak."

"The bastard's leaving? Damn him to hell, this isn't over yet!" Myles spun on his heel and raced across the ballroom.

The entryway was deserted except for a handful of servants savoring a rare moment of quiet by leaning against the wall telling bawdy jokes. The youngest among them was returning from the room where the guests' wraps had been kept, the broad-faced Scottish lad looking more than a little disgruntled at having been deprived of the joke's conclusion.

In his arms he carried a billowing cloak of black velvet shot with silver, a cloak Myles recognized all too well.

Fire burned in his gut afresh. "Where is he? The man who summoned this cloak?"

The youth's grumpy demeanor shifted into one that was stunned and more than a little fearful.

"He—He is waiting outside, milord," the footman stammered, clinging to the folds of the cloak. "The man, he was calling for a coach . . ." But before the lad could finish, Myles was charging out the huge doors and back into the arms of the night.

His gaze swept the carriage circle, the numerous coaches crouching like beasts in the shadows. A brace of servants was stationed at either side of the door, waiting to rouse carriages for guests tired of revelry later in the night.

Frustration built as Myles saw no one else, but suddenly, there was a rustling sound at the edge of the ring of lantern light. Myles's gaze flashed toward the noise and lit upon a tall, spare figure in white, pacing with a controlled fury that fueled the inferno of Myles's own.

Myles charged, slamming his palm into Tracey's shoulder.

Tracey staggered, wheeled, his eyes burning cold, fire entrapped in ice.

"You bastard," Myles rasped out. "What the hell have you been saying to Devlin?"

Tracey's face was a pale mask, lines carving beside that cool, mocking mouth, his eyes frosted over in a deadly chill. "What affair is it of yours what I say to her? Ah, forgive me, I had forgotten. You are to serve as her husband now."

"You urged her to become your mistress after I'd bedded her as wife! Told her I'd not give a damn were you to cuckold me."

"It has never troubled you before to cast women to your friends. How was I to know your scruples would assert themselves at such an inconvenient time?" Tracey's lips thinned. "Of course, I have proof enough that such moral pap didn't trouble you earlier, by God's blood! Devlin kisses like a courtesan now. All hot lips and seeking tongue. Did you think I wouldn't know who taught her thus?"

Myles felt as if Tracey had struck him in the chest with a mace. The bastard had been kissing her, tasting her sweetness, knowing, all the while knowing he was going to cast her aside.

"What I want to know is just how long you have been set on seducing her, Myles. Months? Years? Or was this just one more of your careless dalliances, an entanglement you plunged into without thinking?"

"It wasn't that way at all. Neither one of us meant to—"

"To what? Betray me? Is that supposed to absolve you of guilt? Devlin was mine, Myles. You knew it, and yet you couldn't keep your hands off her, could you? Well, now she is yours. You can teach her all the intriguing little tricks you taught your harlots. It's obvious she is a most apt pupil."

The whole courtyard seemed awash in a red haze of fury, blood pounding in Myles's head, his palms sweating with the need to strike out. To hurt the man who had devastated Devlin, to dash away the shattering truths Tracey had flung at Myles, truths that challenged everything Myles had ever believed about himself.

Myles grasped the hilt of the dragon sword, the steel

hissing, deadly against the quiet as he yanked it from its scabbard. Lantern light danced down the tensile blade, and Myles burned to feel it crashing against Tracey's own weapon, burned to feel it driving the jewel-encrusted dress sword from the man's hand. "Draw steel, you bastard!"

"I regret to disappoint you, but I must decline your little invitation." Tracey swept a scathing glance down the length of Myles's blade. "It would be passing rude to stain the carriage circle with blood. It might ruin the ladies' slippers when they make their departure. Besides, you've not won more than a dozen matches at swordplay since we were twelve, and I've not the time to bother with disposing of your corpse."

Blinding rage jolted through Myles. His sword swept out, just catching the sleeve of Tracey's frock coat. The material tore a gaping hole in the rich cloth, revealing the lawn shirt beneath. "Draw steel, damn you!"

Tracey's face hardened into a mask of fury—a fury even more daunting because it was contained, its power leashed, lethal.

"You want to die so much, Myles?" Tracey said, stripping off his coat with restrained violence. "Then far be it from me to deny you."

Tracey cast the garment aside, then rolled up the sleeve of his sword arm, freeing his wrist in the classic preparation of the master swordsman.

In that instant Myles knew he could be looking at his own death in Tracey's pale eyes. But he did not care if he went to Hades as long as he could have the pleasure of taking Tracey to the devil's gates with him.

Affection and loyalty battled with hatred. And as Tracey turned to face him Myles could see the same emotions reflected back at him from Tracey's eyes.

"Let it begin," Tracey said, bringing his sword up in the briefest of salutes.

The swords crashed together, the blades clanging.

Cries of alarm from the footmen split the air, but Myles focused only upon the clash of the weapons.

The blades rang as Myles thrust and parried, the emotions

surging through him, leaving his concentration ragged-edged while Tracey's blade flashed out like quicksilver, every movement deliberate and calculated as its point danced in murderous arcs against the night.

A hundred times Myles and Tracey had locked in practice combat, but this battle was no jest. It was deadly, in earnest, each man knowing every thrust, every parry, every trick with body or blade that the other man possessed.

Sweat beaded upon Myles's brow, the frock coat he'd disdained removing clutching at his arms, restricting movements already made more awkward because of the savage haze of his wrath. The shouts of alarm welled louder, but Myles ignored them, ignored the guests spilling out into the carriage circle.

But suddenly one voice pierced through the dull roaring. "Tracey! Myles, no!" Myles twisted toward Devlin, her haunted face flashing before him.

At that instant fire blossomed in Myles's thigh as Tracey's blade found flesh. A grunt of pain escaped between gritted teeth. He stumbled, barely righting himself in time to fend off a murderous thrust.

But Tracey yanked his blade aside at the last moment, barely missing Devlin as she hurled herself between them.

"Stop it!" she shrieked, her face stiff with horror. "Stop it, both of you!"

It was as if that command had the power to freeze both men. They stood, their chests heaving with exertion, their eyes still seething hate.

Myles glimpsed Harry behind him, felt Cameron's hands on his arms to restrain him, saw two burly Scotsmen dragging Tracey back as well. The courtyard spun into focus, the circle of stunned faces making Myles's stomach churn, his leg all but giving way beneath him.

But it was nearly worth the pain as Devlin wrapped her arm around his waist, shoring him up while she pressed the handkerchief he'd given her earlier to the welling blood staining his breeches.

"Oh, Myles . . ." Her voice was broken but threaded

through with a hint of her old outrage as she turned on his glaring opponent. "Tracey, how could you?"

"It was easy enough once he attempted to shove his sword-point down my throat."

"Would that I'd succeeded!" Myles snarled. "Never, if you live a thousand years, Tracey, will you understand how much you lost when you cast her away."

"Ah, but you *do* understand, is that it?" Tracey spat. "Tell me, Myles, where did you unearth this sudden empathy with my betrothed? Behind the flap of your breeches?"

The words were wielded like a sword-blade, cutting, deliberate, wounding Myles in places no mere length of steel could reach.

He surged against the arms that restrained him, fury washing acid-hot down his spine, but Devlin clung to him, her hands holding him when chains of iron could not have.

"No, Myles! No!"

He stared down into those green eyes, eyes filled with pain that he had put there.

The tiniest sorrowful smile curved her lips. "I've been deprived of my wedding once in the month past. If you fling your life away, who will suffer to be my husband?"

"Your . . . husband?" Myles stiffened, wary of the sudden fragile hope that whispered in the darkness roiling inside him.

Devlin nodded, her fingertips, soft, trembling, touching his sweat-sheened face.

Myles's heart broke at the feel of her, the sight of her, tumbled and tearstained and so very brave, and he knew that all the stubborn masculine pride in Christendom was not worth adding to the pain in her eyes.

He let his lashes drift shut, fingers closing convulsively about the sword hilt for one more instant. Then he let his sword clatter to the ground.

CHAPTER

19

*M*yles tugged at his neck cloth for the tenth time in as many minutes, the elegant embroidered lace threatening to close off all but the slightest trickle of breath. Already the air seemed far too thin within the antechamber of the ancient stone kirk, as though the thrifty Scots had nailed the excess into kegs and tucked it away so it would not be wasted. And with each tick of the clock ensconced upon a table in the corner of the room the chamber seemed to grow smaller, tightening about him in an unyielding fist of stone.

It seemed an eternity since he and Harry had been let down from a coach before the building, an eternity during which Myles had paced, chafing at hidden fears. Sick dread gnawed at him, driving him all but mad with the uncertainties that had tormented him during the two days his wounded leg had held him virtual prisoner within his bedchamber at the Cameron house.

Where was Tracey? Rumor insisted he'd not left the inn since the duel at the ball. Was he brooding over wrongs done him? Plotting some way, in that deceptively quiet fashion of his, to avenge himself? Or was he truly grieving over what he had lost in Devlin? Was he even now deciding to risk all on her behalf? Driven by the knowledge that she would soon belong to Myles?

And Devlin . . . was she hoping, praying that it might be so? Was she watching out the window for the man she truly loved to come claim her?

No! Myles raged inside himself. After what Tracey did to her, she could not still love him.

And yet how quickly could a woman like Devlin forget a love she had nurtured for five long years? How quickly could she recover from a betrayal that ran so deep? And how long would it be before Devlin—ever most cautious with her affections—would dare risk them again?

Myles closed his eyes, his mind filling with images of Devlin as she had been since the ball. Reeking of efficiency, hellaciously busy, she had bustled in for brief spans of time to change the dressings upon his wound, her day gobbled up by everything from overseeing the last-minute arrangements for the wedding celebration to supervising the household, the strain of the past week finally telling upon the pregnant Bella.

Twice he'd attempted to talk to Devlin about what had happened, but she'd shut him out, pouring bitter concoctions down his throat that made the time pass in a drugged haze. She'd all but forced the brew down him, insisting that he needed it to ease the restlessness that had kept him tossing and turning, aggravating the wound hour after hour. But Myles had known that restlessness was not from the pain or of fever, but rather of guilt and anger, hope and hopelessness.

Always before he had reveled in the uncertainties of life, but now his former pleasures turned their teeth against him, tearing at him, taunting him, until he would have sold his soul to the demons of hell to peer into his future for but a heartbeat.

And through the muzzy haze spawned by one of Devlin's foul brews he had watched her, suffered with her as she cocooned herself from her pain in a chrysalis of industry as she had so many times before.

And Myles had suffered, then, his own agonies, knowing that there was no way he could reach her.

Myles cursed, yanking again at the Dresden lace chafing his throat.

"Keep going on that way and you'll strangle yourself before the preacher even begins." Harry's grousing made Myles jump, and he turned to see Cameron, appearing decidedly uncomfortable in formal attire. But Myles must have looked even more miserable, for the Scotsman's expression softened as he said, "Don't get yourself in such a blather, man. 'Twill be over before you know it."

That is what I am afraid of, Myles wanted to shout. That it will all be over, and that she will slip through my fingers like moonbeams on a summer's night. But he couldn't even begin to voice such fears to Harry, as if saying them aloud might somehow make them come true.

He gritted his teeth, pacing to where the chamber's door stood half open, and peered out into the sanctuary. A hundred candles drizzled rivulets of light across drifts of white roses, their stems woven through with gilt ribbons.

Pale tapers had their bases buried among the velvety petals, heating them until the room was filled with the scent of the flowers, whisperings of the garden where Myles had spun so many dreams. Reminding him of the dreams he longed to spin with Devlin.

But today even his most carefully laid plans could not conceal the fact that this was a wedding that whispered more of nightmare than of any such romantic fantasy.

The pews beyond the half-opened door were abuzz with whispers, the multitude of people Myles had invited in his first rush of enthusiasm now seething with curiosity. Invited guests and scandalmongers alike rustled about, impatient to see the wedding of the runaway lady and the notorious viscount, the more bloodthirsty among them hoping for yet another altercation between the bridegroom and the Honorable Braden Tracey—an altercation Myles was none too certain would not occur.

He had cursed himself a hundred times in the days that had passed since the debacle of the ball, ruing the fact that he had stubbornly insisted upon filling the church to bursting with friends and comrades to witness his joy. For when he had seen the lingering of hurt, of disillusionment ghosted across Devlin's face in unguarded moments, he had wanted nothing more than to steal her away to a deserted chapel and take their vows far away from prying eyes.

The blinding love, the need that would be jolting through him as he made his vows, would not touch Devlin. She would doubtless be thinking of another altar, at the chapel where she and Tracey were to have been wed. Would she be imagining herself in the half-finished gown she'd been dressed in the day he rode through the gates? And when he slipped his ring on her finger, would she be feeling the cool gold clasp of Tracey's token of love, hear his voice saying the vows they had planned to make for so long?

Myles's chest clenched at the thought. What would she be thinking, feeling as she became Lady Devlin Farringdon, Viscountess Liancourt?

Despair? Hopelessness? Resignation? Or worse still, would the pain of Tracey's betrayal, and Myles's own part in the destruction of her dreams, make it impossible for her to go through with this marriage she didn't want? Had never wanted?

"You needn't look so grim, Liancourt."

Myles started as Harry clapped him on the shoulder with a hearty chuckle.

"Many a better man than you has survived matrimony, my friend. I promise you, it will not be *much* more painful than the stitching up of your leg two days past. Remember, you told me as much when I was to marry Bella. But you compared it to a visit to the tooth drawer."

"You hadn't been obliging enough to have your leg slashed open at the time," Myles replied in a feeble attempt at jest, but his hand fell away from the ripples of lace as he was struck with the poignant memory of his place in Cameron's wedding ten months before. Harry had insisted that Myles be accorded the honor of groomsman because of the part Myles had played in getting Bella's father to agree to the match. And Myles had enacted the role with the greatest relish, enjoying the task of diffusing the bridegroom's nervousness with jests and raising a toast to the newlywed couple.

It was a part he was to have played at Liancourt as well, when Tracey made Devlin his bride. Tracey had pressed the role upon him from the moment the betrothal to Devlin had been announced. And despite the odd ambivalence Myles had experienced, he had been ready to do so—hell, *anxious* to have the affair over with as the years drifted past, leaving Myles with the uncomfortable suspicion that somehow Devlin was being taken advantage of. And when Myles had ridden into London to tell Tracey of his quest for the legendary crown, he was certain that a part of Tracey's anger had been that Myles would not be present at the ceremony as planned.

Myles forced away thoughts far too miserable, suddenly aware that Harry was watching him intently. "You should've taken some draughts of that claret I tried to press upon you while you were getting dressed this morn," the Scotsman said, scratching at a sprinkling of powder that had drifted from his fresh-curled wig onto the sweat-beaded hollow of his temple.

Myles gave a forced laugh. "Meet Dev at the altar half foxed? She'd crack me over the head with her prayer book."

"The spirits would have numbed your leg a little, made it easier for you to stand," Harry said with a worried frown. "It will be a long day, and you barely up from your sickbed."

Myles grimaced, gingerly flexing the muscles of his thigh. Though it had only been a flesh wound, it still throbbed, the healing tissue pulling uncomfortably tight whenever he moved.

"No, Harry. I don't want to be numbed even a little this day. I want to be able to remember everything."

He looked down at the circlet of gold in his hand—the wedding ring he had commissioned from the same goldsmith who had mended the miniature of Lady Brianna. It was a wreath of roses, delicate, whimsical, almost as beautiful as the kiss they had shared within Liancourt's garden walls.

"I've been dreaming of this day for longer than even I suspected, old friend," Myles said softly to Harry. "I only wish that she had, too."

Cameron cleared his throat noisily, clapping one warm, solid hand upon Myles's shoulder. "I think that—that your Devlin is a very lucky lady, Myles. Someday she'll know it. And when she does, I vow that the two of you will more than make up for the time lost."

He slipped the ring onto his little finger, the circle barely sliding over the first joint. "Time may be the one thing Devlin and I don't have."

Harry's eyes clouded, and Myles knew Cameron was thinking of his own wife, who was even now off fluttering about Devlin, making her ready for the ceremony. Arabella was growing heavier each day with Cameron's child. A child Harry was all but certain would come into the world while its father was marching through England.

The prince was becoming increasingly impatient with those who bade him use caution, and there were whispers among those in power that before a fortnight had fled Charles's army would be on the march. Myles should have been ecstatic. God knew he'd deafened the prince with enough urgings to take action. But now Myles could only see what little time he and Devlin had slipping away. Days in which he might never be able to tell her he loved her. Show her that what he felt for her was rare, precious, real.

How many times during those few cognizant moments he'd managed to grasp through his drugged haze had Myles warred with himself? At one moment he'd wanted to drag Devlin down onto his bed, forcing her to listen as he spilled out everything that was in his heart; the next moment he was certain that to do so would be to cause her even greater grief.

She needed time—time to heal wounds so deep they still showed in the luminous green of her eyes. Yet how much longer could he afford to wait if at any moment the prince might give the command to march?

Myles paced to where the chamber's door stood half open and peered out into the sanctuary.

His musings evaporated as he saw the dour-faced clergyman draw near, his bushy gray brows crashing together over the bridge of a formidable hooked nose.

"'Tis time, my lord."

Myles's pulse lurched, his fingers straying yet again to tug at his neck cloth. "Harry, it's time."

"I'm not deaf, man," Harry said with a strained chuckle. He walked to stand in front of Myles. Harry smoothed a wrinkle from the scarlet ribbed silk of Myles's frock coat and straightened the griffin pin that glinted in the fall of lace at Myles's throat.

"Many a maid will be mournin' the loss of the rakehell Viscount Liancourt this night," the Scot said, tipping his head up to peer into the face of his much-taller friend. "And as for your Devlin . . . 'twill all come right in the end. I'm certain of it."

Myles nodded, clasping his friend's hand in gratitude for a moment. But as Myles stepped into the sanctuary it was as if the chamber was filled with phantoms that seemed to tug at his coat sleeves, to cling like spiderwebs upon his fingers. So much pain, so many misunderstandings, mistakes he had made in his dealings with Devlin.

Was this marriage just one more? One that would be even more torturously permanent, longer lasting than any of the others?

He scarcely noticed the expectant rustle go through the guests at his presence, his eyes shifting to where a shaft of light set dust motes aglow from a high-flung window, scattering the silvery light across the altar.

"Please, God," he whispered, his heart full. "Please let it be all right. Blast it, I know I don't deserve any aid from You, but Devlin . . . Devlin does, and . . ." The prayer faded as he heard something stir at the back of the church: Bella slipping through the door.

Myles met her eyes for an instant and knew a coiling dread that she would gesture to him, call him back to the rear of the church to tell him that Devlin had changed her mind. But Bella only slid into her place upon the hard pew while Myles stared at the wooden portal, willing Devlin to come charging through it, determined, stubbornly resolved, with that spark in her eyes that told everyone who dared question her to go straight to the devil.

But none of his jumbled thoughts of the past days had prepared him for the moment when the panels carved during the age of knights errant swung wide and everything but the ache of love that dug deep into the core of him ceased to exist.

His breath froze in his throat, his heart careening crazily as he caught his first glimpse of his bride. And in all the fantasies he had woven, never had even the most winsome rescued princess or fairy queen held such beauty as the woman framed within that ancient door.

Her gown was of taffeta embroidered with tangles of rose vines. Snow-white blossoms, from the heaviest full-blown flower to the most timid of buds, were strewn across a background as blue as a summer sky. Her gold underpetticoat shimmered like sunlight from beneath the back-sweep of her skirts, the satin quilted in whimsically wrought scenes from the legends Myles had always adored.

Tristan was clutched in the arms of Isolde, oblivious to the betrayal that was to come; Lancelot knelt to Guinevere; Orpheus, his lute in hand, spun a ribbon of music to guide Eurydice from Hades.

Devlin's coppery hair caught fire in the sunlight, trapping the golden glow beneath a crown of creamy-white roses. But it was Devlin's face that seared its image forever within his mind, filling him with wonder, confusion, and a very real hope. Nowhere was the hard edge of determination he had expected, that fierce resolution he had seen upon her features when confronting one of life's necessary evils, like sorting through apples to find one that was spoiled or stitching up a petticoat that had torn. Her face was all soft, sweet curves and vulnerable rose tints, the delicate heart shape as fragile and beautiful as an exquisitely carved cameo. Every line, every curve was flawless, except for the wisps of sadness that clung about her lips, the painful uncertainty that shone beneath her lashes.

A murmur went through the crowd, and Myles saw her

hesitate for but an instant, the hue in her cheeks deepening with a shyness Myles had never seen in her before.

He knew full well that he should wait for her, solemn, decorous, as she made the long, solitary journey down the aisle to reach his side, but in a heartbeat he was striding toward her.

Her eyes flashed up to his, and she hesitated, her gaze fluttering to the hand he extended to take her own. Then she placed her trembling fingers in his and held on tight, and he felt as if she'd given him the most precious gift he'd ever known.

"You look like an angel," he murmured, only for her, his voice thick in his throat.

Her lips tipped in a heartbreaking smile. "You're devil enough for the both of us, my lord."

Myles reached up with his fingertips, tugging gently at a sunset-red curl, a mockery of all the childhood pranks they had played upon each other. "Chin up, girl," he whispered. "It can't be much worse than the time our raft fell apart in the middle of Sproule's eel-infested lake."

A tiny laugh caught in her throat, and gratitude shone brilliant green in her dark-lashed eyes.

Her jaw jutted up at that pugnacious angle that had always tempted the boy Myles to poke her or tease her and, more recently, had filled the man with the unquenchable desire to kiss her until her knees were weak as water. But this time it was intense respect that welled up inside him because of her courage and that infernal, stubborn pride.

His own shoulders squared, and he turned to lead her to where the holy man stood. The preacher's ruddy face was a study in disapproval, his woolly brows knit above piercing falcon eyes. Myles suspected that the man might be entertaining thoughts of putting a stop to this unorthodox wedding, but Myles fixed the man with the glare that had made the most ruthless of brigands, the most reckless of duelists, take pause, and the man merely vented his censure in a distressingly swinelike grunt and riffled through his prayer book.

"We ar-r-re gather-r-red together-r-r," the man began in

stentorian tones that nearly sent Myles into gales of laughter, "to join this man and this woman in holy matr-r-rimony. A most *ser-r-rious* estate, not to be taken lightly—"

The Scotsman drilled Myles with a quelling frown, and Myles felt a sudden quiver where his arm was pressed against Devlin's ribs. He glanced over to see tears glistening in her eyes—but not the melancholy tears he had so feared when anticipating this ceremony; rather, they were tears of barely suppressed mirth.

He swallowed hard. Images, like cherished paintings, flitted across his mind: Devlin laughing when he had taken a fall from his horse, him chasing her, tumbling her onto the meadow grass, and stealing the pins that caught up her hair.

He could see her, years later, battling *not* to laugh, as she was now, when he had told her a mildly ribald joke, or when he had made a kitten dance by dangling one of her hair ribbons above its tiny cream paws. And as he repeated the vows generations of lovers had spoken before him, he made one promise to her within his heart, more solemn than any other: to gift her, not only with all the love he held in his heart, but also with joy, with laughter, with all the heady, sweet pleasures she had denied herself for so very long.

I love you, Devlin, he said inside himself. Who the blazes would have thought it?

"Harrumph!" The clergyman cleared his throat with deafening force, and Myles started. "Take her hands, milord."

He turned to her and grasped her other hand, his eyes feasting upon her upturned face, her lips no longer curved with laughter. The miniature glowed rich, exquisite against the velvet swell of her breasts, and he was touched again by the magic of that other love story, wondering whether Lady Brianna's bold cavalier could have loved her half as much as Myles did the woman before him.

"Devlin Chastain," the clergyman demanded, sounding like St. Peter determined to keep sinners from befouling heaven's gates, "do you take this man to be your lawful husband? Do you vow to love him, honor him, comfort and obey him, *as long as you both shall live?*"

Myles heard her breath catch. An almost desperate light shone in Devlin's eyes. "Oh, Myles, I—I can't—" she choked out. "I—"

Myles's heart crashed against his ribs, his gut churning, and he was suddenly aware that he had been expecting this moment from the very first, waiting for this quick, sharp pain driving deeper than any sword thrust.

Devlin couldn't marry him. He'd been a fool to think she could.

He dug deep into his soul to steady his voice. "It's all right, Dev. I understand." His hand strayed up, his knuckles smoothing away the tears that clung to her lashes. "I guess I don't blame you. I'd make the devil of a husband."

"No! It's not you. It's me, Myles," she quavered. "I can't . . . can't promise the—the obey part . . ."

"The obey part?" Relief made Myles's head swim more wildly than any brew Devlin had forced down him. He laughed aloud, and she gasped as he caught her by the waist, swooping her high, holding her above him.

"Is that all?" he demanded, ignoring the clergyman's sputterings, the roar of approval from the crowd. "You needn't fear, Dev. I promise I shall never hold you to *the obey part,"* he said, drifting her lightly back to the ground. "After all, I'd not want to be responsible for the damning of your immortal soul when you broke the vow."

"This is a sacrament! Not a game of dicing where you can change the rules at will, my lord!" Eyes bulged beneath thick brows, the clergyman's face as red as a boned salmon.

"Well, then, my good man, consider that my wife shall obey my wishes by *dis*obeying whenever the devil bids her."

The man began to sputter, but his mutterings were cut short by the sound of Devlin's voice, clear and sure and infinitely sweet.

"I promise to—to love you, Myles," she said, painfully earnest, "honor you, comfort and . . ." The solemnity in her eyes wavered into a glimmer of amusement, a whisper of kindred spirits to each other. "And I promise to obey you by not obeying you, as long as we both shall live."

Myles withdrew the ring from his waistcoat pocket and

took up her hand. Without waiting for the clergyman's grudging prompts Myles slipped his ring onto the tip of her finger. "With this ring I thee wed."

Let me be husband to you, Dev, he prayed silently. Let me laugh with you, love you.

Myles's voice went ragged with emotion. "With my body I thee worship."

Let me gift you with every lover's dream you've ever dared, he begged inwardly. Let me kiss every sweet hidden place inside you.

"And with all my wordly goods I thee endow."

Everything I have, he thought, everything I am is yours. I'd be content to stay with you, love you, if we had naught but the ruined hulk of the Dower House to shield us. Hear me, Dev. In your heart.

Fingers unsteady, he eased the ring back into place, his gaze fixed upon the shimmering gold, his dreams filled with images of the future, of children and grandchildren racing about Liancourt, of dozens of Christmastides to delight Devlin with gifts, and of countless simple nights, more precious than any other vision, shared beneath the red velvet bedcurtains of his chamber in the castle tower.

A simple dream but a precious one, because he might not live long enough to hold it in his hands. He reached out, cupping her cheeks with his palms, then lowered his mouth to hers in a devastatingly gentle kiss.

He felt her lips part beneath his and half expected her to pull away. But her fingertips stole up to smooth his hair, then slid down the corded muscles of his throat in a caress infinitely tender because it was so unexpected.

Myles drew away from her, staring down into her face as if he could find some secret within it, now unguarded. "Dev . . . Dev, there's something I have to tell you. I love—"

The sound of applause cut through the sanctuary, a dry, bitter voice making Myles wheel, Devlin caught protectively in one arm.

"Prettily done. Very prettily done, the both of you." Tracey, resplendent in court dress, strolled down the aisle, his gloved palms clapping together in dramatic fashion.

"Tracey." Myles groped for the hilt of the dress sword affixed to his waist, wanting nothing more than to kill him for daring to upset Devlin further. But Devlin's voice broke in, low but firm.

"Braden, go. You're not welcome here."

Tracey held up his hands in a guise of innocence, but Myles could smell the brandy upon his breath. "I've but come to offer my condolences . . . I mean, *felicitations* to my dearest friend and the loveliest—if most faithless—bride in Christendom," Tracey purred. "That can hardly be counted objectionable."

Harry's voice cut in, furious. "It can be when you nearly killed that friend two days past! Leave before I cleave out your gizzard!"

"Of course I will leave if I'm causing anyone distress. However, before I do, you will surely permit me to wish the viscount and viscountess joy upon their wedding night. It will be the last night they ever have."

"Braden, what do you mean?"

"It seems that your self-named prince has chosen this most inopportune time to march upon London, my dear. The only lover your bridegroom will take to his bed upon the morrow will be Dame Death."

CHAPTER
20

Cries of disbelief mingled with whoops of excitement, men and women alike leaping up from their seats. Devlin glimpsed Bella, clasped tight in Harry's arms, while other young lovers who had imagined they had all the time in the world rushed to each other across the room. Youthful fools blinded by visions of glory shouted tributes to their courageous prince.

In the midst of the mayhem all around her Devlin clutched at Myles's coat sleeves, stricken, and stared into Braden Tracey's impassive eyes, eyes far different from the ones she'd dreamed about the past five years.

"No," she breathed; Myles's uncharacteristic silence amid the chaos was more damning than Tracey's words. "They can't march out tomorrow."

"Can't they?" Tracey drawled. "I understand your unwillingness to relinquish Myles so soon after your nuptials, but your bridegroom has been laboring quite energetically to bring this campaign about, from what I have been told. How charming that he should get his wish upon his wedding day. Consider this news my gift to you both." Tracey sketched an insolent bow. "Now, since I am so obviously unwelcome, I bid you adieu. And let me say that I look forward with eager anticipation to meeting you again, Myles, when you . . . *arrive* in London." Tracey's words were a velvet-sheathed threat, a knife stroke to Devlin's already frayed nerves.

She stared in stunned confusion at Tracey's retreating back, then turned pleading eyes to Myles. "You can't possibly go. Not now. The wound in your leg isn't even healed! And winter is coming. Surely the prince has sense enough to wait."

Myles's hand gripped her numb fingers, guiding her into the antechamber where he had awaited the ceremony. When he turned to face her his features were hard with regret. "Dev . . . what Tracey says must be true. We've been expecting this for a long time now."

Panic welled up inside her, the church, the gawking guests, even the departing Tracey fading into nothingness. "You knew?" she demanded.

"I didn't *know*, exactly. I've been locked in my bedchamber, drugged with that vile stuff you were pouring down my throat for the past two days. I *suspected* the prince might be getting ready to move, but I wasn't sure."

"And you didn't bother mentioning any of this to me?"

"You had been driven to distraction already with all that happened. I didn't want you worried any more than necessary."

"Any more than *necessary?*" she echoed, quivering with outrage. "How thoughtful of you! And how blasted kind of the prince to delay this ridiculous march until we were wed! That way, when you ride off on this fool's errand you can widow me instead of merely breaking my heart with grief over your worthless hide!"

A fierce, hot flame ignited in Myles's eyes, and he grasped her by the arms. "Would you?" he demanded in a gritty voice. "Grieve for me?"

She glared up at him through a blur of tears. "Yes, damn you! I—"

"Then the devil himself couldn't scoop me into hell. I'm not going to die, Devlin!"

"Oh, yes you will," she sobbed, thunking a knotted fist

against his chest. "Now that you've started being . . . tolerable . . . you'll do it just to spite me, and—and—"

She heard Myles curse, then she was crushed in his arms, his mouth on hers, hot and hungry, draining away her fury, leaving despair in its place. After a moment his arms gentled.

"Hush, sweeting, hush," he breathed, wiping away her tears with his gloved finger. Devlin tried to resist, but he forced her chin up, looking into her face with a gentle sorrow. "I'd give my sword arm if it would buy me more time to be with you now—hell, if it would only allow me to scoop you off alone this minute, with the vows all said. But we have to brazen this out, girl, get through the celebration as best we can."

He leaned his forehead against hers. "Dev, there is nothing we can do to change this. Nothing we can do to hold back time. All we can do is make the time we *do* have as perfect as we possibly can, so we have something to remember."

His thumb ghosted over her lips, and she felt the dampness of her own tears. "I'm afraid, Myles," she confided, and she saw a flicker of understanding in that face that was so dauntingly masculine, every plane and angle bespeaking arrogance, courage.

"Know what, Dev?" His voice was whisper-soft. "Suddenly, so am I. I never had anything to lose. Until now."

The roses bedecking the Camerons' ballroom were faded, wilted petals littering the floor like wings of fallen angels. The guests, their merrymaking feverish in the face of the danger looming before them, had trampled on the fallen blossoms as they had whirled in cotillions and minuets.

Most of the men and women knew of the danger. Saw it as clearly as their loved ones' faces. But they were willing to sacrifice all to do what they felt was right.

There was beauty in their courage. A beauty Devlin had never suspected.

She leaned against the back of the settee, watching as the more intrepid revelers kept time in yet another country dance. Myles was at their head, with Bella in tow, Devlin having pleaded with him to allow her a moment to catch her breath. Her feet ached from countless dances, her head whirling from the glasses of punch Myles had pressed upon her to quench her thirst.

He had been as attentive as even the most starry-eyed of brides could have wished, straying from her side only long enough to ply her with the choicest sweetmeats and the most cooling drinks before sweeping her off yet again to dance.

A dozen times she had heard hushed whispers from the disgruntled matrons complaining that it was scandalous the way the viscount had spent the night in his new wife's pocket, ignoring the other ladies with whom his sense of duty should have bid him to dance. But the young daughters of those dowagers regarded Devlin with envy, thinking that the dashing viscount, so bedazzled by the bride he was to leave upon the morrow, was the very thing of which deliciously forbidden novels were fashioned.

As Devlin watched Myles move through the set of dancers, so vital, so young and reckless, so alive, she wondered if those same girls realized how unromantic war truly was. She wondered if they understood that the bravest of men could be made to scream in agonies far worse than mere death.

She closed her eyes against the images, fighting to banish them from her mind. Myles had urged her to let this night be as perfect as they could make it, and since the moment Tracey had strode from the church Myles had done all in his power to see that it was so. Dwelling on what was to come would only fill these hours with dreary gray. Hours in which she wanted to memorize this man who had been her nemesis for so long.

This man she had known forever.

This man she knew not at all.

Her husband.

Always before the word had conjured images of a partner with whom to plan a solid future. Someone serious-minded and stable to share the worries of maintaining a vast estate and the raising of industrious sons and capable daughters. It had always brought to mind long, companionable evenings before a fire, reading or mending or going over accounts.

But as she looked at the man circling now with Bella in the dance, it was impossible to think of him content with such staid pastimes. He would be forever upsetting the household with his hounds and his horses and his incessant jests. Instead of reposing in a chair by the fire, he was more likely to shove the furnishings aside to indulge in impromptu theatricals, or to challenge her to games of dicing. And instead of reprimanding his sons and daughters for sliding down the stair rail, he would more probably delight in demonstrating for them how to go down with the greatest of speed.

She had thought she'd known what she wanted for so long, had been so certain of everything. Why was it that her own dreams suddenly seemed so lackluster beside the jewel-bright ones that Myles had conjured? Why was it that the home she had imagined now seemed as dreary as last night's dishwater, while thoughts of the one she might make with Myles someday were bright splashes of happiness and warmth?

Devlin looked at the wedding ring on her finger and traced the masterfully worked roses.

As a child, with her own dreams lying in ashes, Devlin had envied Myles his ability to look at the world and to see beauty. And watching him now as he bowed out of the dance with Bella, she wondered if the gift she would find hidden in this marriage would be the ability to look through his eyes. To see whatever it was that made him smile that heartbreakingly beautiful smile and laugh in that deep, rich music that seemed touched by the angels.

She pasted a smile on her face as Bella hurried over, Myles but a step behind her. Bella's face was drawn, her smile brittle.

Devlin patted the seat beside her. "Sit down at once and rest yourself, Bella. You've been worrying yourself to a frazzle all day."

"Have I?" Bella asked, breathless. "I cannot think why."

She averted her eyes, and Devlin sensed in her a plea not to spoil this time by talk of the parting to come.

"There never was such a beautiful wedding," Bella went on. "The flowers and the—the way Myles came down the aisle to fetch you, as if he couldn't bear to wait."

Devlin sighed, acceding to her friend's unspoken wishes. "More likely he was coming to chain me to him so I wouldn't run away," she attempted to tease, and she was stunned as Myles's face went very still.

After a moment he shrugged, paying a deal of attention to straightening the lace at his cuffs. "I've always been . . . impatient." He gave a pointed look at the clock ticking in its place against the wall.

Bella followed his gaze, and color splashed into her cheeks. She looked away, flustered. "I suppose it is . . . getting late."

"My point exactly," Devlin said. "You should be getting to bed."

Bella dimpled, her smile teasing yet shy, her eyes sparkling with mischief. "So, madam bride, should you."

Devlin felt a sudden catch in her breast, flame seeming to spill into her cheeks. "I . . . oh" was all she could squeeze through a throat suddenly constricted. She looked at Myles, and the heavy, hot light in his eyes made something stir in her center, grow weightier and more compelling until she understood what it was that lured so many women, like gauzy-winged moths, into the heart of Myles Farringdon's flame.

When Bella linked her fingers with Devlin's and pressed her hand, it was all Devlin could do to drag her gaze away from the mesmerizing one of the Viscount Liancourt.

"Shall we go upstairs?" Bella's voice seemed to come from somewhere far distant. "I'd love to help you . . . brush your hair and things."

Devlin's tongue felt too large for her mouth, and she didn't know what to do with hands and feet suddenly stricken with awkwardness. From the first you knew it would come to this, she berated herself inwardly. Don't show yourself a coward now.

"I'd be grateful for the help," she said, surprised that her voice sounded steady.

She stood, and Bella linked arms with her, the gesture reminding Devlin poignantly of the first night she had come to the Cameron house, bedraggled and stubborn and piteously misguided. The night Myles had given her the gift of Arabella Cameron's friendship.

"Bella." Myles reached out to stop her. "Whenever you two are finished . . . arranging Devlin's hair, I'll be in my chamber."

"Pacing, no doubt. Well, I shall contrive to hurry so that you'll not wear a trough in the floorboards, sir. But it takes time and care to ready a bride for her husband."

A hundred butterflies seemed to beat gossamer wings within Devlin's stomach, and she all but dragged the giggling Bella toward the stairs.

Not even her friend's artless babbling could dull the pitching nervousness that bubbled inside Devlin as Bella and Annie, the maid, stripped away the wedding finery and settled a nightrail as thin and delicate as a spider's web over Devlin's red-gold curls. Her hair was brushed until it cascaded in a tumble of molten sunset down her back, while across the neckline of her delicate gown Devlin's initials and Myles's were embroidered in silver thread, entwined in a way that was somehow so intimate it made Devlin's cheeks burn. She fingered the letters as Bella dabbed essence of roses upon the heated skin beneath the fall of red curls.

At last Bella stepped back to see her handiwork. She smiled a smile as pleased and guileless as any child's. "Perfect," she pronounced. "You will take his breath away."

Devlin tried to fight the sense of panic building inside her.

It had seemed as if the wedding day would last forever, but now, as she watched Bella hustle Annie out of the room, it felt as though it had been over in a heartbeat.

Suddenly Bella turned and gave Devlin an affection-filled hug.

"Well, now is the time that your mama should give you some tender words of wisdom before you become, in truth, a married lady."

"I much doubt my mother would do anything but scold me about everything from the way I look, to . . . to how I must be a paragon of womanhood to deserve her precious Myles," Devlin said, thoughts of her mother bringing forth the old pain.

Arabella's face grew solemn. "I feel very sorry for her. She must have had a great sorrow to lock away her love from a daughter as special as you."

Devlin tried to smile but failed. "I think she was just disappointed. She would have done wonderfully well if someone like you had graced her cradle."

Bella ran the palm of her hand lovingly over the swell where her own child was growing, an almost pensive light in her eyes making Devlin concerned. "If I have a daughter, I hope she is just like you. Brave and—and strong, with a mind so sharp no one can ever take advantage of her. And so kind."

Tears spilled down Arabella's wan cheeks, and the girl turned away, dabbing at her eyes with the ruffle of her sleeve. "I only wish that—that Harry was going to be here to—to see her."

Devlin went to her friend, cursing herself as a selfish beast for being so preoccupied with her own troubles she'd not remembered that Bella, too, would be sending her husband off to war. She hugged the girl, petting her golden hair as if Bella were a child.

"Just think what a splendid surprise you will have for him when he returns home."

"You mean . . . *if* they return at all," Bella said in a small voice.

"Myles says that there is time enough to think of that when tonight is over. He's right. I've spent my whole life planning for a tomorrow that might never come—or that comes and is worlds different from anything I could have foreseen. If these weeks with Myles have taught me anything, it is to live for now."

Arabella gave a watery chuckle. "Here I was going to give you words of wisdom from a long-married lady, and you end in comforting me."

"I hope I did. Comfort you, I mean. But Myles is much better at such things than I am."

"I think you did wonderfully well." Bella bristled, defensive. "And as for Myles, it would be hard for him not to be practiced in the art, considering the droves of court belles who fairly fling themselves at his feet in an effort to elicit his sympathies." Arabella's cheeks flushed, and she twisted a bit of galloon trim at the edge of her petticoat. "Do you know . . . well, anything about what is to . . . to happen tonight?"

Devlin fought to suppress a smile, not wanting to hurt her earnest friend's feelings. "I think I have some idea."

"When Harry and I were wed, my aunts had told me so many stories about wifely duty and male urges that were painful and degrading and . . . and . . . well, awful, that I half expected Harry to emerge from his dressing room with fangs and cloven hooves. I was so relieved to see just my Harry in a nightshirt that I all but flung myself upon him, sobbing with relief."

Devlin closed her eyes, trying to reconcile her image of Myles the Tormentor with that other persona she'd heard whispered about from the time she was thirteen: the Viscount Liancourt, a notoriously skilled lover who had only to brush his lips across a woman's fingertips to make her his slave.

Devlin's fingers clenched in the folds of her nightgown, a kind of hopelessness washing over her.

Always before, when she had thought about Myles's rakehell escapades, she had felt the same twisting sensation deep inside her. Always she had told herself it was disgust for his behavior, but now, as that feeling gripped her more fiercely than ever before, she recognized it as something else entirely.

Jealousy.

Where in God's name had it come from?

"Why should it matter so much?" she murmured. "It's not as if I loved him."

"Devlin?"

She opened her eyes to see Bella watching her, confused.

After a moment Devlin gave a weak laugh. "I've always thought Myles sported horns and a tail. So no matter what, I'll not be surprised."

Bella's tear-sheened eyes sparkled. "I wager you will be more than surprised. What happens between you and Myles tonight will be like nothing you've ever imagined. And even when it is over, you will scarce believe . . ."

"We only have tonight. There is no time for mistakes. And I . . ." Devlin looked away. "I'm not sure what to do."

"Myles will show you. Trust him." Bella stood on tiptoe to brush her cheek with a kiss, then the girl turned and left the room.

Devlin stared at the half-open door Bella had disappeared through. "Myles will show you. Trust him." Bella's words echoed in Devlin's head. She turned and paced to where the window was open to the sweet night breeze.

"The last time I trusted Myles I nearly ate a beetle he'd slipped into my syllabub," she muttered aloud.

"It was a very small beetle." The sound of Myles's voice made her wheel to see him lounging against the door frame. "Besides, you never really eat syllabub anyway. You only stir it around to make your hostess think you've taken some."

Devlin knew she should think of some witty retort—one of the verbal thrusts she and Myles had become so adept at through the years. But all she could do was stare at him as though she had never seen him before.

His frock coat and waistcoat had been shed, doubtless cast negligently across a chair back in his own bedchamber. A rich robe of crimson satin stretched across his broad shoulders and swept to the floor in elegant ripples. The exquisite needlework caught the light of the tapers pooled about the room. Rampant lions reared up on their hind legs, their white silk teeth bared, their carefully stitched claws gleaming against the satin. The garment was the perfect foil for the arrogant, aristocratic planes of Myles's face and the recklessness in his eyes.

Devlin caught at the inside of her lip with her teeth, aware of him in a way she'd felt but briefly in the Dower House. For ten years she had heard whispers of the legendary

Myles Farringdon—the rakehell gambler who would wager all he owned on the turn of a single card, the dashing viscount women fought to make their lover.

But as she stared into the eyes of the Viscount Liancourt this night she saw for the first time what other women had seen—the latent power, the sensual promise—and she knew that tonight she would discover those forbidden mysteries hidden in Myles Farringdon's eyes for herself.

CHAPTER

21

Devlin's heart tripped as Myles strode lazily toward her, and she flinched when he reached up with his fingertips to trace the curve of her mouth.

But when he spoke there was no shadow of the practiced seducer. "Do you know what it's like, Dev, to hold a dream in your hands? A real dream, so damn perfect it tears you apart inside?" His fingers threaded through the wispy curls at her temple, the intensity in his eyes seeming to probe into her very soul. "That is what it's like, Dev. For me. Now."

The words hurt because she wanted so much for them to be true. She pulled away from him and walked to the fire. She hugged her arms tight against her, hating the strained sound in her voice.

"Myles, I know you're doing this . . . going through with this marriage out of . . . out of obligation, because you hold yourself responsible for what happened. You don't have to pretend—"

"Pretend?"

"That—that you think I'm . . . pretty," Devlin breathed. "That you . . . want me."

"Oh, I want you, Devlin."

She felt his eyes upon her as certainly as if he had caressed her, and the heat that flooded her body had nothing to do with the flames inches from where she stood.

"I want you more than I've ever wanted anything in my life."

She smiled sadly. "If that is how you always begin . . . this," she said, gesturing to the bed, "it's little wonder you've been so successful in breaching ladies' virtue."

"I've never said those words to another woman, Dev." There was a watchfulness in his eyes that unsettled her.

"Haven't you? Then what do you say?"

"Does it matter?"

"I'm not sure. I just . . . just feel like you're cheating somehow. That it's not fair, because you know all the rules to this game, while I . . . I know next to nothing. You know I could never stand it when you were more . . . informed about any subject than I was."

"I thought at the ball you said that you and Tracey had—"

"He kissed me, and . . . and maybe a little more. But we never . . ." Devlin felt her cheeks burn. "Well, you were acting so infernally smug that I couldn't help misleading you!"

"Sweet God, Dev. Then no one has ever touched you?"

"Not for lack of my trying." Devlin gave a shaky laugh. "I was as impatient to learn about . . . well, what happens between a man and a woman as I have been about learning everything else in my life. But Tracey would have none of it after that first tryst in the stable. He said that he was protecting me from scandal. That as much as he wanted to—well, to mate with me, we had to wait until we were wed."

"I see," Myles said softly.

"I admit I was disappointed, but I thought it was kind of him, wanting to shield me that way. Now . . . now I am certain that he was just afraid of stirring up your grandfather's wrath."

"Dev, I'd be a liar if I said I was sorry I'll be the first man ever to make love to you. There is something special in that—a gift a woman can give but once."

Devlin walked to a stool and sank down on it, but she smiled just a little. "Isn't it the same for men? I mean, the first time, isn't it a gift?"

Myles laughed, and the sound warmed her. "Maybe for some men. But for most, I think virginity is like handling a horseshoe still glowing from a blacksmith's fire—they want to get rid of it as quickly as they can, and they don't much care who they throw the blasted thing at."

"Who did you . . . throw your virginity at? Or were there a multitude of females squabbling over who would be the first to catch it?"

"My first?" Myles walked over and lowered himself to the floor, stretching his long legs out before him. "I was but fifteen, and she was a dozen years older—one of the Traceys' chambermaids, buxom and bonny, and blessed with a sense of humor, which was a good thing for both of us, considering." His lips formed a wry curve.

"Considering what?"

Myles favored her with a devil's grin. "Dev, only you would expect a man to dredge up memories of his first awkward fumblings and expose them for you to dissect." He shook his head. "The truth of it is that it was over the moment Peggity got my breeches undone."

"Oh! Oh, Myles . . . it must have been awful for you," Devlin stammered, but she couldn't suppress a giggle. "Are you better at it now?"

Myles choked on his laughter. "I certainly hope so."

Devlin leaned her chin upon her palm and looked down at him. "I suppose you would have to be better, what with all the practice you've had since."

"Tell me, Lady Farringdon, am I to be insulted or flattered by that comment?"

"Neither. It's only logical."

"There is nothing logical about making love, Dev, I promise you."

"Tell me about it, then. What . . . what does it feel like?"

"For God's sake, Dev!" Myles started to rise, but his gaze locked with hers, and after a moment he sank back down. He picked up a silver-gilt ribbon at the hem of her nightrail and toyed with it, his lashes lowered, his voice soft. "I don't know if I can describe it. It's like nothing else in the world, Dev."

"Try. Please."

He stared meditatively down at the bit of ribbon, running it back and forth between strong bronzed fingers. "It is as close as you can ever be to another person. Like becoming a part of the other. And I believe that if you're in love with that person, you can never be quite alone again."

He raised his eyes to hers, and she stared down into that heartbreakingly handsome face, a wistfulness gripping her until her throat seemed tight.

"When I was little I used to hide and watch you laughing and racing about. It seemed there were always people around you—crowds of children laughing with you, playing, the servants, the grooms—everyone adored you. I wanted that, too, but I could never . . . never seem to risk reaching out." With a hand that trembled she bridged the space between them, skimming the corner of his mouth with the soft tip of the finger that wore his wedding ring. "I don't want to be alone anymore, Myles."

His lashes drifted closed, and he turned his face until his lips pressed soft against the vulnerable cup of her palm. He levered himself to his feet, and his warm hands closed about hers, drawing her up until she stood before him, the night shift a cloud of spun mist about her body.

"Dev, I told you from the first that I'd not—not force myself upon you. If you don't want this . . . I'd be content to do nothing but hold you in my arms."

"But then you would ride away tomorrow. And I would be alone."

In a heartbeat he reached out, scooping her off of her feet, his heart thrumming against her as he held her cradled to his chest. Gently, so gently, he carried her to the bed. With one hand he swept back the coverlets, and tearful laughter bubbled in Devlin's throat as a shower of rose petals floated up to meet her.

He lowered her down onto sheets of fine linen, the rose petals kisses of velvet against her skin. And the fragrance spun around them, weaving an invisible bastion through which no war or ugliness or despair could seep.

Devlin felt the featherbed give as Myles lowered himself down beside her, the candlelight seeming trapped in his eyes, softening them with gentleness, sorrow, and a hope that made her want to cling to him forever, shield him from the madness that was to come.

"You're so beautiful, Dev," he said, smoothing the tendrils of hair back from her face. "Like a dream."

"I've never been very good at dreaming, Myles," she whispered. "Dream a wedding night for me. A perfect one."

"Nothing could be more perfect than being here with you." His eyes glistened, overbright, his fingers stroking every curve, every hollow of her face, as if to memorize it, to carry it with him. And then he was kissing her, his lips seeking, soft, so soft, gentling away all her fears.

Devlin flattened her hand against the brocaded silk that sheathed his chest, her fingertips learning the hard ridges of muscle and bone.

He tasted like honey warmed by summer sun, he smelled of meadows and wild, racing stallions, and as he took tiny sips of her cheek, the fragile skin behind her ear, the hollow at the base of her throat, Devlin felt as if she were being sucked from the safe, sandy shore into some mystic sea she had never known existed.

Slow, so slow his hands and mouth were, so patient as they whispered across her skin.

It was his gift to her, this gentleness, when she knew Myles was more a man of fire and raging passions. When he spoke his voice was raspy, achingly sweet. "Dev, I want to see you. Touch you." He pressed a long kiss to where her nightrail was tied primly at her throat, and his breath, hot and moist and just a little ragged, seemed to penetrate through the cloth to her skin, sending ripples of sensation through her body.

"Is that what . . . what people do? When they're . . . making love?"

"It doesn't matter what other people do, Dev, what other

people want. It's just the two of us here. Me. You. There aren't any wrong answers between us. You tell me what you want, what you need of me, and later . . . I'll tell you."

"I want you to tell me now." There was a catch in her voice. "Tell me what you want."

"Just to look at you, sweeting, to kiss you, to touch you. Just to give you miracles."

It took Devlin a moment to realize that he was waiting— this man who had made countless conquests, this notorious rakehell who had bedded the most beauteous courtesans in Europe. He was waiting for her to tell him what she wanted, what she needed. But she didn't know. Not anymore. It was as if she had never known, as if she had always been waiting, too. Waiting for Myles to take her hand and lead her into this mystical abyss.

Catching her lip between her teeth, she reached out and grasped his hand, carrying his long fingers to the satin tie at her throat. She felt a tremor go through him, and the tips of his fingers closed upon the wisp of satin, slowly tugging it free. The loop of ribbon slid through the knot, gave way, the cool night air trickling across the sliver of flesh he had bared. Then his hand quested downward, slipping free another bow, and another, smoothing the ribbons flat against her breasts before he moved on to yet another delicate tie.

When all were undone he traced the line of rosy flesh with his lips, leaving kisses across the place where her heart seemed to be trying to beat its way from her chest.

Devlin threaded her fingers through the dark mass of his hair, impatient when her journey through the luxurious river of silken strands was stopped by a tie of black velvet at his nape. With fingers far more awkward than Myles's she unfastened the tie, and she heard a moan low in his throat as his hair cascaded into her hands, filling them, the texture a mind-shatteringly sensual contrast to the hard, hot cords of his neck.

She gasped his name as he rubbed his face gently against her breasts, inhaling the scent of her, kissing her through the thin layer of cloth. Then he raised his head, and she saw beneath his inky lashes a smoldering passion as he brushed away the veil of embroidered fabric that shielded her from his eyes.

She knew a moment of panic as she felt cool air on nipples that were agonizingly sensitive, breasts that seemed swollen, aching beneath that hooded gaze. And she hated herself for wondering how many times Myles had done these things that were to her so wondrously splendid, so miraculous, so new. How many women, far more beautiful than she, had displayed their bodies proudly before the Viscount Liancourt for the taking?

Then his voice came, awed, his hand skimming across milky-pale skin with such reverence it drove all thoughts of his many lovers from her mind.

"Sweet Jesus, Dev," he murmured, his fingers tracing the alabaster curve of her breast. "Sweet Jesus, you're more beautiful than any dream I've ever had."

"I'm not beautiful," she whispered. "I'm intelligent, I'm capable . . . dependable . . ."

His voice was savage suddenly, harsh with need. "You're so damn beautiful it makes me burn, Dev, way down deep. Makes me ache in ways I've never felt before." His face contorted, and he arched his head back as if groping for the words to say to her. "It's as if . . . as if the gods dipped into the well of my dreams and fashioned you . . . made you just for me." His eyes were so bright Devlin lost herself in them, drowning in that blue that seemed liquid, glossed with . . . could it be tears?

"Do you know what it's like, Dev, to finally hold something real after all this time of dancing with meaningless shadows, trying to fill the empty places inside me with nothing but mist? I've wanted you forever, Devlin Chastain. I just never knew it . . . until I kissed you in the garden."

Devlin's breath caught in her throat as she stared at him, but there was no jesting in those lips that were suddenly so solemn, only longing.

With her fingertips she traced the lines of his face, the stubborn jut of his jaw, the cheekbones, slashed high, arrogant, the straight, patrician nose, as if learning them for the first time. And her voice broke as she whispered, "You are the one who is beautiful, Myles. Every part of you . . . your face . . . your body . . . but most of all . . . most of all, here." She slid her hand down the front of the banyan, the brocade parting in its wake until her palm rested upon his heart.

He groaned at the contact, then he was kissing her, his mouth moving across hers with a hunger that sent bits of raw pleasure shattering through her. She gasped, her lips parting, and Myles's tongue stole past them, dipping into her mouth, tasting her as if he were starving and she were the sweetest honey.

Tracey had thrust his tongue into her mouth before—a gesture she had found disconcerting, yet thrilling, too, because it seemed forbidden.

But never had the plunging of Tracey's tongue drugged her with mind-numbing pleasure the way Myles's caresses did; never had she felt the heavy, aching sensation at the apex of her thighs.

She gripped Myles's wide shoulders as if to brace her courage, then she let her own tongue venture out to brush tentatively against his firm lips, the straight ridges of his teeth. He opened his mouth wider, and she explored the secrets that lay beneath that bedeviling smile, tasted him in a way that made her thighs melt, her skin burn through the cloth wherever his big body pressed against her.

"Myles . . ." She whimpered his name, her whole body trembling, and he rained kisses across her cheeks, her eyelids, trailing them down the pale arch of her throat.

"I don't want anything between us tonight, Dev. Not the darkness, not the war, not even this thin gown wrapped about you, hiding you from my eyes."

He stared into her face for a moment, and she struggled to free herself from the nightrail that had suddenly become so constricting, keeping her from feeling the brush of Myles's sword-callused hands. But the garment she had shed every morning to begin her tasks suddenly tangled around her, imprisoning her until Myles's fingers clasped her wrists, drawing them away from the fabric.

With agonizing patience his hands worked to unveil her, and when at last he brushed the embroidered material from her shoulders and eased it down the slim length of her legs to pool at the foot of the bed, Devlin was trembling with eagerness and a sudden fierce pride that she could bring that rapt expression, that hot flush of desire to the man before her. She shivered, wondering what was to be next, eager to taste, to learn, to delve into the secrets Myles had promised with his eyes.

But he only cupped her bare foot in his palm, his long, sinewy fingers dark against the ivory of her skin, her foot seeming incredibly fragile against the hard, callused strength. He skimmed the delicate arch of her instep with his thumb, then lowered his lips to kiss her toes, the inside of her ankle, the incredibly sensitive place behind her knee.

Devlin whimpered as he brushed a kiss against the skin of her inner thigh, his fingertips skimming over soft red-gold ringlets that seemed to weep with want of him.

"Myles . . ." she managed to squeeze through a throat tight with emotion. "I want . . . I need . . . to—to see you . . . now that you've seen me."

A strained chuckle rumbled in his chest. "Believe me, Dev, there is nothing I want more. In fact, I remember when I was ten and you were studying anatomy with our illustrious tutor. You wanted to examine a male specimen, if you recall, and tried to impress me into service."

"You refused. I couldn't understand why. It was only in the—the interest of . . . of education."

"And this, sweeting—is this in the interest of education?"

"No. Yes. I—I don't know. I just feel so queer inside. Like if I don't . . . don't get to see you . . ." She reached out to the fastenings at the front of Myles's garment. As she slipped them free one by one she could feel Myles's muscles clench beneath the brush of her knuckles, she could hear Myles's breath rasping, harsh with need. The thin chain of the holy medal she had given him ran in a tempting rivulet of gold across the tensile cords of his throat. The sinews of his chest and flat, hard belly knotted beneath her touch.

Myles seemed to hold his breath as she smoothed the fabric back across the width of his shoulders, the brocade falling to the bedclothes behind them. One powerful tanned thigh was spanned by a thin strip of linen—the bandage she had knotted about his wound that very morning. But nothing in the fluttery sensation she had felt then had even hinted at what she felt now, this wild, racing sensation that left her breathless.

"Does it hurt much?" she asked him, trailing her fingertips across the hair-roughened flesh.

Myles's jaw was clenched, but not in pain, a muscle at the side of his mouth jumping. "How could I feel anything so commonplace as pain when you're touching me at last?"

His words made a shiver of anticipation go through her, and she cast her gaze down, her cheeks heating. But instead of easing the tension cinching tighter inside her, what she saw made her mouth go dry.

Only a single fold of the brocade obscured his final mysteries from her view, a leaf of gold and scarlet pooled across his powerful thighs, dusting the line of dark hair that flowed down from his navel.

Devlin stared down at the long ridge of Myles's masculinity, evident beneath the brocade, and felt an untameable urge to touch it.

"There are no wrong answers between us. Only what you want . . ." She heard Myles's voice echo in her head. Then, before she could lose her courage, she took the edge of the brocade between her fingers and slowly drew it away. She was aware of Myles sitting there, torturously still, was aware of her own mouth gaping. But she couldn't stop herself from taking in the beauty of him, a beauty beyond anything she had ever imagined.

In her years of study she had examined countless images of men—paintings, statuary, anatomical drawings. But they all seemed to pale beside the magnificence of Myles Farringdon's body.

His skin was smooth and sun-darkened, pulled sleekly over the play of his muscles. His shoulders were broad enough to rein in the wildest stallion, his thighs powerful enough to clasp onto its back as it reared and plunged. His hips were impossibly narrow, his belly flat and hard as a slab of granite. And though she knew little of a man with passions roused, that part of him that was so new to her thrust up proudly, beckoning her.

"You told me . . . told me to do whatever I wanted," she said, a little breathless. "I want to—to touch you."

He gritted his teeth and took up her hand, slowly laying her spread fingers upon the center of his chest. She brushed her hand across the prickly mat of hair, the roughness intensely pleasurable as she stroked it. Then curious fingers skimmed the flat disk of his nipple, the nub at the center pebble-hard in the dark aureole. Myles gasped when she touched it, and she looked at him, remembering the wondrous sensations he had evoked in the Dower House that forbidden night he had nearly taken her in sleep.

By instinct alone she dipped her head down, kissing him upon the hardened nub, touching it with her tongue.

He cursed and moved to grab her, kiss her, but she evaded his hands, smiling and shaking her head with a heady sense of power she'd never experienced before. "You told me to tell you what I want," she teased. "And I want you to hold still and let me—"

"Let you drive me insane?" he growled. "Just remember that turnabout is fair play."

But he let her hands stray across his skin until a fine sheen of sweat dampened it and the muscles in his jaw knotted with the restraint it was taking to keep his big body still.

Devlin gloried in it, this sweetest vengeance for all the torment he had caused her in years past. This wondrous amusing game that he had shown her. And when she wanted his hands on her the same way, wanted his mouth savage and hot upon her, she purposely set out to push him over the ledge of his self-control and into a lava-hot sea of passion.

With her fingertips and her lips she traced the curve of his rib cage, smoothed kisses down his belly. Her hair pooled in a veil of red-gold across his lap, and he moaned at the silky caress upon that part of him that pulsed, throbbed with need. Devlin let her fingers catch in her own red-gold tresses as she touched the burning hot center of that need.

He cried out, half in anguish, half in ecstasy as she brushed her fingers across its tip, ran one finger down its length, then up again, savoring the softness of it, the hardness of it, the newness of all she had unveiled.

"Damn it, Dev, if you're . . . making some infernal study of the . . . tolerance of a man pushed beyond endurance, I promise you've reached the . . . breaking point."

"Have I?" Was that temptress's voice really hers? Was that teasing, light brush of taunting fingers across his hardened length practical Devlin Chastain pleasuring her lover?

"Damn right you have."

"Then show me, Myles. I dare you."

A hundred times the word *dare* had been flung between them, a gauntlet for the other to snatch up, defiant. This time it was as if the word itself were some black, sizzling powder that burst into a conflagration within Myles's hands.

In a heartbeat his arms closed about her, his weight ramming her back against the pillows, his naked body crushing hers deep into petal-spangled sheets. There was nothing of the gentle wooing, the patient schooling that had characterized his lovemaking before. His mouth devoured hers, his hands roved over her breasts with a desperate hunger that fired the thirst sizzling even now in Devlin's soul.

She whimpered as he kissed her, deep and long and hard, his mouth slanting down the line of her throat to where her breasts thrust up against his chest, the nipples painful with need, begging for his mouth. Devlin delved her hands into his hair and guided his lips to the rosy crests.

Myles groaned, his lips closing hot and wet around the aching nubs, his teeth raking them with exquisite tenderness, devastating hunger. A low cry tore from her throat as he drew upon her breast, suckling it deep, lavishing it with long, drugging swirls of his tongue.

When she felt she couldn't bear the stark pleasure another moment without shattering he kissed a path to her other breast, shaping it with his hands as he praised it with his mouth, his tongue.

"You taste . . . taste so good, Dev," he breathed against her heated skin. "So sweet."

Then his hand smoothed down the indentation of her waist, down the flare of her hip, easing over to the melting-hot center where all sensation seemed to arrow.

She clasped her thighs tight together at the intimate touch of his fingers, but Myles murmured low in his throat.

"You're so pretty, Dev. Every part of you. So soft and sweet. Let me touch you, love. Touch you like you touched me."

"Myles, I don't . . . don't think I can bear it. Feel like . . . like I'm rolling downhill in a barrel. I can't . . . can't stop it."

"Why would you want to, sweetheart? Just let it go, Dev, faster and faster. Let it take you there."

"Take me where?" she asked a little desperately as his fingers smoothed down the crease between her clenched thighs.

"Soaring, Dev. To a place beyond imagining, where only we can go."

And she wanted to go with him. Anywhere. Everywhere. Wanted to become lost in the beauty that he offered. With the greatest of effort she forced her thighs to relax, her legs to part. Her cheeks blazed with embarrassment as she felt the candle shine drip over her nakedness. But then Myles's hand sheltered her from the unfeeling night, his callused fingers threading gently through the curls, finding the sleek, wet center hidden in their midst.

A shock seemed to jolt through Devlin as the tip of his finger found a place she hadn't even suspected existed. A place that sent pleasure spearing through her, that set loose waves of wantonness so wild and primal they tore a low scream from her throat.

She heard Myles groan at her response, his finger dipping lower, into the font of moisture, toying with her, teasing her until her hands knotted in the coverlets, her breath coming in short, pained gasps.

She didn't know what to say, didn't know what to do as Myles continued his wicked torture, but it no longer mattered, for she couldn't have squeezed words through her throat to stop him, couldn't have forced her leaden hands to push him away.

Then he was entering her with his finger, moving it gently in and out of her tight, virginal passage.

His breath was like a dying man's, harsh, grating, sweat slickening his muscle-hewn body. "Dev . . . we've only one night." There was a hopelessness in his voice. "Only this time. I have to—to taste you."

A shiver of disbelief shook Devlin to her very core as he lowered his head between the pale lengths of her thighs to the center of her desire.

Fire raced in jagged bursts through her veins, setting her whole body to shaking, her head thrashing against the pillows as Myles abraded the sensitive nub with teeth and tongue, the caresses exposing an emptiness, a void inside her, burning to be filled.

She was spiraling down into Myles's world with terrifying speed, catapulting out of control to a place she'd never been before. She was mesmerized, frightened, elated as Myles ministered to her with selfless passion.

And when she seemed to be hurtling wildly into nothingness, lost in the labyrinth of primal need, primitive desire, Myles pulled away from her.

The emptiness screamed inside her, and she cried out in frustrated passion, reaching for him with a desperation such as she'd never known. But he knelt between her quivering thighs, his powerful body towering over her, his shoulders limned with candlelight, his face as glorious as a pagan god's.

She grasped his rock-hard biceps, tugging him down until he covered her, the thick length of his arousal pressed against her thigh.

"I want . . . want you to . . . to fill me, Myles," she whispered, drowning in need. "Now."

But he held back, indecision glinting dark through the sapphire blaze of his eyes. "I don't want to hurt you, Dev. If you're not ready . . ."

"I don't—don't care, you bloody oaf!" she all but sobbed, arching her spine, writhing beneath him. "Please—"

He braced himself on his elbows, and Devlin felt the blunt, warm hardness of his sex press against the petals of her womanhood, hover there. She let her thighs fall farther apart, opening herself completely to Myles. She ran her hands down the curve of his back to the hard muscles of his buttocks and reveled in the tension in them, the trembling in Myles's whole frame.

And then suddenly he drove his hips forward, searing pain lancing through her as he buried his shaft deep. She bit down on her lip until it bled, confused, angry at having her pleasure shattered, tears of disappointment trickling from the corners of her eyes.

But then Myles kissed her and raised his head to peer into her face with such concern, such tenderness, that the pain faded into nothingness beneath the sapphire beauty of his gaze.

"I hurt you." It wasn't a question. His fingertips gathered up her tears. "I wish to God I could have spared you that."

"I didn't—didn't want to be spared. I want—want you to make me feel the way I did when . . . when you were . . . were toying with me . . . down there, Myles. I want . . . want the stars to shatter, to feel them raining down on me in a thousand glittering fragments. Take me there, Myles. Please."

No explicit urgings from the most practiced courtesan could have set Myles's pulse more ablaze. With every art he had gained in the beds of other women he strove to please this one woman that he loved, strove to shatter the stars for them both.

With smooth thrusts he set himself against her, heedless of the dull ache in his half-healed wound as he accustomed her to the feel of him plunging deep, his finger stealing down to the slick center, rubbing it, teasing it in time to the throbbing rhythm he had set.

He watched her, her eyes clenched tight, her head thrown back in a tangle of sunset curls. Her lips were parted in breathy gasps as she writhed against him, her hands locked upon his hips, struggling to draw him deeper, as if she wanted to take him inside herself, wanted him to mate with the very essence of her soul.

And he wanted to—wanted to touch every part of her, inside and out. Wanted to brand his image into her mind, into her heart, driving out dreams of any other man but him.

He sought out her breast, suckling the tip deep, driving his sex into her dark, velvety wet sheath again and again. And with each movement of his body against hers, with each savage-sweet fiber of restraint as he held his own release in check, he willed his body to tell her the things he could not say.

I love you, Dev, it told her. My wife, my bride. I love you more than quests for glory or dream worlds spun of legends. I love you more than life.

He felt the tremors take her as she buried a scream in the hard curve of his shoulder. She writhed, clutching at him as shudder after shudder of ecstasy bolted through her, and he drove himself into her hard, strong, wanting only to prolong the heaven she had found.

When the last ripple of joy had faded Myles clutched her against him, concentrating on his own release. And when it came it was shattering, crushing in its power, devastating him with the knowledge that in scores of meaningless affairs he had never found the world where Devlin had taken him—had never lost himself in another's soul.

His eyes burned as he buried his face against her breasts, wondering if he would ever have the chance to find his way there again with this woman who had stripped away all that he was, then given it back again.

Myles rolled carefully to one side, the dull throbbing in his thigh subsiding as he pillowed Devlin's head upon his shoulder, his hand stroking the tousled silk of her hair.

They lay there, silent, for what seemed forever, the only sound the call of a night bird through the window, mournful, lost. And Myles knew that he had been wrong. That tasting Devlin, touching her, while knowing he had to leave her, had made him feel more alone than he'd ever been in his life. Had made every dream, every quest, every cause that had set his heart ablaze seem cold and worthless when set against the treasure he'd found in her arms.

I don't want to leave you, Dev. Don't want to lose you, he wanted to tell her. I love you, girl. Damn but I do.

And yet, as he peered down into her face—a face glossed with a gentleness, a peace he'd never seen there before—he knew he dared not tell her. She had already lost one love because of him, had felt the jagged hole it had torn in her soul. How could he condemn her to another such loss? How could he pledge undying love to her, and wring the words from her, if she was only to bury him, a grieving widow, when this war was past?

It was the hardest thing he'd ever done, holding back the words that were clamoring inside him. It was the only gift he could give her.

He clenched his jaw at the injustice of it, knowing all the while that there was nothing else he could do.

"Myles?" Her voice was muzzy with sleepiness as she cuddled deeper in the crook of his shoulder.

"What, sweeting?"

"I knew . . . knew you would dream it . . . perfect."

"Did you?"

"Umhumm. And you weren't . . . obnoxious . . . even once."

"Your flattery overwhelms me, fair lady."

"I know that . . . that my other wedding night . . . it wouldn't have been like this if I'd married Tracey."

Myles swallowed hard, the muscles of his throat so tight they seemed ready to snap, but he didn't trust himself to answer.

Quiet draped about them again, the guttering candlelight weaving it into a quilt of flickering shadow.

Myles thought her asleep when she spoke again, a whisper that raked at his heart.

"Myles?" Her breath stirred the fine hairs upon his chest, and she tipped her face up until he could see the smoky green of her eyes. "Can you . . . tell me something. Want to . . . to know . . ."

Myles groped for the shield of humor that had protected him from Devlin's past rejections, wondering if it could preserve him from the softer, gentler Devlin who lay dreaming in his arms. "I'm afraid the calculus of finite differences or Boerhaave's theory of inflammation are a trifle beyond me right now. Maybe in the morning—"

But he wouldn't be there in the morning, he realized. He might never be with her again.

"It's nothing like that," she said, oblivious to the roiling emotions inside him. He could feel her tired smile. "What . . . what happened between us . . . when we were together . . ." Her words trailed off, and he stroked the silky skin of the naked arm draped across him.

"Myles, is that . . . what it would be like . . . if you loved me?"

Myles felt his heart shattering into tiny pieces as he held her in his arms.

"Yes, Dev," he whispered into the cloud of her hair. "That is exactly what it would be like . . . if I loved you."

CHAPTER
22

*M*yles was gone.

Devlin jolted awake. Disbelief, terror, and blinding fury suffocated her as she fought her way from the tangle of bedclothes, slivers of light from the window slashing eyes still fogged with sleep.

Her heart thundering, she hurled back the coverlets as if somehow they could be concealing Myles's long frame. But only a hollow in his pillow and the scent of him on her skin hinted that he had ever slept upon the spacious bed at all.

"Myles?" she called out, scrambling to her feet. "Myles, plague take you—" She snatched up her nightrail, scarcely feeling the draft that sent shivers scuttling across her bare skin as her eyes searched the chamber and the small dressing room adjoining it.

Panic knotted in her chest as she dragged the garment over her naked body, the dark suspicion that had jolted through her the instant she'd opened her eyes burrowing deeper inside her, making her eyes burn, her breath catch in ragged gasps.

No! It was impossible! she screamed inside herself. Myles had ridden days out of his way to bid his mother farewell before he rode off to war. Surely he'd not leave his wife without so much as good-bye.

She heard the creak of the bedroom door, and relief made her knees go weak as she wheeled toward it. "Myles Farringdon, I vow I'll have your hide for frightening me like that," she railed. But as the panel slid slowly open it was not Myles's long, hard-muscled frame that filled it, but rather a small, disconsolate figure in a pink satin morning gown, her hands clasped over the swell of her unborn babe.

"Bella." Devlin breathed the name, knowing in that soul-sickening instant that her worst fears were true.

Tears coursed down her friend's face, a face blotched and reddened from weeping.

"Bella, where is Myles?" She fought to keep her voice level, knew by the way Bella flinched that she had failed.

"He—he's gone, Devlin."

"Gone?" she echoed.

"He and Harry rode out before dawn. Myles . . . Myles didn't want to wake you."

"He *didn't want to wake me?*" Devlin all but shouted. "The man is going off to war, and he *didn't want to wake me?*"

Bella swallowed convulsively, tears overflowing her thick, childishly curled lashes afresh. Devlin felt a stab of guilt but couldn't seem to stop herself.

"Damn him to hell, how dare he—"

"I don't think he could bear to—to say good-bye to you. I think it hurt him too deeply."

"Hurt him?" Devlin heard a note of hysteria in her own voice. "How many times have I told you, Bella, he doesn't love me? He's never loved me! He could have done me the common courtesy of—"

The sound of Bella's broken sobbing jarred Devlin from her fury, leaving her feeling hideously bereft, lost in a way she had never felt before. She spun away from her friend, her hands knotted in the folds of her nightgown, the embroidery abrading her palms.

Devlin closed her eyes, remembering her wonder when

she had first seen the garment, a gift from Myles. Her stomach clenched with pain as she remembered Myles's hands, feverish with need, as he had stripped the garment away, his lovemaking dazzlingly passionate, yet heartbreakingly tender. A night that had changed Devlin forever, yet obviously not touched Myles even deeply enough that he felt compelled to tell her good-bye before he rode off to an uncertain fate.

Having done his husbandly duty and consummated the marriage, he had doubtless been too diverted by other things to bother with her—things like packing his neck cloths or his dice for the long march to London, or working with that ridiculous dragon sword they had found at the Dower House, trying to make the thing fit his hand.

And now he was marching off to get himself killed, and she'd not even had a chance to tell him . . .

Tell him what? a voice inside her jeered. That last night was the most beautiful thing that has ever happened to you? That he was the most tender, the most gentle, the most perfect of lovers? That when he had spilled his seed inside you he might not have conceived the heir his grandfather so desired, but he had planted some of his own dreams within your soul, so deep that you will never be free of them?

She buried her face in her hands, hating the tears that ran between her fingers, hating herself for being stricken with a bout of sentimental idiocy to rival any such madness Myles had ever known.

There was a soft shushing sound as Bella crossed the room, and Devlin felt the girl's hand drift down upon her shoulder in a tentative gesture of comfort.

Bella's voice was soft, thick with her own sorrow. "Devlin, I don't know what passed between you and Myles last night. I don't know what he's—he's told you . . . about how he feels. I only know that when he came to me before dawn broke he looked as if he'd already fought a war and lost. As if he'd lost everything when he left your bedchamber this morn."

"Don't, Bella. I can't bear hearing about how Myles

looked, what words he said, when he didn't even bother to say them to me."

"But he did, in the best way he was able, I think," Bella said, sitting beside her on the bed and withdrawing a small package from the pocket affixed to her waist. "He gave this to me and asked that I bring it to you the moment you awakened."

"Another infernal present?" Devlin raged. "I don't want another pen case or sewing box or brooch. I don't want anything but—"

To have Myles here with me, she thought. To see him smile one more time, to listen to his laughter. To have him kiss me and tell me that heroes never die, that they always come back to their lady loves.

She glared down at the carefully wrapped parcel in Bella's hands, wanting to dash it to the floor, fling it in the fire. She battled to keep her voice steady. "I don't want it, Bella. I don't want anything from him."

"Yes, you do, Devlin. And I think that it terrifies you. But Myles is nothing like . . . like that other one, that Tracey person you fancied yourself in love with."

"Of course he isn't! And I'm glad. But Myles and I . . . You don't just—just wake up one morning, desperately in l—" She couldn't seem to squeeze the word from her throat. She thrust her chin up, defiant. "You don't fall in love with someone in a heartbeat, like lightning flashing."

"Why couldn't it be that way? For both you and Myles? You thought yourself in love with Tracey for five years. How long did it take you to know you didn't love him at all?"

"Don't be ridiculous! The moment he slashed Myles with his sword I—" She leapt to her feet, pacing to the window, stunned to realize that it was true. Within the shelter of the arbor she had been devastated, shattered, uncertain how to claw her way through the rest of her life loving Tracey, a man she would never have. But when she had plunged out into the carriage circle—had seen Myles fighting because of her pain, seen Tracey's expert sword bite deep into Myles's flesh—all love had died. Died in the flash of time it had taken to see Myles's face contort in pain, died in the moment it took her to reach his side, fling herself between him and the point of Tracey's sword.

Yes, she'd fallen out of love just as Bella had said. And that coupled with Tracey's betrayal should have taught her the most painful of lessons: that it was foolhardy to trust her own instincts where love was concerned, idiocy to put her faith in a man who could cast her aside with no more thought than ridding himself of a torn neck cloth.

But Myles was not like that; the certainty streaked through her. Myles, who had always been staunchly loyal to anyone who had gained his affection. Myles, who had boxed the ears of a stable boy who had been tormenting a crofter's child. Myles, who had wiped up Bella's tears the night of her coming out and had tossed her bastard of a suitor into a hedge. Myles, who had taken to wife a woman he didn't want and had introduced her to the marriage bed with more tenderness and more fervor than any love-stricken husband could have managed.

Devlin caught her lip between her teeth, but even that slight pain couldn't drive away the swirling panic building deep inside her, the disbelief, the sick sense of shock.

Sweet God in heaven, it was impossible, she thought wildly, one hand clutched to her throat. She couldn't—by God's blood, she *wouldn't* fall in love with Myles! She absolutely refused to do something so ridiculous! So—so . . .

She leapt up from the bed and all but raced to the far side of the room as if to put as much distance as possible between her and the bed where Myles had made her his wife.

But still ghosts from the night before seemed to jeer at her, her own voice, hazed with sleep, whispering against his skin:

"Is that what it would have been like . . . if you loved me?

The blood drained from her face, leaving her dizzy, and she wanted nothing more than to be left alone, not able to bear having anyone—even the gentle Bella—see her this way, starkly vulnerable, stricken with soul-deep terror, trembling with both fear and wonder.

"Bella, thank you for bringing Myles's gift to me," she managed. "I . . . I don't mean to sound ungrateful, but I need to be alone for a little while."

Bella rose in a swish of pink petticoats, her angelic face wreathed in her own grinding sorrow. "Of course. I'll be in the grand salon if you . . . if you need anything."

Devlin sensed her friend's pain, wanted desperately to go to her, comfort her, but her own heart was too raw. She listened as the door shut, then turned to where the parcel lay upon the tumbled coverlets.

Slowly she crossed to the bed, her fingers reaching out to take up the package.

Sucking in a steadying breath, she slipped free the ribbon that bound the package and eased the paper away from the small rectangular object.

The light of the morning sun picked out the glow of gilt embossing pressed into the fine leather cover of a book. She opened it with trembling hands, running her finger over exquisite illustrations, the even rows of print.

A field was full of cavaliers who charged toward their destinies. Richard III stretched out his fingers toward the crown lost at Bosworth Field.

A sense of familiarity struck her in a jolt, and she battled to remember where she had seen this volume before. In a heartbeat she could picture it in her father's big hands, could hear Josiah Chastain reading the stories to her upon a summer's evening. The volume had always fascinated her— filled not with tales of history, but with the legends surrounding those who had ruled from England's throne.

Devlin stroked the leather binding, her heart aching. Myles must have retrieved it at the Dower House that night she had first tasted his passion. He must have tucked it away until her pain was no longer raw, saved it for her until now.

Her throat constricted as she traced a painting of Lancelot kneeling to Guinevere, Arthur pulling the sword from the stone.

Legends, those legends she had scoffed at years later, that she had brushed aside, impatient, vowing that both Arthur's wife and his friend deserved the destinies fate had dealt them for their faithlessness.

But now, as she stared down at Lancelot's face, at the devotion, the devastation caught by the artist in his eyes, Devlin found herself aching for him, and for the woman torn between two men, loving them both, able to let go of neither.

She closed the volume, the image too painful, somehow too close to her own emotions to bear, but as the pages flipped closed she glimpsed Myles's bold scrawl upon the frontispiece and quickly opened to the page, reading:

To my wife, Mistress Devlin Chastain, upon the occasion of our marriage. Some pieces of dreams. Catch them, Dev, if you dare. Myles.

A drop of moisture bloomed upon the script, smearing it. "Oh, Myles," Devlin whispered, turning the pages as though she could find a piece of him hidden inside them. And yet, in a very real way it was as if he had given her some part of him to hold in the pages of the book. A part of himself that she'd never touched before. Never wanted to touch, until now.

She started as a leaf of paper slipped from the pages, and she set the book aside, taking up the bit of paper. Her fingertips ran over the Liancourt seal pressed into the sealing wax, and she could picture the ring that never left Myles's finger. The ring that generations of his ancestors had worn before him.

Careful not to break the wafer of wax, she eased it away from the edge of the paper and unfolded the missive.

Dear wife,

The words were bittersweet, beautiful, written in his hand.

You are most likely vexed with me for leaving without bidding you farewell, but as I watched you sleeping, so peaceful, I found I could not bear the thought of saying good-bye. I have left ample funds in the care of Harry's solicitor, John Campbell, for your convenience, and in the event that you should have need of more, I drafted letters to my banker in England, and to my grandfather, apprising them of our marriage. Anger gave way before a kind of aching tenderness that Myles—the ever-impulsive—had been so careful to provide for her.

As for the Dower House jewels, I have dispatched them to my grandfather as well, so they will await your pleasure in a place where the war cannot touch them.

Most importantly of all, I wanted you to know that the terms of my will—Devlin winced at the word—*have always been in your favor, everything save the entailed estates bequeathed to you—a large enough competency to make you "quite independent," as you've always wanted.* Disbelief and tearing grief dug into her chest as she heard the echo of her own oft-repeated words and knew that Myles alone had sensed the desperation in them, and the pain.

Always before, she continued to read, *I had wanted to make certain you would benefit, should your dire predictions about my breaking my neck or being shot in a duel come true. But upon the event of our wedding I also wanted to make certain that you would receive the rights due you as my wife, as well as those of the mere beneficiary. Also, if God should bless us with a child, I wanted there to be no doubt that it is mine—to be accorded all the rank and privilege the heir of the Viscount Liancourt deserves.*

For now, Dev, I think it best that you accompany Bella to Harry's country estate of Thistlewould and remain there, safely out of the path of the war. With the babe coming I know Bella will be grateful for your company, and I'm certain no one could usher the newest Cameron into the world with more dispatch than you.

Regarding last night, I want you to know that it was everything I could have wished for. And that I—there was an unsteadiness to his hand there before he had plunged on in his usual scrawl—*hold you in higher esteem and affection than any woman I've ever known.*

Your husband and obedient servant,

Myles Farringdon, Viscount Liancourt

Devlin clutched at the edges of the letter, felt the paper tear in her hand, but she couldn't shake the horrible sense of foreboding rippling through her.

Always before she had been incensed, furious when Myles had ridden out, heedless, thinking only of glory and adventure, his eyes blinded with idealism. But now, staring at the letter in her hand—the lines filled with careful plans, directions given in the event he should die—she was more terrified than she'd ever been in her life.

She clutched the letter an instant more, then thrust it aside, charging to her feet. Within moments she'd dragged out fresh petticoats, determination flooding through her.

Perhaps the viscount would prefer that she remain behind, but he had spent his whole life being hopelessly spoiled. This time he would not get his way. She was going to ride after him, find him, and . . . She swore. She didn't have the slightest idea what she would do when she found him, but it didn't matter. Nothing mattered except reaching him, his laughter wiping away the horrible dark shadows that frightened her so.

She had struggled into the bodice and was battling the laces of her riding habit when the door burst open, the stricken, pale face of Annie making terror race through Devlin's veins.

"Mistress Devlin, hurry," the girl choked out. "It's my lady. She's bleeding, and I fear—"

Within an instant Devlin had shoved the girl aside, racing for the salon where Harry and Bella had spent so many hours. Face ashen, Bella was curled in Harry's favorite chair, her slight frame racked with sobs of pain and terror.

"The babe," Bella cried, her fingers clenching about Devlin's until they ached. "Oh, God, I can't . . . can't lose the babe—"

The soft pink skirts of Bella's gown were splashed with small stains of crimson, the dark moisture spreading until alarm streaked through Devlin.

She forced her voice to be steady, reassuring. "You're not going to lose the baby, Bella. You're just overwrought with Harry's leaving." She turned to shout out the door. "Jacob! Carry your mistress up to her bedchamber. And Annie, go into my room and fetch up my pouch full of possets at once."

The servants scurried to do her bidding, but as Jacob lifted Bella from the chair the girl gave a cry of such agony it drove like a knife into Devlin's heart.

Please, God, don't let anything happen to her! Devlin pleaded silently. Help me.

She took up Bella's hand, walking beside Jacob as he carried the girl up the stairs, settling her in the big bed she had shared with Harry Cameron.

Hour after hour, day and night, Devlin fought a war of her own, fighting against Bella's emotional anguish and nature's implacable will to keep the child tucked safely in Bella's womb.

Soothing possets and compresses were brewed and dispensed with more care than Devlin had ever given before, every mixture containing large doses of desperate, heartfelt prayers.

In all the years Devlin had served as healer about the Liancourt estate, the illness of only one other person had touched her this deeply, frightened her this badly.

But even when Lady Caroline had been at her worst, when the physicians had shaken their heads like vultures over her frail body, and the servants had gone to the corners of the big castle to weep in grief for their dying mistress, Devlin had never given up. She was not going to give up with Bella now.

All of her own strength, her knowledge, she poured into helping this woman she loved. And when at last the pain had subsided and Bella slept like an exhausted child herself, Devlin felt again the weary triumph she had known with Lady Caroline, the sense of victory tempered by the most mind-numbing exhaustion Devlin had ever known.

She sat at Bella's bedside and stared into the girl's translucent face, a face so pale that the tracery of blue lines was visible where her veins carried life beneath her skin. And as she peered down into that beautiful countenance, Devlin knew that she would never be able to leave Bella now, to ride off after Myles, hoping somehow to find him in the vast countryside between Edinburgh and England.

Even when the danger of miscarriage was truly past for Bella, Devlin could hardly abandon the girl to the care of frightened servants and unfeeling physicians or clumsy midwives who might well cost the girl the child she so wanted. Especially when Myles had trusted her to care for this woman he loved like a sister.

Devlin stared out the window in Bella's room, watching the last wisps of night dance with the dawn. Somewhere out across the heather Myles was riding with his prince, the Stuart banner unfurling proudly above their heads. The fifes were playing, the beat of the drum urging the warriors onward, the skirl of bagpipes singing, mournful, upon the wind.

Somewhere he was sitting astride his Barbary stallion, his dark hair tossed by the breeze. And she might never know what he was thinking, feeling as he rode toward the country he so loved, to wrest England from the German upstart's hands. She might never know that he was fighting, that he was dying, until all was past, the names of fields as yet unchristened with rebel blood being scribed in history books for generations to come.

She turned away from the window, the empty void beyond seeming to swallow her, to make her ache, and she slipped away from Bella's bedside just long enough to go into her own chamber and scoop up the book she'd abandoned in her haste to reach Bella's side days before.

Returning to her chair, she leaned toward the candle and opened the book to the frontispiece, skimming her fingertips over Myles's script.

"I need those pieces of your dreams now, Myles, since you're not here to show them to me in your eyes," she whispered to the night.

And as she read the beautiful stories, the romantic tales Myles had given her, it was as if she could feel him surround her, enfold her in his arms. Every hero was gifted with his sapphire eyes, every word spoken came from the mouth that had kissed her into madness. And every time the conqueror knelt before his lady, offering up the fruits of his quest, it was Myles she saw, kneeling before her in a garden filled with Stuart roses, offering up a crown woven of legend, the Stuart crown that had disappeared into the mists of time generations ago.

When at last she finished the final page the beauty of the words still held her, caressed her. And she knew then that she loved him.

Her tormentor.

Her husband.

Myles.

If only somehow the fates would let him live long enough for her to tell him so.

CHAPTER

23

*T*he fire crackled upon the hearth, filling the library at Thistlewould, the Camerons' country estate, with a cozy golden glow. April breezes heavy with rain buffeted the window, the countryside beyond the panes greening with the coming spring.

The beauty of life renewing itself was everywhere. But nowhere was it more evident than in the manor house itself, where six-week-old Master Henry Myles Cameron held court among an adoring throng comprised of devoted family retainers, his enchanted mama, and Devlin herself.

From the moment she had eased baby Hal's wriggling, sturdy little body into the world she had been entranced with the tiny being, her arms aching to hold him, to discover everything about him, from how to soothe him when he cried to what colored ribbons would make him burst into that winsome toothless grin.

She had helped with the birth of over a dozen infants while assisting the midwife at Liancourt, had scrubbed their wrinkled, red skin clean and wrapped them up warmly before putting them into the arms of their mothers. She had tidied up the little crofters' cabins and had left potfuls of soup or stew bubbling over a fire. Then she had left the family alone to marvel at their newest member while she went off, her attention drawn to the next pressing task.

She had always deemed infants rather boring—tiny, demanding bundles with a distressing propensity for wailing at the most inconvenient times.

But that was because she had never stayed long enough to see them kick out with dimpled legs or reach up with tiny fingers. She had never heard the soft sucking noises the baby made in its sleep or seen the sparkle of delight in eyes that were heartbreakingly innocent.

And she had never witnessed mother and child while the little one suckled at the breast, the two seemingly held in a magical circle of love.

It might have been perfect, the picture Bella made with her son, were it not for the fact that Master Hal's papa had never looked upon that cherubic little face, nor had the boy's namesake, the Viscount Liancourt, been present to dangle an elegant coral and bells above the little one's cradle, to see the babe's delight at the silvery jingle the toy made.

The weeks at Thistlewould might have been an idyll of beauty and peace were it not for the fact that sometimes Devlin caught Arabella bending over the cradle of her tiny son, weeping when she thought no one was about. Or were it not for the fact that both women's hearts stopped each time a messenger rode up to the door, fearful that he would bring them the most dreaded news of all.

Five months it had been since Myles and Harry had ridden away—five months of sporadic news, rare, treasured letters, and conflicting reports that had driven both women wild with worry. Five months in which they had been determinedly cheerful, neither allowing the other to guess how fearful they were, how filled with sick dread and gnawing loneliness.

Ever since the day the hired coach had rumbled up the winding road, bringing Devlin and Bella to Harry's ancestral home, time had crawled by at an agonizingly slow pace.

They had kept busy, forcibly optimistic as news of the march into England filtered back to their secluded haven.

They had rejoiced as the Stuart army had charged through England all but unchallenged, occupying Carlisle and Derby. They had thanked God fervently at the news that the army's few losses were mostly deserters wearied of adventure and hungering for their own cozy hearths.

As Christmas had neared it seemed certain that Myles's predictions of glory were to be realized, only the most meager chain of defense still standing between Prince Charles and the capital city of England. Devlin had never been more grateful to be proved wrong in her life.

The two women had packed a chest with festive gifts for their husbands—warm knitted stockings and gloves to shield fingers chilled by the bite of the wind, shirts stitched through long, sleepless nights, flasks of brandy and tins of chocolates for Myles's insatiable sweet tooth. And lastly Devlin had slipped in the final gift that she had sewn him, a gift she hoped would tell him more than mere words could say: a white Stuart cockade, the symbol of the cause for which Myles had risked so much, the knot of ribbon to be affixed to his dashing tricorn when he "marched, triumphant, into London Town."

The box had been sent off in ample time, and the two women had steeled themselves for the strain of waiting once again, praying that the holiday would bring them word that the forces were safe within the city walls and that the prince sat upon the throne generations of Stuarts had held before him.

When a messenger garbed in the Cameron plaid had ridden up the carriage circle three months earlier Devlin had rushed out to meet him, but one look at the expression beneath the Scotsman's shaggy russet hair had sent her spirits plunging.

She'd all but ripped Myles's letter from the man's hand, tearing it open, her hands shaking. As she scanned the familiar scrawl her stomach churned, her eyes stinging at Myles's furious, confused words.

They had turned back in full retreat. Not in the face of superior forces or because they had suffered defeat, but because Charles's council had turned against him, refusing to go on. News of French reinforcements and another army of Scots and Irishmen amassing, anxious to join the Jacobites, had not fed the fire of their victorious march, driving the council to strike swiftly at the nearly defenseless capital city. Rather, the elder Jacobites had decided that there was no reason to risk the existing army in such a military push when by spring their numbers would be doubled.

It was military suicide, Myles wrote, his bold scrawl filled with fury. It had slaughtered the morale of the soldiers more certainly than any Hanoverian army could have done. Most had not even been told of the decision to pull back into Scotland. They had merely begun to march out of Derby before dawn, following their commanders, and when the sun had risen they realized that they were not upon the road to London, but rather traveling back in the direction that they had come from weeks before.

It had mattered little that the prince himself was outraged at the direction the campaign had taken. The clan chieftains had stood firm in their refusal to risk their men. But despite Charles's anger, despite the fury of men like Myles and Harry, despite the fact that London yet dangled before them like an overripe plum waiting to fall into their hands, they retreated through the wintry countryside, defeated in spirit, yet not defeated by the sword.

There would be another campaign, the councilors assured them, one guaranteed to end in victory. But Myles had written that with each step he had taken away from the heart of London he had memorized the countryside: the churches, with their spires pointing to the heavens; the rows of stone fences; the wattle and daub cottages, with their gardens sleeping in winter. And he had sensed that he would never see the rows of cabbages and carrots standing like sentries in the rich earth, would never again watch an English mist whisper across lands that the druids had once walked. That he would be exiled forever from this country for which he had been willing to sacrifice everything he loved—even his life.

Tears had seared Devlin's cheeks, and she had sobbed until her chest ached, wanting nothing more than to find

Myles, rage with him, hold him, tell him that she cared not if the whole of England sank into the sea as long as he still smiled at her, held her in his arms.

But the letter had ended with his saying that the one thing he took comfort in was the fact that she was far away from this cause he had thought so glorious, that she could not see the disillusionment that festered among the ranks like the plague. And Devlin had sensed the words he could not say—that he didn't want her to see him thus, thwarted, furious. That he didn't want her to witness his anger at his ultimate helplessness to change things.

She had paced about, indecisive, tempted to disregard his request and ride to meet him. But that had been before Hal was born and Bella had been so stricken by what had been in Harry's letter that Devlin feared the babe would come too early. Again she had quelled her own fierce need, loathing the sense of resentment, of being trapped, that sometimes crept through her, despite her love of Bella.

Devlin had paced about the house like a tigress caged in some collector's menagerie those final weeks before Hal's birth. Half mad with worry she had been, torn in a way that made her burst into tears or slam the toe of her slipper into walls in raw frustration.

In the end she had done the only thing she could think of to keep herself sane. She had flung herself into Harry Cameron's library, wanting to lose herself in the learning that had always numbed her pain. But neither history nor science could divert her.

Disconsolate, she had huddled before the fire, attempting to stem the tide of her loneliness, depression, the aching need for Myles that never seemed to ease.

She had been watching the patterns of the firelight upon the hearth, attempting to play Myles's childhood game of seeing pictures in the shadows—a game at which she had been decidedly awful. But that night, as she had stared down at them, willing them to take some form, she had frozen, stunned, as the patterns had suddenly seemed to shift, rosy embers starring the bright gold reflections of the flames. A crown. For just a heartbeat it had been so clear that it made a chill scuttle down her spine.

She blinked, rubbing a hand across swollen eyes, and when she looked at the place where the image had been it was gone. Even so, she couldn't shake the uneasiness that gripped her, couldn't stop herself from darting wary glances about the room, probing shadows pooled in the corners as if she expected to see some ethereal figure garbed in a cavalier's hat, some ghostly keeper of legends reaching out to her with skeletal fingers.

She shook herself in aggravation and disbelief that she should be prey to such absurd fancies, and she had taken herself off to bed, resolutely telling herself that it was merely lack of sleep that was making her so impressionable.

Instead of donning the wedding nightrail she had favored in the months past because it made her feel somehow closer to Myles, she had rummaged through her things until she found a serviceable white lawn garment fashioned with as much imagination as a nun's stark habit.

She had tucked herself in bed, dragging the bedclothes up to her chin. But the moment she closed her eyes the glimmering gold and glowing red of the crown image wavered in the darkness until it seemed the thing had somehow branded itself upon the insides of her eyelids.

Midnight had passed, sleepless, and she had lain abed, listening to the silence—a silence that seemed to sing to her some siren's song that she alone could hear. She wanted to plug up her ears with bits of cotton, wanted to sever the thread that tugged her back to the library against her will. But when the clock in the hallway struck the hour of two Devlin had clambered out of bed and yanked on a dressing gown. By the light of a single candle she had rummaged from one of her trunks the material Myles had amassed about the Stuart crown—books and letters, diaries of those who had sought it before, and a bundle of vellum with a notation at the top saying that Myles had taken it from the priest hole.

Devlin had carried it all down to Harry's library, sifting

through the information about the legend with a hunger that was suddenly insatiable.

All the skills she had learned from Lady Caroline and the stern tutors who had resented having to teach a mere girl Devlin applied to the mystical story. And in the weeks that followed it was the one thing that eased her restlessness, her loneliness. The hope that she might somehow unravel the obscure clues Myles had documented with such uncharacteristic care gave her a feeling that she was doing something tangible to help him.

For she sensed that nothing would ease his battered spirits more certainly than for her to write him with the news that she had somehow furthered the quest that the rebellion had forced him to abandon. Nothing would bring that amused smile to his lips more quickly than knowing that she had been consumed by the magic of the story, that she had discovered whatever link was missing from the careful web of clues that he had constructed.

That was when it had begun—her own obsession with Myles's dream. She had delved tirelessly into unearthing any information she could find about the legend. And after little Hal was born she attempted to learn all she could about babies as well, hoping desperately that when Myles was with her once again they could set themselves to the joyous task of filling numerous cradles with their own blue-eyed babes.

She had drafted him letters, telling him of small triumphs she had made amid the stacks of research. And when letters had come from him, only the paragraphs containing his reflections upon the crown had seemed to hold any of his accustomed enthusiasm, optimism. But still the final piece of information that would solve the puzzle dangled just out of her reach.

And as her own frustration increased the sense of urgency that had niggled at the back of her mind seemed to grow as well, edging past her usual calm sense of logic.

She had sat in the dimly lit library, her fingers tracing the golden flowers wreathing the miniature Myles had given her the night of the ball. The eyes of the painted lady had seemed to stare up at her, attempting to relay some message she couldn't understand, filling her with a sense of frustration, yet of union as well, a link with this long-dead woman who had also watched as her beloved husband charged off to war.

But today, as the rain beat against the window, the wind crooning a mournful tune to the heather, the sense of doom Devlin had felt seemed to fill the room until she felt she couldn't breathe.

The door to the library creaked, and Devlin jumped, turning to see Bella hovering in the doorway. The weight she'd gained in her pregnancy had been lost due to the twin forces of fussing over baby Hal and worrying over the absent Harry. Her shoulder was damp, doubtless from little Hal's enthusiastic gnawing, and her golden hair was in disarray. Often during the weary months past, just the sight of Bella's, face had cheered Devlin. But today the young woman's expression only tightened the noose of unease that seemed to hold Devlin in its grasp.

"Hal is sleeping," Bella said, fidgeting as if she were a guilty schoolgirl invading Devlin's private domain. "Do you—do you mind if I come in? I mean, if I'm disturbing you, just tell me, and—"

"Don't be a fool, Bella," Devlin snapped, impatient. *"You* are the mistress of this house. If you wanted to build a pile of books in the center of the floor and set fire to it, no one could say you nay."

Bella blanched, hurt washing over her gentle features. "I'm sorry. I can see you'd rather be alone. It's just that you burrow yourself away so often of late, and I . . . the babe keeps me so busy, I . . ."

A rumble of thunder rolled over the hills, and Bella jumped, outwardly as skittish as Devlin felt inside.

Disgusted with herself, Devlin hastened over to her friend's side. "I don't know how you put up with me. It's little wonder everyone at Liancourt dived beneath the wall hangings whenever I was in a surly mood."

"You're not . . . *so* very surly," Bella sniffled. "And I'm not such a fool that I don't know that you are the one who has been 'putting up' with me these many months. If I hadn't been so sickly, and so frightened, and so lonely, you would have charged off to join Myles long ago."

Devlin looked away quickly, attempting to hide the sharp pang she felt at the truth in Bella's words.

"You know I wouldn't have left you until the baby was born. And as for Myles . . . even if I had been strapped to his middle like his sword and pistols, we'd only have spent the time fighting."

"And you would have been having a w-wonderful time of it, too. Debating military strategies, and—and arguing about everything from the color of the sky to which direction his tent should face. You would both be worlds happier than you are now, so far apart." Tears trembled on Bella's lashes, then fell free.

"Myles doesn't want me with him, Bella. He's made that abundantly clear. With every letter he expounds on how glad he is that I am safely far away."

Bella smiled a little through her tears. "If he writes it often enough, he might even convince both of you that it is true."

"What are you talking about?" Devlin protested. "Of course it is true!"

"Come now, you cannot have thought that Myles would ever ask a woman he loved to share the hardships of a military campaign. Suffer the uncertainties, the peril."

"It didn't seem to bother Myles to drag me across England with not even a tent to shield us. I cannot see why this should be any different."

"You were not his wife then."

"Are you trying to tell me that wives are not expendable? There is a baronet near Liancourt who has been married six times. He keeps outliving his wives in turn. It never seems to bother him in the least. They stuff the dead one in the family crypt and start fitting out the new one with bridal clothes three weeks later."

Bella giggled, the amusement in her eyes a reminder of days gone by. "Be that as it may, most men feel it is their duty to protect their wife—a mistress lost is inconvenient, a lover lost is the stuff of tragedies, but a wife lost . . . it is somehow a reflection upon the man himself, the whole world feeling that he has neglected his duty. And even were it not for this husbandly peccadillo, Myles would not risk you in such a venture because no matter how desperately he wants you, he would see such a request as the height of selfishness."

Devlin pressed her teeth into her lower lip, her mind whirling. How many times since childhood had she stubbornly clung to the belief that Myles was selfish? How many times had she comforted herself with that knowledge while she had dashed about feeling superior to him as she took care of the many tasks about the estate? It had confused her, hurt her, that everyone from the lowliest spitboy to Liancourt's most august guests had favored Myles's careless kindnesses to her own meticulous tending to details.

But now, as she heard the distant rumble of thunder roll in across the Scottish hills, it was suddenly all so clear. Myles's gifts had always been gifts of the heart—as natural and freely given as the scent of the roses in Liancourt's gardens. Her 'gifts' had not been gifts at all, but fiercely made bargains designed to wring loyalty from the people she served, since she could not even manage to win the loyalty of her own mother.

And all the while Devlin had been meddling, she had cared little about the dreams and hopes and quirks of those she aided. Rather she had crammed them into whatever shape she, in her inviolate wisdom, saw fit.

Devlin paced to where the fire crackled upon the hearth and stared at her shadow outlined upon the floor. It was as though she were staring, not at the shifting pool of darkness upon the stone, but rather at a mirror, looking at her own reflection for the very first time.

She had bullied and tyrannized until she had gotten her own way, and afterward she had been resentful when those around her hadn't thanked her for her efforts.

While Myles—Myles had always rejoiced in everyone's uniqueness, had accepted people upon their own terms. He had allowed them to be angry, foolhardy, giddy, or stubborn, whatever their particular demon dictated. And yet he had still welcomed them into the circle of warmth to be found in that bedazzlingly loving grin.

He had even welcomed her—resentful, belligerent, lashing out in her pain—and had cared for her in spite of her prickly facade, while she had spent a lifetime dredging out the slightest of his shortcomings, recounting them to any who would listen.

Fierce loneliness tore at her with savage teeth, and she realized that she had always felt alone except when Myles was teasing her, tormenting her, making her far too angry to realize how sad she was inside.

And now *he* was the one who was alone. Alone with his doubts, his frustration, alone with the guilt she had sensed in his letters. Guilt and fury and soul-searing regret for what had happened to her and to Tracey and to the cause Myles had devoted himself to.

She closed her eyes, imagining the interior of his stark tent, the yawning silence of it, oilcloth walling out the laughter. And she wondered if he was taking the only comfort available to him, in the form of one of the buxom women who trailed along in the wake of the army. God knew she'd gleaned enough from overhearing the servants' gossip to know that half the wives of the Stuart officers would have been willing to cuckold their husbands for a tumble in Myles Farringdon's bed, and many of the officers themselves would have encouraged such dalliances, prideful that their mates should be chosen for such an exalted position as a viscount's mistress.

Yet such thoughts could do little but sadden Devlin further, because she was certain that even should Myles want to seek out the forgetfulness he had found in so many meaningless beds, he would never betray her. Even through his pain he would remember her anguish over Tracey's perfidy and would want to spare her from suffering more on his own account.

"I love him, Bella." She said the words aloud for the first time, her throat constricting.

"I know. The only marvel is that you didn't realize it years ago."

"Do you know that I nearly broke my nose once? I was attempting to finish a volume of Machiavelli before my mother set me to a basket of mending. I ran into the branch of an apple tree, face first."

"That must have come as a surprise."

"It did. I vow it knocked me clean off my feet. It bled abominably, and of course I'd forgotten my handkerchief."

"What happened?"

"Myles had been hiding in the tree to avoid his lessons. He clambered down and gave me his handkerchief. He said that I always had my nose stuffed so deep in my books that I never saw what was dangling right before my eyes." Devlin's voice grew soft, remembering. "I thought he meant the tree branch, but he meant other things, didn't he? Things I never suspected."

"I can't say. I only know that when he came to us at the vicarage there was something in his eyes whenever he spoke of you. Nan said from the first he was nursing a broken heart."

"Broken? Over me?" Devlin shook her head, incredulous. "Look at me, Bella. Do I seem the sort of woman that a man like Myles Farringdon would break his heart over? I'm plain and—and I haven't any tact. I'd rather burrow away in a corner and read than attend the king's own ball. Myles . . . he—he's dazzling to the eyes, and he could charm the keys to hell out of the devil himself. Besides that, there is nothing Myles loves better than to be neck-deep in frivolity."

"Are you certain of that? I'll grant you, Myles is beautiful to look upon, but most of the women who flock to his bed fail to see beyond that to how beautiful he is inside. And as for loving frivolity—have you ever thought that might be his way of burying his hurt, the way that you bury yourself in your books?"

Devlin gaped at her friend, her memory reeling with images of Myles at soirees or balls or musicales when he thought no one was watching him. Gazing out the window, his face touched by some emotion Devlin had not been able to name. She had been so angry as the years had flown by and Myles's visits to Liancourt grew rarer and rarer. She had thought it heedlessness, selfishness, the height of villainy for him to deprive his sick mother of his company. Surely it wasn't possible that Myles had been attempting to avoid the pain of . . .

Of what? Of seeing Devlin? Of knowing that she was betrothed to his best friend?

No. It wasn't possible that Myles—Myles of the sparkling eyes and teasing grin—might *need* Devlin. Might *want* her.

"Do you know what it is like to hold a dream in your hands?" he had asked her when they made love.

Pretty words they had been, his handsome features as ardent as any bride could have wished. Yet she had believed Myles was only being kind, spinning her out a perfect wedding night as expertly as any weaver of legend had ever fashioned a fantastical story.

Could it be that Myles had meant the things he said? That the hunger in his kiss had come from a need that had smoldered in him long before he had kissed her in the rose garden at Liancourt? Perhaps even before Braden Tracey had hidden away with her in the stables, to give Devlin her first taste of that heady wine called desire?

She searched her memory, dredging up the musty, hay-scented room where she and Tracey had lain, slivers of sunlight piercing the cracks between the boards. Tracey had kissed her into dizziness, frissons of excitement fizzling through her as that perfectly manicured hand toyed with her breasts beneath her loosened stomacher.

Her face had been afire with embarrassment, but her mind had been churning, carefully recording every sensation, every emotion, to be taken out and examined thoroughly at a later time, when suddenly Tracey had all but flown away from her, launched by Myles's furious hands.

She had looked up into those eyes that could be so filled with amusement, affection, and had seen in that heartbeat the Myles Farringdon who had become notorious throughout England for his deadly temper and savage skill at the duel. And for a moment she had feared that he would draw steel upon Tracey where they stood.

But Tracey had claimed to love her, and she had blurted out that she felt the same, though now, looking back, she was uncertain whether she had acted because of her feelings for the elegant Tracey or to drive away the frightening ferocity in Myles's eyes.

No, she *had* loved Tracey—the *idea* of Tracey, a man who cared for her. Countless times she had been witness to women flinging themselves at Myles's head—everyone from Mary Maginny to the local baronet's gap-toothed daughters, who fairly swooned at the sight of him.

But except for Myles, there had never been a man who had looked upon Devlin with anything but a wary kind of awe, a kind of mistrustful unease that was at once aggravating and disappointing. Though she'd never wanted men slavering over her and simpering the way they did around brainless, fan-fluttering females, she had longed for some kind of attention. If only to fling it in Myles's laughing face.

Devlin fingered the binding of *Paradise Lost,* her lips twisting in disgust. Even when Tracey had struck up a flirtation with her upon holiday at Liancourt, hadn't she mainly grabbed up his offer because Myles was flaunting his *affaire de coeur* with a pretty little dairy maid possessed of the most adoring doe-brown eyes? And even now, five years later, Devlin could not say whether or not she would have dared slip off with Tracey to the stable at all had she not stumbled upon Myles and his light o' love in the buttery that morning, skimming off a good deal more than last night's cream.

She had been so angry, unsettled, feeling as if she were dancing barefoot upon a sun-seared stone. But until now she had never suspected why.

"Bella, I have to go to him," she blurted out.

"Of course you do." Arabella's laughter rang out, and she flung her arms about Devlin in an exuberant hug. "First thing in the morning we'll begin preparations for the journey. I'll have Jacob ready the coach, and he and William can escort you while Annie tends to the rest of your needs. With all the servants who are fixtures here at Thistlewould, we'll not even miss the three of them. Before two days are out you'll be on your way to winter camp in Inverness."

A grin spread across Devlin's face, the thunder that had seemed so ominous a while ago now seeming little more than a rumbling echo of her joy.

"Myles will be furious," she said, her mind already whirling with dozens of comforts she could bring him, her tongue already forming the words she could say if she but had the courage.

"I doubt my lord Farringdon will be able to cling to his anger after he looks at you . . . sees . . ."

"Sees what?"

"This." Arabella trailed her delicate fingertips in an affectionate path down Devlin's cheek. "There is a softness in your face that wasn't there before. A . . . a gentling. And a certain sense of peace."

"He gave me that, didn't he? Mystical legends to dream about, and acceptance of me despite my thorns. No, not merely acceptance." *Love,* Devlin wanted to say, but the word was too precious to say aloud, even to Bella.

Her eyes full of tears, she turned to the window. The scene outside blurred as she fought not to cry.

But a point of light wavering in the darkness made her shake herself, dash the back of one hand across her eyes to clear them. Devlin stared until the picture before her became dauntingly, terrifyingly clear.

It was a coach careening along the rutted road. Its lanterns bobbed crazily against the darkness, the driver seeming to be in an alarming hurry to reach the carriage circle at Thistlewould.

Both women stared at each other for a moment, stricken. But already shouts were going up from beyond the huge front doors.

Within a moment Bella and Devlin were running, Devlin outstripping her friend by a dozen lengths as she dashed out into the pouring rain. Jacob had already flung wide the coach's door, and Devlin's heart stopped as the unmistakable stench of sickness struck her nostrils. She peered within the coach's interior, terrified.

A makeshift bed had been fashioned upon the cushions, the surface now holding a linen-shrouded figure whose face was hidden by shadow.

"Myles? Sweet God, he cannot be dead," Devlin cried out, desperate, then hated herself for the relief that shot through her as the voice that spoke was shaded with an unmistakable Scottish burr.

"Nay," Harry Cameron said, slowly sitting up. "But unless God works a miracle, I fear that Myles soon will be. That they all will be . . . and me of no infernal use, weak as a bloody babe." Harry's voice broke, and in the lantern light Devlin saw him drive shaking hands back through his shaggy hair.

"Harry?" Bella shoved past Devlin and climbed into the coach, flinging her arms about her husband. "Are you hurt? Sick? Oh, my God, Devlin—"

"Easy, now, love. 'Tis nothing fatal," Harry soothed, clutching his wife against his chest. "'Tis but a bout of dysentery—months of it, sickening me until I can scarce move." Cameron's eyes met Devlin's, fierce. "But even still I wouldn't have left him. Not even then. Save for the fact that . . . that I was too weak to fight. And Myles . . . he claimed I'd only be in the way if I stayed with the army. I'd be naught save a burden to them when . . . when it comes."

Devlin pressed her hand against Harry's clammy brow, the sound of Bella's muffled sobbing feeding the frantic sensation building inside her. "When what comes?"

"The end, girl. The end of it all." Harry's chest was racked with a hideous sob. "They're cold, the men are, an' starving, feeding their horses what little whiskey they have to keep them from freezing to death this winter past. But even that wouldn't matter, save for the fact that their spirits . . . their spirits already lay bleeding from the thrust their own commanders' swords dealt them at Derby."

Devlin's blood turned to ice at the terrible picture Harry had painted with his words.

Myles drizzling liquor between the lips of his Barbary

stallion with freezing fingers. Myles, his stomach churning, gnawing, torn by hunger. Myles watching the end of his dream.

"'Twill be like casting babes to the slaughter." Cameron buried his face in Arabella's golden hair. "And Myles is sending away everyone he can. Sending them to safety while he . . . Oh, sweet Jesus . . ."

"Damn it, Harry, what are you talking about? Tell me!"

The Scotsman looked up at her with vacant eyes, his mouth as twisted as the features of the damned toppling into hell.

"Haven't you heard, girl? That butcher the Duke of Cumberland is marching for Inverness, his army fat and rested and hungering for victory. Even now Prince Charles's advisors are scurrying about, attempting to find a fit battlefield on which to meet him."

"Where, Harry?" Devlin demanded urgently. "Tell me where."

The Scotsman let his eyes fall closed. His voice was deathly quiet as he said, "'Tis a place called Culloden Moor."

*F*lickering lights winked in the mist across Culloden Moor. The sounds of grief and despair echoed through the air as anguished women waded through the destruction all around them in search of brothers, sons, husbands, or lovers who had been devoured by the Stuart cause.

Devlin sat astride her exhausted mare and stared numbly at the scene before her. The face of war glared back.

For days Devlin had ridden, changing exhausted horses at post houses, scarcely pausing to eat or sleep as long as she could cling to her mount's back, pushing on to Inverness as if she alone could stem the tide of disaster threatening to sweep away the man she loved.

But it was too late. Too late to stop it. Too late to shield Myles from the horror of what had happened. For surely no one could have survived the carnage that littered the battlefield of Culloden Moor. They were dead. All dead. If not in body, then in spirit.

Devlin closed her eyes against the sight, her mind filling with the laughter and the magic of the ball given on the night she and Myles had married. How many of these men had danced that long-ago night? How many of them had drunk

toasts to her and Myles? How many of them had made
frantic love to the women they would leave behind, then
ridden off upon their grand adventure, bold and laughing,
never suspecting that this horror would await them instead
of a hero's crown?

There had been no glorious legend spun upon the ground
of Culloden Moor. There had been only despair, death, and
defeat.

Myles was dead. She knew it with a certainty that ripped
the heart from her breast. He was dead without ever
knowing that she had forgiven him for all the madness that
had befallen them since they had fled Liancourt. He
was dead without knowing she understood now about magic and beauty and hope. And never would she be able to
cup that strong, stubborn jaw in her hands, kiss those
arrogantly curved lips, watch eyes as blue as the heavens darken with passion as she told him that she loved
him.

Devlin closed her eyes against the image of the greedy
demons of war sucking Myles's lifeblood into the unfeeling
earth, glazing those laughing blue eyes with a veil of death.

Even now she was certain Myles was not among those few
who had escaped, because Myles Farringdon would never
have abandoned the men who had died here.

Myles might even have been grateful for the peace death
offered after such destruction.

"My lady, come away."

Devlin started at the pleading voice, aware that she had
forgotten the sturdy Jacob, who had kept pace with her upon
this crazed flight—her one concession to Harry and Bella's
concern when she had shunned the elaborate preparations
of coach and trunk for the far faster mode of horseback and
a light-packed valise.

In the light of the lantern he held, the footman's face was
so stricken she feared he might be sick.

"M-My lord Farringdon . . . cannot . . . cannot be here,
lost in this." Tears trickled from the corners of the boy's
eyes, and Devlin remembered with a pang of grief how

many times she had caught Myles spinning yarns for him of mad heroics or reckless adventures, or teasing the boy about the apple-cheeked kitchen maid who was much smitten with Jacob's charms.

"P-Please, my lady," the youth choked out. "You cannot stay here."

Fury blazed hot, sudden, and she wheeled upon him.

"Would you have me leave him here?" she raged, "to be torn apart by night creatures, or robbed by the scavengers that pick dead men's pockets?"

She recoiled inwardly at the image her own words had painted: an unfeeling thief closing his fist about the holy medal she had given Myles so long ago, the villain yanking upon the chain, snapping it free from the corded muscles of Myles's neck. Grimy hands rifling through Myles's pockets or, worse still, stripping away the fine clothes that had garbed Myles's beautifully honed body—the neck cloth, the shirt, the fine-tailored breeches—to be flaunted before the thief's fellows in some dank, reeking tavern. That prospect was far more devastating than the thought of wading through the carnage to find Myles, to give him the only gift left within her power—that of loving hands laying him within the crypt where generations of Farringdons had found eternal rest. Feral protectiveness as fierce and primitive as the desire he had stirred in her jolted through Devlin. Her jaw clenched, her eyes searingly dry.

"If you've not the stomach for it, Jacob, go back to that inn we passed," she said, swinging down from her mount, defiant. "Ride all the way back to Thistlewould, plague take you!" By instinct alone she snatched up the haversack filled with her herbs and powders. Flinging its strap across her shoulder, she stalked to where the youth sat astride a dappled gelding and tore the lantern from his hand. "I'll not leave without Myles, do you hear me? Not if I have to search every face upon this moor."

"But milady, you don't . . . don't know what you'll find. My lord Myles would not want—"

"Lord Myles is dead, Jacob. Dead!" Devlin felt as if she

were about to shatter, grief slicing like shards of glass within her tortured throat. "He cannot be ordering people about anymore."

She spun away from the footman and scooped up the skirts of her riding habit with one hand, holding the lantern aloft with the other. She strode to the edge of the battlefield, resolute.

A sea of suffering spread out before her, torment beyond human comprehension. The broken bodies had faces; the hands that had caressed lovers' cheeks lay lifeless upon the earth. The lips that had once kissed children and wives were now slack, the bodies that had been vital and alive such a brief time ago bloated, grotesque.

The thought of finding Myles thus nearly drove Devlin to her knees, but there was no time for such weakness if she were to spare him the final horrors she had described to Jacob.

She reached deep inside herself, searching for a well of courage she was not certain she possessed, and then she stepped to the side of the nearest body, all but ripped in two by cannon fire.

Relief flooded through her as the lantern light illuminated the dark gold of the soldier's hair, a hue far too light to be Myles's dark tresses.

She had thought she'd known terror before, thought she understood destruction. She had spent a lifetime attempting to force Myles to see her vision of the glorious crusades he had so adored. But not even in her own relentlessly practical mind had she been able to create the true reality of war as she forced herself to press deeper, deeper into the heart of Armageddon.

She heard Jacob trailing behind her, sobbing quietly into the sleeve of his frock coat, saw the other women she passed, also searching for their loved ones in that abyss of agony and death.

Faces. They would haunt her forever. A lad of sixteen, lifeless arms clutched about the neck of his fallen horse, his face pillowed against the beast's bloodstained coat. A grizzled man scored with a hundred wounds, his hand knotted in the banner of his clan. An old woman, her skirts soaked with blood, crooned a lullaby to the boy in her arms who stared up at the heavens, unseeing. "An' will ye come home, my bonny, bonny son? An' will ye come home, my Johnnie?"

A cry of anguish pierced the old woman's song as a girl, heavily pregnant, flung herself upon the contorted form of a foot soldier, a child of no more than three summers clinging to her skirts.

Oh, God, Devlin thought. If they had known, these Stuart soldiers, if they had seen the torture their course would leave in its wake, could they ever have abandoned their hearth fires and the arms of the women who loved them? Could they ever have marched to Edinburgh and Carlisle and Derby?

But the dream had been strong then, shimmering just beyond their reach, as luminous and mesmerizing as the image of the legendary crown Myles had sought, Devlin thought numbly, remembering his impassioned letters. Was it possible that Myles had been right—if they had merely had the courage to push forward, this moor would still slumber in the mist-veiled night? Innocent of blood, only the sigh of the heather in the wind, the cry of birds, the whisperings of the stars within the heavens, breaking the serenity?

No matter what might have happened if the troops had marched on to London, it would have been better than the fate that had awaited them here. Even defeat, after a campaign fraught with astounding victories, would have lent a sheen of glory to what they had accomplished. While this—to have been within reach of their dream and merely turned and slunk away—must have been the most searing pain that they could know.

Devlin trudged onward, the lantern growing heavy in her hand, her whole body quivering with exhaustion, revulsion, despair, and grief.

Never before had Devlin been troubled by her imagination, but now it was as if she could hear the clash of sword against sword, feel the jarring impact of leaden balls burying themselves in flesh. She could see the powder smoke, hear the explosions, the death screams, the battle cries of men who knew already that their cause was lost.

What had Myles been thinking, feeling as he plunged into the hell that was Culloden? The only thing Devlin could pray was that he had been cut down swiftly, mercifully, before he had seen the full extent of this massacre.

She closed her eyes for a moment against the painful thought that in the midst of the confusion, the horror that had forever stained this patch of ground, Myles might be lost forever.

Switching the lantern to her other hand, Devlin forced herself onward, unaware of the sweep of time, dawn oozing sullen colors across the sky. The mist was burning away, and Devlin wanted nothing more than to reach up and draw it back like a shroud to shelter the Stuart dead. Hundreds upon hundreds they blanketed the earth, stretching as far as she could see, swallowing her up in hopelessness, desperation. Her search for one man in the carnage was as futile as that of a child attempting to find a single shell in the whole vast ocean.

Yet she couldn't stop, wouldn't stop searching until she could cradle Myles in her arms one last time. Until she could carry him away from this place that had stolen his life.

She paused for a moment, leaning against a huge stone that seemed adrift in a lake of Cameron plaid. Harry's people, she thought with sick despair. The slaughter here had been even more vicious than in the other places she had passed, the chances of anyone escaping the fury of battle that had beset them in this place all but impossible.

A dozen women moved like wraiths through the destruction, their faces muddy, their bare feet splashed with blood. Devlin steeled herself to move into the thick of the carnage. But as she passed the huge stone she heard, not a cry of grief, but one of desperate fear, yet miraculous hope.

"Please, help me! Somebody help me! Me boy's alive!"

Slipping, sliding on the blood-slickened ground, Devlin rounded the boulder to find a woman of about forty years clutching a boy whose face was as smooth and innocent as that of Arabella's little Hal. Red hair curled riotously about hollow cheeks, bruised circles framing long-lashed eyes. Freckles spattered a small, pugnacious nose, the lips beneath bluish and trembling. The woman had wrapped her shawl about him, as if to ward off the plucking fingers of death, and Devlin could just make out the broken-off shaft of a pike bristling obscenely from his shoulder.

"H-Hurts, m-mam . . ."

Devlin barely made out the croaked whisper.

"M-Make hurt g-go away. . . ."

The chance that one small boy might be snatched from the jaws of this monstrous battle jolted hope through Devlin. And she rushed to his side, as though in saving him she could give Myles's death some small meaning. She fell to her knees at the moaning boy's side, and the mother looked up at her with wide, desperate eyes.

"Please . . . please, help us! He's so hurt. . . ."

"I will. You must let him go so I can see—"

The mother clutched the child even tighter. "I told him not to go! I barred him in his room, but he climbed . . . climbed out the window. . . ." She sobbed, gesturing to a shattered drum. "He said . . . said he would pipe his brothers into battle. . . . He said . . ."

Devlin's heart broke at the image of the valiant man-child going off to be a drummer, seeking out adventure and finding only death. He could have been Myles as a boy, could have been Myles's son, *her* son, filled with the tales of heroism that had sent generation after generation of children into the heat of battle, seeking something they could never find.

"If you want him to live, you must let him go," Devlin commanded. "I cannot reach him."

Reluctantly the woman lowered the boy to the chill, hard ground, and Devlin found herself wondering how many times those same arms had tucked him safely in his cradle an eternity ago, in a world that seemed secure. How many times had this woman stolen in under the cover of darkness to soothe away nightmares or tend fevers? But this nightmare was one that even her loving hands could never banish from the child's memory. This fever of despair, defeat, could not be cured with bitter teas or compresses.

In all her years of healing Devlin had found that often a frightened parent only terrified the injured child more. And the helplessness of distraught parents made them quarrelsome and questioning, often interfering with the treatment of the wound. This little boy could stand no such hindrance, his life already teetering in the balance.

She turned to Jacob and the mother. "The two of you go off and find some way to fashion a litter, to get the boy out of this hell once we are done."

"Nay! I'll not leave him!" the mother protested, but Devlin grasped her arm, quelling her outburst with a steady glare.

"Do you want to get him away from this? Or do you want him to lie here until King George's soldiers decide to scour the battlefield once again for prisoners?"

The woman's face whitened. "But he needs me . . . the boy—"

"He does need you. More than ever before. He needs you to find a way to get him out of here."

"But his wound . . ."

"I'm a healer. I vow to you, I'll take care of your son."

The woman seemed to waver, then trust lit her eyes. She clambered to her feet. Jacob took the woman's hand. Devlin watched for a moment as the two figures wound their way through the mass of destruction.

Then she looked down at her small charge. The child peered up at Devlin with frightened eyes, his pale little face racked with confusion.

She smoothed her hand lightly over his clammy brow, the wispy red curls clinging to her hand. "My name is Devlin. I'm going to help you."

The child must have found something reassuring in her face, because he suddenly stilled. "I—I'm . . . Andrew. G-German scum s-stuck me."

"I can see that he did."

The boy shifted again, restless. "H-He told them not to.

Told them to—to leave me alone. Tried t-to make me run. But I—I wouldn't leave . . . wouldn't leave him."

Devlin imagined the boy clinging to the master drummer who commanded him. Imagined the child resolutely refusing to flee, even in the thick of battle. The man who had held the boy's loyalty must have been mad with desperation to see him safe, yet he had possessed no magical way to transport the child from the midst of this butchery. She glanced around at the Cameron dead, wondering which of the men had been burdened with that final hell of fighting, knowing that this child would fall beneath some blade.

She swallowed hard, searching for the words the boy needed to hear. The words that Myles would have found to comfort him. "I'm certain that . . . that you made him very proud."

With hands more gentle than efficient Devlin smoothed back the shawl that had wrapped the boy. The pike's wicked point was buried deep, sheathed in the child's narrow shoulder. From the direction of the wound Devlin could tell that the thrust had been intended to kill but had glanced off bone. Still, the only thing that had saved the child was the fact that the pike's owner had not thought his broken weapon worth tearing back out of the boy's flesh. For with a wound not stopped up by the biting steel the child would most likely have bled to death long before his mother had managed to stumble upon him.

Sliding the canvas pouch from her own shoulder, Devlin rummaged among her herbs and possets to find what she needed. Clean strips of linen for bandages, foul-smelling mixtures of herbs to draw out the poisons festering in the torn flesh. A flask of brandy Myles had supplied her with years ago. A sharp stab of loss pierced her as she remembered him leaning against the drawing room mantel, telling her that it would help to ease the pain of someone wounded, and that it could cleanse away the filth in torn flesh that brought on fever and often death.

Devlin had been scornful, jeering that he should pretend to know anything about such nonsense. But Myles had only laughed at her, saying that his presence at countless duels had made him something of an expert on those sorts of wounds. Then he had flashed her that insufferable grin and said that even if she chose not to believe him, she should at least use the spirits to deaden her patients' wits before she began working upon them. Otherwise, one day some poor victim would revolt and pour her disgusting brews down her throat.

She'd wanted to dump the contents of the flask over his head, but there had been challenge in those blue eyes. A subtle taunt that questioned which was more important to her—her patients' comfort or her pride.

She'd replenished the flask countless times in the ensuing years, but she'd never quite been able to bring herself to tell Myles what a valuable tool the brandy had become. Had never been able to bring herself to tell him he'd been right. Why? It seemed so unimportant now, the stubbornness, the pride. She'd have cast it all to the winds just to have Myles torment her once again.

Shaking herself free of the memories, she turned back to Andrew. Withdrawing a bottle of water from her pouch, she dampened the shirt that was stuck to his skin and the jagged wound by dried blood. With scissors she cut away the edges of the shirt, then tested the fabric to judge how much pressure would be needed to tear it free of the wound.

It was all but congealed to the torn flesh, and Devlin dreaded having to put the child through the torture of ripping it away.

"Andrew, I fear this is going to hurt you, but I promise to be as quick as I can. Do you think you're able to hold still, sweeting? As still as you can?"

"I'll just . . . just hold on to the dragons," the child breathed. "H-He called me a good, brave l-lad. Told me . . . had courage of twenty . . . men full grown."

Devlin's eyes stung, and she gently raised the boy's head, pressing the rim of the brandy flask to his lips. "Take a drink of this. It will ease the pain."

The boy gulped down a draught, then sputtered and

choked weakly, making such a horrible face that Devlin's hope was renewed.

Steeling herself, she talked to the child as she worked, listened to his babblings about the battle and the courage, the terror and brutality and the oft-mentioned, mysterious *him* who the child seemed to regard as half god, half father.

And when it was done—the pike lying upon the ground, stained with fresh blood, the wound cleansed and stitched and poulticed—Devlin couldn't stop herself from bending over the child and kissing his sweat-soaked forehead.

"W-Was I brave?" the little one whispered.

"Braver than twenty men full grown," Devlin said, and she meant it. "Now, as soon as Jacob and your mother return, they will take you back home where you can rest and get your strength back." Devlin bundled together the things the woman would need to tend the boy, scratching out instructions upon a bit of paper with the small bottle of ink and the half-crushed quill stuffed in the bottom of her pouch.

When she poured brandy into a vial for them to use to brace the boy upon the journey home, she felt something tug at her sleeve.

Andrew was looking at the brandy, his eyes shining. "W-Wasn't the . . . the brandy . . . eased pain," he said. "The dragons."

"Dragons?" Devlin echoed.

"He said they'd . . . help me . . . magical." The child pulled his other arm from the shielding of wool, and Devlin's heart stopped as the light of the new-morning sun skated down the blade of a rapier. The tip was broken off, the blade nicked and scratched, the metal dulled by the grime of battle. But two exquisitely fashioned dragons writhed up the blade.

The dragon sword. Myles's dragon sword.

Devlin's head whirled, and she struggled to speak. "This sword. Where . . . where did you get this sword?"

"From *him*," Andrew said. "M-My lord Farringdon. He gave it to me when . . . when all was lost."

"What happened to Lord Farringdon?" Devlin demanded, grasping Andrew's hand, desperate. "Sweet Christ, tell me—"

"German . . . scum all around us. M-My lord said dragons . . . magical. It made me . . . not afraid."

It made me not afraid.

Tears streamed down Devlin's face, the image of Myles aiding this boy breaking her heart—Myles, doing the only thing within his power to ease the child's fear. Painting the sword with magic, pressing it into the child's hand as death closed in all around them.

"Andrew," she said, her hands knotting in her petticoats, her whole body trembling. "My lord Farringdon. How . . . how did he die?"

The child's eyes flooded with confusion. "He didn't die." Tears trickled down those grubby child-cheeks. "They took him. Took him away. A dozen of the bastards hurt him, and—"

"Where, Andrew?" Devlin demanded, desperation and wild hope mingling in her breast. "Where did they take my lord?"

"T-To that butcher. Cumberland. Said my lord was . . . was prize. Reward if . . . alive."

"But he *was* alive? When they took him away he was *alive?*"

"B-Barely," Andrew choked out. "They b-beat him and beat him, and . . . bastards. Cursed bastards."

A sob tore through the child's small body, his hand clinging to Devlin's sleeve.

"If my lord had . . . had kept his magic sword . . . they never could have hurt him, could they? It was my—my fault they . . . hurt him."

"No, Andrew. It wasn't your fault. Myles . . . Lord Farringdon wanted you to have the sword."

The child stared at her intently. "You . . . you're his lady, aren't you? His lady wife?"

Devlin nodded. "Yes. I'm his wife."

The pain-racked face brightened, the eyes shining with feverish hope. "Will you . . . take the magic back to him?

316

The—the sword. He needs it, you see . . . more than I do now."

Devlin stared down into those gray eyes as he pressed the sword hilt into her palm, the weapon seeming to settle into the curve as if it were fashioned for her hand.

"Yes, Andrew," she said, steely resolve washing through her. "I'll take the magic back to him. I'll take the magic back to him right away."

CHAPTER
25

*M*yles braced himself against the harsh stone wall of the castle ruin that was his prison, feeling he would gladly barter away his soul to draw a deep breath of meadow-scented air or feel the wind on his face. In the days before Culloden Moor his worst fear had been being caged, helpless. But now, as he lay within the stone walls, he knew that there were far darker, more sinister prisons than ones made of stone—prisons that threatened to entrap not only his body, but his soul.

He shifted, his whole body afire with agony. Fathomless blackness seemed to crush his chest in the windowless chamber, the painful imprints of countless boots and fists and bludgeons sending agony spiking through his muscles. Manacles sawed deep into the flesh about his wrists, the rattle of the chains that bound him grating upon his nerves whenever he moved.

But he welcomed the pain, embraced it. For it was the only thing that could stave off the relentless tug of exhaustion that threatened to pull him back to Culloden Moor again, back to the horror and the screams and the hideous waste of it all. Back to the dream.

Myles leaned his face against his palm, the cold bite of metal abrading his jaw.

No, not a dream, a nightmare, just as Devlin predicted it would be. Sweet Jesus, why hadn't he listened to her? There in the rose garden an eternity ago. Why hadn't he listened while the scent of flowers filled his nostrils, instead of the stench of death and defeat? Why hadn't he understood the things she had tried to tell him—that leaders often betrayed those they led, that a battle can never prove what is good, what is right. It can only prove who is willing to cause the most destruction to get his own way.

But even Devlin had not suspected the most horrible affliction of war—the fact that when the glorious leader was defeated and raced across country, across continent, across oceans to reach safety, he left thousands of his people, loyal men and women and children, to the mercy of the conquering army. Abandoned them with no place to hide, no palace to shelter them in exile. No, not even the means to carry them to a hovel upon some foreign shore.

Sacrifices. They were human sacrifices upon the field of battle. And later, when their leaders fled, they were nothing but debris to be cleared away by the victors' blood-drunk men.

Myles closed his eyes against the disillusionment that was more acid-hot than the pain. He struggled against the pull of that nightmare world that always consumed him in sleep, struggled to force his eyelids open once again. But the tides swirled him away, merciless, feasting on his helplessness. A moan escaped his lips as he felt himself letting go of consciousness once more.

In the claws of the nightmare, Myles fought like a madman, trying to reach Devlin through a sea of destruction. "Dev!" he screamed. "Sweet Christ, Devlin!"

"Crying out for your bride within your prison cell?" A familiar voice raked Myles through mists of confusion. "It is so touching, I vow it brings a tear to my eye."

Laughter seemed to surround Myles, and he struggled to claw his way through the mists to the sound.

A hard blow to the ribs jarred him, and light pried at his eyes. He came awake with a wrenching clarity that plunged him afresh into fury.

Manacles held his wrists and ankles, their heavy chains weighing him down. He could feel a score of wounds beneath the filthy ruin of his clothes. Eyes still a little blurred focused upon a maze of scarlet coats and jeering faces illuminated by the light of several lanterns. Hanover's beasts, the men were.

But it was not the sight of those guards that stunned Myles. It was the man who lounged before them, turning an elegant riding crop in white-gloved hands.

Tracey.

Sweet God, had he somehow become embroiled in the rebellion? Had his link with Myles trapped him in this morass of suffering as well? Or was this something far more sinister—the retribution Tracey had promised with his eyes upon the day Myles had made Devlin his wife?

"What the hell . . ." Myles started to rise, but a beefy guard yanked on the chains that bound him, sending him crashing back to the floor.

"Now, now, no need for such . . . er . . . crude tactics, Lieutenant," Tracey said. "After all, the Viscount Liancourt and I are . . . the closest of friends."

Guffaws filled the room, and Myles stared, disbelieving, into Tracey's features. They were a mask laced with the same feigned boredom, the same intelligence, the same unflappable control they had held since childhood. Not so much as a single line carved into that smooth skin; not the briefest glint lit those cool eyes to hint that this was another one of Tracey's constant games, ruses, that this was some sort of jest that would vanish with a wave of his hand.

"Damn you, Tracey, what the devil are you doing here?"

"I'm here at the behest of your . . . host, the Duke of Cumberland."

Myles reeled at Tracey's careless words.

"You see, His Grace is most enthralled by the stories of the crown you were seeking. The Stuart crown. Rebellions, you'll allow, are expensive. Even for the victor. And as payment for the trouble you and your fellow traitors have caused God-fearing Englishmen, the prince is determined to exact the price of one legend-shrouded crown."

"He can go to hell! I'll not—"

"Myles, Myles. I know how difficult it is for you to be reasonable, but you must attempt it. The crown can surely be of no value to your Jacobite friends. Prince Charles's cause has been crushed. Even now the pretender is being hunted all across Scotland. And I assure you the duke will not allow anything so sloppy as Charles's escape to blight the glorious victories he has won."

"Victory? It was a cursed slaughter—women, children— they killed anything that moved."

"Regrettable, to be sure. But these things *will* happen when idealists like you insist upon fomenting rebellion instead of tending to their estates and paying their taxes to the king Parliament has seen fit to place over them."

"Even if I knew where the cursed crown was, I'd not tell you—not even if you flayed me alive."

"I'd be cautious about giving these gentlemen any ideas. I fear they are still a trifle blood-drunk, and one more atrocity in the wake of so many others would be distressingly insignificant."

"And you, the grand schemer, the great politician—you would stand by and watch, doubtless. Always ready to tackle the most unpleasant of tasks as long as it furthers your political career."

"Exactly." Tracey steepled his hands in front of him, his eyes upon Myles opaque, unreadable. "Now, in light of our former friendship I shall demonstrate my goodwill toward you by requesting that these gentlemen free you of your shackles. I fear they will prove distracting to both of us, what with all that noisy clattering."

The guard grumbled a protest, but Tracey dismissed it with a wave. "Believe me, sir, I have wanted this crown for far too long to let the dregs of friendship stand in my way."

A portly private, sweating profusely, wiped the moisture from his thick lips. "'Tis all right, Smee, you horse's arse. Didn't ye hear that the viscount here snatched up Mr.

Tracey's bride from practically under his nose? Married her himself, the traitorous bastard did. Show ye just how much milor' Farringdon, here, clings t' the virtue of loyalty, eh, Mr. Tracey?"

Tracey's lips curled in an ugly smile, and Myles was tempted to tell the oafish guard to close his mouth unless he wanted Tracey's rapier thrust through his gullet. But Tracey only spoke in that smooth, dangerous voice of his, quiet, deadly quiet. "You see, sir, there is no love lost between Myles Farringdon and myself. Besides which, I'll want at least three of you to remain present during this . . . interrogation."

Myles watched Tracey, wary, as a pockmarked guard hastened to do the man's bidding.

The manacles clattered to the floor, and Myles rubbed at the raw flesh of his wrists.

Tracey motioned for the guards to move away to the far corner of the cell. Then he turned back to Myles, his beringed fingers straightening the fall of pristine lace that tumbled across his smooth hand.

"What the hell do you want from me, Tracey?"

"What I've always wanted. The crown. The Jacobite treasure."

A sick suspicion stirred inside Myles. "What treasure?"

"The one that Devlin's father hid before he died so long ago."

"You knew? About the jewels in the Dower House?"

"Is that where they were? How astonishing. And of course you found them. Very resourceful of you."

"Damn you, I asked you a question!"

Tracey raised one eyebrow. "You are scarcely in a position to make demands, Myles. But in light of our former friendship, I shall humor you. How could you think for even a moment that I would fail to discover the existence of such a treasure? I am not a careless man. Especially in matters of finance." Tracey's lips curved in a thin smile. "After Devlin and I became betrothed at your grandfather's somewhat inconvenient insistence, I raked through all the files I could find about my future bride's family. Most dangerous, should there be any skeletons lurking in closets that I didn't know about. Imagine my surprise when I discovered that Josiah Chastain was a hero—a secretly revered hero of the Jacobites."

"Josiah Chastain? That's impossible! The man went bankrupt and killed himself."

"A convenient misconception bought by the government for a most exorbitant price. Sir Josiah's wife, it seems, was not pleased with her husband's clandestine activities and was more than happy to keep silent for a generous stipend."

Myles's hands knotted into fists, fury on Devlin's behalf tearing through him. How many times had he seen the lurking grief, the agony her father's supposed suicide had caused her? How many times had he sensed how deeply her dependence upon the Farringdons' charity galled her? How many times had Lady Agatha scorned her, ignored her, belittled her, attempting to take away Devlin's pride as certainly as she had stolen the girl's loving memories of her father?

Loathing filled Myles, choked him, every loving gesture Agatha Chastain had lavished upon him now making him feel somehow tainted by the wrong she had done her daughter.

"What could she have done with her blood money?" Myles snarled. "She never spent a farthing upon Devlin."

"Why should she have bothered, when you Farringdons were so eager to pay off your life-debt to hero Josiah's daughter? And how long do you suppose your father or grandfather—or even your mother—would have tolerated Agatha Chastain's presence if they knew she was profiting from the death of the man who had saved so many lives? From what information I can glean, Sir Josiah cheated the axeman out of half the nobles in England through his courage—your father among them. Did you know that?"

Myles scrambled to gather pieces of the puzzle that had always so frustrated him—the enigma of the Chastains' residence at Liancourt, Agatha's neglect of Devlin. The child must have been a constant reminder of the way she had betrayed her husband's memory. A living accusation with flaming red hair and a stubborn-set jaw.

Tracey's voice intruded, the note of pleasure in his tones fraying Myles's already thin nerves. "There was a list of those pledged to help James Stuart regain his throne. A tally sheet containing all the names paired with the amount of silver plate, jewels, or gold they had given to the cause."

"My father's griffin pin," Myles muttered. "It was there among the treasure. It must have been his contribution to the Stuart cause."

"No doubt. In truth, Sir Josiah would have been wiser to donate the pin, along with the rest of the baubles, to the Hanover treasury. But being a brainless, honorable sort— not unlike you—he hid the treasure and destroyed the list just as the authorities rode through his gate. It put them in a somewhat surly mood, I am afraid. While they were attempting to, shall we say, jar his memory, they became over-enthusiastic and bludgeoned him to death."

Tracey removed a snuffbox from his waistcoat pocket and held a pinch delicately to one nostril. "Were I you, Myles, I would take warning from that unfortunate occurrence and tell us what we want to know."

Myles reeled beneath the force of Tracey's revelations. "You bastard! You used Devlin! All those years—"

Tracey shrugged. "Even you must admit she was more than willing to be used by me. You should be thanking me, Myles, instead of reviling me as a villain. It is only because of my considerable self-control that she came to your bridal bed a virgin."

With a bellow of fury Myles launched himself at Tracey, his hands closing about the man's throat. He crushed the flesh in his hands, heard Tracey gasping, choking. The guards shouted in alarm, and Myles glimpsed them lunging toward him, dragging him away. Something heavy cracked into the back of his skull, and the room whirled, Tracey's reddened face in its center.

A beefy fist slammed into Myles's ribs, and he doubled over in agony, but even the pain could not douse the fiery pleasure he'd taken in throttling Tracey, the desperate wish that he could have snapped the man's neck before the guards had yanked him away.

Myles saw the man called Smee draw back his fist again and braced himself for the blow, but it was Tracey's voice that stopped the man in mid-swing. "No, Smee," Tracey said in a raspy, breathless voice. "No more entertainment at my lord Farringdon's expense—despite his ill-advised heroics."

"But the traitorous bastard tried to kill ye!" the man exclaimed, giving Myles a bruising shake.

"Yes, yes. And I understand your urge to kill him in return. But that would hardly please the Duke of Cumberland, now, would it? After all the trouble the two of us went to in order to see that Lord Farringdon escaped Culloden Moor alive?"

Smee scuffed the toe of his boot against the stone, his jaw thrust out belligerently. "I suppose not. But he—"

"Release my lord now, and carry yourself back to the far side of this cell. Until you become more intimately acquainted with lye soap and Hungary water, I've no desire to have you near me. Besides which, I am certain that the blow you dealt him has left my lord Farringdon less inclined to indulge in any more such stupidity."

"Bastard!" Myles rasped, his hand clutched over bruised ribs. "I'll break your neck! I swear—"

Tracey bent within inches of his face, his voice a cutting hiss. "That would be most ungrateful, considering all I have risked for you."

"For me? What the hell have you risked for me?"

"Who do you think sent your grandfather to Liancourt that day, to warn you the soldiers were hunting you? That they had learned of your Stuart sympathies? And about your quest for the crown?" Tracey said, low. "Of course, I judged that it was only sporting for me to do so, since I was the one who informed the authorities of your involvement in the first place."

Myles stared into the face of the man he had seen as his friend for a score of years, the man for whom he would gladly have sacrificed his life. The man who was now a stranger. "You told them. Sweet God, of course it had to be you."

"You were far too trusting to consider that possibility at the time, weren't you? I depended upon that. But why, Myles, why did you not follow instructions and board that ship for France? It would have taken you out of danger and saved you from your own idiocy. You see? I am not without my own brand of chivalry."

"As long as it doesn't infringe upon your purpose," Myles spat.

"Ah, we understand each other better and better. Well, I could hardly have you knocking about, chasing that infernal crown when I wanted it for the greater glory of England."

"You mean the greater glory of Braden Tracey."

"What harm will there be in my benefiting from unearthing the treasure? It's not as if I were going to keep it for myself. If I can garner some adulation, some political support for my efforts, it is nothing less than my due. If you had merely been sensible, I would have hurt no one."

"What about Devlin? You all but destroyed her!"

"She seems to have recovered with remarkable haste." Was there bitterness in Tracey's voice? A flicker of something in his eyes? Myles struggled to decipher the mystery of the man's face.

"What the hell do you mean?"

"She arrived in the Duke of Cumberland's encampment three hours ago, blistering His Grace's ears with demands that she be allowed to see you."

Sick horror careened through Myles. "No! Damn it to hell, I don't believe you! Devlin would never . . . never . . . do something so reckless!"

"I admit it was most ill-advised, what with her part in your escape from Liancourt being so notorious. The girl might as well have stuck her head through a noose and been done with it. I always thought her too intelligent to make such a mistake."

"Where is she? Damn it, Tracey—"

"Why, she is waiting outside with the two men who guard

your door. They are searching that sack of herbs she insists on carting about."

Myles staggered to his feet, his stomach rolling with the sudden certainty that she *was* outside the cell, at the mercy of forces whose savagery she did not even suspect. "Devlin?" He shouted her name. "For God's sake, Dev—"

Desperation. It sliced into him as he stumbled to the door, slammed his fists upon it.

"In my opinion, you've managed to get yourself battered enough. I wouldn't waste my energy pounding upon the door. The guards will not allow her in until I give the word."

Myles wheeled on Tracey, rage filling him in a seething red wave. "Damn you, if you hurt her—"

"Believe me when I tell you that Devlin's ultimate fate lies entirely in your hands."

Myles glared at Tracey, more helpless than he'd been in the lengths of chain. Suspicion ate at his gut. "What do you mean?"

"Wha' 'e means, ye traitorous scum," Smee guffawed, "is that ye ain't goin' t' see yer lady till ye tell us what we want to know!"

"Mr. Smee, please do not attempt to guess my plans. It will only frustrate me and humiliate you."

"Tracey, even *you* couldn't be such a bastard to her, for God's sake."

"Oh, I am quite accomplished at quelling inconvenient attacks of scruples, as you should know. And if I thought that withholding Devlin from you would work in my favor, I would not hesitate to do so. However, I always prefer to take the most effective, most expedient course to get what I desire."

"What accursed course? Damn you, tell me!"

"I've decided to address the fact that the two of you had such a brief time together following your wedding. My gift to you, in a manner of speaking, will be a considerable length of time in this cell together. I wonder how precious your Stuart crown will seem when the rats begin crawling on Devlin. You know she'll never complain—it's not her way. But you'll know what she's thinking, won't you, Myles?

Know what she is feeling? That was always your curse, to be attuned to the feelings of others. When her terror consumes her, you will know it, won't you? You'll taste it upon your tongue, feel it slip, icy-cold, through your veins."

"I'll kill you, Tracey. My hand to God—"

Tracey's eyes pierced his in the lantern light, shimmering, intent. "Why waste time in such a futile quest, Myles? This stubbornness . . . it will gain you nothing. And now Devlin is to suffer as well. Just a few words that chafe that stiff-necked pride of yours are all it will take to spare her."

"You would let her go? Free her? If I—"

Something darted across Tracey's face, something startling, unreadable. "What do you think, my friend?"

"I think you are a liar." Hate blazed through Myles.

"We shall see, shan't we? And now, being a most considerate fellow, I shall introduce Lady Farringdon to her new bridal chamber."

"Tracey, don't." There was a plea in his voice. "Don't bring her in here! For Christ's sake, don't make her a part of this."

"She made herself a part of this by dumping herself upon the Duke of Cumberland's doorstep. But I'll concede this much: I'll leave a lantern for the two of you, to accustom her to her new surroundings. And, of course, so that you can see the terror begin to cloud her eyes, see her face grow pale before I put you both in darkness."

"Shall I chain 'im afore we leave, Mr. Tracey?" Smee asked, rubbing his hands together. "So his lordship can't escape?"

"Oh, his lordship isn't going anywhere." Tracey turned toward the guard. "He can scarcely move himself, and even if he entertained such an idiotic thought while alone, he would never risk his wife in such a venture. Myles, I have given orders to shoot to kill should either you or Devlin make . . . ahem . . . an unannounced appearance."

Tracey angled a glance at Myles. "The whole place is crawling with guards and is far distant from Cumberland's encampment. I convinced the duke that it would be better if no one was able to carry tales back to England of the

Viscount Liancourt's screams, should torture become necessary. You are twenty miles from the nearest village, stranded in the middle of nowhere. A brilliant choice, don't you think? Nothing like opportunities for escape to distract you. Now I shall bid you adieu. Smee, you may escort the viscount's lovely bride to her new quarters."

Tracey strode to the door and rapped upon it. The portal swung wide, sounds of a heated argument from the corridor beyond spilling into the cell.

Devlin.

Despair and feral protectiveness gripped Myles, and he attempted to reach the open door, but Smee grabbed him by the arms and flung him to the stones with gleeful violence.

"Mr. Tracey said that I could bring these with me!" Devlin raged. "You've no right to meddle—"

She must have seen Tracey, for Myles heard her appeal to the man. "They've pawed through everything I own! Drank the brandy, and—it was for Myles, blast it, and—"

"Be glad it was the only price they exacted, my dear. I fear these men are accustomed to levying a somewhat higher forfeit from women they deem traitors."

"Dev?" Myles shouted, desperate to get her away from the animals in the corridor, the cell suddenly seeming safer than where she now stood. "For God's sake, Dev—"

In a heartbeat she appeared in the opening of the door, her ransacked canvas bag clutched to her breasts, her hair tumbling in a riot of red about her face. A face even more beautiful than he had remembered, scored with outrage and so much courage it broke his heart.

With a cry she ran to him, flinging herself against his chest with a force that sent pinwheels of pain catapulting through his battered body. But he only clutched her tighter, trying desperately to believe that she was real.

"Myles," she choked out, her fingertips tracing his face, his lips. "Oh, God, they hurt you." She was crying. For him. And the knowledge tore Myles apart.

"Tracey, how could you?" She wheeled upon the man like a fury. "I'll never—never forgive you for this!"

"I shall probably never forgive myself," Tracey said

cryptically, his mouth twisting in a wry smile. "But for now I must bid you both good night. Myles, I shall leave you the lantern tonight. But as for tomorrow . . . remember what we've talked about while you're holding your bride in your arms."

Rage, resolve bolted through Myles, his grasp about Devlin tightening, fierce as the last of the guards exited the room.

"I won't let you do it, Tracey," Myles snarled. "I won't let you break her."

"You are the one who brought her to this pass, Myles. You. And if I'm forced to break her, every agony she suffers will be your doing, as certainly as if you wielded the lash."

The words armed with an acid edge of truth drove with crippling force into Myles's soul as the cell's heavy door crashed shut.

330

CHAPTER
26

Devlin stared at the door for a frozen instant. Then, suddenly, she was whipped about to confront a Myles she had never seen before—a Myles seething with desperation, and with a fury that made her want to pull away from the bruising grip of his hands and skitter to the far corner of the cell.

"Did Tracey hurt you?" Myles snarled. "I swear I'll see him dead if he so much as touched you!"

"No! Myles, I'm fine. I—"

"Fine? In the middle of a goddamned dungeon?" An ugly laugh tore from his lips. "What the hell are you doing here, Dev? For Christ's sake, the only thing that kept me sane was knowing that you were safe. I trusted in your wits and your resourcefulness and your strength. Was certain that you would manage to slip free of this madness. And instead you ride straight to Cumberland and throw yourself into his hands!" He flung her away from him, and the torment in his face seemed to crush Devlin's voice. "The one thing I never took you for was a reckless idiot, girl!"

Tears bit at the backs of Devlin's eyes, no hint of the love she had hoped for showing in Myles's war-savaged face. "I fear recklessness must be a contagious condition," she said, glaring back into his glittering blue eyes. "I caught it from my husband."

Not even a hint of a smile touched lips hardened by betrayal, misery.

"Blast it, Myles, I had to—to see you. Help you. I had to tell you—"

"*Help* me? You can't be stupid enough to believe that! You've managed to double the danger, the difficulty of any escape just by being here. Do you think I'd risk . . ." He swore, spinning away from her, driving his fingers through the dark tangle of his hair. "You've given Tracey and his dogs the exact weapon they needed to break me! You've walked blindly up to the block and all but laid your head beneath the axe."

"I don't care." She said the words quietly, her gaze locked upon broad shoulders that trembled with fury and fear for her.

He wheeled, his voice tortured in his throat. "You don't care? Have you ever seen an execution, Dev? Heard the roar of a crowd greedy for your blood? Hanover's loyalists will be hungering for traitors to tear apart. And Cumberland and his commanders will be duty bound to hurl sacrifices to them. Who better than the Viscount Liancourt and his wife? What a spectacle it would make, notorious as we've both become."

Devlin shuddered at the picture his vivid words painted. What she had seen in her hours amid Cumberland's command had sickened her, terrified her. The troops that had been repeatedly deprived of victory by their poorly armed Stuart enemies were now wreaking their vengeance, making all who had fallen under their heel pay for their former humiliation.

Only the fact that they had believed her to be just one more of their own camp followers had spared Devlin from the force of their wrath.

No, they hadn't suspected for an instant that a traitoress was in their midst. A traitoress who was plotting desperately to save the man she loved. But before she could put any of her schemes into action she had been grabbed by a set of

familiar hands and found herself staring up into the implacable face of Braden Tracey.

She had begged him to help her. Insisting that after all
Myles had been to him, Tracey could not mean to let him
die. But Tracey had only dragged her before the Duke of
Cumberland and insisted that she be taken to the ruin of
Lochshannon Castle to be used to batter down the resistance
of the Viscount Liancourt.

Betrayal and fury had both raced through Devlin, yet
mingled with those emotions was a fierce sense of joy that
she would see Myles once again. And in the journey to the
castle ruin, and through the maze of twisting stone corridors, she had scrambled desperately to form some plan, find
some way to free Myles of this horrible place.

Fear? She had felt it in abundance. Knowing the chance
she was taking, the fate that would await her. Yet more
cutting still was the possibility that Myles might go to his
grave, never knowing that she loved him. And the chance to
say those words to him had been worth any forfeit the fates
could demand.

Devlin shook herself inwardly, and met Myles's gaze with
defiance.

"I'm afraid those bloodthirsty crowds you spoke of will
just have to be disappointed," she said. "The Viscount and
Viscountess Liancourt have better things to do with their
time than provide entertainment for the vulgar herd."

"The viscount and viscountess won't have any damn
choice in the matter if Cumberland and Tracey have their
way."

"I suppose it all depends."

"Depends? In case you hadn't noticed, you've gotten
yourself trapped in a bloody dungeon! With guards and a
sea of wilderness around us. Didn't you hear a word Tracey
said?"

"Do you remember when we were children how you
always managed to wriggle out of any disaster you had
caused?"

"Christ, are we back to that again? This is hardly the time
for reminiscing."

"Oh, but you're wrong. If you are still as good at such dramatics as I remember, I promise you we can be through that door before a quarter hour has passed."

He gaped at her, incredulous. "Free? But how—"

Devlin couldn't quell the grin of satisfaction that curved her lips. "Do you remember that brandy I was squawking about when Tracey opened the cell door?"

"Brandy? Hell, no—I was a trifle distracted by the fact that you were about to be imprisoned."

"The guards drank it."

"Christ, Dev, this is no infernal jest!"

"No. I made certain they knew that it was most distressing to me. Being loyal subjects of German George, duty bound to protect his interests—and make life hell for rebel scum—they were most eager to distress me as much as possible."

"Blast it, girl, have you waxed mad? This whole thing is so damned senseless—"

"No, they are the ones who will soon be senseless. You see, the brandy was most definitely drugged."

"God in heaven, you've drugged the cursed guards?" Myles's face was white beneath the stubbled growth of beard. "Did it occur to you that a drugged guard could hardly open the cell door? Or have you mixed up some disgusting brew that will shrink us down to the size of mice, so we can slip between the cracks?"

"Don't be absurd. I used a potion with a somewhat delayed action that I discovered while studying the Borgias . . . an interesting family, the Borgias. Quite poison-happy, the lot of them, and—"

Lightning-fast, he grabbed her, his face dark, tormented, carved with confusion as he glared down at her with eyes full of pain. "Why, Dev? Why are you doing this?" His voice broke, his face contorting with anguish. "You have to know how ridiculous this is, how futile! Christ, girl, you could die because of this insanity!"

Her fingers stole up to trace the stubborn curve of his jaw, and she stared at the lips that had kissed her to madness, wishing there was some way to soften them again, drive away their pain.

"I would die for you, and welcome," she said, her heart racing, her fingers trembling. "Because I . . . I can't imagine living without you."

She raised her gaze to his, hoping to see some flicker of joy, some answering blaze of passion. But the blue was glazed with such wrenching bitterness she felt as if he'd struck her.

"Damn you, Myles, I'm trying to tell you that I love you, and you're not cooperating in the least!"

"What do you expect me to say?" His voice cut deep, jagged, and Devlin stumbled back, feeling something precious shatter inside her. In the arbor, when Tracey had rejected her, she'd felt pain, and upon Culloden Moor she had looked upon the face of despair. But staring into Myles's unreadable eyes at that moment was the worst torture that she had ever known.

"I don't know. I—"

"Son of a bitch!" He slammed his fist into the wall, his knuckles tearing, bleeding. "Just tell me the rest of this infernal plan of yours so we can attempt to make it work. Because I promise you this, Dev: If it does not, Cumberland and Tracey won't bother waiting to cart us back to London and put us on trial! They'll kill us where we stand."

"You—You're to feign sickness. Writhe and . . . and groan just before the guards feel the effects of the drug. I'll summon them to help you."

"I see. And doubtless Crully and Ragnor will bustle in with hot compresses and a hartshorn pillow for my head."

"You're a valuable prisoner. Cumberland would not want you harmed."

"Don't be so sure of that. A brace of his minions convinced me of the contrary with fists and clubs just this morning."

"Then you will have to pretend you are dying. There could be no amusement in torturing a dead man!"

Always before her blunt outbursts had brought gales of

laughter from Myles, but his mouth remained hard, angry. "Fine. I had best get in practice, since that will doubtless be the state I'll soon be saddled with. Now tell me how much time we have before the drug will take effect."

"I—I'm not certain. The sleeping potion is not an—an exact science. We shall have to contrive to . . . do the best we can to judge."

"Do you mean to tell me you don't even know how long it takes for this poison to take effect?"

"I know approximately."

"Approximately. But we have to keep both guards in this cell until it does."

"Yes."

"And if St. Jude should smile on us, and we should miraculously pass through this first disaster, pray tell, what is our next course of action to be? I don't suppose you know the corridors of this monstrous ruin. The place is supposedly crawling with guards. How do you propose to get through them? With a wave of a magical wand?"

"I would think you could bestir yourself and come up with something to help!"

"I wouldn't dream of it, considering all the forethought you've put into this wonderful scheme. Tell me, though. After we escape the castle, what then? I suppose you have a pair of horses hidden under your skirts?"

"Blast you, Myles, stop it!" A sob breached her lips. "I don't know. I don't know. But you'll think of something. You always have."

"Not at Culloden, I didn't. Not in that butchery. Christ, I couldn't save anyone . . . not anyone." The anguish in his voice shook Devlin from her own pain, and she suddenly stilled, peering into his bleak features.

"You did save someone. That was how I found you."

"What the—"

"In fact, he wanted me to return something to you." She raised the hem of her petticoat, the lantern light exposing a long, cloth-wrapped bundle she had tied to her thigh with strips of linen. With deft fingers she untied it. Then she laid the bundle in Myles's reluctant hands.

His fingers closed convulsively, as if he suspected. Hope and fear streaked like quicksilver through his eyes. With shaking hands he unrolled the wrapping, then hesitated just a heartbeat before pulling the last bit of fabric free.

Dragons danced across the blade, battered, nicked, and yet still beautiful. In some ways more beautiful, because now they seemed far more real than they had, all glistening bright, untouched. His eyes widened, shimmering with what could only be tears as he raised them to her face. "Andrew." He choked out the name, and in that instant she understood the depth of what Myles had suffered. "I saw the bastards strike him down. I saw the pike thrust, saw him fall—"

"He should have died, what with his wound, and lying there near that rock for God knows how long," Devlin said softly. "But he's on his way home with his mama and Jacob. In fact, by now he might be sleeping upon his own little pallet, thanks to you." She stroked Myles's trembling arm. "It was the dragons that made him keep fighting to live. He thought they . . . protected him. If you could have seen the light in his eyes, Myles, when he told me." Her voice cracked. "He asked me to bring the magic back to you."

Myles ran his fingertips down the flat of the blade. "There isn't any magic. You always knew that."

"That was before I was kissed in a rose garden. Before a hero fought a duel over me. Before I spent a night learning how beautiful a dream could be through his eyes, in his arms."

"Dev, I—"

A grating sound from outside the cell made them both wheel, hearts pounding. "The drug. We need to hurry, in case . . ." Without a word Myles lunged for the rotted straw that served as a pallet and jammed the dragon sword beneath him. The flush that stung his cheeks lent a realism to the feverish guise he was to adopt.

Devlin hastened to the cell door. With a last look at Myles she pounded upon the panel, her voice shrill with what she prayed would pass for panic.

"Help!" she shrieked. "For the love of God, help us! The viscount is . . . oh, God, I fear he's dying!"

There was a grumble from outside the door, the scrape of the heavy bar being lifted free. The door was pulled open a crack, but it was not Crully or Ragnor who poked his head in the opening, it was the foul-smelling Smee. Devlin's pulse tripped. Merciful heavens, the man hadn't taken so much as a sip of the brandy. Where in God's name were the guards she had drugged? Her mind filled with images of the two men in the common room above suddenly keeling over, unconscious. The whole castle would be alerted that something was afoot. She listened, half expecting to hear the thunder of heavy boots racing toward them, shouts of alarm echoing through the aged stone halls.

"What be the problem, me lady?" Smee's voice yanked her back to the present. She could feel the blood drain from her cheeks. There was no need to pretend fear. She was terrified.

The guard stepped into the cell, one hand on the butt of his pistol. "Be the viscount not man enough to satisfy ye after so long? An' what with Master Tracey even leavin' you a lantern t' play by."

There was something bestial and dark in the guard's piglike eyes. But Devlin met his glare with one of her own. She hastened to where Myles lay upon the pallet, groaning and clutching his stomach. The muscles in his face stood out in hard ridges, beads of sweat trickling in rivulets across his skin.

"The viscount is ill! I fear . . . fear he is dying."

Smee shrugged one hamlike shoulder. "Makes little difference whether he dies now or later. Traitorous scum—"

"Perhaps not to you, but your masters would not be amused should he die! He is the only one who knows the whereabouts of the crown they are so greedy to find! If he dies because of your negligence—"

Smee's heavy features flushed, his eyes narrowing. He stalked over to where Myles writhed. Despite the fact that Devlin knew it was a ruse, she felt her own sense of unease mount as she looked down at that pain-racked face. She knelt beside the pallet in an effort to be convincing and pried Myles's hands away from his filthy, tattered shirt.

"Blast you, we have to help him! Do something!" she appealed to Smee as she spread open the fabric. But at that instant her gaze snagged upon something unexpected. Horrible. A choked cry tore from her throat, her senses reeling.

The bronzed flesh she had exposed was splashed with horrible colored bruises, sickly green and yellow, deep purple, bluish gray, while across those same battered muscles were several gashes.

God in heaven, if any of those wounds had been deeper . . .

She wheeled on Smee, shrieking, "Do you want him to die? Don't just stand there!" A sob racked her, and she scrambled to retrieve her canvas bag, rummaging for something inside it. "I need hot water, and brandy! The guards outside stole all that I had! Send the other guards in here to help me, and go get Mr. Tracey."

Smee stared one last instant at Myles, then at Devlin. "Go, you bloody fool!" Devlin bellowed in Smee's face.

There was a scuffle as the big man wheeled and fled, barking out orders to the men outside the door. The answers from the other guards were a little slurred, and Devlin was terrified one of them would collapse at any moment.

But Smee must have attributed his fellow guards' unsteadiness to the purloined brandy. Devlin heard the thundering sound of his footsteps racing away from the cell, and a shaft of relief shot through her.

But when she glanced up to see the figures entering the door her heart plunged to her toes. Crully wove toward her, an idiotic grin upon his face. But behind him was again the surly countenance of Mr. Smee.

"God's blood, the bastards are drunker than a monk on Sunday!" Smee raged. "Can't be of any help to you, either of them. Bloody viscount dies, 'twill be *my* head that rolls."

Devlin searched her mind, desperate for some way to rid herself of Smee, some way to get the oaf out of the cell before all was lost.

"Ragnor will never find the things I need if he's drunk! You'll have to go after him."

"Oh, no, missy, I'm not so dense as that!" Smee's lips

pulled in an ugly snarl over his teeth. "I've seen how long a woman's faith'll last when she sees the rats a-crawlin' and senses the bite o' the headsman's axe upon her pretty neck. You'd run like an arrow-shot deer if I left ye alone."

"I'm not going anywhere! If my husband dies—"

"If the viscount dies, I'll just tell them ye tried to escape, I will. An' I shot the both of ye . . . just like I was ordered."

Terror, black, suffocating, washed through Devlin. She sensed the sudden tension in Myles, wondered what he was thinking, if there was anything they could do to avert this disaster. The sword was shoved beneath him, if he could reach it . . . but there was little chance he could grab it and draw it out before the fully alert Smee was aware something was afoot.

Desperation clawed in Devlin, and she looked into Myles's narrowed eyes, trying to decipher what he was attempting to tell her.

Suddenly she looked down to where his hands were clawing at the straw. Disbelief and a wild hope sprang to life within her. Myles's fingers were knotted in a pool of chains. The shackles in which they had doubtless bound him when they were beating him.

Outrage made Devlin's whole body shake, but she fought to keep the aura of pleading in her face, to play the role of the terrified wife begging her dying husband's captors for aid.

She let her glance skate past Crully, who was leaning against the stone wall, the black of his pupils all but swallowing the muddy brown irises around them. Then she glared up at Smee. "What would you rather be? The soldier who shot two prisoners supposedly attempting escape? Or the man who saved the life of the prisoner who will lead Cumberland to the Stuart crown?"

Smee's lip curled. "I'd have to think on it."

"While you're thinking, help me get my lord out of this shirt. We have to put compresses upon—"

"I'd rather take ye out of yer bodice, milady, I vow." There was lust in Smee's eyes as they fastened upon her neckline. Smee reached out a beefy hand and closed it roughly about Devlin's breast.

At that instant the world seemed to explode. Myles hurled himself at the guard, the heavy chains cracking into that lust-suffused face. Smee bellowed in fury, staggered, the half-drugged Crully fumbling for his sword.

One of Smee's huge fists connected solidly with Myles's ribs, and Devlin saw him pale, a guttural sound tearing from his throat. But Myles didn't even pause to draw breath. He attacked Smee with a savagery that stunned Devlin, bewildered the huge guard. The manacles cracked into Smee's skull, blood spurting in their wake.

"Run, Dev!" Myles shouted. "For God's sake—"

But at that instant Dev saw the sword half buried in the straw. She lunged for it, the hilt slipping into her hand. Crully was staggering toward Myles, the gleaming blade of his weapon still lethal, even in the soldier's unsteady hand.

Smee struggled against Myles's onslaught, and Devlin could feel Myles's own strength ebbing away.

She gripped the dragon sword tight, then, with all her strength, slammed the cutting edge of the blade deep into Crully's side.

The man screamed, fell, horror bolting through Devlin as he toppled to the stone floor. She heard a hideous cracking sound and wheeled to see Smee tumbling to the stones as well, his eyes rolling back in death.

Myles was on his knees, his breath rasping in his chest, his body shaking with exertion. Devlin flung the dragon sword aside as he struggled to gain his feet.

"Myles, oh God, Myles," she was crying as she ran to his side, jamming her shoulder beneath his arm, attempting to help him rise.

"It's all right, Dev," he gasped, his breath ragged, one arm clutched tight against his ribs. "Have to . . . to hurry." He sucked in a shuddering breath. "The sword. Don't leave . . ."

Devlin scooped it up and pressed it into his hand, needing both of her own to help brace him upright. And she prayed that some of Andrew's magic would strengthen Myles, steady his legs beneath him.

She plunged out into the corridor, terrified, not knowing which way to turn. Myles had been right—the only way out she knew was the one that led straight through the common room where the soldiers Cumberland had given Tracey lounged over their flagons of rum.

What if there was no other path to freedom? She and Myles, armed with a length of chain and a broken sword, could hardly defeat a dozen men.

"I don't—don't know where to go," she said, desperate.

"Neither do I." Was there a ghost of Myles's old teasing in that pain-taut voice? "We'll leave it to Dame Fortune. Roll the dice, Dev."

She gaped at him for a moment, realizing he was placing both their lives in her hands. From the time she was eight she had been blessed with unshakable faith in herself, a toughness of spirit that had shielded her from the worst her mother had dealt her. But not until this moment had she realized where that strength had come from, who had nurtured her inborn stubborn will after her father had died.

Myles.

She closed her eyes, feeling as if she were again teetering upon the stable rafters, Myles's voice drifting from below: "Jump, Dev, I won't let you fall."

But they would both fall, into the arms of death, if she made the wrong choice now.

Devlin glanced desperately at the branches of corridors, feeling precious seconds slip between her fingers. "This way." She angled them to the right, hastening away from the dungeon. Myles was moving faster, and Devlin could feel less and less of his weight lean upon her as they rushed onward.

Hope bubbled up, a heady sensation, as they ran. Splintered bits of wood, shattered crockery, fragments of iron littered the way, refuse from centuries past catching at Devlin's petticoats.

Myles's breath was rasping, her own side aching with the effort of helping him, traveling as fast as they were able.

"We're almost there now, Myles," she choked out. "We have to be."

Light beckoned from around a corner, and Devlin raced toward it, praying that it would be a doorway to the Scottish countryside and freedom.

But as they rounded the bend horror iced Devlin's veins.

A single taper flickered eerily upon the dank stone walls, the narrow path blocked by Braden Tracey, an unsheathed sword gleaming in his hand.

CHAPTER

27

*I*n a heartbeat Myles had whipped her behind the shield of his broad chest, the dragon sword at the ready. "Bastard!" Myles snarled. He lashed out with the blade, but Tracey's own weapon shot out, blocking the thrust.

Panic rocketed through Devlin with the knowledge that Myles was weak, wounded, on the brink of collapse, while Tracey stood pristine in the lantern light, not even his golden hair out of place.

The night of the disastrous ball flickered into her memory —the night Tracey had pierced Myles's leg, could have killed him if he'd wished it. Tracey, who had always preened over the fact that he could best his friend with a sword.

"Myles, don't make me kill you." Tracey's voice was low.

Myles circled Tracey in the narrow stone confines, the dragon sword gleaming as if it possessed a light of its own. "You leave the killing to curs like Smee and Crully, don't you? We all know how squeamish political supporters can grow when they see blood on a man's hands."

Myles rained murderous blows upon Tracey, the broken tip of the sword clashing again and again with the flashing steel of Tracey's rapier.

Never had Devlin seen Myles attack with such fury, a fury that would doubtless break through even Tracey's formidable guard before long. But Tracey was not fighting back, not seeking advantage. He was only parrying the blows as deftly as possible, leaping out of the path of Myles's more aggressive blade.

"Damn it, Myles, listen to me!" Tracey snarled. "You're going the wrong bloody way!"

"You're going straight to hell, Tracey. You'll not have to worry."

"There are a dozen men . . . at the end of this hall," Tracey ground out, his voice ragged. "Go on and they'll . . . shoot you before . . . you've taken three steps."

"So what? I should surrender to you? Let you kill us at your convenience?"

"I was coming to help!"

"Bastard! You drag Devlin into this, and you expect me to believe—" With a masterful stroke Myles sent the rapier flying, the weapon skittering into the shadows. Tracey dived for it, but it was lost in the darkness. He rolled onto his back, his mouth setting in a hard line as the broken tip of Myles's sword pressed against the exposed cords of his throat.

Devlin tried to cry out, to speak, but her own throat seemed locked, time itself frozen as the two men faced each other for what would be the last time.

"We were friends," Myles grated, "brothers in a way no mere blood tie could offer. I loved you, damn you, but I promised to send you to hell."

Tracey's voice was level, his eyes meeting Myles's gaze. "Myles, listen to me. I was coming to get you out—you and Devlin. I swear to God."

"What kind of a fool do you think I am? You watched them beat the devil out of me. You brought Devlin into this hellhole."

"How else could I have gotten her away from Cumberland's camp? And as for the other, I had to make them all believe that I hated you—a man the whole of

345

England knows was my foster brother, my best friend. To make *them* believe it I had to make *you* believe it. Don't you understand?"

The blade of the sword pressed a fraction deeper, blood welling at its point. "What about the crown? The fact that you betrayed me?"

Tracey's eyes seemed to hold Myles's gaze for a long minute. "That part was true. I did want the crown. Badly."

"Badly enough to set the whole goddamned English army upon my trail?"

"Yes. But not badly enough to kill you for it."

"What did you expect them to do when they found me? Invite me to a blasted musicale?"

"I knew you'd find a way to escape them. Christ, how many times have the two of us managed to slip through such nooses before? In France, in Italy—blast it, Myles, I was sure you'd get away, and then you'd be safe. How was I supposed to know that you'd snarl Devlin up in this madness? That you wouldn't just take yourself off to France and spend the whole rebellion reveling in the charms of one of your mistresses?"

"Damn you to hell, Tracey," Myles ground out between gritted teeth. "I'll not let you use me again, manipulate me."

"Kill me, then, if it will make you feel the better," Tracey said, desperate. "But don't take Devlin out this way! Don't, Myles, for the love of God. You'll be slaughtered. I have horses waiting behind the stone wall behind the west gate. I made certain no one would be there."

The sword shook, Myles's hand ice-white, his features drained of color. "You're a liar. You betrayed me. Betrayed her."

"There is a bag affixed to the horse. Some of my things are in it. There is enough coin to carry you out of Scotland."

"Don't do this to me, damn you . . . don't." Myles's voice thrummed with animal pain. He drew back the sword, and Devlin could see his jaw lock, feel him steeling himself to drive it home.

She flung herself at him, grabbing his arm. "Myles, no!"

He wheeled on her, his eyes clouded with primal anguish, his features so tortured tears poured from her eyes.

"Blast it, Dev, you saw what he did! You heard—"

"I believe him."

He stared at her as if she had driven Tracey's sword through his heart. And maybe she had—placing her trust and both their lives in Tracey's hands rather than Myles's own. Love she had offered Myles, freely. But in that instant she sensed that her faith at this moment, after so many years of scorn, would have been a far greater gift.

Myles's face contorted with anguish and indecision as he hovered upon the brink of madness bred at Culloden Moor and within the dank confines of the dungeon where Cumberland's beasts had tortured him. His terror for her was a living thing, pulsing beneath the sheath of his muscle under the palm of her hand.

For long minutes she didn't know who would win, the beast war had loosed inside him or her love for him.

A sound tore through him, half agony, half sob, and he whirled away from Tracey, slamming the dragon sword against the stone.

She had shattered him, devastated him in a way even the war and Tracey's betrayal had not been able to. She only prayed to God that the pain she had caused him would save his life.

Tracey scrambled to his feet, one hand covering the tiny wound at his throat.

"Devlin, this way," he said. Then they were running again. But as they seemed to wind deeper again into the ruined castle's depths Devlin wondered if she had somehow doomed both herself and Myles to a traitor's death.

It felt as if they'd been racing through the dimness forever when suddenly Tracey slammed the palms of his hands against a heavy oak door, the sunlight all but blinding them as it spilled across the stones.

As if the crash of the door itself had sent up a signal, a roar of alarm echoed from behind them.

"You bastard!" Myles wheeled on Tracey, one hand going for his throat. "You betrayed—"

Tracey dashed his hand away, shoving Devlin forward. "Hurry! For the love of God!"

They raced across the strip of open ground, the sound of pistol fire and muskets reverberating all around them. Beyond the stone wall a dozen yards away Devlin could hear the nervous whickering of the horses and wondered fleetingly if the sound heralded their means of escape or the closing of the jaws of yet another trap—a trap set by Tracey himself.

She stumbled upon a stone and felt Myles jerk her upright, keeping her on her feet, the space between the deadly musket fire and the shelter of the wall seeming to yawn in an unbridgeable chasm before them.

She glimpsed Myles's pain-haggard face, his hand still clutching the dragon sword, his other arm curled protectively about wounds that must be throbbing with agony.

Shouts rang out closer, the red-coated soldiers spilling out of the ruins.

"They'll overtake us the minute they mount their horses," Myles snarled.

And Devlin was stunned to hear Tracey give a short bark of laughter. "I slit the cinches, like we did that time in Cannes. They'll ride three feet and fall on their arses."

Already Devlin caught fleeting glimpses of the soldiers attempting to swing onto their mounts, falling, cursing. She felt a surge of hope that they might truly evade their pursuers if they could but reach the horses Tracey had promised.

She stumbled as the thunderous rain of gunfire split the air yet again. Murderous lead balls whizzed past. One caught her petticoat, and she felt the tug of it tearing through the fabric, her heart tripping at the knowledge of how close it had come to finding its mark. But before she could utter so much as a prayer of thanksgiving another sound made horror streak through her—a horrible thud as lead struck flesh.

She cried out, terrified that Myles had been hit. But it was Tracey who crumpled to the ground, Tracey's coat that blossomed with the red stain of blood.

Tracey who she'd still feared might prove their betrayer.

She started to turn toward him, but Myles was already at his side, yanking him up, though Myles himself could barely stand.

"Get up, damn you, Tracey!" Myles bellowed, the sound of the soldiers' pursuit growing nearer, nearer. "Run!"

Tracey staggered, attempting to pull away. "Can't . . . can't make it . . . Myles! Have to . . . to leave me."

"I'm not bloody leaving you!" With strength born of desperation Myles half dragged, half carried Tracey the distance to the wall and flung him up onto one of the waiting horses.

Devlin swung astride a skittish mare, the creature terri-fied by the explosions, the stench of gunpowder and blood swirling around them.

"Ride, Dev!" Myles shouted, struggling to drag his own battered body on behind the limp form of Tracey. "Ride!"

The instant she saw him manage to catch the swinging stirrups she drove her heels into her own mount's barrel. The horse surged forward, both animals thundering across the countryside.

Tears blinded her, grief wrenching through her as she glimpsed the two men upon the sturdy black gelding. Tracey leaned limply against Myles's chest, Myles's arms battling to balance Tracey's considerable weight before him.

She had seen them together a hundred times, laughing over some private jest, racing across the hills upon the hunt, playing at dice or hazard or faro in the drawing room, Myles's long, booted legs draped lazily upon the polished tabletop, Tracey's graceful fingers curled about the stem of a goblet full of Liancourt's finest wine.

It seemed an eternity ago that those two rakehells had gone about their revels, consummately confident that the world and all its treasures were theirs for the taking.

Who would have dreamed that the neck cloth Myles had always taken such pains in tying would be crumpled beneath Tracey's head, that Tracey's blood would be seeping into Myles's waistcoat, the moisture mingling with Myles's sweat, making his wounds burn? Bruises, cuts that Tracey might as well have inflicted with his own two hands.

How had it happened? This madness that had hurled the three of them into these vast wildlands so far away from the garden and the drawing rooms, the gaming hells and the hunting lodges? How had it come to shatter them as certainly as the rebellion had shattered Scotland?

It seemed impossible. But it was agonizingly real. Devlin could feel it in the way her heart was breaking.

"Tracey, don't die, damn you!" She heard Myles's voice, broken, hoarse. "Damn you, don't you die!"

But long before they had drawn rein at a cave to shelter for the night, Devlin knew that not even Myles's fierce will would be able to stave off the tide of death that was slowly sweeping Tracey away.

Myles climbed down from his horse, Tracey in his arms, and eased him down upon the turf gently as a mother laying a babe in its cradle.

The lazy arrogance that had always clung about Myles's features was gone, lines of grief, fury carving deep beside his mouth, his hands trembling as he ripped open Tracey's shirt.

"Get a poultice, Dev!" he pleaded. "My hand . . . I kept my hand upon the wound . . . stanched the blood as best I could."

Devlin had seen death a dozen times among the crofters at Liancourt, had always been able to sense it. And as she looked at Tracey she was certain he already could feel its chill kiss upon his brow.

"It's too . . . late, Myles." Tracey's voice. Faint. Resigned. "Surely wouldn't . . . condemn me . . . to spending last moments . . . choking on Devlin's . . . weeds."

"Blast it, don't say that! She can work miracles."

"Not . . . this time."

"You've been shot before, damn it, and you were fine."

"In Genoa, wasn't it? Jealous husband. You never . . . trifled with . . . married ladies. A most . . . sage . . . policy."

"Damn it, Tracey! Breathe!" Myles was cradling him in his arms, his dark head bent over Tracey's golden one. "You're not going to do this! Make me mad as hell—betray me—and then goddamn die before you can tell me why!"

"You'd never . . . understand . . . if had . . . lifetime to explain. Power . . . craved it. Would've sold . . . my soul for it. Astonished to . . . find . . . in the end . . . couldn't sell . . . yours."

Tracey's lips twisted in a weak smile. "From time we were . . . boys . . . you were my conscience. Damned inconvenient things, consciences are . . . sometimes."

"Just fight this, man!"

"You . . . always one . . . to fight when all was lost. I . . . never had that . . . kind of courage." A racking shudder went through Tracey, death trailing her chill fingers down his spine.

"Myles, in bag . . . a . . . list," Tracey gasped out. "Spies for . . . French. Gathering it . . . for months."

"Tracey, I don't give a damn about—"

"You have to—to take it. Send it to . . . grandfather." He grimaced, and Devlin could see him battle to form the words. "Meant to . . . present it . . . to authorities at most . . . auspicious time . . . for career. But don't have career . . . anymore, do I?"

"Of course you do! You will! Damn it, Dev, help him!"

"Dev . . . Devlin . . ." Tracey choked, the death rattle sounding in his throat.

She knelt beside him, catching up one pale, limp hand. She had once thought she loved him. As she looked into his face she saw all he might have been, instead of the man he had become.

"I'm here."

"I . . . hurt you."

"Don't think about that now." She swallowed the tears and stroked a lock of dark gold hair from his brow. "It's over. Forgotten."

"I can't . . . forget it. Have to . . . tell you."

The words were agony now, his eyes fluttering shut, pain contorting his features. "Have to tell you . . . I loved you . . . in my way."

Devlin laid her cheek upon his hand, her tears warming the chill of his skin.

"Dev . . . Myles's way . . . is . . . better."

His fingers tightened about hers for a heartbeat, and she saw his eyes, glazed with pain, catch Myles's one last time.

Tears seared her cheeks, burned her spirit as she watched the transformation she had witnessed upon so many others: death sweeping her mystical fingers across that pain-tortured face, granting Braden Tracey peace.

CHAPTER
28

A million stars spangled the sky above Thistlewould, as though some wayward goddess had snapped a necklet of diamonds and scattered them across the heavens. Devlin leaned against the ledge of the open window, the breeze threading through hair still damp from the bath Jacob had carried up for her an hour before.

She and Myles had arrived at the estate at twilight, bedraggled, dispirited, exhausted, to find the Cameron home abuzz with activity. Trunks crowded the entryway, with what few loyal servants still remained stuffing the containers with the Camerons' treasures.

It had warmed Devlin's heart to see the retainers working so tirelessly on behalf of a master and mistress who were already gone. The surprisingly resourceful Bella had scooped her ailing husband and little son out of danger five days before, boarding a ship bound for Italy.

Jacob, recently returned from his trek with little Andrew, had seen them safely aboard but had not fled Scotland himself. The shy youth who had jested with Myles in Edinburgh was gone, lost somewhere upon the battlefield at Culloden Moor, or on the hazardous journey he had taken with the wounded child Devlin had placed in his care. The Jacob who now strode about the halls, rapping out orders, was a man with an uncommon strength in his face.

He had seen a dozen horrors, the knife edge of the war slicing deep into his soul. It had made him angry, made him resolve to snatch away the spoils Hanover's greedy men would attempt to steal from his beloved master. Jacob had returned to Thistlewould determined to carry the treasures the Camerons had left behind to Bella's father in England for safekeeping. And there was something in the change in this youth that touched Devlin's heart.

Yet not even the fact that Thistlewould's treasures would be snatched from Hanover's hands, nor the knowledge that Bella and Harry and little Hal were safe, could rid Devlin of the sadness that robed her as tangibly as Bella's amber silk dressing gown. Not even this place that she had come to love second only to Liancourt could banish the horrible feeling that she had somehow lost Myles—her laughing, gallant rogue—forever.

It was as if he had stepped through some enchanted mirror, a gallant knight wreathed in legend, and had emerged on the other side bitter, disillusioned, all but broken.

He had shut her out, shut everyone out, with the bitter line of that mouth that had once curved with such bedeviling humor. He had barely touched her upon the journey to Thistlewould, had barely spoken, barely slept, never once alluding to the words she had spoken to him in the dungeon: that she loved him.

But she wondered if this Myles was capable of loving anyone anymore. If he would ever again be able to make himself vulnerable to the anguish he'd felt watching Andrew at Culloden Moor, or to the desperation he'd known with Devlin in the dungeon, or to the torturous self-doubt that had been Tracey's final legacy.

A part of Myles had died as certainly as Tracey had within that rugged stone cave upon the barren sweep of moor. The blue of his eyes that had shone with the same stark pleasure upon the sight of a crofter's moppet splashing in a rain puddle or a glorious masterpiece wrought in gold or silver or stone had been robbed of all dreams, all joy, all hope.

From the time she was a child Devlin had wanted to drive the dream-dust from Myles's eyes.

But never had she suspected what it would be like to see Myles this way. Never had she known that all the beauty she had seen—the rainbow tints gilding the clouds, the fragrance of the roses in the summer wind, the rippling sound of laughter—had been magnified a hundredfold because they had been reflected in Myles Farringdon's eyes.

Devlin walked to the dressing table and picked up the necklet she had removed during her bath, the miniature of Lady Brianna glowing richly in the candlelight. The cavalier's lady stared back at her with eyes that seemed filled with understanding. It was as if this woman from a century past were reaching out to Devlin with the abiding strength of eyes that had seen defeat at Worcester, that had watched Cromwell's New Model Army shatter life as she knew it, and then, after years of exile, had doubtless rejoiced at the restoration of that most gallant of all cavaliers, Charles II, to his rightful throne.

In the years between tragedy and triumph, what had this woman endured? What joy had she found? For there was a strength shining in those eyes that proclaimed she had survived it all with new dreams, better dreams, tucked safely within the palms of her hands.

Devlin's fingers closed about the painted image.

Dreams. She had always thought they were such fragile things, a kind of blindness embraced to keep the harsh realities of life at bay. But now she knew that dreams were what had made Myles stronger than anyone she had ever known.

Dreams were what had carried him through the days when his father had died and his mother had lain ill. They had glossed his rakish smile during the time Devlin had loathed him, and blamed him for things that were not his fault. They had given him hope when she had wed him—not out of love, but out of despair.

Dreams. He had given them to her the night he had made

love to her, the morning he had left the leather book for her to find.

She closed her eyes, remembering his bold script upon the frontispiece, the writing she had blurred with her tears.

Pieces of dreams . . .

If only she could give them back to him.

The library's shelves were all but bare, Harry Cameron's treasured books waiting to be loaded on the wagon Jacob was taking to England. Portraits of Camerons from generations past had been stripped from their places of honor, leaving shadowy imprints upon the walls where they had hung.

Shadows. They seemed to be everywhere, crowding about Myles's shoulders, hovering in the corners, creeping about the hearth. Images of Harry downing a draught of brandy, of Bella shy and smiling, her golden hair framing her face like a halo.

Shadows of Tracey, negligently wagering a fortune upon a curricle race, or grimacing over some inferior wine set forth by an eager host.

In the poolings of darkness, Myles could see Devlin, bustling about Liancourt, her keys jingling at her waist, as she sent the servants about their tasks, or other times, sequestered in his mother's rooms, the sunlight toying with the red-gold strands of her hair, a blot of ink upon her nose.

Safe in her own castle tower, where the outside world could never touch her.

Myles sat at the desk at which he had seen Harry so often and twisted a bent quill one of the maids had rummaged from a corner of the house.

How long had he been in this room, haunted by images his pen could never capture? How many times had he attempted to dip the quill into ink, to draft the letter that now lay drying upon the desk?

The fire crackling upon the hearth had greedily devoured a dozen efforts, searing away the words it had been torture for him to write. But at last he had penned the direction upon the final draft of the missive—to be delivered to the Duke of Pothsby, at Pothsby Hall.

He stared at the letter, thinking of all he had left unsaid. But how could he explain what had happened these past weeks? How could he untangle the web of Tracey's lies and betrayal, his plotting and his sacrifices? How could he transcribe into mere words the pain of it, the hurt, the anger, the outrage he had felt when Tracey had taken years of friendship and tarnished them forever for nothing more than greed?

In the end he had written only the briefest of letters. He had enclosed Tracey's list of French informers and had transcribed detailed instructions on how to find Tracey's grave, knowing that his family would want to bring him home. Not a word had Myles written about the perfidy, the betrayal. He had shielded Tracey from that slur upon his honor, some small repayment for the way Tracey had sacrificed his life to make things right.

Myles only wished that he could rid his own memory of what had happened—that he could write down all the hurt, all the villainy that Tracey had done and fling it into the fire to be burned, leaving the image of his friend clean once again.

Myles cast the quill down upon the table and buried his face in his hands. Sweet God, how had everything gone awry? Why was it that everything he touched had been destroyed? Everything he believed in turned to ash?

Devlin . . .

Her name formed in his mind, but he brushed it aside with angry pain. Hadn't he destroyed her as well? Taken all that she loved, and given her in return the horrors of Culloden Moor and the castle ruin where she'd almost died? He had wanted to give her dreams, but instead he had given her nightmares that would haunt her forever. He had shown her blood and hate, betrayal and destruction. He had ripped down the wall inside her stone by stone, stealing away the defenses that had kept her safe these many years.

He had left her defenseless against the hurt that now shimmered in her eyes, the vulnerability that touched those lips that had always faced life with such fierce determination.

He had saddled her with a future cast in exile.

How painful was the knowledge that any children she might bear him would be raised in some land where they would never see the beauty of an English springtime or know how the scent of flowers clung to the air after rain.

And most worthless of all, he had given her his heart—a heart filled not with dreams, but with bitterness, anger, despair.

What a paltry offering in return for all that she had been cheated of.

"Damn you, Myles, I'm trying to tell you that I love you. . . ."

The words echoed in his mind, the desperation in her face when she had said them raking at his soul. How many times had he imagined her saying those words to him? How many times had he played out the scene in his mind? The way her eyes would shine, her lips would tremble. The way she would lift her face to his to be kissed.

He had imagined what he would say to her, how she would laugh when he told her how long he had loved her, how even he had never suspected that was the reason he had tormented her for so long—the only means he had of gaining her attention.

He had pictured her garbed in gauzy white lawn, framed against the backdrop of the tumbled coverlets of their bed, her hair a silken flame against his skin as he made love to her again and again, telling her that he loved her with each brush of his lips, each touch of his hand, each thrust of his body, joining his with hers.

But there hadn't been bedsheets scented with wildflowers or gauzy lawn skimming the curves of her body. There had been harsh stone walls and an axe blade hovering over her head. There had been chains and foul bastards wanting to hurt her.

And all he'd been able to think when she said those precious words to him was that *he* was responsible for her being in that dungeon, trapped in deadly danger. His love hadn't cocooned her in security, seared her with passion. It had been the poison that lured her from the safety of Thistlewould into the hell of war and bitterness and peril.

All his life he had read hero tales, stories of ladies fair who had sacrificed everything to go to the men they loved. Never had he suspected what it might be like for the men they went to. What it would be like to be helpless as they walked into dungeon or dragonfire, and to know that it was love that would lure them to their death.

A soft snapping sound made Myles start, and he stared at the quill, broken in his hand. Broken, like so many things he had believed in.

"Can I make you another one?" Devlin's soft voice came to him. "I was always better at it than you were."

Myles turned to see her in the doorway. An amber silk dressing gown draped around her, skimming the arches of her bare feet. Her hair, caressed cheeks still pale, eyes still shadowed, a mouth so soft and vulnerable it wrenched his heart.

"You were better at everything than I was," he said, tearing his eyes away. "Everything that mattered."

"Not everything."

He could hear the soft shush of her feet against the floor, smell the scent of roses that always clung to her skin.

"I wasn't any good at laughing. And I never saw anything beautiful unless you thrust my nose smack against it."

"Maybe that was because there wasn't anything beautiful in your life. A mother who neglected you. Tutors who resented you because you were a girl. And me . . . constantly tormenting you. Never giving you peace."

"I didn't need peace. After my father died . . . I wanted to curl up inside myself, never feel anything again. I was so scared, Myles, and lost. My father was dead, and my mother . . . she couldn't even look at me without . . ." The pain in her voice made Myles's throat raw.

"It wasn't your fault, the way she treated you."

Devlin gave him a soft, sad smile. "I wasn't a lovable

child, all laughter and mischief. Maybe that is what my mother needed when we came to Liancourt. Maybe that is what she found in you."

"Your mother was a witch who hurt you because of her own sins," Myles said, savage, his hands closing on Devlin's arms. "Christ, when I think of the way she treated you—I swear, I should have demanded my mother send her away instead of going off to Tracey's myself." He broke off the sentence, cursing himself for a fool. Those green eyes that had always been far too wise locked upon his face, and it was as if she could see his very thoughts.

"That was why you badgered your mother to send you away. Because of me." Her hand reached up, velvety softness skimming the hard line of his jaw. Tears were shimmering in her eyes.

"Your mother wanted to send you away because . . . because we were fighting so much. I was in my mother's room, working some devilment upon your inkwell, when I overheard them."

"So you left Liancourt. Left everything you knew, everything you loved to spare me."

"I didn't understand how your mother could be so cold. I never understood it until Tracey told me." Hate and fury welled up in Myles again. "Your father . . . he didn't kill himself, Devlin."

She gasped, her face waxen as he rushed on.

"He was murdered by soldiers who were seeking information on King James's supporters in England. The Jacobites had gathered up a fortune in jewels, gold, and silver plate to finance his return. There were lists kept of those who had contributed, so that they could be rewarded when the rebellion was over. Your father was entrusted with both the fortune and the list."

"The treasure. At the Dower House." Devlin stared at him, incredulous. "That is where it came from."

"He must have hidden it just before the soldiers arrived. And then stayed to destroy the lists."

"The dreams . . . I remember . . . remember fire . . . my mother hiding with me . . ."

"They killed him, Dev. Because he wouldn't give them the information they wanted. And through his courage he saved the lives of half the nobles in England. My father among them."

He had expected bitterness to shadow her face, had expected all the pain of her mother's neglect to burst forth like a wound that had festered far too long.

Never had he expected her face to shine, her lips to curve into a tremulous smile. Never had he expected the joy that rippled through her where her hands pressed against the wall of his chest.

"Dev, you should be mad as hell!"

"It doesn't matter. Don't you see, Myles? He didn't leave me. All these years . . . I thought my father didn't love me enough to keep fighting. That he'd killed himself because of financial ruin. Coin that meant nothing. But he did love me. He did."

Her hand strayed up to the miniature caught about her neck by a thin amber ribbon. And Myles could feel the peace in her.

But suddenly her brows lowered, a crease of confusion carving between them. "But I don't understand why my mother lied all these years. If there was treasure, and my mother knew where it was, why didn't she go to the Dower House herself and take it? My father might have been noble, but I doubt my mother would have shrunk from using Jacobite gold—she would have thought it her due, payment for the death of my father."

"She didn't need the gold, Devlin. The authorities knew what an uproar there would be if the truth about your father's death was ever known. They had murdered him, a knight of the realm, without a trial, without ever proving his guilt. They paid your mother an exorbitant sum to hold her peace. And as for the other Jacobites, they wouldn't have dared to come forward with the tale, because to do so would incriminate themselves. No one save a Jacobite traitor who was involved with the scheme could possibly have known the truth."

Those dark-lashed eyes were wide. "But if she was taking

the government's money, what could she have done with it all these years? We lived off of your family's charity all this time, when she—"

"I don't know what she's done with the money. But I hope she's invested it well. Even if I never return to claim my birthright, her days at Liancourt are over."

"Because she lied?"

"Because she tried to break you," he said, his fingertips caressing her face. "But she couldn't do it, could she, Dev? No. She couldn't do it."

Only I could, he thought.

He turned away from her and walked to the window to stare out into the darkness. An emptiness, a void as far as he could see. If only he could scrub away the mistakes he had made and start again. He would be twenty, and Devlin would be innocent of all that had hurt her. He would carry her off to the Stuart garden, and kneel before her, and tell her . . . tell her he loved her. And she would laugh, and fling her arms about his neck, and . . .

He swore, slamming his fist against the window frame, dashing away the visions that seemed to carve a jagged hole within his soul.

"Myles, don't do this to yourself. All that happened with my mother was a lifetime ago. All that matters now is that I'm with you."

"Oh, yes, you're with me. Racing across Scotland with a price on your head, with nothing save the coin Tracey gave us and the gown upon your back."

"In truth, this is Bella's dressing gown. Perhaps I should remove it at once."

Feral anger ripped through Myles, desperation to drag her into his arms, tear back the amber silk folds so he could lose himself in her body for just a little while. He despised himself for his need to use her that way, to escape his grinding pain.

"Don't." A muscle ticked in his jaw. "It's no good, Dev. I can't."

"Can't what? Make love to me?" Her fingers strayed to the fastenings, slipping them free, the fabric gliding down the ivory curve of her shoulders, skimming past the coral tips of her breasts. "I'm your wife. I want you. Why shouldn't we—"

"Because I don't want you, damn it! Not like this!" Swearing, he closed the space between them, yanking the garment back into place with barely leashed violence. His fingers accidentally snagged upon the thin ribbon about her neck, and it snapped. The miniature tumbled to the floor with a sickening sound.

Devlin gave a cry and scooped up the miniature in her hand. Myles winced at the sight of a crack cutting jaggedly across the portrait.

"I broke it," he said, his fury ebbing into regret, self-recrimination. "I'm sorry, Dev."

But the eyes that had been so pleading, so soft, snapped with anger, scarlet staining her cheekbones. "You're sorry. Sorry about everything, aren't you, Myles? You're sorry you came to Liancourt. Sorry you married me. Sorry you fought in the Stuart cause. Well, I'm not sorry. And I never will be!"

"Devlin, for God's sake—"

"Do you think you're the only man who ever lost in his bid for some infernal quest?" she raged at him. "For every hero basking in a glorious victory there is a man somewhere seared with defeat. How many times have I tried to tell you that battles do nothing to prove who was right or who was wrong?"

"They only show who is willing to cause the most destruction to get his own way," he said wearily. "I've heard your opinion a hundred times."

"Well, you've not heard *this* opinion, Myles Farringdon! This time you were *right.* Charles should have been King of England. The rebellion should have succeeded. It would have, if Charles's advisors had listened to you and hadn't forced him to turn back at Derby."

"You can't know that."

"Don't tell me what I can and cannot do! I've been thinking about it a lot, Myles. And if you had struck swiftly, I'm certain you would have triumphed. *You were right.* But you lost, Myles, through no fault of your own. Does that make you less of a man? Does it make you less noble? Less loving?"

"Dev, I don't want to hear this. Not now."

"Well, you're going to. Do you know that while you were gone I spent hours staring at this miniature you gave me? I would sit and stare into the woman's face, wondering about her. What had made her laugh, cry. Whether she had children. Whether she loved her husband half as much as . . . as I love mine."

"Dev—" He rasped out the plea.

"She must have watched her husband go off to war as well. A cavalier's lady. She must have waited for news of Marston Moor and Nasby and had her world shattered at Worcester when the Royalists were defeated."

"What the hell does this matter to us?"

"Everything, Myles. Don't you see? It wasn't the end of the world for her. And this doesn't have to be the end of our world either. We're alive. We have each other. And I know your dreams are still there if you will reach out and take them."

She cupped his hand in hers. Her fingers trembled as she lay the broken miniature in his palm.

Myles skimmed his eyes across the portrait, wanting to see the magic Devlin had found there, wanting to feel the sense of comfort. But instead alarm streaked through him as he saw a smear of blood upon the woman's golden hair.

"Damn it, Dev, you've cut yourself!" He dumped the miniature upon Harry's desk and scooped up Devlin's hand, holding it to the light. A small wound pierced her skin, a drop of scarlet welling from the cut.

"It's nothing," she protested. "Really."

Myles searched for something to bandage it with, finally tearing a bit of the hem from the shirt he had borrowed. Gently he wrapped the cloth about her hand, tying it off in a knot.

"If only other wounds were so easy to heal," Devlin said, her voice soft, sad. "If only you'd let me ease them."

Myles cradled her injured hand in both of his and kissed the tips of her fingers. "Dev, I want—want to let you. But I can't . . . can't seem to . . ." The words trailed off. "It's like my heart is encased in ice. So damned cold. And every time I close my eyes, all I can see is blood and death and you, shattered because of me."

"Myles, because of you I have a life. Without you . . . there is nothing." She looked down, trailing her fingertips over the golden flowers twined about Lady Brianna's image. "Give me something more beautiful than this miniature to dream about. Give me all the magic inside you. The enchantment."

Her words were gentle, healing. He could feel them seeping into his heart, his soul. "There isn't any magic anymore, Dev. I don't think there ever will be."

"Myles, I—what in heaven?"

His gaze flashed, stunned, to where her fingers had stilled upon the image, a wisp of something fragile and yellowed with age peeking from the crack in the portrait. A bit of paper tucked there many years before.

He reached down, ever so gently pulling the paper free. Cramped handwriting filled the square. He unfolded it and held it to the candlelight.

The crown of dreams lies sleeping beyond the veil of tears. Tears so precious my two dragons guard them, only their fire whispering the way. Brianna Devlin Wakefield.

"The crown," Myles said, his eyes meeting Devlin's astonished ones. "It's about the crown. But it doesn't make any sense. Tears? Dragons?"

Devlin snatched it from his hand, her hair spilling over her shoulders, her eyes blazing, intent. "Of course!" she gasped after a long minute. "Of course! It has to be!"

She snatched up the miniature, heedless of her injured hand, and caught at him, tugging at him to follow.

"Dev, what the hell—"

"Don't you see, Myles?" she cried, racing up the stairs, her bare feet flashing against the dark wood, her nightrobe flying back from the silken columns of her legs. "That was why you could never fight well with it!"

"Fight with *what?*" he demanded, but she was babbling on, as she always did when she'd discovered the solution to some enigma, solved some riddle that had been rattling about her mind.

"That was why it made no sense! Why no one ever thought of it and found the crown! In all the records about the search for the crown they were trying to trace it through a man. But it was *hers!*"

"You're the one who is not making any sense! What was hers?"

"The sword! The dragon sword! It belonged to Lady Brianna." Devlin burst into the room where Myles had bathed hours before and dashed to where his things lay upon a crewel-worked chair.

Myles felt his own pulse leap. "Of course! The location of the crown must be inscribed somewhere on the sword. We've had both clues in our hands the whole time!"

Myles shoved aside his things, grasping the sword's jeweled hilt. Together he and Devlin rushed to where the fire crackled on the hearth. He held the weapon in the light of the flames. The orange tongues sent fountains of red and gold flowing up the metal of the blade, catching in the facets of the etching some master craftsman had worked a hundred years ago.

There, between the battling dragons, was a far cruder inscription, so tiny it seemed to be a part of the dragon's flame.

" 'Heatherspray'?" Myles read. "It's no solution—it's another goddamned riddle."

"No, it isn't!" Devlin looked up at him. "I've heard of it before. It's a place in Ireland that used to belong to the woman I was named for. It was passed down through the Wakefield side of the family—and went to one of my father's cousins. Brianna Wakefield must have taken the crown there for safekeeping."

"You know how to find this place?"

"I think so." Her eyes were shining with hope and a kind of watchfulness, as if she were waiting to find something in his face.

He stood, his hand still gripping the hilt of the sword. "Take me there."

Devlin's lips parted, her eyes glistening with tears. "Of course I'll take you there. Your quest, Myles. It's not over. It hasn't failed. It's another chance to—"

Myles hated himself for hurting her but had to make her understand. "This isn't about any quest, Devlin."

"But the crown," she faltered. "If you find it—"

"If I find it, it will be only to take it to the nearest goldsmith and have it broken up so the jewels and gold can be sold."

"Sold?" Her face was more stricken than it had been in the dungeon, and Myles sensed that her eyes must have held that same expression when she looked out across Culloden Moor. "I don't understand."

He turned his back to her, unable to bear the pain in her eyes. "It's the only way, Dev. The only way I can make things right. I'm going to use whatever coin I can glean from it to buy a fleet of ships."

"Ships?"

"To carry the people who fought for Charles away from Scotland, out of the path of Cumberland's sword. We abandoned them. All the simple men who fought for the Jacobite cause. We aristocrats—we privileged few—had the coin and the power to buy our way to freedom. But those men and their families have nowhere to run."

"I think you're wonderful for planning to help them. It's one of the things I love most about you—that sense of honor. Have your grandfather send you the money once we're safe. You could buy a hundred ships. But the legend . . . you can't shatter it."

Myles rounded on her. "Do you want some other poor fool to ruin his life searching for the damned thing? Do you know how dangerous a legend can be?"

He stared into those eyes that had borne so much, shown such courage, such heart-wrenching love, and the silent grief in their forest-hued depths loosed his own crushing pain anew.

He cast aside the sword and went to her, taking her in his arms. "I have to do this, Dev. My hand to God, it's the only way."

He had crushed something inside her. He could see it, feel it crumbling beneath his hands. But he was helpless to stop it.

She pulled away from him and walked to the tiny table where she had dropped the miniature in her excitement.

"I suppose I had better put this on," she said quietly, "before you decide to destroy it as well."

He swore, driving his fingers back through his hair, feeling raw inside. He watched her fasten the ribbon about her throat once again. Despite the imperfection of the crack, the portrait of Lady Brianna still glowed, beautiful against her skin.

"Dev, please," he said low. "Try to understand."

"I do understand, Myles. Better than you know. There was a time I didn't have any dreams left either. Until you gave them back to me."

CHAPTER

29

The jaunty sea captain who had smuggled them across the sea had named Ireland an isle of enchantment. And as Devlin stared across the land that had once belonged to the woman she was named for, she felt the magic draw her in.

The estate of Heatherspray was a cradle of imagination where dreams were as thick as the violets that scattered the hillsides.

And with every step of bare feet through the meadows, with every sprig of scarlet pimpernel and fragile primrose she paused to caress, Devlin felt the undeniable sensation that she had been drawn here by a thread fashioned generations ago. That she had been destined to come to this tiny cup of land perhaps even before the beginning of time.

From the moment the smiling Eileen Wakefield had opened wide the door of the manor house, Devlin had felt herself being swept into the arms of a family she'd never known—a family history as rich and varied as the most beautiful tapestry.

Her uncle's wife seemed akin to the ancient senachies who had kept the flame of Irish history alive two thousand years. And Devlin had delighted in every story the aged woman had told—tales of wild Irish warriors, of women so beautiful they had lured Viking invaders to leave their frigid shores forever to build homes upon the island they had come to conquer. Stories of rebellions and famines and a people so strong no peril could break their stiff-necked pride.

Devlin had reveled in seeing the portraits that lined Heatherspray's gallery and had marveled at how like her some of them seemed. An image of Lady Brianna rigged out in a man's breeches, her golden hair flowing about her shoulders as she taught a girl-child of about eight to fight with the dragon sword. A portrait that showed Lord Creighton Wakefield, Brianna's husband, surrounded by four strong sons, his cavalier hat a splash of rakish color above eyes as bright and full of laughter as Myles's own had once been.

Devlin had listened for hours as Eileen told their love story. She had walked the halls of Heatherspray imagining Brianna's pleasure when her love, Lord Creighton, had surprised her with the lovely manor house he had built for her upon the land that had belonged to her ancestors for five hundred years.

As Devlin walked the corridors, wandered the rooms, it was as if she half expected to hear their laughter, they were so real to her.

"'Tis an island o' magic," Eileen had warned her, her eyes sparkling in a webbing of tiny lines. "Once it enchants your soul, it will stay there forever."

And Devlin wanted to stay forever.

It was a fortress of dreams, this Ireland, walled off from the rest of the world by the protective arms of the sea. Yet while Devlin wandered through meadows splashed with blue gentians and stooped in pools of shade to pluck shining yellow kingcups and cradle them against her palm, she ached because even this wild and primal magic could not bring the light back to Myles's blue eyes.

He had been like a man possessed from the moment he had set foot upon Irish shores, pacing across the land that had been Brianna Devlin Wakefield's birthright, searching desperately for any clue that would prove the key to the crown's location. And with every step he took Devlin could see him tallying the days the Scottish Jacobites had suffered, could see him torturing himself over the fact that they would have to suffer longer still before he could aid them.

Even the news of Prince Charles's daring escape with the aid of a woman named Flora MacDonald had not eased the bitter lines about Myles's mouth. Rather, the lines had deepened, as he enumerated a dozen other men, simple fighting men under his command, who were doubtless still imprisoned by the Scottish hills, manacled by poverty and helplessness, with no dashing Flora to save them.

Only when it grew too dark for him to range across the countryside searching for the key to the riddle did he return to the manor house. And despite Eileen's urgings, he barely tasted the rich, fresh milk, the nutty flavored bread and the thick, creamy butter that Devlin devoured at each meal.

He would thank Eileen, still courtly and gallant as any knight, but there would be no joy in his eyes as he made his way to the bed he and Devlin shared. There would be only a haunted light in the dark blue depths as he drew her head onto his shoulder and stroked her hair far into the night.

They would lie there, silent, clinging to each other, their bodies as close as they could be, their spirits in worlds distant from each other. For though Devlin would have given her very life and gladly to give his dreams back to him, she couldn't bring herself to scour the hills and glens for the *tears* Brianna Wakefield had written of so long ago. Couldn't bring herself to wrest the mystical crown from this land of enchantment. For she sensed that when Myles placed the crown beneath the goldsmith's hands to be shattered and melted, he would be destroying himself as well— purposefully exorcising the last vestiges of the gallant knight errant to whom Devlin had given her heart.

She raised her eyes from the crown of blossoms she had been weaving beside a bilberry bush and watched him pace the bank of the stream a dozen feet below. His hair was caught back at the nape of his neck with a thong of leather, a billowing white shirt pressed by the wind against the muscles of his chest. The sleeves were shoved up powerful forearms, the neck open, baring a V of sun-darkened skin. Fawn-colored breeches clung to the taut cords of his thighs, boots of black leather reaching his knees.

He was beautiful.

Beautiful as a fallen angel.

Beautiful as a pagan god cast down into the realm of mortals.

He stood there, oblivious to the beauty that held him in its hand—the laughing ribbon of water that tumbled over smooth polished stones, the white-flecked spray that played at hoodman blind with boulders marking the stream's path. He didn't see the way the sun caught upon the waves, or marvel at the silver waterfall that spilled into the crystalline pool at his feet.

Ever since the day Devlin had watched him bury Tracey, she had allowed him to turn inward, giving him space to heal. She had waited for time to smooth away the grief, waited for him to reach out to her for comfort.

But as the weeks had passed, the torment of allowing him to wander alone in darkness grew beyond bearing. The thought of possibly losing him forever the greatest terror she had ever known. If only there was some way to show him how deeply he had changed her. Was it possible he might find a way to struggle through his hopelessness?

If she could give to him just a fraction of the wonder she had found the night he had made her his wife, was it possible that he might find himself again?

And yet, Devlin thought, with a sharp sting of fear, what if she managed to get him to make love to her and he still peered back at her with that emptiness, that pain, would that mean she had lost him forever?

It was the most terrifying risk she had ever taken, and she trembled at the thought of it.

Jump, Dev . . . The words drifted back to her from a lifetime ago. *I won't let you fall* . . .

She steeled herself, then tossed the ring of flowers into the stream, watched as the current swept it up, carried it away.

Scooping up her petticoats, she ran down the hill, her hair streaming out behind her.

At the sound of her approach, Myles angled his face toward her, his eyes filled with a silent longing. She saw him struggle to smile, the slight curve of his lips more eloquent than any words that he could say.

"Devlin." He said her name, as though it were some talisman, and she wanted to go to him, smooth back the hair from his brow, kiss away the sadness that clung to his lips.

But she didn't pause for an instant, only ran on to the bank of the pool, peering into the waves.

"Dev, what is wrong?"

"I lost it. It tumbled into the water, and—" The distress in her voice was real, caused by the pain she had seen in Myles's face.

He hurried to her side, his gaze searching the water. "What did you lose, love? Your wedding ring? The miniature?"

"No . . ." She plunged into the water, her petticoats dragging about her legs as she waded deeper. "I'd worked upon it a whole hour, and now it's— Oh!" The bright ring of blossoms bobbed up from the waves, the petals miraculously unbruised, the colors glittering jewel-bright with the spangles of moisture that clung to the flowers.

Myles swore as he watched her, the current tugging at her petticoats, the weight of them all but carrying her feet from beneath her as the flower crown bobbed just out of her reach.

It dipped beyond her fingertips, the waves threatening to carry it away, but at that instant there was a sloshing sound, Myles diving to capture it with his long brown fingers.

He stood there with the wreath dangling from his hand, his clothes clinging, wet, against his skin, even his hair damp, dark wisps stuck to the hard lines of his jaw.

"*This* is what you almost drowned yourself to save?" he demanded. "The whole meadow is full of flowers. You could have picked more, woven a basketful of these if you'd cared to."

"It wouldn't have been the same," Devlin said, facing him, her whole body trembling.

"A wreath of flower is hardly worth drowning for."

"But this isn't a wreath of flowers," she said, staring up into that beloved face. "It's a crown, Myles . . . a crown of dreams."

A wariness stole over his features, and she could feel him shuttering himself against her. "Dev, I'm tired and frustrated and I don't . . . don't have the energy for—"

"They *are* dreams, Myles," she insisted. "You of all people should be able to see them. You're the one who gave them to me."

"That should give you cause enough to hate me," he said with a bitter laugh.

But she shook her head, drifting her fingertips across the bud of a tiny pink flower. "This one is the garden where you kissed me the first time. Can't you smell the roses? See them trailing across the stone walls? I can. And I can feel the buttons of your frock coat against my breasts. I can taste your lips, all heady-sweet and searching against mine."

"You'll never go back to that garden. I took it away from you."

"Nothing can take it away from me. I'll have it in my heart forever." She drew out a bit of wood sorrel and trailed the blossom down the rigid line of Myles's cheek. "This dream is bathed in starlight, the night you gave me the miniature of Lady Brianna. You had dreams in your eyes then. I could see them. Touch them, if I had just reached out."

"Devlin, don't." His voice was ragged as she drew the petals over his lips.

"This is our wedding night. And here, here is the book of legends that you left for me. Did I ever tell you that when I finished reading the pieces of dreams you left me, I knew that I was in love with you? They were like holding pieces of you in my heart, Myles. And I needed something to hold on to so badly, when I was terrified that you would die before I had the chance to tell you I loved you."

He was agonizingly silent, a muscle in his jaw pulsing, his eyes pools of torment.

"And this dream," Devlin whispered, suddenly unable to meet his eyes. "This dream is the most special of all, because it hasn't come true yet. For a little while at Thistlewould I hoped, but . . ."

She was hurting him. She could feel it. The knife blade of his sense of guilt and regret sliced deeper and deeper with every word she spoke. And she couldn't bear the thought of driving it further still, when not even the tiniest flicker in his expression showed that she was reaching him at all.

The silence seemed to stretch out, endless, filled with all the pain they'd shared between them.

Tears filled Devlin's eyes, spilled over her lashes. She had lost. The magic she had tasted on the night Myles had made her his bride had slipped between her fingers. She let her lids drop closed, despairing.

But at that instant she felt the sword-toughened warmth of Myles's finger gather up the moisture from her cheek. He tipped her chin up, just as he had a hundred times before, his face darkly handsome, a bare whisper away from her, his own eyes overbright.

He looked down at her, his chestnut hair capturing the sunlight filtering through the veil of water, his hand just a little unsteady. "What was it?" he asked softly as he laid the crown of flowers upon her tumbled curls. "The dream that hasn't come true?"

"That . . . that you would give me a child . . . a little son or daughter . . . with eyes like a summer sky, and a mouth fashioned for laughter. That I would feel life growing inside me, a part of you . . . mine forever. That I could lay the baby in your arms and watch you teach it . . . teach it to see beauty . . . magic . . . the way that you taught me."

"Dev . . . oh, Dev . . ." His face contorted as he dragged her into his arms. Fire. Passion. They ignited the instant his mouth crashed down on hers. And she opened to him, gloried as his tongue plunged deep, a savage groan racking his body.

With fingers hungering for the satin of his skin Devlin fumbled to open his shirt, her palms skimming over the planes and hollows of rock-hard muscle, the delicious roughness of the web of dark hair that spanned his chest.

He gave a shudder of longing, his hard palms cupping her buttocks, his hips arching against her, leaving her no doubt about how savagely desire raged through him.

"Make love to me, Myles," she pleaded. "Give me this one perfect dream."

"We can't . . . not here."

"This is *my* dream, Myles. Mine." She pressed her lips to the pebble-hard tip of his nipple, let her tongue swirl once around it. "I want you. Here. Now."

He swore, and she could feel something snap inside him. His hands shot out, awkward, racing to unlace her bodice. Bunches of satin fell away and were caught by the hands of the water, but Devlin didn't care if they were swept all the way to England. Didn't care if she were trapped within the chill stream waters and Myles's fire-hot embrace for all eternity.

She battled to unfasten the wet breeches that clung in an unbearably erotic sheath to the hardened shaft of Myles's sex. He tore away from her for a moment, yanking off his boots, the rest of his clothing, hurling them toward shore.

With a laugh Devlin turned and splashed toward the waterfall, hungering for the rush of silver over her naked skin, the rush of Myles's hands and mouth devouring her.

He chased her, caught her just as she reached the cascade of water. He spun her around, myriad rainbows dancing across his skin, trapped in the droplets that gilded his broad shoulders, trickled down his flat belly. They stood for a moment, then he was lifting her, catching her to him. She let her legs drift open in the pull of the water, a delicious weightlessness making her head spin as Myles positioned himself at the soft center of her. Velvety, hard, he sheathed himself inside her in one swift thrust.

Devlin leaned back against his arms, feeling the water flow over her skin, ripple through her hair, feeling Myles inside her, deep, so deep.

The waterfall was a curtain of crystal, the sky blindingly blue, and Myles's lips—those bewitchingly sensual, mind-shatteringly tender lips—were taking tiny nips of her throat, her breast, circling nipples that ached for the touch of his tongue.

He teased her, tormented her, worshiped her with his mouth, his hands, until she couldn't bear it. And then he took one hardened rosette in his mouth, suckling at her breast in a rhythm that sent her heart slamming against her ribs.

She arched against him, her hands grasping at the hard curve of his buttocks, a sob racking her as he began to thrust again and again.

She had known a perfect sweetness upon her wedding night, tasted magic in his arms. But this, this was a different flavor of wonder, one dark and dizzying, one that fused their bodies together in a primal mating so fierce it seemed to meld their very souls.

As the tide of sensation rose, swirling inside her, Myles buried his face against the lee of her neck, driving into her body with a tender savagery that made her head toss against the wavelets, her hands clutch at him for purchase as he hurtled her into a madness such as she'd never felt before.

The rainbows burst, scattering their colors across the heavens in vivid hues. She felt Myles stiffen, bury himself deep as his own release burst upon him and he spilled his seed inside her.

They clung together for long minutes, unable to speak, their breathing ragged, the sound of the stream a sweet music all around them. His face was buried in the wet strands of her hair, but instead of the chill rivulets of water dripping down her skin she felt something warm, wet upon her cheek. Felt those shoulders that were so powerful shaking as she held him.

Was he crying? This man who had always been so strong? So sure?

She could feel the anguish pouring from him, feel the waters sweep it away, cleansing the bitterness from inside him.

She held him, stroking his back, his shoulders, his hair, her own eyes burning with tears.

After a long time Myles raised his head, his eyes, crystal-blue, probing hers. "We lost your crown," he said, brushing his knuckles against her curls.

"Don't you see, Myles? We can never lose it. We can only weave new dreams into the wreath. More beautiful dreams."

"There can't be a more beautiful dream than you. Here. Loving me." Myles smoothed his fingertips down her face, and she felt the magic enfold her. "Do you know that I've kissed you, made love to you, and—if dreams come true—conceived a child with you, and I've never once told you . . . told you that I love you?"

Devlin swallowed the knot of joy in her throat. "You always did find new and creative ways to irritate me."

A ghost of a smile crooked his lips. "I do. Love you, Dev. I always have." There was a shadow of sadness in his eyes again; she longed to banish it forever. "That was why I felt so damned guilty about you . . . about Tracey. The truth was, I wanted you for my wife. And I would have done anything to have you. Sometimes I still wonder if I could have made other choices, more honorable choices when the soldiers came to Liancourt and I stole you away. I wonder if I snatched you up on purpose, hoping . . ." He looked away. "If things had been different, Tracey might still be alive."

"But I wouldn't be. Not here." She dragged his hand up, flattened his palm against her heart. "That was your gift to me. Making me feel . . . feel anger and pain, but most of all joy—when I didn't want to feel anything at all. You didn't drag me into that courtyard, Myles. I went myself. And Tracey . . . he had buried himself in his scheming long before you entered Liancourt's gates. Maybe this was our dragon fire—our test—before the story ends in wonder. And if I'd known . . . known all that would happen . . . everything, from that first kiss under the rose tree, I would have passed through that fire a hundred times to find you waiting on the other side."

Myles pulled her to him, kissing lashes now misted with tears. "Dev . . . I love you . . . I love . . ."

The sudden bleat of a lamb and the sound of a gruff voice

on the hillside above made them both jump, eyes wide with alarm.

"Damnation!" Myles swore, looking desperately around for their things. Most of the clothes they had shed in such haste had drifted down the stream a dozen yards; Devlin's shift had snagged upon a branch an arm's length away and Myles's breeches were tangled on an outcropping of stone. The other garments were doubtless already within the shepherd's line of vision.

With a muttered oath Myles snatched up the breeches and shift, then grabbed Devlin's hand.

"The waterfall," he bit out, splashing toward the cascade of water. "We'll have to try to hide, or your Aunt Eileen will have her ears singed off with gossip."

Devlin laughed as they plunged through it and emerged laughing and sputtering upon the other side. Myles shook the water from his hair like a wet hound, dashing the dark strands back from his face.

Eyes bright with love, sparkling with laughter, he slipped the linen shift over her head, smoothing the woven lace about the collar tenderly around her throat. As he maneuvered into his breeches Devlin stared, mesmerized at the magic of his smile. Another dream, infinitely precious, to be woven among the blossoms of the crown.

"Do you know how long I've waited to see your smile again?" she asked, smoothing her fingertips over his lips. "I was afraid it was gone forever."

"You gave it back to me. You . . ." His words trailed off, his eyes widening, lips parting. Alarm shot through Devlin.

"Myles, what is it? What—"

He grasped her shoulders, and he turned her gently so she was peering at the back of the tiny room nature had fashioned of stone and stream.

A trickle of sunlight pierced the waterfall and pooled in a cache carved into the stone. There upon the ledge was a chest banded with iron, some of the wood it was fashioned of rotted away by dampness and time. Devlin's breath caught as the sparks of sunshine danced with spangles of red and gold, blue and ice-white fire.

With unsteady hands Myles grasped the lid of the chest and opened it, the diamond-bright sunlight flooding over a circlet of gold, rubies and emeralds, diamonds and sapphires all set in glorious chains about the most stunningly beautiful object Devlin had ever seen.

The crown. The Stuart crown, tucked away so long ago by Brianna Devlin Wakefield's hands.

A thrill of discovery rippled through Devlin, followed by a swift stab of fear. Her foreboding about this crown and Myles's plan to destroy it made her whole body tense.

"The crown lies sleeping beyond the veil of tears." Myles murmured the words of the riddle, his fingertips reaching out to touch a glittering jewel. "The waterfall. Of course."

Devlin watched him as he picked up the ornament so many men had sought, those long, strong fingers tracing over the intricate workmanship. And in that instant Devlin knew how Galahad must have appeared, his fingers curved reverently about the Holy Grail.

"Do you know what we could do with this, Devlin?" Myles asked softly. "I could buy Liancourt back for you . . . a pardon that would let us return to England. Or we could commission two hundred ships. Supply food and blankets and clothes for half of Scotland. This emerald alone could buy a man a new life in the Colonies, or on the Continent. A new beginning."

"But it couldn't buy him dreams, Myles. It couldn't buy him hope."

He looked at her, his face solemn, achingly beautiful. "What are you saying?"

"Just that . . . that children like Andrew will need dreams to fill their hearts in the hard days to come as much as they'll need food to fill their stomachs. They'll need the beauty of legends, and the hope . . . hope that one day they might discover . . . magic. For themselves."

"But the ships . . ."

"There is still plenty of the Jacobite treasure in the priest hole at the Dower House. Use that to aid them, Myles. Give it all to them. It's fitting that it should be so. But leave them one dream, Myles. To keep forever."

Myles stared down at her a long minute, then his hands gently placed the crown back into the nook where it had slept a hundred years.

"I'll let the mists keep it for all eternity," he said softly, his love shining bright in his eyes. "I've already found my dream, Dev. Here." His lips took hers in an achingly tender kiss. "A dream I can keep forever."

EPILOGUE

*T*he roses were blooming again, sprays of velvety white petals splashed against the garden's stone walls. Devlin hurried along the path toward the gate, her fingers unfastening the pins that held her hair tucked beneath a blue-ribboned bonnet.

Myles was waiting there, in the banks of roses, that devilish smile upon his lips, his eyes bright at the thought of stolen pleasures to come.

It had been ten whole years since he had first kissed her there, in the shadow of his dreaming tree. And eight years since the letter had arrived from the Duke of Pothsby announcing that King George had been induced to grant the Viscount and Viscountess Liancourt a pardon because of their part in bringing the ring of French spies to justice.

Myles had protested that it had all been Tracey's doing, and yet there had been a rightness about the fact that Tracey—whose betrayal had sent them on their flight from England—had unwittingly given them the means to return. It was an irony that would have made Tracey smile.

Five times Myles had laid a new babe in the Farringdon cradle, the halls where Devlin and Myles once battled now filled with shouts and squabbles and squeals of delight.

It was as if the very sound of so much joy echoing up to Lady Caroline's rooms had suffused that fragile body with strength, allowing her to make ever-lengthening forays while leaning upon the sturdy shoulder of seven-year-old Arthur, while twin moppets Lancelot and Elaine frolicked in their wake.

Even Devlin's mother had softened with the years, allowed, at Devlin's request, to remain in the castle that had been her home for so long. Though Myles had acquiesced to Devlin's wishes, he had insisted upon holding a private interview with Agatha Chastain the very day they had returned home, three-month-old Guinevere Brianna Farringdon asleep in Devlin's arms.

What passed between Myles and her mother Devlin never knew. But afterward Agatha had come to her and in halting tones attempted to explain what had happened on the horrible night when Devlin's father had been killed. A wealth of bitterness had remained in Agatha Chastain's voice as she told of her loathing for her husband's Jacobite activities, her countless pleas for him to cease.

But most unforgivable of all in Agatha Chastain's eyes was the fact that Josiah had stayed behind to destroy the list of names rather than carry his wife and daughter to safety. Agatha had hated him for that, had wanted her daughter to share that hatred. She had attempted to spawn those crippling emotions the only way that she knew how—by a lie so agonizing, she had been certain Devlin would never be free of its pain. But nothing Agatha said had been able to drive the love from Devlin's eyes.

And Agatha had known that somewhere within Devlin's ceaseless defiance after their arrival at Liancourt the child still adored the big, laughing father who had carried her about on his shoulders and spun her stories of fair maidens and hidden treasures.

With baby Gwenny in her arms Devlin tried to imagine how she might have felt were she the one who had been forced to flee on the night of the Dower House fire. She knew the nearly feral protectiveness that would have thrummed through her toward her child. And yet how could she have expected a man with any honor to do other than her father had done?

Dozens of families would have been shattered without her father's selfless act. There would have been hundreds of children bereft of their fathers, scores of wives grieving for their husbands.

No, far more painful than the belief that her father had committed suicide would have been the knowledge that he had hidden in the shrubbery while the authorities confiscated enough evidence of treason to keep the axe blades at Tower Hill busy for half the season.

But no matter what the differences between the opinions she and her mother held about Josiah Chastain's Jacobite activities, Devlin could never imagine lying to her child to wound her more deeply still. Could not imagine watching that child suffer beneath the weight of those lies, nor imagine any mother blaming that child for loving a parent who had died.

In the end Devlin forced herself to tuck the hurt away, resolving only to be grateful that she knew the truth, and to make certain that Lady Caroline would never be saddened by learning the harsh facts about the friend who had lied to her, used her, and yet still loved her after twenty years.

If Agatha Chastain could not offer love to Devlin, it didn't matter. For love spilled out everywhere within the castle, joy soon to be magnified by yet another tiny voice, another set of curious hands and busy, running feet.

Devlin caressed the flat plane of her stomach, feeling the tiny stirrings of life there, imagining Myles's face when she told him of the delight to come.

She tossed the bonnet from her head in a flutter of sky-hued ribbons, the last of the hairpins coming free. Her hair tumbled loose about her shoulders, the way Myles had always loved it best.

Feeling young and wondrously alive, she closed the garden gate behind her, bolting it to keep away small, prying eyes.

Then she turned and ran lightly through a wonderland of

blossoms and perfectly trimmed hedges, the most exquisite statues and carefully tended paths. Only the small patch of nettles Myles would not allow to be uprooted hinted at the garden's former state of neglect—a patch that the bewildered head gardener was given stern orders to nurture as diligently as the most perfect bush of flowers.

Never did Devlin think of it without the purest delight rippling through her. Eager, she turned the corner, hastening to where she knew she would find Myles. He lay below the rose tree, his long legs stretched out before him, his tousled hair still dark as sin and thrice as tempting.

His neck cloth was pulled awry, doubtless by two-year-old Tristram, who had recently developed a most decided passion for playing peeking games beneath its lacy folds upon his doting papa's frequent visits to the nursery.

The thick, curling lashes that Myles had managed to pass down to all of his offspring were pillowed upon arrogant cheekbones, those beguilingly sensual lips parted in sleep.

For ten years she had shared his bed, his life, but never would she take for granted the sensations that she felt every time she looked upon that handsome face.

Devlin felt a brief disappointment that their romantic tryst would have to be postponed, but she crept over to where he lay, savoring the luxury of watching him sleep.

A wisp of dark hair had tumbled across his brow, and she reached over to smooth it away. But at that instant she cried out as Myles grabbed her, rolling her over until he was sprawled atop her, his long, hard body pressed deliciously against hers.

White teeth flashed in a salacious grin. "Has no one ever cautioned you about what happens to beautiful maidens who wander in enchanted gardens?" He growled low in his throat. "They become feasts for hungry dragons."

With the fierce snarl that had so often delighted his sons in their favorite nursery game, Myles pretended to gnaw upon the soft curve of Devlin's throat. Sparks of desire snapped beneath her skin, but she laughed as he tickled her unmercifully.

She arched against him, attempting to drag his lips up to hers when a long-suffering groan from the branches above them made the passion heating her blood turn to ice.

"Not the dragon game again! Cannot a person find *any* peace in this place?"

In a heartbeat Myles rolled off of Devlin, the unflappable rakehell looking adorably disconcerted as they both scrambled to their feet and peered up into the face of their oldest daughter.

A dusting of rose petals clung to dark ringlets that rioted about features astonishingly like her father's—the same blue eyes, the same straight nose, the same dark sweep of brows.

From the instant she had been born, Guinevere Farringdon's face had held a certain royal aura, as if the status of her namesake had been transferred to her within the womb. At the moment "Her Royal Highness, Queen Gwenny," as Myles often called her, was a study in regal displeasure.

"Gwenny, what the blazes are you doing here?" Myles demanded, but his arms were gentle as he plucked his daughter from the crook of the tree. Despite the dignity of her years she looped her arms about her father's neck, cuddling closer, one of the child's ubiquitous books clutched in her small hand.

"I was sitting in my dreaming tree," she confided.

"Your dreaming tree?" Myles's lips curved into a smile.

"I found it a week ago when Arthur was laughing at me. Nobody was using it."

Myles caught Devlin's eyes with a wry grimace, and she knew he was remembering the countless times during past years when they *had* used it . . . with deliciously wicked intent.

Devlin's own grin tickled the corners of her mouth, but she sternly quelled it as she stroked the stubborn chin that had been the only feature of hers to find its way into her daughter's face.

"So you came here to escape Arthur, then?"

As though suddenly aware of her jealously guarded status

as the eldest, Gwenny clambered down from Myles's embrace.

"Arthur is the most repre—reprehensible boy that ever was! You should have—have given him away to some Gypsy king the minute he was born!"

Myles's rumbling laugh echoed out, and he tugged at one dark ringlet. "I am certain Arthur would be quite agreeable to such a proposal. Especially since Mr. Lenning informed me that your brother has once again neglected his Latin."

"It's not funny, Papa! I hate him! He takes my books and laughs at them. He says that I'm a goose to believe in such faradiddle. But it's real. I know it is!"

"I'd not hold your brother as an expert upon any such matter, Your Highness, considering his present state of disgrace," Myles said. "Perhaps I can be of assistance."

Myles reached out for the book, and for an instant Gwenny clutched it protectively against the bodice of her white cotton dress. But after a moment she surrendered it into Myles's strong brown hand, allowing the father she so adored to leaf through the much-worn pages.

Devlin saw his smile widen, a kind of wistful tenderness wreathing his face. "Where did you find this, sweeting?"

"Tucked away in a corner of the library among Mama's special books," Gwenny said. "The tale is about a crown lost a hundred years ago. The most beautiful crown that ever was, with diamonds as big as a man's fist and sapphires—"

"As blue as the lakes of Killarney," Devlin said softly.

Gwenny looked up, astonishment flushing her cheeks. "Yes, Mama! However did you know?"

"Your papa gave me that book the morning after our wedding. A long time ago."

"Did you read it, then? About the crown?" Gwenny asked eagerly. "It's hidden away somewhere magical, like the Grail in the Galahad story Papa put under my pillow last Christmastide. There are riddles and such that lead the way, and—and all sorts of stories of people trying to find the crown. But nobody ever has."

"Is that so?" Myles asked her, attempting to regard her with the expected level of seriousness.

"Arthur says it's just a story someone made up," she said with the greatest of scorn. "But I know it's real. And when I'm big enough, I'm going to have a grand adventure and find it. I am going to have a dress of blue satin, like the one Mama wore to court last spring, and I'll put the crown on my head and walk right into a ballroom, with Arthur standing there. And he'll be drinking punch, and it'll spill all over his shirtfront because he'll be staring at me."

"It will serve the little rogue right," Myles managed, his eyes twinkling.

Gwenny pulled the book out of his hands, her lips thinning. "You're laughing inside again, Papa. I can hear it."

"I'm sorry, sweeting. It's just that I think you are quite possibly the most delightful creature in Christendom, and I can't help myself."

"It's all right," the child conceded, shaking her head in resignation. "I knew I could never make either of you understand." Gwenny chewed at her lower lip, her eyes filled with such beautiful dreams that Devlin caught Myles's hand.

"It is just that . . . I *know* the crown is out there, Mama, waiting for me," the child whispered. "I can feel the magic."

Unexpected tears stung at Devlin's eyes as she leaned against the warm strength of her husband, felt his love shimmer around her like the cascade of an Irish waterfall, warm her like the velvety kiss of a flower wreath in her hand.

"I understand perfectly, angel," she said, trailing her hand down her daughter's tumbled curls. "I feel the magic, too."

508

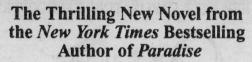

The Thrilling New Novel from
the *New York Times* Bestselling
Author of *Paradise*

Judith McNaught

"Another incomparable love story Judith
McNaught's readers are sure to cherish"
--Dallas Times Herald

*P*erfect

POCKET
BOOKS

Available in hardcover from Pocket Books
May 1993